continued . . .

Acts of Vengeance

"As exciting as the first book. Readers are immediately drawn in and kept on edge. . . . This is a great story . . . another marvelous, action-packed tale . . . with its all-too-real dangers. It is sure to increase his well-deserved following."
—*Flight Journal*

"Gandt, who knows his stuff, provides the reader with a plethora of whiz-bang techno-action and old-fashioned knife and pistol duels. . . . The real excitement is in the fast-paced action. There is something for most military junkies here. . . . The climactic dogfight is authentic in action and terminology. . . . But the main enjoyment in this book is Gandt's pleasurable story telling and authenticity."
—*The Hook*

"Gandt is a rare treasure, a Navy jet jock with the rare gift of being able to tell a compelling story in a believable and exciting manner that leaves the reader exhausted at the end. If only some movie studio mogul would take this book—I guarantee you everyone would forget *Top Gun*."
—*Pacific Flyer*

With Hostile Intent

"I thoroughly enjoyed [*With Hostile Intent*]. . . . Characters are believable. . . . Combat scenes are excellent. Great job!"
—Dale Brown

"A red-hot aerial shoot-'em-up by an aviation pro who has done his homework."
—Stephen Coonts

FICTION BY ROBERT GANDT

*SHADOWS OF WAR**
*ACTS OF VENGEANCE**
*WITH HOSTILE INTENT**
*BLACK STAR**

NONFICTION BY ROBERT GANDT

FLY LOW, FLY FAST:
Inside the Reno Air Races

BOGEYS AND BANDITS:
The Making of a Fighter Pilot

SKYGODS:
The Fall of Pan Am

CHINA CLIPPER

SEASON OF STORMS:
The Siege of Hong Kong

*Published by Signet

THE
KILLING
SKY

★

ROBERT
GANDT

A SIGNET BOOK

SIGNET
Published by New American Library, a division of
Penguin Group (USA) Inc., 375 Hudson Street,
New York, New York 10014, USA
Penguin Group (Canada), 90 Eglinton Avenue East, Suite 700, Toronto,
Ontario M4P 2Y3, Canada (a division of Pearson Penguin Canada Inc.)
Penguin Books Ltd., 80 Strand, London WC2R 0RL, England
Penguin Ireland, 25 St. Stephen's Green, Dublin 2,
Ireland (a division of Penguin Books Ltd.)
Penguin Group (Australia), 250 Camberwell Road, Camberwell, Victoria 3124,
Australia (a division of Pearson Australia Group Pty. Ltd.)
Penguin Books India Pvt. Ltd., 11 Community Centre, Panchsheel Park,
New Delhi—110 017, India
Penguin Group (NZ), cnr Airborne and Rosedale Roads, Albany,
Auckland 1310, New Zealand (a division of Pearson New Zealand Ltd.)
Penguin Books (South Africa) (Pty.) Ltd., 24 Sturdee Avenue,
Rosebank, Johannesburg 2196, South Africa

Penguin Books Ltd., Registered Offices:
80 Strand, London WC2R 0RL, England

First published by Signet, an imprint of New American Library,
a division of Penguin Group (USA) Inc.

First Printing, November 2005
10   9   8   7   6   5   4   3   2   1

PUBLISHER'S NOTE
This is a work of fiction. Names, characters, places, and incidents either are the product
of the author's imagination or are used fictitiously, and any resemblance to actual persons,
living or dead, business establishments, events, or locales is entirely coincidental.
    The publisher does not have any control over and does not assume any responsibil-
ity for author or third-party Web sites or their content.

To Martin Caidin
who showed the way

ACKNOWLEDGMENTS

A toast and another round of thanks to the crew that keeps Brick Maxwell in the skies. Special credit to Lt. Cmdr. Allen "Zoomie" Baker, fighter pilot and writer; Doug Grad, master editor and story mechanic; Mark Chait, new friend and editor; Alice Martell, old friend and literary agent; Vernon Lewis, buddy and eagle-eyed proofreader.

For their help with my research in Israel and the Palestinian territories, I am indebted to Doron Suslik, Deputy VP for Communications of Israeli Aircraft Industries; his formidable office manager, Hadassah Paz; and to Brig. General Uzi Rozzen. Additional thanks to Yosi Harel, former IAF fighter pilot, and to the patient staff of the Hazerim Air Force Museum.

"The oath is firm to continue this difficult Jihad, this long Jihad, in the path of martyrs, the path of sacrifices."
—Yasser Arafat, former Palestinian Authority President

"Our American friends offer us money, arms, and advice. We take the money, we take the arms, and we decline the advice."
—General Moshe Dayan, Israeli Defense Minister

"I have a premonition that will not leave me; as it goes with Israel so will it go with all of us. Should Israel perish, the holocaust will be upon us."
—Eric Hoffer

CHAPTER 1

FOX AWAY

Negev Desert, Southern Israel
1145, Thursday, 13 October

Speed is life.

It was an old fighter pilot proverb, and it kept flashing like a signboard in Lt. Pearly Gates's brain. He forced himself to ignore it. Like most old fighter pilot proverbs, it wasn't always true. Not in this kind of fight.

Gates grunted against the seven and a half Gs pressing his body into the hard cushion of the ejection seat. The acceleration was causing perspiration to stream from his helmet, stinging his eyes. The muscles in his neck ached as he tried to peer back over his shoulder, straining to pick out the mottled sand-and-brown camouflage scheme of the Viper.

Nothing back there. No goddamned Viper.

Where the hell did he go? The F-16D, called *Barakeet*—Thunderbolt—by the Israelis, was known to the rest of the world as the Viper. The sleek American-built fighter was as hard to see as a gnat in the haze. Gates knew that this particular Viper was flown by a cold-eyed young Israeli captain named Yuri Lebev.

Pearly could already see the derisive look on Lebev's face when they landed back at Hazerim air base. It was the same look the cocky little shit had worn the day before when they went two-vee-two—two U.S. Navy Super Hornets versus two Israeli F-16 Vipers. Gates and his flight lead, Lt. Cmdr. Flash Gordon, had gotten their butts kicked by Lebev and his flight leader.

That was day one—and the low point for the Americans—of the exercise between the VFA-36 Roadrunners from the USS *Ronald Reagan* and the 109 Squadron of the Israeli Air Force. Gates was still simmering from the encounter. Sure, the Israeli fighter pilots were good, but he hadn't expected them to be *that* good.

It was natural, at least the first day, that the Israelis would have an advantage, flying over their home turf, using their own controllers. What *was* surprising was that they knew exactly how to fight the F/A-18 Super Hornet.

Technically, of course, the fight should have been over before it started. Both the Super Hornet and the Viper carried high-aspect, off-bore sight air-to-air missiles. The Americans were armed with AIM-9 Sidewinders and AIM-120 AMRAAMs—advanced medium range air-to-air missles. The Israelis were also carrying AMRAAMs as well as their own heat-seeking Rafael Python missiles. In a real fight, either could have killed the other long before the turning fight began.

But this wasn't a real fight. Fighter pilots didn't settle personal accounts with forward-quarter radar missiles. By unspoken agreement, this would be an old-fashioned, kick-ass dogfight, each pilot trying to lock onto the other guy's tail. Their only high-tech edge was the HUD— Heads-Up Display—that showed radar range and a shoot cue and a little image of your inertial path through space.

In this kind of fight, you maneuvered behind your adversary's tail to get a shot at him. It was that single, gut-squeezing, neck-wrenching skill that distinguished a fighter pilot from a button pusher. The winner got to fly home with a video shot of the loser's tailpipe.

Where the hell was the Viper? The two flights—Gates

and his squadron skipper, Cmdr. Brick Maxwell, Lebev and his own squadron commander, Col. Lev Asher—had merged, passing nose-to-nose at a closing speed of over a thousand knots. They went into a high-G reversal, each converting energy into angles to lock onto the other's six o'clock.

For the moment Gates had lost sight of his leader, a tactical sin for which he knew he'd catch hell from Maxwell. He'd worry about that later. His objective in life at this moment was to nail that snake-eyed little shit, Lebev.

Gates kept the turn in, peering over his shoulder, letting the Super Hornet's flight control computer maintain its 7.5-G limit. Everyone knew that the Super Hornet couldn't outrun or outclimb or outaccelerate a Viper. For pure, balls-out, eyeball-flattening energy, nothing could touch a bigmouthed, GE-engined F-16 Viper. The F-16 could accelerate going straight up, pull over the top, and shoot you in the face on the way back down.

But the Hornet had one thing going for it that made it deadly. It could turn. None of the hot fighters—not the F-14 Tomcat or the MiG-29 or the F-15 or even the F-16—could beat a Hornet in a turning fight. When the other guy was falling out of the sky trying to match your radius, the Hornet would still be there, pivoting, standing on its tail, pirouetting like a hummingbird.

Of course, that was the tricky part—getting the other guy to play your game. Most U.S. Air Force F-16 pilots had already learned about the Hornet, and they played a different game, using their jet's raw power to leave the fight, only to reenter with the numbers in their favor. But according to the air intel briefer, the Israeli Air Force didn't have any real experience fighting Super Hornets. Pearly still didn't believe that this Israeli jock—

Pearly saw him. *Shit.* The reason he hadn't spotted the Viper through the back of the canopy was because the sonofabitch wasn't there. He was high. Instead of trying to turn with Gates's Hornet, he was going high, using the vertical plane to cut across the circle.

"Hard deck is ten thousand," came the voice of Brick Maxwell. "Acknowledge."

Maxwell was reminding him that the minimum altitude for the exercise was ten thousand feet. They had to knock it off if the engagement descended to the hard deck.

Pearly didn't acknowledge. Lebev was still out there. Fuck the hard deck. He needed another half minute.

Maxwell called again. "Watch the hard deck. Answer up, Pearly."

Pearly caught the edge in Maxwell's voice. The skipper wasn't going to cut him any slack. Gates thumbed his lower mike button. "Roger the hard deck."

He glanced at the altimeter reading in the HUD. *Uh-oh.* Running out of sky. The digital read out was clicking downward through 11,800. He guessed that Lebev was having a similar dialogue with his flight leader, Colonel Asher, on their own discrete frequency. The Israeli squadron commander was even more uptight about rules of engagement than Maxwell.

The Viper was closing in. *Damn.* Another turn and he'd be in firing position. Maybe the F-16 couldn't turn with the Hornet, but the sonofabitch could go up and down like a yo-yo.

"Hard deck, Runners," came Maxwell's voice. "Knock it off. Runner One-two, knock it off."

Saved by the bell, thought Pearly. Maxwell had just given the order to disengage. Pearly saw his digital altimeter clicking through 9,500 feet. At least he'd be spared the humiliation of getting schwacked again by that little prick Lebev.

But Lebev wasn't knocking it off. The Viper was still back there. Gates could see the slim, insectlike shape of the F-16 carving inside the turn.

In the kill zone.

Gates's thumb was on the transmit button to acknowledge the disengage command when he heard Lebev's voice on the radio.

"Fox Two!"

The call for a heat-seeking missile shot.

Maxwell heard Lebev's transmission. A second later, peering downward through his Plexiglas canopy, he spotted the two fighters. They were a couple thousand feet below, a few miles to the east, in the direction of the Dead Sea. Against the brown mat of the Negev Desert, the two fighters looked like blurry mirages.

Yeah, the Viper definitely had gained the advantage on Gates's Super Hornet. He was in the Hornet's rear quarter. Lebev would have had a legitimate simulated kill if he hadn't violated the hard deck. Now all he'd get out of it would be an ass reaming from—

What was that? Maxwell squinted against the glare of the afternoon sun. Something down there, behind Gates's jet. Something glimmering, zigzagging like a bat.

Maxwell felt a chill run through him.

In the next instant, he knew. The tail section of Pearly Gates's jet erupted in an orange, roiling fireball. The Super Hornet was disintegrating, trailing black smoke and pieces of airframe and engine.

"Eject! Eject!" Maxwell yelled into his microphone, knowing that it was a useless call. If Pearly hadn't already punched out, he was toast.

What the hell happened? Maxwell shoved the Hornet's nose down toward the burning fighter. *That sonofabitch Lebev fired a real missile. Why?*

In his peripheral vision he glimpsed an F-16 off his right wing. It was Asher, still keeping his silence. Maxwell felt a wave of anger sweep over him. He resisted the impulse to tell him to stay the hell out of the way. He and his idiot wingman had done enough damage.

The flaming carcass of Gates's F/A-18 Super Hornet

was plunging toward the desert. Maxwell kept his eyes fixed on the descending debris field. Where was Pearly? Did he have time to grab the ejection lanyard when the missile hit him?

Yes. He saw it, a white puff, just beneath the cloud of swirling smoke and shattered airplane parts. At first glimpse it looked like a fluttering ribbon; then it swelled into the hemispherical shape of a parachute canopy. Beneath the chute dangled the tiny, doll-like figure of the pilot.

Maxwell lost sight of the parachute as he swept past. He hauled the nose of the Super Hornet up high, then back down for another pass. In his peripheral vision he was dimly aware of Asher's Viper staying with him, high and to the outside of his turn.

Maxwell felt exposed. An Israeli fighter had just shot down one of his Super Hornets. Was he the next target?

"Runner Three and Four," he called to Asher and Lebev, "set up a RESCAP and call for a rescue helo." A RESCAP—Rescue Combat Air Patrol—was unnecessary, he reflected. They were over friendly territory.

Or were they? Why did Pearly Gates get shot down? The RESCAP would at least keep Asher and Lebev busy and out of the way.

He kept his eyes on Asher's Viper. If he was going to take a shot—

"Already done," answered Asher. "An SAR helicopter is on the way from Hazerim air base. Recommend we orbit above ten thousand."

"*You* orbit above ten thousand. I'll stay down here and cover my wingman."

Though Maxwell was the official flight leader for the exercise, Asher, a full colonel in the IAF, outranked him. And this was *his* country.

Tough, decided Maxwell. He wanted the Israelis as far away as possible. Asher could go pound sand.

The joint air combat exercise had begun over the

Negev Desert, which blanketed the lower third of Israel and extended southward into the Sinai. The swirling dogfight had gradually drifted west.

Maybe too far west, Maxwell thought. Beneath his left wing he could see the mottled checkerboard of the Gaza Strip. Once a possession of Egypt, Gaza was seized by Israel in the 1967 war. Since then the strip had become a hotbed of the Palestinian insurgency.

Asher called again. "Runner One-one, are you picking up a locator beacon?"

"Negative. I had it for a few seconds; then it quit. He's not transmitting on his survival radio." The locator beacon was a homing device installed in the pilot's ejection seat. The PRC-112 radio was a handheld device attached to the pilot. Maxwell didn't expect Pearly to transmit until he was down.

The chute was almost on the ground. Maxwell saw that it was descending into a brush-covered wadi. The bottom of the wadi looked like an old stream bed, obscured by a stand of low scrub trees.

Maxwell lost sight of the chute again as he pulled up for another pass. The burning wreckage of the Super Hornet had already plunged into the desert a mile away. A column of black smoke marked the impact site. Smaller pieces of debris were still raining onto the brown earth.

Again Maxwell wondered what the hell had gone wrong. How did a simple one-vee-one air combat maneuvering exercise turn into a blue-on-blue—friendly versus friendly—shoot-down?

He brought the nose of the F/A-18 back around, leveling at a thousand feet over the desert, trying to pick up the parachute. It should be on the ground, Maxwell thought. He peered downward, squinting against the glare. He could see the wadi, the stream bed with the scrub trees, the steep slope where he guessed that Pearly would land.

No chute.

Damn it. He'd flown right over the spot. He was sure

of it. He stabbed the position-hold button on his navigation display, locking the coordinates of the site in the computer's memory. He pulled up, reversed course, swept back over the wadi.

Nothing. No parachute canopy on the ground. No Pearly Gates waving that he was okay. Still no signal on the emergency radio frequency.

He hauled the Super Hornet's nose up and came back for another pass. Nothing. It was as if the desert had swallowed Pearly Gates, leaving not a trace.

Five minutes elapsed. He heard Asher call, "The SAR helo is here, Runner One-one. You can talk to him on guard frequency."

Maxwell climbed to two thousand feet and entered an orbit to the south of the site. To the northeast he saw the distinctive low-snouted profile of the UH-60 Blackhawk skimming the desert, flanked by a pair of AH-1 Cobra gunships. They were coming from the direction of Beer-sheva and the Hazerim air base.

"Runner lead, this is Rescue Four-zero on guard. I'm the Blackhawk at your four o'clock, three miles. Do you have a visual on the downed pilot?"

"Runner One-one, negative. I had a chute, but he's no longer in sight. Stand by; I'll give you the coordinates of where he should have landed."

Maxwell retrieved the position he had frozen in his navigation display and passed it to the Israeli Blackhawk pilot. Five minutes later the Blackhawk was on the ground with the Cobras orbiting around it. Maxwell could see soldiers in battle gear picking their way through the scrub brush.

Another ten minutes passed. Maxwell had nearly reached bingo state—minimum fuel. He'd have to return and land.

The Blackhawk pilot radioed again. "Bad news, Runner One-one."

"You found the pilot? Is he injured?"

"We don't know."

Maxwell felt a flash of irritation. These Israelis and their goddamn games were getting on his nerves. "What do you mean, you don't know?"

"I mean we don't know. He's not here."

CHAPTER 2

HAZERIM

Hazerim Air Base, Southern Israel
1305, Thursday, 13 October

Asher was waiting in the 109 Squadron briefing room back at the air base. In a chair in the first row, looking ashen-faced and sullen, sat Capt. Yuri Lebev.

Maxwell was still wearing his sweat-stained torso harness and G suit. He slammed the door behind him and glared at Asher. "Okay, what the hell happened?"

"I suggest you sit down," said Asher. He motioned to the chair beside Lebev. "Have a cold drink."

"I don't want a cold drink." He fixed his gaze on Lebev. "I'll sit down after this guy explains why he took a shot at my wingman."

"He didn't," said Asher.

Maxwell's temper was spiking. He had reached his limit with these contentious goddamn Israelis. "Then how did one of his missiles manage to blow off the tail of Pearly's jet?"

Asher walked over to a covered window. He yanked open the blind and pointed outside to the flight line, where a row of Vipers was parked. "Go out and see for yourself. That's Lebev's aircraft, number thirty-three, at the end of the row. It hasn't been touched since he landed. The missiles are still on the rails. None have been fired."

Maxwell stared at the colonel. This wasn't making sense. He had just witnessed the shoot-down of one of his pilots by a so-called friendly. "If it wasn't Lebev's missile, then who—"

"You'll see." Asher picked up a cassette from the briefing desk and dropped it into a digital videotape machine. "This is Lebev's HUD tape. He kept it running during the entire engagement."

Maxwell took a seat. Like all modern fighters, the Israeli F-16s had a video recorder that could be selected to tape the view through the HUD.

A grainy image flashed onto the screen in the front of the room. At first Maxwell saw only the blank sky, with the glowing reticules and the HUD symbols superimposed on it. The nose of the Viper was high, arcing over the horizon.

Then he saw the vertical line of the horizon slice into the picture, and with it a familiar sight. Maxwell recognized the canted stabilators and twin tailpipes of an F/A-18 Super Hornet.

Pearly Gates's Super Hornet. The Viper was pulling in behind him.

As he watched the maneuver, Maxwell had to admire the Israeli's skill as he moved in on his prey. He saw the seeker circle in the HUD inching nearer and nearer the tail section of the hard-turning F/A-18.

Closer. Lebev's jet was already in kill range. The Israeli-built Python missile on Lebev's F-16 had a broad enough kill envelope that Lebev could have declared Pearly dead long before. But Maxwell knew what he really wanted. Lebev wanted indisputable proof on the videotape that he had outmaneuvered his opponent and locked onto his tail.

An old-fashioned six-o'clock kill.

Maxwell saw the altitude readout on the HUD—9,600

feet, descending. Then he heard his own voice on the video soundtrack. "Hard deck, Runners. Knock it off. Runner One-two, knock it off."

No one acknowledged. The SHOOT cue was flashing in Lebev's HUD.

"Fox Two," came the voice of Lebev over the tape.

Maxwell stared at the video. Where was the missile? He strained to pick up the telltale streak of smoke as a Python heat-seeking missile streaked toward Gates's jet.

No missile appeared in the video. Maxwell strained to pick up the track of a missile.

Nothing. The sky between Lebev's Viper and the Super Hornet was empty.

Then he noticed something. *There.* In the far bottom-right corner of the HUD, a glimmer, something coming from down below. It climbed in a zigzag motion, like a bat flitting in the gloom.

Fascinated, Maxwell watched the nearly invisible object race toward Pearly Gates. Then he saw the aft section of the F/A-18 disintegrate in a roiling ball of fire.

Lebev spoke for the first time. "I never saw it," he said. "I saw only the explosion when it hit the Hornet. I thought it came from my jet too." Lebev wore a morose expression, all the cockiness gone from him.

Maxwell shook his head in puzzlement. "A SAM?"

"An SA-16," said Asher. He stopped the video, then backed it up and froze the image. The slender, finned rocket quivered on the screen, a tiny wisp of gray smoke marking its trail. "Code name Gimlet. Russian-made, short-range, shoulder-launched, surface-to-air missile. We heard they were trying to get them, but this is the first one we've seen."

"Who are 'they'?"

Asher shrugged. "The usual bunch. Hamas, probably. Or one of the Islamic Jihad units. There are several. They have different names, different signatures, but they all have the same objective."

"Palestinian?"

"Mostly, but not all. They come from Syria, Saudi Arabia, Afghanistan, Chechnya. Wherever they train terrorists."

Maxwell rose and walked to the window. The late afternoon sun was glinting off the rows of warplanes on the ramp. Two squadrons of F-16s were dispersed on the ramp. A squadron of twin-finned F-15 Eagles occupied a space across the tarmac. Maxwell's own detachment of F/A-18 Super Hornets from the USS *Ronald Reagan* was parked in a neat row facing the Vipers.

Maxwell looked at Asher. He was a slightly built man, trim and lean-faced, with piercing dark eyes. Maxwell had already determined that Asher was a skilled fighter pilot. He also had the sense that Asher was a fast-rising officer in the Israeli Air Force.

"So what happened to Pearly?" Maxwell said.

"A company of IDF troops has been on the ground for over an hour looking for him. They found his helmet and parachute and some survival gear. Also traces of blood. They reported seeing vehicle tracks and evidence of some kind of encampment in a cave down in the wadi."

"So he's a prisoner?"

"If he's alive."

"But they're inside Israel. Where could they take him?"

"Where else?" said Asher. He pointed to the wall-length map of Israel on the wall. "The Gaza Strip." The Strip protruded like a finger from Egypt's border with Israel northward along the Mediterranean coast.

"I thought the border around the Gaza Strip was sealed off."

"It is, and everyone knows that's a joke. The terrorists have a hundred secret routes under the fence. The bunch that captured your wingman is almost certainly inside Gaza by now."

"But Israel occupies the Gaza Strip. You have troops there, right? Can't they search the place?"

Asher gave him a patient smile. "Another joke. Sure, Israel occupies the West Bank and Gaza, but we have almost no control over what goes on inside the villages and the markets and the refugee camps. It's a giant snake pit."

Maxwell felt the frustration gathering inside him. He wanted to lash out at someone, demand that they goddamn *do* something. How could a bunch of terrorist thugs pull off a—

His thoughts were stopped short. The door of the briefing room flew open and banged against the wall. Into the room barged a barrel-chested man in the beige uniform of the Israeli Air Force. He wore a blue-gray beret and two stars on each shoulder epaulet. In lockstep behind him appeared two IAF captains.

Asher drew himself up straight. Lebev catapulted from his seat and stood quivering at attention.

The general's eyes swept the room, pausing for a second on Maxwell, then riveting on Asher. "Asher, damn you, what have you done? You've caused an international incident."

A wry smile flitted over Asher's face. "It's good to see you again, General Zemek."

"Why was an air combat exercise conducted at such a low altitude?"

"The hard deck was a minimum safe maneuvering altitude, General. We received no intelligence warning about a surface missile threat."

"Why were you operating so close to the Gaza border?"

"We were inside the Hazerim range area. And as you know, there is no restriction about overflying the Gaza boundary."

Zemek seemed uninterested in Asher's explanation. He whirled on Lebev. "You, Lebev. You're grounded until there has been a full inquiry into the incident." Then Zemek turned on Maxwell. "I had serious reservations about this exercise with the U.S. Navy. I didn't think anything good would come of it, and I was right. The exercise is finished, as of now."

Maxwell nodded, keeping his silence. There was no point in arguing with General Zemek. Anyway, ending the exercise suited him just fine. He'd already lost one pilot. That was enough.

"It wasn't Lebev's fault," said Asher.

"The board of inquiry will determine that," snapped Zemek.

"It's stupid to ground one of my best pilots without a reason."

Zemek's face reddened. "I'm the commander of the air force. I said he's grounded."

"I am his squadron commander. I should be consulted on this matter."

"You may find yourself grounded too."

"That would be even more stupid."

Maxwell stared at the two Israelis. Asher was either recklessly insubordinate or crazy. Arguing like this with a flag officer in the U.S. Navy would be an instant career finisher. But this was Israel. Apparently they were more egalitarian.

"Damn you, Lev Asher. You are a colonel and I am a major general. When will you learn to respect authority?"

"When you quit meddling with my squadron."

At this, Zemek seemed to reach the limit of his tolerance. His face was turning a darker shade of purple. Maxwell guessed that even in the egalitarian Israeli Air Force, Asher had pushed too far.

Before Zemek could speak, the door swung open again. Each head in the room swiveled toward the woman who strode into the room.

She had thick black hair that fell almost to her shoulders. The designer sunglasses were tilted high on her forehead. The leather skirt stopped well short of her knees, revealing slender, tanned legs.

"Stop arguing, you two. We have work to do."

*   *   *

"Hannah Shamir," she said, shaking Maxwell's hand.

"She's from the Foreign Ministry," said Asher. "A Deputy Minister, I believe." He looked amused.

General Zemek did not. "How did you get on the base?" he demanded.

She smiled, and Maxwell couldn't help noticing the perfectly spaced white teeth. She had the complexion of a woman who spent a lot of time outdoors.

"The Minister gave the order," she said. "Anyway, I'm still a major in the reserves."

"Why are you here?" said Zemek.

"The same reason you're here. The American jet that went down."

"That is a matter for the military, not the Foreign Ministry."

"Don't be a blockhead, Nathan. Didn't the Super Hornet belong to a foreign government? Wasn't the pilot a foreign national? Of course it's a matter for the foreign ministry."

Maxwell watched them, fascinated by the rude familiarity between them. He was beginning to understand that Israel was a peculiar place—more like a big squabbling family than a country.

Zemek sighed and seemed to resign himself to her presence. He turned to Maxwell. "Ms. Shamir served on my staff at one time."

"I was the most efficient aide a wing commander ever had."

"And the most disputatious," Zemek added. "It was a blessing for the air force when she left to join the Foreign Ministry."

"Which is why the Minister sent me here. As a reserve air force officer, I can help with the matter of the missing pilot."

"I don't recall requesting your help."

"The Minister was very insistent."

Zemek mumbled something under his breath. Hannah

Shamir peered around the briefing room. Her eyes fastened on the still-frozen image of the SA-16 on the video screen.

"Was that the weapon that shot down the American jet?"

"It's still being investigated," said Zemek.

She nodded, then turned her attention to Maxwell. She looked him up and down. "You're taller than I expected."

He stared at her.

"And you're better-looking than the photo in your file."

Maxwell was confused. "File? What file? I have a file?"

"We like to gather information about official visitors to Israel."

Again he noticed the shortness of the leather skirt, the bare, tanned legs. She had the hard, trim body of a runner, or someone into serious aerobics. He guessed her to be in her mid-thirties. She didn't look like any Deputy Foreign Minister he'd ever met before.

He wanted to change the subject. "How are we going to get my wingman back?"

"By finding out where he is and who took him."

Zemek's head snapped in her direction. "That's enough. If you have classified information about this matter, you may not discuss it in this room, and not"—he glanced at Maxwell—"in the presence of unauthorized people."

"Commander Maxwell is hardly unauthorized," she said. "After all, he was involved in the incident, and it's a pilot in his squadron we're talking about. Anyway, there's nothing classified about it. It will be in all the newspapers tomorrow."

"Okay," said Maxwell. "Who's got him?"

She gave him another look up and down. She nodded, seeming to like what she saw. "You'll see."

CHAPTER 3

PRISONER

Gaza, Palestinian Territories
1605, Thursday, 13 October

They removed the blindfold.

Pearly blinked his eyes and peered around. He tried to count the people in the dimly lit room. Six. Seven. No, at least eight. Each held a weapon, an AK-47 or some kind of automatic pistol. They were all staring at him.

He was thirsty. And god-awful tired, mostly from the three-hour adrenaline surge, which was now gone, leaving in its place deep fatigue. He'd made the transition from scared shitless to roaring mad to scared again before finally accepting his fate. He was a prisoner.

Now they were going to kill him.

Something hurt like hell. His neck ached, and a dull throb came from somewhere in his skull. Carefully he touched his head with his fingers. They came away sticky with blood.

"It is your own fault," said the man closest to him. He had a dark stubbly beard and wore a checkered kaffiyeh. "Let it be a lesson. Do not resist us."

Pearly tried to think of a clever retort. He couldn't, so he said, "Fuck you."

The man was not amused. "It was stupid of you to

fight. That's why I hit you with the rifle butt. If you co-operate now, someone will treat your wound."

Pearly's brain was still ticking along at minimum speed. He didn't know how long he'd been unconscious. His first awareness after being captured was of being tied and blindfolded, bumping along in the back of a dusty vehicle.

The circumstances of the dogfight with Lebev—the explosion in the tail section of his jet, the belated groping for the ejection seat lanyard, the descent in the parachute—were coming back to him in disconnected fragments.

Lebev. That snake-eyed little shit fired a live missile. Why?

It didn't make sense. And how did these assholes happen to be at the site when his chute hit the ground? How did they know?

Did they do it? Could they have popped me with a SAM?

Maybe.

How could it happen without any warning?

All very confusing. His head still throbbed.

"I'm thirsty," he said.

Hazerim Air Base, Israel

"Watch out for her," said Asher. He reached for another skewer of kebab.

He and Maxwell sat at a corner table in the Hazerim officers' dining room. They were still wearing their flight suits. General Zemek and Hannah Shamir had gone to the base commander's office to continue the argument over her presence at Hazerim.

"Why?" said Maxwell.

"Hannah Shamir may not be what she seems."

Maxwell slid several hunks of lamb and chicken from a skewer onto his plate. "She seems to be a very attractive former air force major who works in the Foreign Ministry."

"You've got the attractive part right," said Asher. "And she knows how to use it. Charms the cabinet members, even the Prime Minister. Which is how she gets away with telling off Zemek."

"Looks like you get away with it too."

"Zemek and I go way back." Asher chomped on a slice of lamb. "He was my flight leader in my first squadron. I was a captain; he was a major. One day over Lebanon I took out a Syrian MiG-21 that had him targeted. He's alive today because of me."

Maxwell nodded. It was something fighter pilots understood about one another. After you'd flown together in combat, you had a special bond. Even if you hated one another's guts.

"There's more to the story," said Asher. "In that same fight, we lost an F-16. The pilot was captured by Hezbollah guerrillas."

"What happened to him?"

"We never got him back. His name was Ron Shamir. He and Hannah had been married six months."

Maxwell vaguely remembered the incident. Israel refused to negotiate with the terrorists. It was a standoff. After several weeks, Hezbollah sent a video of the blindfolded pilot being executed by a firing squad.

"So Ms. Shamir is a widow," said Maxwell. "And now she's a bureaucrat. What else?"

For a while Asher studied the point of his brass kebab skewer. "Let's just say it's rumored that she has another affiliation. Outside the Foreign Ministry."

"Another affiliation? I'm not following you."

"The Foreign Ministry in Israel is a political office. Most of the staff come and go with the elected officials. But some have specialized training, and they stay on. They have connections with the intelligence agencies."

Maxwell was getting the picture. "Mossad?"

Asher just shrugged.

Well, thought Maxwell, it made sense. The Mossad was Israel's equivalent of the CIA. It explained how Hannah Shamir knew things about Maxwell. And, perhaps, about who captured Lt. Pearly Gates.

"You're saying I should be careful around her?" said Maxwell.

"Treat her as you would a snake." Asher held up his skewer, grasping it with two fingers at the stem. "Very carefully."

Gaza, Palestinian Territories

A man in a beige safari suit gave him a carafe of water. Pearly tilted the carafe up and sloshed the water down, spilling it over his chin and onto his flight suit. As he drained the carafe, it occurred to him that the water probably wasn't purified. He dismissed the thought. Getting the shits from bad water was the least of his worries.

"My name is Khaled Mohanor," said the man in the safari suit. "Have you heard of me?"

"No."

"If you were an Israeli, you would have."

Pearly didn't ask why. The guy obviously had a high opinion of himself. He was also trying to get him to talk. He could go screw himself. If they wanted information, they'd have to get it the hard way.

He noticed how the others in the group—he assumed they were Palestinians—deferred to the one who called himself Khaled. Most were young. A couple appeared to be teenagers. One was a young woman in a checked shawl.

Khaled waved for the young woman to come across the room.

"This is Hanadi," he said. "She is a nurse. You will allow her to treat the wound on your head."

The young woman gave Khaled a deferential nod, then produced a bag filled with medical apparatus and bandages. She gestured for Pearly to sit on a stool.

Pearly sat. "Do you speak English?" he said.

"Of course." She tilted his head so that she could examine the wound.

"Where did you study to be a nurse?"

"I didn't." She dampened a compress with a solution from a bottle and began dabbing at his wound. "I was a medical student at the Al-Quds University in East Jerusalem."

Pearly winced at the sharp sting of the antiseptic. "Was?"

"I left six months ago. After the Israelis killed my family in Jenin."

Pearly let the subject drop. He guessed her to be in her mid-twenties. Her face didn't change expression as she spoke. She had bright brown eyes, a soft, pretty face, no makeup.

"Is that why you joined these—" Pearly nearly said *terrorists,* then caught himself.

"Many young people in Palestine have chosen to join Khaled. We call him the Great Leader. Even my brother has joined us."

"Which one is your brother?"

"That one." She gestured with the compress to a teenager standing by the wall. He was watching them with open-faced curiosity. "His name is Saleh. He's seventeen."

Saleh saw Pearly looking at him. His face brightened, and he shuffled across the room, looking embarrassed. He stared for a moment at Pearly.

"Do you know Tom Cruise?" said the young man.

"No."

He looked dubious. "But he is a fighter pilot like you, no?"

"No. He is an actor. He played a fighter pilot like me in a movie once."

Saleh peered at Pearly with renewed interest. He looked younger than seventeen. His face was a male version of his sister's, with the same soft features, the intelligent brown eyes.

Hanadi finished cleaning the wound. She produced a bandage from her bag and began applying it to Pearly's temple. "Saleh wants to be a soldier," she said.

"I *am* a soldier."

"Not yet."

"I am joining the Al-Aksa Brigade."

"Be quiet," said his sister.

"What's the Al-Aksa Brigade?" asked Pearly.

"The Brigade of Martyrs," said the young man. "They have vowed to—"

"Shut up," said his sister.

Before Saleh could say more, a man in a checked kaffiyeh—the same one who had warned Pearly not to resist—noticed them. His name, Pearly had learned, was Muhammad. He strode across the room and seized Saleh's arm. "Why are you talking to the prisoner?" Muhammad slapped him across the face. "Get back to your post. No more talking to the prisoner, do you understand?"

Saleh looked like a beaten dog. He gave Pearly a last glance, then shuffled toward the door.

Hanadi ignored Muhammad. She finished bandaging Pearly's wound. She tilted his head again so she could examine her handiwork. "Does it still hurt?"

"No. Why does your brother want to join the Brigade of Martyrs?"

She returned the roll of gauze and the antiseptic to her medical kit. "He is young. He thinks it is romantic."

"Why would he want to throw away his life?"

She glanced across the room. Muhammad was watching them. "It is something you wouldn't understand," she said.

"Maybe. Try me."

"He thinks it is the only way to fight the enemy."

"And what do you think?"

She considered for a moment, then glanced across the room. Muhammad was watching them with a dark look on his face.

She picked up the bag and turned away. "It doesn't matter what I think."

Hazerim Air Base, Israel

"How the hell did they do it?" said CAG Boyce.

Maxwell knew it was a rhetorical question. Boyce already had as much information as he did.

"We don't know, CAG. We don't even know who they are."

Maxwell could see the light glinting off Boyce's nearly bald head on the video screen. Capt. Red Boyce's official title was Commander, Carrier Air Wing Three. His wing was deployed aboard USS *Ronald Reagan*. Like all air wing commanders, he went by the traditional but extinct label, "CAG"—Commander, Air Group.

"This feels like Yemen all over again," said Boyce. "A bunch of camel drivers with an obsolete Manpad missile, bagging one of our jets."

Maxwell nodded. Neither he nor Boyce would forget the brief war against the Bu Hasa terrorists in Yemen. That time it was Maxwell's jet that was targeted by a shoulder-launched missile. He'd been shot down and narrowly escaped capture.

The satellite link between the Hazerim air base and the *Reagan*, anchored in the bay north of Haifa, Israel, was crystal-clear. The resolution of the video screen was distinctly sharper than the less advanced equipment they used aboard the *Reagan*. Not only clearer, but the image was almost natural, without the jerkiness and fuzziness of the monitors on the carrier. The Israeli military possessed the latest in teleconferencing technology.

"Do you think the bastards just got lucky?" said Boyce.

Another rhetorical question. Maxwell knew it was a subtle message. *Don't say too much.* Even though Maxwell was alone in the room, they had to assume the Israelis were monitoring everything that was being transmitted. Why not? It was their air base.

"Something like that. They happened to be in the right place to snatch Pearly and disappear before the SAR team showed up."

For a moment Boyce didn't answer. He appeared to be deep in thought. Maxwell saw a gray wisp of smoke fill the video screen.

"CAG, do I see smoke in your compartment?"

A grin spread over Boyce's face. He held up a lighted cigar. "Don't you start that crap, Maxwell. There are enough goddamn pure-air freaks on this ship. There's no one here except me and Senior Chief Lester, and he knows better than to rat on me."

Maxwell had to laugh. Capt. Red Boyce was the third-highest-ranking officer on the USS *Ronald Reagan*—and the most notorious breaker of rules.

Boyce clenched the cigar in his teeth. "Here's the scoop. The mishap investigation team from the *Reagan* is going by helo out to Hazerim this afternoon. They'll go over the wreckage of Pearly's jet, take pictures, make their report. They'll want a statement from you, of course. You know the drill."

Maxwell nodded. He knew the drill. Boyce was talking in code again. It was important that the Mishap Investigation Board tag the downed Hornet as a combat loss. Anything else—a pilot or maintenance or command dysfunction—would count against the squadron and the air wing in the ongoing competition for the Battle Readiness "E"—the annual award for the most combat-ready unit in the fleet.

Maxwell's squadron, the VFA-36 Roadrunners, was

one of three Super Hornet squadrons in the *Reagan*'s air wing. Six of his jets, with pilots and a support crew, had been detached to Hazerim air base for Operation Gideon, the joint exercise with the Israeli Air Force.

Now there were five. And Operation Gideon was history.

"When do we go baksheep, CAG?" *Baksheep* was Navy idiom for *back to the ship*.

"Day after tomorrow. As soon as the *Reagan* is under way, I want your five jets back aboard."

"And then what?"

"Then you go back to Hazerim."

Maxwell said, "CAG, I've got a squadron to run. I need some time to—"

"I know you'll find this hard to believe, Maxwell, but the squadron is running just fine in your absence. Your XO, Bullet Alexander, is doing a good job, and your OpsO, Bat Masters, loves being second in command."

"What am I supposed to do here at Hazerim?"

"Get Pearly back."

"How am I supposed to do that?"

"I don't know," said Boyce. "All I can tell you is we've got intel and diplomatic assets working on it."

"What diplomatic assets?"

Boyce blew a cloud of gray smoke at the video cam. "You ready for this? How about Special Envoy Ricardo Solares?"

Maxwell groaned. He knew Solares by reputation. He was a former congressman and a television demagogue who managed to insert himself into every hot spot in the world. His penchant for getting himself televised with military combat units during the Gulf Wars had earned him an unflattering nickname. It had also earned him the admiration of the White House. Now Solares was the President's Special Envoy to the Middle East.

"What's Rambo Rick going to do? Tell the terrorists how sorry we are and give them a billion dollars in reparations?"

"You said it, not me," said Boyce. "I'll fill you in when

you get here. In the meantime, go have a couple of beers and try not to piss off the Israelis. Okay?"

"I'll try."

Gaza, Palestinian Territories

"Do you know Brad Pitt?"

Pearly stared at Saleh. The kid had to be joking.

"No," said Pearly.

"But you have met him?"

"Sorry. Never met him."

Saleh looked disappointed. "But he is very famous."

"I don't know any famous people."

They sat at a long wooden table. One of the Palestinian men had come in with a cardboard box filled with bread, coffee, an assortment of fruit. Half a dozen AK-47-armed Palestinians guarded the barred entry door in the spacious, windowless room. A hallway door led to a primitive toilet facility and opened on another warren of low, plastered rooms. The building was old, with crumbling yellow plaster on the walls and a single bare lightbulb hanging from the ceiling. As far as Pearly could determine, it was a single-story structure.

Pearly helped himself to a piece of the flat, unleavened bread.

"Do you have a girlfriend?" asked Saleh.

"Yes." Pearly gnawed on a chunk of the bread. It was dry and chewy, without much taste.

"Do you have a photograph of her?"

They had taken all his possessions—flight gear, Beretta semiautomatic, PRC-112 mobile radio, survival equipment, his wallet, and wristwatch—when he was captured. Later, they returned the wallet and watch.

He unzipped the breast pocket of his flight suit and retrieved his wallet. He pulled out a photo and handed it to Saleh.

The young man's eyes bulged. "This is your girl-friend?"

"Yep."

"Is she in the movies?"

Pearly laughed. "No. She's a flight attendant."

Saleh's eyes were riveted on the girl in the photograph. She wore short shorts and a tight halter. Her tousled blond hair hung over one shoulder. She was sitting, legs crossed, on the hood of Pearly's Corvette.

"What is her name?"

"Amy."

Saleh's sister came up behind him and peered over his shoulder.

"Western women," she said, shaking her head. "They're all decadent." She snatched the photo from him and handed it back to Pearly. Pearly thought he saw a faint smile flit over her face.

Nearly forty-eight hours had elapsed since he'd been shot down. Whenever Saleh had the chance, when neither Muhammad nor his sister was present, he badgered Pearly with questions.

No, Pearly didn't know Britney Spears. No, he had never met Ozzy Osbourne. No, he did not hang out with Michael Jackson.

"What about Kurt Cobain?"

"I think he's dead."

Saleh didn't seem to care. "But you must know—"

"Stop it," said Hanadi. She gave her brother a shove. "Muhammad warned you not to talk to the prisoner."

Saleh gave her a sullen look, then shuffled away to the far side of the room. He stood with the gunmen, still watching Pearly.

Pearly said, "He doesn't act like a kid who wants to be a martyr."

"No one *wants* to be a martyr," said Hanadi. "It is a matter of honor. And duty."

"Some duty. Throwing away your life for nothing."

"You wouldn't understand."

"You got that right." Pearly picked up one of the pieces of fruit. He didn't know what it was. It looked like a pear, only it was reddish and very hard. "Blowing yourself to smithereens so you can kill a bunch of civilians. Yeah, that's kinda hard to understand."

"It is the only weapon we have."

Pearly could tell by the hard set of her face that she wasn't interested in his opinion. He poured a cup of the coffee. It was thick, filled with a dark residue. He took a sip and nearly gagged.

"*Yuugh.* What is this stuff? It tastes like mud."

"Arab coffee," she said. "You'll get used to it. After a while you will no longer like the weak Western coffee."

"After a while? How long will I be here?"

She looked flustered. "I don't know. I only meant—"

"That they'll keep me alive as long as they can trade me for something?"

She didn't answer. He noticed again the soft, pretty face, unlined and untouched by makeup. He wondered what the slender body looked like beneath the baggy gray-and-black ankle-length dress.

"What will they do to me if they don't get what they want?"

He saw a shadow pass over her face. Still no answer.

"They'll kill me, right?"

The dark eyes looked at him, holding his gaze. Abruptly she turned and scurried away.

CHAPTER 4

BETWEEN
ENGAGEMENTS

Hazerim Air Base, Southern Israel
1545, Friday, 14 October

Maxwell left the videoconferencing room and walked out into the late-afternoon sunlight. The glare stung his eyes. From across the sprawling apron of the base, he heard the cacophonous roar of jet engines.

Through the shimmering heat waves of the desert, he could see the wavy shapes of two fighters. They looked like apparitions moving along the two-mile-long strip of concrete. As Maxwell watched, they disappeared down a swale in the undulating surface of the runway. Seconds later they reappeared. A roiling flurry of dust and jet exhaust trailed them as their noses pointed upward. The torches of their afterburners looked like the plumes of comets.

Maxwell stood frozen, watching the shapes grow smaller in the hazy sky.

"F-16s," said a voice behind him. "Mine, in fact."

Maxwell turned to see Lev Asher standing behind him. He was wearing a freshly creased flight suit with the patch of his unit—109 Squadron—over one breast.

"Another training exercise?" said Maxwell.

"Could be," said Asher. "Or it could be the real thing. This is Israel."

Maxwell kept his eyes on the departing jets. Israel's F-16s were the key to its survival. The highly modified fighters were used for everything from air superiority to targeted killing of terrorists to deep strikes against a neighboring enemy's nuclear weapons factory. Maxwell knew that the IAF was due to receive a new batch of the two-seat F-16I *Soufa*—Storm—fighters from the United States. The new F-16s would be equipped with Israeli-produced weapons systems and would have the range to attack targets in Iran.

Asher said, "The second F-16 in that flight is being flown by your friend, Captain Lebev."

Maxwell looked at him in surprise. "I thought General Zemek grounded him."

"I convinced him that Lebev had to get back in the cockpit. Lebev is a gifted young man, but his confidence is fragile."

"He gave me the impression that he was supremely confident. Cocky even."

"That's his style. Yuri is not a *sabra*—a native-born Israeli—like most of us. He is an immigrant from Volgograd, in Russia. He came here when he was fourteen years old. Like many of our new citizens, Yuri thinks he has to prove himself. As you've seen, he sometimes tries too hard."

Maxwell nodded. He knew what Asher meant. Young fighter pilots walked a thin line between recklessness and professionalism. If they were lucky, they learned the difference early in the game and went on to be competent warriors. Yuri Lebev may have learned. For Pearly Gates, it might be too late.

Asher waited until the specks of the jets had dwindled to nothing and the rumble of the engines was gone.

"I've got news," he said. "Some good, some bad."

Asher handed Maxwell a folded newspaper. It was the Friday *Jerusalem Times*. On the front page was a black-and-white photo of a young man in a flight suit. He was grim-faced, unshaven, and the caption identified him only as a "captured American pilot."

With a shock, Maxwell recognized the image of Pearly Gates.

The article reported that the pilot was being held by Al-Tanzim, one of the extremist units of Hamas. They would release him only if the Israeli government released four hundred Fatah guerrilla prisoners. Otherwise he would be executed.

"Pearly is alive," said Maxwell. "That's the good news. Tell me the rest."

"There won't be a trade," said Asher. "The Israeli government doesn't negotiate with terrorists. Even if they did, they would never release four hundred terrorists."

"Even if it meant saving the life of a captured pilot?"

"They didn't do it to save Ron Shamir. They won't do it now."

Maxwell looked at the photo in the newspaper again. Pearly did not appear to be injured. The eyes were clear, but the face showed no expression. Had he been tortured? *Name, rank, serial number.* Pearly would tough it out as long as he could.

"What happens if the Israeli government refuses to make a deal?"

Asher's face hardened. "Exactly what they said. These are not civilized people."

It was still hard for Maxwell to believe. When the Roadrunners flew to Israel for Operation Gideon, no one imagined one of them would be a prisoner of war. A prisoner of *what* war? This wasn't the United States's fight. This was an age-old blood feud between Jews and Arabs—a feud without an end.

Why did they want Pearly?

Simple, he reminded himself. Asher had just told him. They wanted their own people back—terrorists who massacred villagers and executed captured pilots.

He saw Asher studying him. "We Israelis learned one very useful custom from you Americans."

"What's that?"

"An old fighter pilot tradition. It's called happy hour." Asher glanced at his watch. "It starts in fifteen minutes."

Gaza, Palestinian Territories

Ignorant goat herders, thought Khaled Mohanor. *Brainless idiots.* He forced himself to give Muhammad Khouri a placating smile.

"I believe you are mistaken," he said with all the politeness he could muster. "I must tell you that the Israelis will never negotiate on these terms."

"They have to," said Muhammad. "The Americans will force them."

"The Israelis don't listen to everything the Americans tell them."

"The Americans are sentimental fools. They want their precious pilot back. They will put great pressure on the Israelis."

"Perhaps, Muhammad. But there is not the slightest chance that the Israelis will release four hundred captured Fatah fighters. Impossible."

"So be it," said Muhammad. "Then we give them an example they will not forget."

They were standing in the small anteroom next to the chamber where the American prisoner was held. At Muhammad's side was his lieutenant, a scowling thug named Akram. Akram kept his AK-47 at the ready, glowering at Khaled.

Khaled knew it would come to this. Muhammad Khouri was one of Yasser Arafat's old Fatah commanders. With the death of Arafat in 2004, Muhammad and the other Fatah incompetents became rogue terrorists who understood nothing about negotiation or the subtle forms

of point and counterpoint. They understood only violence. Violence without purpose.

What Muhammad Khouri most of all did not understand was that Fatah was finished. Irrelevant. A laughingstock in Tel Aviv and Washington. So, for that matter,
were all the Palestinian Authority bureaucrats.

But with this prisoner, the American pilot, they had
gained a precious bargaining tool, perhaps more precious
than they realized. Now this pock-faced peasant wanted
to throw it away with his demand that the Israelis release
all his Fatah brothers.

The problem was, Muhammad Khouri was the commander of the unit that had downed the American pilot.
Khaled would have to proceed carefully. Muhammad was
a firebrand. With one stupid act he could destroy the future of Palestine. And of Khaled Mohanor.

"To provoke the Israelis is one matter," said Khaled.
"To anger the United States is quite another. We should
remember the example of Iraq."

"The United States expended all its energy in Iraq,"
said Muhammad. "The Americans have no more stomach
for war."

He's even stupider than Arafat was, thought Khaled.
Muhammad is a delusional idiot.

With that thought, Khaled knew what he had to do.

"Very well," he said in his silkiest voice. "I respect
your authority in this matter. With your concurrence, I
will present your terms to the Israelis."

"The four hundred Fatah fighters. Nothing less."

"I understand," said Khaled. *You mud-wallowing peasant.* "Nothing less."

Hazerim Air Base, Israel

"Mind if I join you?"
The voice came from behind. Maxwell was halfway

through his beer, a surprisingly good local brew called Maccabee. Asher had downed his rum and Coke and had another on the way.

Maxwell saw her reflection in the mirror behind the bar—raven-black hair, sunglasses tilted up on her forehead, large brown eyes set in a tanned face. The short leather skirt had been replaced by a powder-blue pantsuit, tight at the waist. She was smiling.

He turned to face her. "I thought you went to Tel Aviv."

"I did," said Hannah Shamir. "I'm back."

Asher was wearing a bemused smile. "On official business, I presume."

She kept her eyes on Maxwell. "Hazerim is my second home. I have a sentimental attachment to this base."

Maxwell pulled an empty stool between him and Asher. She slipped onto the stool and signaled the bartender, an aging, round-faced man in a white apron. "Special tea, Doron. You know how I like it."

The bartender nodded deferentially and went to work mixing her drink.

"She calls it tea," said Asher. "The rest of the world knows it as vodka and guava juice."

"With a twist of lime," she said. "I learned it from you and Ron." She turned to Maxwell. "Lev and Ron were captains when I was a student in flight training."

"Ron was your husband?" said Maxwell.

She nodded. "If he were still alive, he'd be a colonel like Lev."

"He'd be a general," said Asher. "He was the best officer in the squadron."

Hannah shrugged. "All in the past. I've gotten on with my life." She sampled her drink and flashed a thumbs-up to the bartender. She looked at Maxwell. "That's something you and I have in common, don't we?"

Maxwell didn't get her meaning. "Excuse me?"

"We each lost our spouse."

Maxwell froze. The file again. She even knew about

Debbie. He turned to stare into the mirror over the bar. The death of his wife was a subject he rarely discussed, and never with strangers.

"Yes."

"Then you resigned from NASA," she said. "After one shuttle flight."

"Like you said, all in the past." He said it gruffly enough to make it clear that the subject was closed. He felt Asher's eyes watching him curiously.

She wasn't finished. "So when you went back to the Navy—"

"Enough of that, Hannah," said Asher. "Brick came here to drink, not to be interrogated."

"Sorry," she said. She looked at Maxwell. "We Israelis tend to get callous about losses. Ours as well as everyone else's."

Asher steered the conversation to safer ground with a joke about a rabbi and a taxi driver. Maxwell laughed politely, not sure he got it. Hannah told a story about her boss, the Foreign Minister, who was so absentminded he wore mismatched socks and left his briefcase filled with sensitive documents in limos and restaurants and lounges all over Israel.

More laughter. Maxwell found himself relaxing. The beer and the good humor were cutting through the earlier tension. This woman, when she slipped out of her Deputy Minister's shell, might be okay. Maybe more than okay.

He was aware of her closeness, her leg brushing against his. The silk pantsuit did a good job of displaying her figure. *Careful, Maxwell.* What had Asher said? *Treat her very carefully. Like you would a snake.*

Why was she here? It was obvious that she and Asher went way back. But he sensed that they weren't an item. Anyway, Asher had a wife. Hannah had been a widow for—he did a quick calculation—over ten years. Why had she not remarried? Did she have—

"Why have you not remarried, Brick?"

Off balance again. This woman had a knack for that.

"Probably because I've just never been in one place long enough."

A lame answer, but close to the truth. He might be married now if he had gotten out of the Navy and taken a job like a normal man.

"But you have a girlfriend? Someone you're close to?"

He remembered the file. What else was in it?

"I'm, ah, sort of between engagements."

She nodded. By her expression he guessed that she knew about Claire.

The truth was, he missed the company of a pretty and intelligent woman. How long had it been? Five months, give or take a couple weeks. Since the afternoon back in Bahrain when Claire Phillips, the television journalist whom he had almost married, declared that she was opting out of the relationship, choosing not to be a part-time wife while her fighter pilot husband embarked on a hundred-thousand-ton steel sarcophagus, sticking his neck out so far it was only a matter of time before she was thrust into widowhood, which, thank you very much, was not for her. So good-bye. Or words to that effect.

Asher was saying something.

"Excuse me?" Maxwell said.

"I said, we have to drink quickly. Sunset is coming."

Maxwell was confused. "What's sunset got to do with drinking?"

Hannah supplied the answer. "This is Friday. Shabbat—our holy day—begins at sunset and lasts for twenty-four hours. Most bars and restaurants, including this one, will be shut down."

"What about the Air Force? You don't shut down too?"

"Our enemies wish we would," said Asher. "We learned that lesson in 1973. The Arabs hit us during Yom Kippur, our holiest holiday, when most of the soldiers and pilots were home or in the synagogues. It nearly cost us our existence. Since then, we've become more pragmatic, even during religious days."

As if to emphasize his words, the rumble of jet engines rattled the windows of the bar.

"Hear that?" Asher pointed in the direction of the rumbling engines. "The sound of pragmatism."

Maxwell nodded. A strange country, he thought. Full of ancient traditions and contradictions. He finished his beer. "Okay, so everything here will be closed. What do we do about dinner?"

"I know a good Arab restaurant in Beersheva," said Asher.

"I've got a better idea," said Hannah. "Something more adventurous." She turned to Maxwell. "Have you seen Masada?"

He had to think for a second. *Masada?* Then he remembered. "The ancient fortress? No. I haven't had time to be a tourist."

She glanced at her watch, then looked at Asher. "Quarter past five. Can we do it?"

"It closes at sunset also."

"You're a colonel. Don't they keep it open for the military?"

Asher shrugged. "I could make a phone call."

"What are you waiting for?" She was already off her stool. "Go on; make the call."

CHAPTER 5

GHOSTS

Masada Fortress, Eastern Israel
1855, Friday, 14 October

"Listen," said Hannah. She squeezed Maxwell's arm. "Do you hear them?"

"Hear what?"

"The ghosts."

Maxwell listened. The wind was murmuring through the deserted caverns and battlements. A flagstaff had been erected at the highest point on the plateau, and the blue-and-white emblem of Israel was making a staccato snapping noise in the desert breeze.

He didn't believe in ghosts, but at the moment he wasn't ruling them out.

His shirt was soaked with sweat. They were all breathing heavily from the thousand-foot climb to the top of the mountain.

He sucked in a lungful of the dry air and gazed around him. They were standing on a sprawling plateau atop a sheer-sided rock in the Judean desert. The sun was melting into the jagged western horizon, bathing the desert in a soft orange glow. To the east sprawled the gray shape of the Dead Sea and the high ridgeline of the Jordan shore.

Before they left Hazerim, Maxwell had shed his uniform and switched to jeans, running shoes, and a cotton Izod polo shirt. Asher was in chinos and hiking boots. Hannah had replaced her pantsuit with khaki shorts, a loose cotton halter top, and high-topped running shoes. Once again Maxwell noted the slender, tanned legs. Hannah Shamir was a woman who spent time outdoors.

Over Asher's objections, she insisted that they go in her blue Jaguar X-Type. She sped through the sleepy town of Beersheva, then eastward into the desert. Sitting in the right seat, Maxwell tried to ignore the speedometer, which she kept pegged at 150 kilometers per hour.

The desert had swept past in a brownish blur. She barely slowed as they passed through the desert town of Arad. At Neve Zohar, she turned north and followed the shore of the Dead Sea. Maxwell had smelled the acrid sulfur fumes from the mineral springs along the seashore.

In less than an hour they were standing in the gravel parking lot, staring up at the brown mass that filled the western sky.

He knew the basic story—that in the first century A.D., after a failed rebellion against their Roman conquerors, a group of militant Jews took sanctuary in the mountain fortress called Masada.

Hannah filled him in on the rest while they slogged their way up the snaking path toward the summit. In its final stages, the battle came to a standoff between two driven leaders—Flavius Silva, commander of the Roman Tenth Legion, and Eleazar ben Yair, leader of the Zealots, the band of Jews who defended Masada.

With the overwhelming advantage of fifteen thousand legionnaires versus fewer than a thousand Jews, the Romans still could not take Masada. Silva's ultimate solution was hugely expensive and, in the end, effective. He built an earthen ramp up the western face of the mountain. To keep the defenders from killing the construction workers with well-aimed arrows, he used captured Jews. When the ramp was high enough, the Romans brought up their siege engines and prepared to breach the upper fortress walls.

The night before the final battle, the Jews burned their houses and all their possessions. Ten were chosen by lots and given the task of executing all the others. One was then selected to slay the remaining nine, then kill himself.

Hannah finished the story as they climbed the last steps to the summit. She pointed across the plateau. "There is where the Romans broke through the walls. When they entered the fortress, they found only bodies."

Within twenty minutes, darkness had overtaken the mountain. Floodlights were coming on, illuminating the excavated chambers and anterooms and berthing areas. Maxwell walked over to the western fortification where the wall had first been breached. The ramp that Silva built still sloped up to the western face. Maxwell peered down, trying to imagine seeing fifteen thousand legionnaires camped on the plain below. And reaching a momentous decision: *They won't take us alive.*

Fanatics, he thought. Unbelievably courageous. Or unbelievably crazy. Or equal parts of both.

Hannah came up beside him. Her thick black hair ruffled in the wind that blew over the ramparts.

"Well?" she said.

"I thought Jews didn't believe in suicide."

"We don't. But we believe that freedom is more valuable than our lives."

"Sounds good on paper. In the real world, it means losing your people."

She looked out into the darkening desert. "Yes, sometimes that's what it means."

Maxwell was aware of Asher standing on the other side. "I know what you're thinking," said Asher. "That Israel would rather sacrifice lives than make concessions to get prisoners back."

Maxwell gazed around the floodlit fortress. "Isn't that the way it works?"

"It's the only way that works for us," he said. "Israel wouldn't exist if we weren't willing to sacrifice lives. Our own included."

"Pearly Gates isn't one of your own."

"The terrorists don't care. To them he's a bargaining chip."

"So Israel will let them kill him?"

"Not my decision," said Asher. "I'm a fighter pilot, not a diplomat."

Maxwell turned to Hannah. "You're a diplomat. What do you say?"

She regarded him for a moment, then shook her head. "I say going down this mountain is going to be tougher than climbing it. Follow me."

She started down the darkened path. Maxwell paused at the top and looked back over the windswept plateau. The wind was murmuring through the empty chambers.

"Do we have to drive so fast?" said Maxwell. The speedometer read 160 kilometers per hour.

"I thought fighter pilots were brave," said Hannah.

"Only in the air. We're chickens on the ground."

"This isn't fast," said Hannah. "You want to see fast?"

Before he could say no, she stepped on the accelerator. The tires squalled as the Jag hurtled through a turn.

Darkness had come to the desert. Silhouettes of mounds and dunes were blurring past the headlights. The signpost to Arad flashed by too fast for Maxwell to read it.

She handled the car well, he had to admit, even if she was scaring the crap out of him. Asher, in the backseat, didn't seem to mind. He was conducting a lecture about the history of the Roman occupation and the many failed rebellions of the Jews.

She slowed only slightly to pass through the outskirts of Beersheva, then sped up again on the road that led to Hazerim air base. At the main gate, the sentry checked their IDs, then waved them through. She pulled into the parking lot of the officers' quarters.

"It's early," said Hannah. "Shouldn't we have a night-cap?"

Asher was already climbing out of the backseat. "You two are on your own. I've got a poodle and a wife at home."

From the darkened interior of the Jag, they watched him walk across the parking lot to his car, an old BMW cabriolet.

"Well?" she said to Maxwell. "Do you have a poodle also?"

Maxwell looked down at his jeans. They had turned the color of the Judean desert. He could feel his polo shirt sticking to his chest in a mixture of sweat and grime.

"No poodle, no wife, but I need a shower." He glanced at his watch. "How about the club bar in, say, half an hour?"

"I have a better idea. My quarters on the third floor. It has a bar."

He hesitated, remembering Asher's warning. *Watch out for her.* Hannah Shamir was in the intelligence busi-ness. She wasn't inviting him to her room because she ad-mired his scintillating wit. After all, he wasn't called "Brick" for nothing.

Then another thought. Who gave a damn? So she was a spy. Everybody needed a job. He was alone, she was alone, they were adults. And she had great legs.

"Make it twenty minutes," he said.

It took him twenty-five.

He arrived at Hannah Shamir's door wearing clean chi-nos, a fresh cotton shirt, boat shoes, no socks. The hot shower had not only removed the dirt and sweat, but it had had the effect of clearing his brain.

Asher was right. He had to be very careful. Never mind the great legs. He'd have one drink, no classified talk, get the hell out. *Don't get intimate with a spy, even if she's friendly.*

She opened the door.

Maxwell stared. The great legs were displayed beneath a short silk wraparound that stopped well north of the knees. She was barefoot. Her hair was wet, and she carried a towel in one hand. The white lines from her halter straps showed against bare shoulders.

"I, ah, can come back when you're—"

"Come in. The bar's open."

Following her into the room, he caught a fresh lavender scent. His eyes locked onto the rhythmic motion of her derriere beneath the thin silk. *One drink, no classified talk, get out fast.*

Well, maybe not too fast. Check it out, then leave.

The quarters were the same as his, plainly furnished in the style of military officers' quarters on bases throughout the world, a decent-size living room with a view of the opposite building, a door that led to a bedroom that he presumed was just like his own. The difference was that her quarters showed a woman's touch. Vases filled with flowers were positioned around the room. Brightly colored bedouin rugs covered the tiled floor.

As promised, there was a bar. It was in the corner, four feet long, with two padded stools.

He took one of the stools.

"Sticking to beer?" she said.

"I've developed a taste for Maccabee."

"A fine Israeli product."

She retrieved a brown bottle, expertly poured the beer into a tall glass. She swirled together her own drink— guava juice, shot of vodka, twist of lime—and dropped in the ice.

She took the stool beside him. Her bare knees brushed against his leg.

"To Masada." She clinked her glass against his. "And to your new understanding of Israel."

"To Masada." He wasn't sure about his understanding of Israel, but he knew that the story of the ancient fortress somehow went to the very heart of these people. Fight to the death, never surrender, never be enslaved. Easy to say, excruciatingly difficult to live by.

She seemed to be reading his thoughts. "Israel is a complicated country. To an outsider, it doesn't make much sense."

"Letting prisoners of war be executed because you won't negotiate doesn't make sense."

"In case you were wondering, I don't agree with everything my government does."

Actually, he was wondering something else. He toyed with the question, trying to find the right words. *To hell with it,* he decided. *Put it on the table.*

"Hannah, I need to ask you something."

"Something intimate?" A smile flitted over her face.

"Not exactly. I want to know, do you work for an intelligence agency?"

"Intelligence agency? Like what?"

"Like the Mossad."

She stared at him. "Did Lev Asher tell you that? That I was some kind of spy?"

"It doesn't matter who said it."

"It was Asher, that fink. I know it was."

"Well? Are you?"

"Why do you want to know?"

"I want to know why I'm here. Do you work for the Mossad?"

She didn't answer right away. She stirred her drink and turned her gaze toward the curtained window. "No," she said. "Not in the way you think. But it's true that officials in the Foreign Ministry are sometimes assigned to do intelligence work."

"And you? Are you one of those assigned to do intelligence work?"

"Does it matter?"

"Yes, if you're doing intelligence work now."

The brown eyes blazed at him. "So you think that's why I invited you here, to obtain information?"

"It crossed my mind."

"You can relax, because it isn't. You may find it impossible to believe, but I actually wanted to be with you. If you are worried that you may be compromised, then you should leave."

He didn't move. For a while neither of them spoke. Her brown eyes weren't blazing any longer. They were somber and dark.

"Go on," she said. "Leave. You shouldn't be here."

He still didn't move. *Okay,* he thought, *you put it on the table.* Now they understood each other. She knew that he knew that she was an agent, that she'd use him for classified information if he were careless enough to spill it. But he wasn't careless, of course, and, anyway, that wasn't why she invited him to her room.

Or so she said.

So why *was* he here? He wasn't sure, but he knew that being this close to Hannah Shamir was a bad idea. He shouldn't have come. He really *should* leave. Get the hell out.

He set his glass on the bar and rose from the stool. He was turning to leave when he glanced again at the long tanned legs, knees together, on the stool next to him. Bare shoulders with white strap marks. Wet, raven-black hair.

He felt the brown eyes on him. Not blazing, not accusing, just somber and watchful. Waiting to see what he would do.

What he did was lean forward and kiss her. It was a tentative kiss, lips just brushing hers. Then she was kissing him back, rising from the stool, pressing herself into him, fingers gliding over his back.

Through the thin silk he could feel the tautness of her body. He felt her hands unbuttoning his shirt, pulling it off his shoulders. She was guiding his hands, helping him unfasten her wraparound, slipping it over her hips, letting it rustle to the floor.

He realized that she wore nothing beneath it.

"Hannah . . ."

She put her finger to his lips. "No talk. That way we're safe. If we don't talk, we don't tell secrets."

Well, how could he argue with that? It made perfectly good sense. He took her hand and followed her to the bedroom.

CHAPTER 6

BAKSHEEP

"Yes, Mr. President," said Ricardo Solares. "I will make your position very clear to the Prime Minister."

Solares held the phone an inch from his ear while the President of the United States repeated for the third time what was foremost on his mind—that this was a fucking election year and the voters by God expected—no, *demanded*—that this administration do whatever it goddamned well took to get that downed Navy pilot back from those ragheads. Was that clear?

"I couldn't have said it better, sir," said Solares.

The President reminded him, also for the third time, that the prima donna Israelis had better quit fiddle-fucking around and start goddamn *talking* to the Palestinians about the unimaginable wave of shit that was going to roll down on all of them if they didn't get this prisoner thing over and done with. Did everyone there understand that?

"I will make sure of it, sir," said Solares.

With that, the President calmed down. He reassured Solares that he had the authority to do whatever was necessary. He was the President's Special Envoy, which meant he had the full backing of the White House.

"Thank you for your confidence in me, Mr. President."

He heard the click on the other end, then the empty crackle of the satellite connection.

Solares was alone in his suite in the U.S. embassy compound in Tel Aviv. For a while he sat in silence, reflecting on his dialogue with the leader of the free world. He wondered what the voters would think if they ever heard the President off the record. In public, he was a Bible-quoting Midwesterner, a prim Baptist whose favorite epithet was *shoot* or *dang* or sometimes, for special emphasis, *cripes amighty*. In private, as Solares and a few insiders knew, his tirades could peel paint from the walls of the Oval Office.

Solares knew the real reason for the President's vehemence. It was an election year, and he was dropping like a shotgunned pigeon in the polls. Besides the mess in the Middle East, the Dow had just dumped two thousand points in the last quarter, unemployment was shooting through 6 percent, and it didn't help that the White House Deputy Chief of Staff had just been caught soliciting little boys in a Capitol Building men's room.

Now the Navy pilot and the terrorists. *Correction,* thought Solares. *Can't call them terrorists anymore.* The current party line was to distinguish the mad-dog crazies like Al Qaeda and Islamic Jihad from the more nationalistic factions like Hamas and Fatah. Those were now "Palestinian militants." Sooner or later, one of them would replace the corrupt Palestinian Authority and become the de facto government of Palestine. Today's militant could be tomorrow's negotiating partner.

And that was precisely where Special Envoy Ricardo Solares would step in. At the correct moment, he would enter stage center with the full might and influence of the United States behind him. He would oversee the creation of a Palestinian state.

Destiny. He could hear it beckoning. And it was hinged to the fate of Lieutenant What's-his-face—Solares had already forgotten the Navy pilot's name—who was shot down by the Palestinians.

In the short term, thought Solares, it would be nice if he got credit for getting the prisoner released. In the bigger picture it might be even better if the prisoner never saw the light of day. Let him become a cause célèbre. It would just give Solares the leverage to bring the full might of the United States down on Palestine.

If he *did* somehow manage to extract the pilot from captivity, of course, Solares would be acclaimed as the greatest negotiator since Kissinger. And he could parlay that into something even greater. It would give him the mandate to bring a lasting settlement to the longest-running war in the Middle East. Perhaps he would even preside like a benevolent dictator, in the way MacArthur once ruled a conquered Japan.

Solares caught his reflection in the wall-length mirror. He tilted his head, smiled the old killer smile, imagining his face again on television. It was still there—the Hispanic good looks, long, straight nose, dark mustache, metallic brown eyes that he could change to suit the occasion. He could be intense, amused, compassionate. Whatever the scene required. *You've still got it, Ricko.*

Yeah, he hadn't changed much from the old days when he was a crusading television reporter with a viewership of forty million, a majority of whom adored him and a small minority who would like to fry him in oil. When he exited television to run for Congress, his mixed popularity followed him. Two years later one of his ardent fans, the newly elected President, tapped him for the Special Envoy job.

It was a nothing job at first. He was dispatched to shit holes like Ghana and the Ivory Coast and, for three terrifying months, Afghanistan. As the President's representative he was supposed to sweet-talk the belligerents, smooth ruffled feathers, leave them all smiling. And he did, more or less. Nothing much else came of it.

Then came the Colombia hostage crisis. Freeing the fifty-three American hostages thrust Rick Solares back on the nightly news and put his face on every newspaper front page. The fact that it was a done deal with the insurgents before Solares ever set foot in their jungle camp was never revealed. It didn't matter. The President thought he crapped gold bricks. So much so that he had lately been dropping Solares's name in public during off-the-cuff press briefs.

And that had been enough to start the nightly pundits ruminating about the President's choice of a running mate on the next ticket. His previous selection had been an egregious mistake, not only because the Veep was concealing an advanced case of prostate cancer, but because of his constant squabbling with the press. The media hated the Vice President and loved to goad him into one embarrassing gaffe after another. It was no secret that the President was shopping for a new running mate.

Rick Solares, of course, was still a distant dark horse. There were plenty of candidates with far more political qualification, but Solares could sense the tide turning in his favor. What he—and the President—needed was a dazzling display of statesmanship.

And a Nobel Peace Prize for the Special Envoy.

It was so close he could taste it. Freeing the American pilot was just the beginning. An accord between Israel and the Arabs that resulted in Palestinian statehood would establish Solares as the greatest peacemaker in modern history. The Vice President's slot would be his. And after the President's final term in office, who would be the inevitable choice to succeed him?

The thought made him almost giddy.

Solares looked again at the mirror. He tilted his chin upward, again flashing the famous grin. Minus the mustache, he thought, he bore a striking resemblance to FDR. Same confident grin, same intent gaze, same *You can trust me* expression. Hyde Park with a splash of Spanish Harlem.

A rap on the door interrupted his thoughts.

Vernon Lewis, his administrative assistant, came into the suite. Lewis was a heavyset man with shaggy hair and an IQ that ran off the scale.

"Your meeting with the Israeli Prime Minister is set for tomorrow, two o'clock, Mr. Solares."

"I thought someone was going to brief me on the prisoner situation."

"In the morning. He'll give you all the information before your meeting with the Prime Minister."

"Who is it? Another CIA spook?"

"No, we told them to send a Navy officer. Someone familiar with the details of the incident."

Solares had already stopped listening. He didn't care who briefed him on the downed pilot. It was only a formality. His thoughts had returned to the image of himself and the President and the Nobel Prize.

Hazerim Air Base, Israel

"Runner Zero-one, Hazerim tower, wind is two-four-zero degrees at twelve. Your flight is cleared for takeoff."

"Roger, Hazerim, Runner Zero-one and flight cleared for takeoff."

Maxwell's jet was aligned on the left half of the runway, with Lt. B.J. Johnson on his right. Behind them were Lt. Cmdr. Flash Gordon and his wingman, Lt. Hozer Miller. In solo position behind them was Lt. Bud Spencer.

Maxwell shoved the two throttles up to 80 percent thrust, holding the brakes against the thrust of the two GE engines. He glanced once more at B.J. Johnson. Her jet was powered up, ready to roll with him.

He nodded his head and released the brakes. In unison, the two Super Hornets lurched forward and accelerated down the runway. Maxwell eased the throttles forward, stopping just short of full military power. As the jets reached takeoff speed, they tilted their noses upward and left the long concrete strip at Hazerim.

Climbing into the desert sky, Maxwell raised the gear, then the flaps. He glanced over his shoulder to make sure Johnson was hanging on to his wing. She was. Behind them Gordon and Miller were in their own takeoff roll, followed by Spencer.

"Runner Zero-one, contact Storm Bird Control on two-eight-nine-point-five. Shalom, Commander Maxwell."

"Runner Zero-one and flight switching. Shalom, Hazerim."

Forty-five minutes later, Maxwell and his flight were skimming over the sea at six hundred feet, tailhooks extended. Ahead was the craggy gray shape of the *Reagan*, trailing a ribbon of white foam.

In echelon formation, they swept past the starboard side of the carrier. Half a mile beyond the bow, Maxwell banked hard to the left, grunting against the four-G turn, entering the downwind leg of the pattern. At six-second intervals, the other jets followed, slowing to gear and flap speed.

Halfway through the turn to final he picked up the shimmering yellow blob of the Fresnel lens—the yellow optical glide slope indicator mounted on a lens at the left edge of the landing deck.

"Runner Zero-one, Rhino ball, nine-point-three."

"Roger, ball," answered the Landing Signal Officer.

That was the ritual: Rolling into the groove, approaching the carrier deck, you announced your aircraft type, that you had the "ball"—the optical glide path reference. *Rhino* was the call to distinguish the Super Hornet from its smaller Hornet predecessor. Then fuel quantity. The LSO completed the contract by acknowledging "Roger, ball."

The contract was complete. The LSO had control of the pilot's approach to the ship.

Maxwell recognized the LSO's voice—Lt. Cmdr. Big

Mac MacFarquhar, the air wing LSO. For a moment Maxwell thought about Pearly Gates. Gates was the VFA-36 squadron LSO, whose voice Maxwell had heard more than any other as he landed aboard the *Reagan.*

He forced himself to stay focused on the ball. If the ball was in the center of the lens, aligned with the horizontal row of datum lights, it signaled that the jet was on the ideal flight path to the deck. If the ball went high on the lens, the jet was high. Unless the pilot corrected, he would overshoot the arresting wires.

A low ball was worse. It meant that the jet was settling dangerously close to the ramp—the blunt end of the flight deck.

The ball was drifting upward. With his left hand, Maxwell nudged the throttles back an increment. *Just a touch. Not too much or . . .*

It had been nearly three weeks since his last carrier landing. He was overcontrolling the stick and throttles.

"A liiiiittle powerr," said Big Mac, using his best LSO sugar talk.

Maxwell squeezed the throttles forward a tiny increment. The jet's descent flattened slightly, and the shimmering ball returned to the center of the lens.

The gray mass of the carrier swelled in Maxwell's windshield. The ramp swept beneath him.

Whump. The hard steel deck slammed into the Super Hornet's wheels. By instinct, Maxwell shoved the throttles forward. If the hook missed the wires, he wanted the engines at full thrust to hurtle back into the sky.

Maxwell felt the hard, reassuring tug of the harness against his shoulders as the tailhook grabbed a wire. The jet lurched to a stop, and he snatched the throttles back to idle.

He knew he'd snagged the number two wire. In the debriefing, the LSO would give him a "fair" grade. Not an ugly pass, but not good. He was out of practice.

Obeying the urgent signals of the plane director, he

taxied to the forward flight deck. When the jet was
snugged to the deck with tie-down chains, he shut down
the engines.

Maxwell opened the canopy and felt the warm twenty-
knot breeze flowing over the deck. He gazed around. Another Super Hornet—it should be B.J. Johnson—was just
rumbling forward from the arresting wires. More fighters
were spotted around the forward deck, on the elevator
forward of the island. High up in the carrier's superstructure he could see the faces on the captain's bridge peering through the thick glass.

He was home. *Baksheep.* Back aboard the hundred-
thousand-ton thrumming steel warship that he loved and
hated in equal amounts. He had expected that he would
return to the *Reagan* with the warm feeling of a mission
accomplished, but Operation Gideon had not turned out
the way he expected. His squadron had lost a pilot. Nothing would remove the bitter taste in Maxwell's mouth.

Petty Officer Third Class Laura Hensley, the plane
captain—the Navy's appellation for crew chief—was
standing on the boarding ladder. Hensley had just turned
nineteen. She was responsible for the cleaning, fueling,
and general airworthiness of the $100 million strike
fighter.

"Welcome back, Skipper," she said. "XO says he needs
to talk with you right away. He's waiting for you in
Ready Three."

Maxwell had a sinking feeling in his gut. Cmdr. Bullet
Alexander was Maxwell's executive officer and second
in command. He'd been running the squadron for three
weeks in Maxwell's absence. If he had to talk to Maxwell
right away, it had to be trouble.

He was right.
"I can't believe this shit," said Maxwell.
"I knew you'd say that," said Bullet Alexander.
Maxwell felt a headache coming on. He sighed and

rubbed the bridge of his nose with his thumb and forefinger. He could still feel the indent of the oxygen mask on his face.

They were sitting on the last row of seats in the back of the ready room, out of earshot of the junior officers clustered in the front. Maxwell saw them sneaking glances back at him. They looked worried. And for good reason, damn it.

"Okay, let me get this straight," Maxwell said. "The squadron was having a party in the admin in Haifa and—"

"More like . . . you know, a reception," said Alexander.

"Yeah, right. Reception. I don't suppose there was drinking involved?"

"Well, you know how it is. There might have been a few libations."

"How many guests were at this bash?"

"Maybe a couple dozen. Some chicks the guys invited from town. Some other air wing guys, a few ship's officers."

Maxwell knew the scenario. It was a tradition that when a carrier entered a foreign port, the officers of each squadron pooled their money and rented a hotel suite, called an "admin." The admin was stocked with abundant refreshments and served as social headquarters and crash pad while the squadron officers were ashore.

"Which hotel?" said Maxwell.

"The Carmel Beach, of course."

"Of course."

The Carmel Beach was the location of choice for squadron admins. It had a beach filled with bikini-clad scenery, music, and a bar that stayed open late.

"With a sea view, I presume?"

A pained look crossed Alexander's face. "Yes, sir, and in retrospect, I suppose that was a mistake. That was probably what inspired the . . . ah, catapult."

Maxwell kept his silence while Alexander told him the story. At some time well after midnight on their last night ashore, someone in the Roadrunner admin conceived the idea. It was supposed to simulate the real thing on a carrier—a catapult that launched jets. Using a coffee table, they erected a ramp over the rail of the first-floor balcony. For a launch vehicle, they purloined a laundry cart from hotel housekeeping.

Then came the choice of *who* would occupy the cart.

"How badly was he injured?" said Maxwell.

"Depends on who you talk to. The flight surgeon, Knuckles Ball, says that the guy's got some abrasions but he's basically okay. He claims to have neck injuries, and he's been wearing a brace around to prove it."

Maxwell shook his head. Of all people for them to pick on, why did it have to be Lt. Cmdr. Norbert P. Scudder? As the *Reagan*'s public affairs officer, Scudder had made it his personal crusade to reform the Roadrunners. In particular, he wanted to sanitize their use of raunchy call signs. This had come about after newspapers around the world published a photo of the USS *Reagan*'s catapult officer proudly wearing his float coat emblazoned with the call sign the Roadrunners had bestowed on him: Dog Balls.

Scudder failed. Not only was he unable to eradicate Dog Balls Harvey's offensive call sign, he discovered to his horror that the Roadrunner junior officers had given *him* a call sign. One day in the officers' wardroom, with an appropriate ceremony, the JOs presented him with a jersey with his new name on it. Scudder threw the jersey away. They gave him another. He threw that one away. Then the call sign appeared in the form of a placard on his stateroom door. He removed it. It reappeared.

And so on. Scudder was discovering a truth that every strike fighter pilot in the Navy had already learned. Call signs were like superglue: The more you resisted them, the more they stuck.

"Scrotum Scudder," said Maxwell. "What am I missing here? Scrotum hates the Roadrunners for hanging that call sign on him. Why was he there? And how did they get him into the laundry cart?"

"You know our JOs," said Alexander. "Those sneaky little shits could charm birds out of a tree. They invited Scrotum to their party on the pretext that they wanted to shake hands, make up, let him be one of the bubbas. Maybe even change his call sign. After he got shit-faced, someone convinced him it would be really cool if he got into the laundry cart."

Maxwell could visualize the rest. He could see Scrotum Scudder soaring like a wingless jet into the night sky, yelling in terror, crashing his laundry cart onto the hard-packed sand of Carmel Beach.

"So he got some scrapes and a sore neck. What's the big deal?"

"He's pressing charges. He wants somebody court-martialed for assaulting an officer. He's got JAG involved, and now they're conducting an investigation to identify the perpetrator." JAG—Judge Advocate General—was the legal branch of the U.S. military.

"And who might that be?"

"That's the problem," said Alexander. "They *all* want to be the perp. At last count we have twelve JOs who each swear he's the guy who launched Scrotum. Even Dog Balls Harvey, who isn't in the squadron, wants to be a perp."

Maxwell felt his headache worsening. This was the part of commanding a squadron that he hated. "Damn it, Bullet, where were you and Bat Masters? Those wild-ass JOs should have had adult supervision."

Alexander nodded and rubbed the dome of his glistening brown skull. "Yes, sir, I know that. Bat and I thought that it being their last night ashore, we'd cut them a little slack and get out of the way. My mistake, Skipper. I accept the blame."

Maxwell gave it some more thought. Of all the problems on his plate right now, Scrotum Scudder's crash in a laundry cart didn't even register on the scale.

But, he reminded himself, this was the new Navy. Since the Tailhook scandal, no commanding officer could afford to appear insensitive to the improper behavior of his junior officers.

"Okay, Bullet, this happened on your watch, right?"

"Right."

"Then it's your problem. Fix it."

"Yes, sir." Alexander sighed. "Somehow I knew you'd say that."

CHAPTER 7

GREAT LEADER

Gaza, Palestinian Territories
0930, Monday, 17 October

Here comes trouble.

Pearly could see it in Muhammad's face as he stormed into the room. Something had changed. The Palestinian gunmen posted at the doors and along the far wall saw it too. They scurried like mice to open a path for him.

The door slammed behind him. Muhammad stomped across the room to where Pearly sat, his left wrist still fastened with a chain to the leg of the wooden chair. For several seconds Muhammad said nothing. His chest was heaving as though he had just exerted himself.

Abruptly he swung his arm in a sweeping backhanded slap. Pearly's head snapped back.

"Hey, asshole. What do you think—"

Another blow, this time with his fist. It caught Pearly on the cheekbone, toppling him from the chair. He hit the floor, and the chain from his wrist yanked the chair over on top of him.

Pearly's vision clouded. He tasted blood trickling from the corner of his mouth. Looking up at Muhammad, he had a blurred view of the man's face. The nostrils were pinched and the eyes looked like burning embers. *Okay, he doesn't like being called an asshole.*

"Uh, we may be having a misunderstanding here. Don't you think we can—"

The toe of Muhammad's boot hit him in the stomach. The air wheezed out of him. Pearly gasped from the sudden pain.

Another kick. Pearly rolled away from it. He felt the boot brush his face, shattering the wooden leg of the chair.

He heard a woman's voice from across the room, yelling in Arabic.

Hanadi? Pearly couldn't see. He was doubled over, rolling on his side and clutching his arms around his midsection to ward off the next kick. He heard himself making wet sucking sounds, trying to regain his breath.

The voice was nearer, more shrill. She was arguing with Muhammad. It was Hanadi's voice. He was sure of it. Muhammad had gone off his rail and Hanadi was getting into it.

Muhammad said something in his harsh, guttural voice. Hanadi replied; then a *whack* cut her voice short. Pearly heard the sound of a hand against soft flesh.

He rolled over to see what was happening. Hanadi was glowering at Muhammad. Her shawl was knocked away and her short black hair hung in disarray over her forehead. A trickle of blood ran from her nose.

Muhammad's hand was raised to strike her again. From across the room came a blurred figure, flying like a wraith.

The slender form of Saleh collided with Muhammad, nearly knocking him over. Muhammad regained his balance and flung Saleh like a rag doll across the floor.

Muhammad had his pistol out. He was waving it at the two of them, yelling at them in Arabic. He turned back to Pearly.

Pearly sat, bracing for the next blow. The wreckage of

the chair was still chained to him. His gut ached from the kick to the stomach. His breath was coming in short wheezes.

Muhammad shoved the pistol within three inches of Pearly's eyes. It was a semiautomatic, heavy and clunky-looking. The barrel looked like the muzzle of a howitzer.

"Americans." He spat the word as if it were acid on his tongue. "You are worse than the Jews."

A fresh wave of rage seemed to come over him. He swung the pistol at Pearly's face. Pearly tried to duck, but the hard ridge of the weapon's frame caught him across the right ear. The blow made a shrill ringing sound that penetrated his skull. A flash of white light ignited in his head. He felt himself topple to the floor.

A deep voice, filled with authority, rang out from across the room.

Muhammad turned to confront the newcomer.

Pearly raised himself up on an elbow. His eyes were clouded again. Dimly he saw a man walking toward them. Through the watery blur of his vision, he recognized Khaled Mohanor.

The two men argued, their voices rising to an urgent pitch. Muhammad muttered something in a low voice and glowered once more at Pearly. He still held the semiautomatic in his right hand. He made one more threatening gesture with the gun, then shoved it back inside his shirt.

He whirled and stomped out of the room. His boots pounded like hammer blows on the tile floor.

Khaled waited until he was gone.

"He wants to kill you."

No shit, thought Pearly. His ears were ringing. His rib cage felt like it had been caved in. *He almost succeeded.*

"Why?"

"Because the Israelis have refused to release prisoners in exchange for you. Muhammad says you are of no further value to us."

Pearly felt his heart sink. "So why did you stop him from killing me?"

"It would have been an act of rage." Khaled nodded to where Hanadi and Saleh and the young Palestinian gunmen stood watching them. "It is not good for them to see their leaders behaving in such a way."

"What's the difference? You're going to kill me anyway."

"Yes," said Khaled. "But not until it serves my purpose."

USS Ronald Reagan, *Eastern Mediterranean*

Maxwell groaned. "Why me?"

"Very simple," said Boyce. He paused to take a bite from his doughnut, then washed it down with coffee. "You're our man in Israel. And because you know better than anyone the circumstances of how Pearly Gates got shot down. That makes you the logical guy to brief Solares."

Maxwell shook his head. Rambo Rick Solares. He had met Solares on one other occasion, and that was enough. During Operation Iraqi Freedom, Solares had landed aboard the carrier with an entourage of two dozen cameramen and staffers. As it turned out, he had no interest in interviewing pilots who were flying combat missions. Solares spent most of his time with the admiral and the ship's captain. Then he had himself filmed in full flight gear, posing in the cockpit of a strike fighter.

Maxwell and Boyce were seated at a back table in the officers' wardroom. It was midmorning. Maxwell's bag was already repacked for the trip back to Hazerim. The COD—carrier onboard delivery aircraft—that would take him back to Ben-Gurion airport was launching in a little over an hour. From Ben Gurion he would be driven out to Hazerim air base.

And then Boyce caught up with him in the wardroom.

"What am I supposed to tell Solares?" said Maxwell. "Anything sensitive?"

"Just enough so that he can sound knowledgeable when he preens for the television cameras tonight. Better leave out the stuff about the low-altitude dogfight with the Israelis. All he needs to know is that the goons who grabbed Pearly are the same species of scumbag that we've been fighting since September eleventh, 2001."

Maxwell nodded. He had mixed feelings about returning to Hazerim. Losing one of his pilots in the brown maw of the Israeli desert made it hard for him to like the place. But, he reminded himself, he still liked the Israelis. They were a bright people, industrious and outspoken. He had been impressed by the officers he met—Asher, Lebev, even the bellicose General Zemek.

An image flashed across his mind—thick black hair, tanned legs beneath a leather miniskirt.

Hannah Shamir. Yeah, he had to admit, he liked her too. Even if she was a spy.

Boyce reached for another doughnut. "You oughta try one of these things."

"No, thanks."

"They're not Krispy Kremes, of course, but what the hell. This is—"

He stopped. His eyes riveted on something across the room.

Maxwell looked up. Scrotum Scudder was standing in the front of the wardroom. He was wearing a white brace that looked like the neck sheath of a turtle.

Scudder caught them looking at him. He tilted his chin upward and marched over to the coffee urn.

"Behold, the walking wounded," said Boyce in a low voice.

"Do you think Scudder's neck is really injured?" said Maxwell.

"Doesn't matter," said Boyce. "He *says* it is, and Sticks

Stickney believes him. Whoever did it is in a world of shit."

Maxwell nodded. Captain Stickney was the *Reagan*'s captain and Scrotum Scudder's commanding officer.

Damn, thought Maxwell. Laundry carts and catapults and immature junior officers. Boyce had just done him a huge favor by sending him back to Hazerim. He should feel guilty that he was leaving the mess behind him. But he didn't.

Gaza, Palestinian Territories

Khaled took his time. He wanted Muhammad in a calmer mood. Muhammad was a ticking bomb. The man was unpredictable when he was enraged, which was most of the time.

It was necessary that he be alone with Muhammad. That was the hard part. What happened in the next few minutes was critical to the future of the movement. And to Khaled's future.

He waited until he figured no more than three or four were in the next room. He opened the door. They all stopped talking and turned to look at him.

The space was nearly as large as the front room. There was a dilapidated wooden table, a few chairs, a sink with a rusty tap. Large chunks of plaster were missing from the walls. A bare lightbulb dangled from the ceiling. Wooden crates lined one wall. Weapons, Khaled guessed. Small arms and AK-47s, maybe some RPGs. There would also be the material of bombs—nitroglycerin, ball bearing shrapnel, wire, and fuses—the stuff with which they obliterated themselves along with their enemies.

With Muhammad was his lieutenant, Akram. Khaled knew him only by reputation. Akram was a thug, like most of Muhammad's foot soldiers. Fanatic, vicious, surpassingly stupid. The two others he didn't know by name.

They were young, trying their best to look tough, openly worshipful of Muhammad.

"I need to speak with you," Khaled said to Muhammad.

"About what?"

"About the prisoner."

"Then speak."

"Alone."

Muhammad looked wary. "Why alone?"

"Because it is a very sensitive matter. What I have to tell you is for your ears and no one else's."

Muhammad looked unconvinced. "Akram is my lieutenant. He sees what I see, hears what I hear."

Akram's head bobbed up and down, signifying his agreement. He gave Khaled a menacing glower.

Khaled expected this. It would be more difficult, but it was necessary. Sooner or later Akram had to be dealt with. Better sooner.

"Very well," said Khaled. "If he must stay, then send the others out."

Muhammad hesitated for a moment, then motioned for the two younger Palestinians to leave. They skulked out of the room, closing the door behind them.

Muhammad and Akram stood facing Khaled.

"The prisoner is mine," said Muhammad. His voice still had an angry, defiant tone. "I intend to kill him, with or without your consent."

"We have not finished interrogating him," said Khaled. "He may still have information of value to us."

"That is not for you to decide. You are a political figure, nothing more. Go have your photograph taken with the Israelis and the Americans and pretend that you are someone important. It is I who captured the prisoner. I will dispose of him."

Akram nodded his head in support. He loosened the strap of the AK-47 over his shoulder and gave Khaled a menacing glower.

Khaled sighed. He gave them a look of resignation. "Very well, Muhammad. I must concede that you are correct."

Muhammad looked surprised. "You concede?"

"Yes. When you explain it that way, I understand clearly. The prisoner is your responsibility, not mine."

"You will not interfere?"

"No. I realize now that I acted impulsively. It was improper of me to question your judgment in this matter."

"We are in the same struggle," Muhammad said. His voice was less strident now. "You and I have separate duties. I am the commander of this unit."

"And you are an excellent commander. You deserve more respect from your subordinates. From me also."

Muhammad nodded his agreement. The hard lines in his face seemed to soften.

I was right, thought Khaled. *He loves flattery.*

"Then we are in agreement that the prisoner has no more value?" Muhammad said.

"We are."

"And you agree that he should be killed?"

"Of course," said Khaled. "I would only offer a humble suggestion."

Muhammad's eyebrows arched upward. "And that is . . . ?"

"That it be dramatic and excruciating. The execution should be videotaped and delivered to the Israelis and Americans."

Muhammad's face came alive. "Exactly," he said. "Let them see the price they pay for oppressing us."

At this, even Akram's countenance changed. Something close to a smile flitted over his face.

It was as Khaled expected. Nothing warmed the hearts of these idiots like a good execution. Despite their swagger and fondness for titles, they were illiterate peasants. None, including Muhammad, possessed more than a rudimentary education, and that consisted mainly of the teachings of Islam. They had no notion of Western culture except what they saw on television. Their world view was simplistic. Love Allah, hate Israel. Kill everyone who doesn't hate Israel.

Kill the prisoner.

"I leave it in your hands," said Khaled. "Do with the prisoner as you wish."

"As Allah wishes," said Muhammad. *Inshallah.*

"As Allah wishes."

He gave Muhammad a deferential bow of the head. Muhammad replied with a curt nod. Akram wore a curious expression, as though he might have missed something.

The two turned to exit the room. Muhammad's hand was on the door lever when Khaled, standing behind him, said, "There's one more thing."

Both heads turned. Akram recognized the danger first. In a single practiced motion, he lifted the stock of the AK-47 with his left hand, right hand slipping into the trigger cage. The movement took only a millisecond.

A millisecond too long.

Khaled shot him first. The range was less than three meters. The nine-millimeter bullet from the Browning semiautomatic struck Akram's forehead, opening a cavity just above his left eye.

Muhammad was dancing sideways, groping inside his shirt for his own pistol. Khaled took his time. In his peripheral vision he saw Akram going down, the Kalashnikov clattering to the floor beside him.

He put a bullet into Muhammad's chest.

Muhammad stopped dancing. His own pistol, a large-caliber Makarov, fell from his fingers. His face was filled with disbelief. This couldn't be happening.

"You deceived us. . . ."

"Of course," said Khaled, and shot him between the eyes.

*   *   *

Pearly heard the shots. *Here it comes. I'm next.*

The Palestinian gunmen in the room heard it too. For a long moment they stood frozen, staring at the closed door. The two AK-47-carrying young men, the same pair who had just left the room a few minutes earlier, rushed to the door.

"Muhammad?" one called.

Nothing.

"Akram?"

No answer. The door swung open. Khaled appeared, looking grim-faced. He carried a pistol in his hand.

From ten meters away Pearly could hear him arguing with the young men. Pearly didn't understand what they were saying, but it was clear that there had been a shootout. Khaled? Muhammad?

Now what? The young men were unhappy about what happened.

There was more argument, much gesticulating, and through the din Pearly could hear the deep, mesmerizing timbre of Khaled's voice overriding the shrill sounds of the gunmen.

Pearly was aware of Hanadi's presence. Her face was tense, watching the confrontation across the room.

"What happened?" Pearly said.

She kept her eyes on the arguing men. One of them, a young man with the beginnings of a fuzzy beard, was waving his Kalashnikov like a baton. Khaled was watching him, still holding the pistol.

"Muhammad and Akram are dead," she said in a flat voice.

"Let me guess. Those other guys aren't happy, right?"

"There was a disagreement," she said.

Yeah, and he could figure out what the disagreement was about. Muhammad and the other dude, the one called Akram, wanted to blow him away. Khaled wasn't ready for that. Not yet anyway. So he settled the argument with a pistol. *Way to go, Khaled.*

Except that the other guys, who looked like kids dressed up like badass terrorists, seemed ready to do the same thing to Khaled. They had enough firepower between them to shred him like a paper target. And when that happened, Pearly knew who was next on the killing agenda.

He listened while the argument ebbed and flowed, gathering heat and then simmering down. The young men were excited, waving their weapons and hopping from foot to foot. Khaled remained calm, lecturing them like a stern schoolmaster.

The confrontation seemed to lose its intensity. The one who was waving the Kalashnikov slung it back over his shoulder. The young Palestinians stopped chattering and listened to Khaled, who was explaining something to them in Arabic. His voice had a strong, resonant ring that seemed to fill the room.

Hanadi was nodding her head, listening to Khaled speak.

"What's he saying?" Pearly asked.

"He says Muhammad and Akram would have brought destruction down on all of them. By killing the prisoner and defying the Israelis and Americans, they were inviting a mass retaliation. Khaled says that Muhammad wanted nothing but revenge and destruction, that he had no interest in a Palestinian homeland. Khaled wants a free Palestine. A country of our own. So he told the young men they must make a choice."

"And they did?"

She nodded, and her eyes seemed to glow as she gazed at Khaled. "They know he is the Great Leader. Khaled will lead us to freedom."

CHAPTER 8

HARDBALL TIME

USS Ronald Reagan
Eastern Mediterranean
0920, Monday, 17 October

Bullet Alexander peered down at the flight deck.
Through the thick glass of the captain's bridge, he saw
the C-2A COD hurtling down the track of the number two
catapult. The blunt-nosed turboprop cleared the bow and
lifted into the morning sky.

Maxwell was on his way back to Israel. Alexander was
running the squadron again. And the Scrotum Scudder affair was metamorphosing from a minor tremor to a full-
scale earthquake.

Behind him, CAG Boyce was arguing with Captain
Stickney.

"Damn it, Sticks," said Boyce, "doesn't it matter that
the dumb shit wasn't really hurt? Knuckles Ball says
Scudder is just faking it with that neck brace."

"What matters," said Capt. Sticks Stickney, "is that Mr.
Scudder *claims* he's hurt. Even though he's technically
one of my officers, he works for the U.S. Navy Office of
Information. I don't have to remind you that they, more
than anyone else, take the Navy's public image very seri-
ously."

Alexander watched the exchange between Boyce and Stickney. The two men were contemporaries in rank, one responsible for the air wing and its eighty-plus aircraft embarked aboard the *Reagan*, the other responsible for the ship itself.

But Alexander knew also that they were opposites in style and temperament. Capt. Sticks Stickney was a cautious, by-the-book carrier skipper who had a reputation for meticulous attention to detail. Boyce was more of a maverick, a fighter pilot who didn't mind bending rules that he thought needed bending.

One such rule concerned smoking. Stickney was frowning at Boyce's cigar. Everyone knew that Stickney hated all forms of tobacco, particularly cigars, lit or unlit. Which, of course, was why Boyce liked to have one clenched in his teeth when he came to Stickney's bridge.

Boyce removed the cigar and studied it for a moment. "So we're going to let that supercilious little prick ruin someone's career because he got drunk and accepted a ride in a laundry cart?"

Stickney gave Boyce a sour look. "It's out of my hands. JAG is pursuing the investigation. If the person who committed the assault isn't identified and charged with a violation of the UCMJ, then you can assume that everyone involved with the incident will receive a letter of reprimand." The UCMJ—Uniform Code of Military Justice—was the Navy's basic body of laws.

Stickney paused and peered at Alexander. "Including the commanding officer and executive officer. Do I need to explain what that means, Commander Alexander?"

It was the first time Stickney had acknowledged Alexander's presence. "No, sir," said Alexander.

He knew exactly what it meant. A letter of reprimand was the kiss of death. Dozens of such letters had been issued to attendees of the 1991 Tailhook convention. Most of the recipients had seen their careers crash and burn. Officers on a fast track to command had found their names deleted from promotion lists. Senior officers selected for fleet command saw their orders rescinded.

Boyce snorted. "This is turning into a witch hunt, Sticks. Brick and Bullet weren't even there. Why should they get tagged with reprimands?"

Stickney gave him a humorless smile. "You know the rules, Red. This is the new Navy. Zero tolerance for scandal. Someone has to be responsible."

At this, Boyce snorted and turned to the heavy glass pane. "What a crock of shit," he muttered.

"Excuse me?" said Stickney. "Did you say—"

"I said thanks for your time, Captain." He turned to Alexander. "C'mon, Bullet. Let's go find us a perp."

U.S. Embassy, Tel Aviv

Maxwell waited while Solares posed for the camera. Solares turned his head, giving the camera a shot of his profile. He held the pose until he heard the shutter click.

He turned to Maxwell. "I'm sorry, your name again? Commander . . . what was it?"

"Maxwell, sir."

"Nice of you to come, Commander." Solares peered at him. "Have we met before?"

"Briefly. During Operation Iraqi Freedom."

"Oh, yes. A lot has happened since then. So you were with the chap who was shot down. Lieutenant, ah . . ."

"Gates. I was his flight leader, and I'm the commanding officer of his squadron."

The COD had delivered Maxwell to the military ramp of Ben-Gurion airport. He was picked up by a driver in a plain white Toyota and delivered to the U.S. embassy compound in Tel Aviv. Vernon Lewis met him at the security checkpoint, then walked him up two flights of stairs to Special Envoy Solares's temporary office.

Maxwell and Ricardo Solares were seated at the end of

a long conference table. Several chairs away by himself sat Lewis. He had a yellow legal pad in front of him. The photographer was roaming the room, snapping candid shots of Solares.

Maxwell couldn't help staring at Solares. *Rambo Rick*. He was in full costume—boots, khaki trousers, creased military-style shirt with epaulets. He looked like the great white hunter.

Solares asked about the mission, why Navy fighters were flying in Israel, how it was that the Navy pilot got shot down. Maxwell told him about Operation Gideon. He described the downing of Pearly's jet, leaving out the details about the engagement with Lebev's F-16.

Lewis was making notes on his pad. In the center of the table, a tape recorder was running. The photographer moved silently around the room, getting more shots of Solares.

Solares said, "So you saw the pilot being taken prisoner?"

"I saw his parachute, but he vanished almost as soon as he reached the ground."

"But no one actually saw him being captured?"

"Only the guys who captured him."

Solares ignored this while he tilted his chin up and turned to give the photographer another shot. From across the table, Lewis watched with a blank expression.

"Well," said Solares. "I think I have all the facts. We should prepare ourselves for the possibility that the prisoner may not be released." After a moment, he added, "Alive, I mean."

Maxwell didn't like what he was hearing. "If a release isn't negotiated, what will be our next initiative?"

"I don't see that we have one."

"We can conduct a military operation."

"Not a chance."

"Why not?"

"Because this isn't our country, Commander."

"Neither was Iraq or Afghanistan or Kosovo. We did what we had to do."

"This is different. Israel is not a hostile country."

"Then why wouldn't they allow us to get Lieutenant Gates back?"

Solares made a show of looking exasperated. "For your information, Americans are in Israel by invitation only. We're guests in this country."

"Yes, sir. But Lieutenant Gates is not exactly a guest, is he?"

Solares gave him a sharp look. "Look, Commander, you're way out of your depth here. Your job is military. Mine happens to be diplomatic. In fact, I'll be conferring with the Israeli Prime Minister about this very subject in"—he glanced at his watch—"three hours. The only way we're going to get the prisoner of war back is through diplomacy."

Maxwell caught the hard edge in Solares's voice. He saw Lewis lower his pen and stare across the table at them, a curious expression on his face. *Okay, Maxwell, you've said your piece. Time to shut up and get the hell out.*

He pushed himself back from the table and rose to leave.

Then he sat down again.

"With all due respect, sir, I think you're missing something here."

"Excuse me?"

"You keep referring to Lieutenant Gates as a prisoner of war. You and I both know that's bullshit. He's a hostage, and the animals who kidnapped him are terrorists."

Solares motioned for the photographer to stop. The grin was gone from his face. "Thank you for the lecture, Commander. For your information, the Palestinians don't consider themselves terrorists. They're nationalists and freedom fighters. If we expect to negotiate with them, we have to give them that recognition. Now if you'll excuse me."

Solares turned from him and directed his attention to the sheaf of papers on the table. The briefing was over.

"Yes, sir," said Maxwell.

Now it was *really* time to get the hell out. He saw Lewis nodding his head toward the exit. Maxwell rose and followed him out. Solares didn't look up as they left.

They walked in silence back down the stairs, through the security checkpoint again, and out to the open court-yard, where the white Toyota was waiting.

"I have to hand it to you, Maxwell," said Lewis. "That was a hell of a show."

Maxwell paused before climbing into the Toyota. "What do you mean?"

"Telling Solares he's full of shit. Nobody here has the guts to do that."

Gaza, Palestinian Territories

Khaled Mohanor sipped his tea as he watched the traffic on the street outside.

"Sheik Hamzeh?" The voice in the cell phone sounded incredulous. "You cannot be serious."

"I am quite serious," said Mohanor. From the sidewalk table he could see pedestrians in each direction.

"You are asking for the impossible," said the man on the phone. "Even though you no longer demand the release of the four hundred Fatah fighters, I can assure you the Prime Minister will never agree to free Hamzeh."

"It doesn't matter what he agrees to. Sheik Hamzeh must be freed. It is the only acceptable condition. The Prime Minister should understand the great symbolism of such an exchange."

"And if he does not agree?"

"You know the answer."

Silence. Khaled waited, sipping again at his coffee. It was thick Arab coffee, with a rich sludge at the bottom of the cup. He knew the man was stalling, probably allowing the electronic surveillance trackers time to refine the location of Khaled's cell phone. Let them, he thought. If they wanted to arrest him here in Gaza, or even kill him, they could have done it already. Both sides knew that it would be a calamitous mistake.

The man said, "You understand that the Americans must be involved?"

"Of course."

He not only understood it; it was exactly what he wanted. Without pressure from the Americans, the Israelis would never release a prize like Sheik Hamzeh.

"I will deliver the message," said the man. "Contact me tomorrow. The usual channel."

"The proposal will be in the *Jerusalem Times* in the morning."

"That would be a serious mistake," said the man, his voice sharp. "It will only complicate—"

"Tell the PM I expect an answer in twelve hours."

"Do not push your luck. You are demanding too much."

"Twelve hours. No later."

"I will relay your message."

Khaled clicked the END CALL button on the phone. As he finished the coffee, he let his eyes sweep the street around him. Two Palestinian men sat at another table, also sipping coffee, pretending to ignore him. Three more stood across the street, and two were loitering in the market stall twenty meters down the sidewalk. Each, Khaled knew, carried a semiautomatic weapon. Each was prepared to use it at the first hint of a threat to Khaled.

It was mostly ritual, of course. Bodyguards were no protection against a rocket fired from an Israeli helicopter. Or a precision bomb from an F-16. But his enemies were not all Israeli. These days an attempt on his life was more likely to come from another Palestinian.

The Palestinian Authority—the so-called government of Gaza and the West Bank—was wary of the rise of Khaled Mohanor. He had become too popular—a folk hero to the demoralized Palestinians. The Great Leader, he was being called, and the PA would do anything to discredit him. They were even circulating rumors that Khaled might be dealing with the Israelis.

With that thought, Khaled smiled to himself. He left ten shekels on the table and left. The men at the next table rose and followed him.

Israeli Prime Minister's Office, Jerusalem

Crotchety old windbag, thought Solares. He kept a polite expression on his face while the Prime Minister ranted on.

". . . and furthermore, you should understand that we Israelis have much more experience dealing with terrorists than the Americans." Prime Minister Shallutz's jowls waggled, and he jabbed the air with his right forefinger as he spoke. "You seem to forget that we have been at war with terrorists since 1948."

Solares waited until Shallutz paused for breath. "I haven't forgotten, Mr. Prime Minister. Nor has the President. But I must inform you, he is most emphatic. The recovery of our pilot must be accomplished."

"We could recover his body. And we could kill most of his captors. There is not the slightest chance that we could rescue him alive." Shallutz spoke with the firm sureness of a military leader, which he had once been. Before being elected Prime Minister, Shallutz had been Defense Minister, and before that he was the senior ranking general in the Israeli Defense Force.

"The President agrees with that position. But he expects that the prisoner's release will be negotiated."

Shallutz's face darkened further. The veins in his neck

were throbbing. Solares wondered how much pressure the old man's heart could take before it exploded.

"We have been down this path before," said Shallutz. "We refused to release the four hundred captured Fatah guerrillas, and we must refuse to consider this latest proposal to exchange Sheik Hamzeh. It is not our policy to negotiate with terrorists."

Sitting with Shallutz and Solares were Dan Shimon, the Defense Minister; Menahem Yoffe, the Foreign Minister; and General Zemek, the commander of the Israeli Air Force. Half a dozen aides sat at the end of the table with notepads. On each side of Solares was a U.S. State Department staffer.

Solares said, "The President strongly believes that you should make an exception in this case."

"We are deeply grateful for the continuing support of the United States. But the President must understand that he does not dictate Israeli policy."

Solares nodded, savoring the moment. He knew it would come to this. Hardball time. He made a steeple with the fingers of both hands and gazed across the table at the older man.

"The President would like you to know that he has ordered a review of the export of the seventy-five new F-16I fighters that Israel has on order. The authorization for the contract will be suspended indefinitely until the review is complete."

Shallutz looked as if he'd been walloped with a mallet. From his shirt pocket he produced a vial of pills. He popped one into his mouth, then chased it with a glass of water.

A silence fell over the long conference table.

Shimon, the Defense Minister, broke the silence. "That comes dangerously close to blackmail," he said, glowering at Solares.

Solares flashed his famous television smile at the Defense Minister. Shimon, like Shallutz, had been a senior general in the Israeli Defense Force. In Israeli politics, the Defense Minister's post was a stepping-stone to the Prime Minister's seat. But not for Shimon. Not since he'd become implicated in a much-publicized bribe-taking scandal. Dan Shimon was a toothless tiger.

Shallutz regained his composure. He banged his fist on the table. "Those F-16s are essential to our security. What makes the U.S. think they can gamble with Israel's survival?"

"The President is strongly committed to Israel's survival," said Solares in a silky voice. "He is also convinced that an accommodation can be found in this matter that will satisfy all our mutual interests."

At this, Gen. Nathan Zemek seemed to come alive. He arched one eyebrow, and for a moment he and Solares locked gazes across the table. Solares knew Zemek only by reputation. More and more, the name of Nathan Zemek was being floated around the Knesset as a successor to Yoffe and perhaps even old Shallutz himself.

Zemek cleared his throat. "Mr. Prime Minister, if you will permit me, perhaps Mr. Solares and I may have a discussion. Just he and I, in private."

Shallutz fixed his beady brown eyes first on Zemek. Solares saw the two men lock gazes; then Shallutz gave Zemek a barely perceptible nod. With a wave of one plump hand, he dismissed him. "Go," he said.

"You're the one to do it," said Zemek.

They were in an anteroom off the cabinet meeting room. Zemek was pacing like a lion, hands shoved into his trouser pockets.

"I'm the one to do what?" Solares asked.

"Negotiate. Deal with the terrorists who are holding your pilot."

"How? The Prime Minister just said—"

"I know what he said." Zemek stopped pacing and pulled two Cokes from the refrigerator. He handed one to

Solares. "He had to say that. If Shallutz said anything else, the right-wing coalition would turn on him like a pack of jackals."

"I'm not sure I follow you, General. What can I do if the Prime Minister refuses to release this Palestinian sheik?"

"That's not what he meant. What he meant was that *he* wouldn't negotiate. He means that it's up to you."

Solares felt a thrill run through him. He knew where this was going now, but he still had to play the game.

"Negotiate with whom?"

"With the only Palestinian who can work with us. His name is Khaled Mohanor."

Solares nodded. He had been briefed by Vernon Lewis about a Palestinian named Khaled Mohanor. The one who liked to be called the Great Leader.

According to the briefing material, Khaled Mohanor was born in Beirut, the son of Palestinians who had been evicted from Israel after the 1948 war. When he was still in the university in Cairo in 1982, both his parents were killed by the Christian Lebanese militia during the Israeli occupation of Lebanon. It was then that Mohanor joined the Hezbollah and became a cult hero.

In one of the rare military successes against Israeli forces, Mohanor and his guerrillas drove IDF troops from a southern Lebanon hilltop, after which they withdrew all their forces from Lebanon. When the second intifada ignited in September 2000, Israeli troops occupied the West Bank, and Mohanor took command of a splinter Hamas faction called Al-Tanzim.

Refusing to ally himself with Arafat's Palestinian Authority, Mohanor and his followers conducted their own clandestine operations. If the intel reports were correct, Mohanor was hated more by the Palestinian government than he was by the Israelis. He had survived at least four assassination attempts.

Solares said, "Will Shallutz order the sheik released if I make a deal with Mohanor?"

Zemek shrugged and opened the tab of the Coke can. "Shallutz is a pragmatist. He will do what is to his advantage."

There was more to it, Solares sensed. This was more than just an exchange of prisoners. Something larger was at stake here.

"How do I make contact with Khaled Mohanor?"

"It will be arranged," said General Zemek.

CHAPTER 9

DOME OF THE ROCK

Hazerim Air Base, Southern Israel
1645, Monday, 17 October

"Message for you, Commander Maxwell," said the sergeant at the desk in the senior officers' quarters. She was blond and petite, with hip-hugging khaki uniform pants. She looked like a teenager, thought Maxwell. But they all did these days.

She scanned his ID card, then handed him a sealed white envelope. The inked stamp read:

FROM: COMMANDER AIR WING THREE,
           USS *REAGAN*
TO: CDR S. H. MAXWELL
VIA: COMMUNICATIONS OFFICER,
           HAZERIM AIR BASE, IDF

It was nearly nine o'clock. He thought he caught a knowing smile on the sergeant's face. The last time he had seen her was when he was on his way to Hannah Shamir's room.

He took the stairs to the third floor and let himself into the room. The Hazerim SOQ had been his home now for . . . how long? Over a week. It was a comfortable accommodation, luxurious by U.S. Navy standards, with a separate bedroom, a small dinette, a living room with stuffed chairs and a couch and a floral-patterned carpet. It even had cable television and a broadband Internet connection. Through the two curtained windows he had a view of the sprawling base and the black emptiness of the desert beyond.

He dropped the envelope on the desk beside his notebook computer. Nothing from Boyce at this time of night could be good news. First he'd take a shower. He could feel the fatigue of the long day in his bones. He was tired from the steady stress of the Pearly Gates crisis, the frustration of his meeting with Solares.

He thought about Hannah. Was she here at Hazerim? No. He remembered that she was going back to Tel Aviv for a few days. She'd call, she said.

He didn't know yet how he was supposed to feel. He hardly knew her. It was unlikely, if not impossible, that anything could come of it. They were from opposite worlds, opposite backgrounds, opposite attitudes. She was a *sabra*, a native Israeli, always would be. He would always be an outsider here. Nothing in common.

Bullshit. Hannah was a smart, sexy woman who made him feel good. What the hell was wrong with that?

Nothing. *Relax, Maxwell.*

When he'd dried off and put on his gray cotton warmups, he went back into the living room. He pulled a Maccabee from the tiny fridge, popped it open, sat at the desk.

He ripped the envelope open and stared at the laser-printed letter. It wasn't from Boyce. Maxwell's heart rate accelerated by twenty beats.

For several seconds he sat frozen. He looked away from the letter, fixing his eyes on the curtained window across the room.

Why now? It was supposed to be over. Or was it?

An unsummoned vision of Hannah Shamir again

flashed through his mind. Dark eyes, olive skin, thick hair rustling in the wind of Masada.

He pushed the image from his mind and read the message.

My dearest Sam,

Captain Boyce on the Reagan *informed me that you are somewhere in Israel and suggested that you might actually be glad to hear from me. He kindly offered to forward this message.*

It has been five months, three days, and a few hours (who's counting?) since I last saw you, but it seems like several lifetimes. As you will recall, I was angry when we said good-bye. Maybe more than angry. When I said I had no wish to be a Navy widow, I meant it. But since then I have come to realize that being apart from you like this is a far worse condition than being a widow. It was selfish of me to demand that you give up what you love. Even if you had agreed, you would hate me for it.

Does this sound like an apology? I'm not good at this kind of thing, you know. For all I know there is someone else in your life. If so, I understand.

By the time you read this, I will probably be in Jerusalem with my network news crew. We're coming to cover the story of the downed American pilot, who, I believe, was from your squadron. Don't worry; I know the rules. No questions.

I will be in the King David Hotel. Phone: 057-970-788. Please call. Better than that, please come.

I know you, Sam Maxwell. You are a proud and stubborn man. But just this once, allow a girl who loves you to tell you that she was wrong.

I miss you terribly.

All my love,
Claire

Maxwell continued staring at the letter, his emotions flowing wildly inside him.

Claire. His first love. She came into his life when he was a rookie test pilot. They'd been young. Too young, he reflected. And too proud, too ambitious. They let their careers come between them, take them in different directions, Maxwell to NASA, she to foreign assignments. He married an astronaut, became a widower, returned to the fleet. She married a journalist/CIA agent named Tyrwhitt, then divorced him.

Nearly a decade passed before their lives intertwined again. But the differences never really went away. They kept coming back to the same old choices. Stay in the Navy, pursue your career until it consumed you or spit you out with a sea trunk full of memories. Or marry the woman you love. Live ashore, lead a normal life, close your ears to the sound of jets overhead.

The eternal dilemma of the warrior.

He no longer felt the fatigue of the long day. His mind was sorting through all the pieces of his life, like a complicated mosaic. Each had a face attached. Pearly Gates. Ricardo Solares. Hannah Shamir. Claire Phillips.

He looked again at the letter. It wasn't too late. Still early evening.

He picked up the phone.

Temple Mount, Old City, Jerusalem

The eyes.

That was it, thought Solares. Most Arabs avoided direct eye contact, but Khaled Mohanor was different. The Palestinian's eyes were fixed on him like lasers.

In the dim light of the mosque, Solares studied the man. He had a lean, handsome face and a dark mustache. He wore a leather jacket and a checked kaffiyeh.

Khaled Mohanor smiled, revealing brilliant white teeth. "You seem nervous, Mr. Solares."

"Not at all," said Solares. His nerves were twanging like high tension wires.

The temperature had dropped as they arrived in the city. At twenty-five hundred feet above sea level, Jerusalem was exposed to frigid autumn winds and the blustery squalls that descended from the north. Solares wore chinos and a fleece pullover against the autumn chill.

With Solares were Vernon Lewis and the three Secret Service agents assigned to Solares's mission. The agents wore bulky down-filled parkas, not so much for warmth but to conceal the stubby Heckler & Koch MP-5 nine-millimeter submachine guns.

Along the walls of the enclosure, Solares saw the shapes of a dozen other men watching them. Palestinians. Even in the dim light he knew they were armed.

"You have nothing to fear from me," said Mohanor. "In fact, we have a common adversary."

"Oh? Who is that?"

"Israel. You want the American pilot back. We want the Palestinian prisoner Sheik Hamzeh released. It is the Israeli government who is obstructing both our purposes."

"It is the Palestinians who are holding the American prisoner," said Solares, "not the Israelis."

Solares and his party had driven in a pair of white Toyotas from Tel Aviv to the old city of Jerusalem. From the Damascus Gate at the northwest wall of the city they went by foot, passing through thousand-year-old covered passageways, through closed bazaars, cutting through the edge of the Muslim quarter.

When they came to the perimeter of the Temple Mount, Solares had stopped, awed as always by the spectacle. The Dome of the Rock rose like a great golden bulb within the enclosure. Constructed in the seventh century by an Arab caliph, the dome enclosed the sacred rock on which Abraham prepared to sacrifice his son and from which, according to Islamic tradition, Mohammed launched himself to join Allah.

Now it was a place for a clandestine meeting. Standing inside the Muslim enclave, Solares fought back the panic that rose in him. He was in alien territory. This was where Ariel Sharon, then the opposition party leader in the Israeli government, forced his way into the mosque with a contingent of IDF soldiers. In the resultant shoot-out seven Palestinians were killed. The second intifada had been ignited.

Why had he agreed to a meeting here? They should have done the deal in Tel Aviv. Or in the new city of Jerusalem. Why hadn't he sent Lewis in his place? He was career State Department. Lewis was expendable.

Mohanor said, "The Israelis are the reason your pilot is not free. Why doesn't the U.S. President order the Prime Minister to release Sheik Hamzeh?"

"The Prime Minister of Israel does not take orders from the President."

"He does when he believes it is to his advantage."

"The Prime Minister believes that Sheik Hamzeh is a danger to the security of Israel."

"Danger?" Khaled scoffed. "What do Israelis know of danger? Every Israeli soldier is a danger to the Palestinian people."

"But the prisoner you're holding is not an Israeli soldier."

"The United States and Israel are as one in this matter."

Solares sensed that this part of the discussion was concluded. Mohanor was reciting his lines as if reading a script. It was time to move on.

"Tell me what you want," said Solares.

"I told you. Sheik Hamzeh."

"And you would release the American pilot?"

"Of course."

"And then?"

Solares could feel the intensity of Mohanor's gaze. The eyes bored into him.

"And then we execute the next phase," said Mohanor.

The next phase. This was the part that wasn't clear to Solares, but he knew he was close to a deal. "Do I have your word that Sheik Hamzeh will not be a threat to Israel?"

The laser eyes flicked around the interior of the mosque, then returned to Solares. "You have my word."

CHAPTER 10

PIANO CONCERTO NUMBER THREE

Jerusalem
1955, Monday, 17 October

She caught the waiter's attention and ordered another vodka-tonic, her second in fifteen minutes. Why was she so damned nervous? No reason. None at all, except that her life wouldn't amount to a puddle of pee if the guy she was waiting for didn't say he still loved her.

Quit acting like an addled schoolgirl. She hated feeling this way. She was a television journalist, poised and unflappable. *Damn it!* Most men were intimidated by her.

Yes, but most men were not like Sam Maxwell.

She wanted a cigarette. Where did that come from? She had quit nearly two years ago, hadn't even felt the need. She sipped at the drink, making herself go slowly, trying to be calm and collected.

Now that darkness had come, it was cool outside. She had asked for a table on the terrace, thinking it would give them privacy. Sprawled beneath the grounds of the hotel was the old city of Jerusalem, glowing now in the softness of the evening. From the lounge inside came the sound of a piano. Something classical that she couldn't pin down. Chopin? Sam would know. He knew more about music than—

She saw him.

Same old blue blazer, button-down oxford shirt, no tie, pressed khakis. Sam Maxwell wasn't into fashion. Someday she'd take him shopping. Nothing flashy, good wool, something dark and nice and tailored to that lanky, long-armed frame.

He was gazing around, looking for her among the dozen or so tables on the long outdoor terrace. She felt a warm glow come over her. Was it the vodka, or did the guy really have that kind of effect on her?

She saw the two women at the table nearest the door, each in her twenties or early thirties, take a long, appraising look at him. Sam Maxwell missed handsomeness by a fair margin, but there was something about him. He had that kind of presence—the craggy looks and tall, almost imperious bearing—that made people notice him.

He spotted her.

She felt her heart race. With long, purposeful strides he came across the terrace to her table. A lopsided grin creased his face.

"Hey, sailor," she said. "Looking for a good time?"

"Maybe. Are you available?"

"Sure, if you promise to stay awhile."

And that was the end of all her glib chatter. She was on her feet, folded into his arms, tears rushing to the surface. "Sam, Sam, I've missed you so much. . . ."

He kissed her, stroked her hair, held her in his arms. She knew the women at the table by the door were gawking. She didn't care. To hell with them. To hell with the whole world. She had nearly lost Sam Maxwell, and now she had him back.

She drew him to the seat beside her at the table. He held both her hands while she told him about the Jerusalem assignment, how the network wanted someone else but she wheedled and cajoled, then threatened to jump ship if they didn't send her. She knew she was rambling incoherently, not at all the composed reporter she was on camera. She didn't care.

Maxwell was nodding his head, smiling at her. She saw furrows in his brow, crinkles around the eyes she hadn't noticed before. A few gray hairs showed at his temples.

"You look tired, Sam."

"Life has been a little hectic."

"I promised I wouldn't ask questions about what you're doing in Israel. And I won't."

"You already know. Pearly. I'm here to get him back."

She nodded. "Do you think that's going to happen?"

"Yes." He said it without hesitation, but she saw a look pass over his face that she had seen before. She knew what it meant. *I will make it happen. One way or another.*

"Have you met Special Envoy Solares?" she said.

"Rambo Rick? Yeah, I've had the pleasure."

"Were you impressed?"

"Hugely."

She smiled, imagining Maxwell and Solares together. A collision of planets. She wished she had been there.

"I know him from years ago," she said. "When I was starting at the network. He was already the big star, hob-nobbing with senators and cabinet members and talking about running for Congress."

"What was he like?"

"A jerk."

"In what way?"

"The usual way. He made a pass at me."

"Well, give the guy credit for good taste."

"I gave him a knee in the groin."

Maxwell laughed. "Really? I love it. And now you're going to interview him, right?"

"Small world, huh?"

"You'd better be nice to him," said Maxwell. "Mr. Solares seems to be headed for higher office."

"Depends on what happens here in Israel. He'd better pull a rabbit out of a hat."

"Or a pilot out of a rat hole."

She nodded, liking the old familiar tone of his voice, warmed by the nearness of him. A pair of candles on the table cast an orange glow over his face. He hadn't changed. Despite the new wrinkles and the gray hairs, it was the same Sam Maxwell.

He ordered a bottle of wine. She persuaded him that they should have dinner on the terrace. It wasn't too chilly, about twenty degrees Celsius, no wind. She had brought a shawl to wrap around her bare shoulders.

They talked about old friends, the ones they both knew from phase one—the Pax River and Washington days—and phase two—Bahrain and Dubai. That was how they defined their truncated relationship. Phase one happened when he was a test pilot at Patuxent River, Maryland, and she was a cub reporter in the Washington bureau. Phase two came later, after they'd broken up, married others, then found each other again in the Middle East.

"Captain Boyce?" she asked. "How is he?"

"Doing his swan song," Maxwell said. "After being an air wing commander, there aren't any more flying jobs. None as good, anyway. With the rank of captain, he's gone as far as he can."

She shook her head. "Such a waste. An excellent commander like him. Why wouldn't the Navy make him an admiral?"

"Red's a dinosaur," said Maxwell. "Never learned politics. You don't make admiral in the U.S. Navy by breaking rules and stomping on toes."

She nodded, thinking about this. "And you, Sam? Will you make admiral?"

He laughed. "I'm a dinosaur too."

"Where will they send you after you've finished your tour as skipper of the Roadrunners?"

"Back to the beach. Some desk job that I'll hate."

She nodded. *And where you'll be home every night.*

She reminded herself to avoid that subject. They'd been there before. It was dangerous ground.

In the silence that fell over them, she heard piano music again floating out from the lounge. "Chopin?" she said.

He listened for a moment. "Rachmaninoff."

"Sure it's not Chopin? That romantic part?"

"Rachmaninoff, Piano Concerto Number Three. Wanna bet?"

She shook her head. "No bet." Sam knew classical music.

Another silence while she listened to the lilting strains of the piano concerto. She wrestled with the question that she was afraid to ask.

"Sam, I have to ask you something. I know we . . . broke up, went our own ways. Are you seeing someone? Someone special, I mean?"

She studied his face while he composed an answer. He seemed to be thinking, gazing out at the lights of the old city. *Of course he's seeing someone. A man like Sam Maxwell wouldn't just sit around and—*

"No," he said after what seemed an eternity. "No one special."

A flood of relief swept over her. "I'm glad."

"And you?" he said. "Anyone special?"

She shook her head. "No one special." Which was true, at least the special part. Howard, the guy from the World Bank whom she'd been dating, was nice company. Definitely not special.

She squeezed his hand. "Sam, do you think we could start all over again?"

"I don't know."

"You mean, you don't know if it's possible?"

"I mean I don't know if we should. You and I have gotten too proficient at hurting each other. Maybe we shouldn't try it again."

She knew what he meant. She could still feel the dull

ache from the past five months. This time it had been her fault.

She said, "Do you still love me, Sam?"

"Yes." He said it without hesitation. A good sign.

"Same as always?"

"Same as always."

"Then I have a suggestion. We could give it a chance. No decisions, no promises. See what happens."

"What do you want to happen?"

"I want us to be happy. That's all. Without demands, conditions, or expectations. Does that sound unreasonable?"

"Not to me."

For a while they held hands, letting the music wash over them, gazing down at the lights of old Jerusalem. She felt a warm glow of contentment settle over her. Life wasn't always fair, she thought. Sometimes you didn't get another chance. Sometimes you had to be lucky.

"How long do I get to keep you, Sam?"

"As long as you want."

"How about all night?"

"Sounds good to me," he said.

A familiar scent. Like lilacs, but more subtle. Chestnut hair splayed on the pillow beside his head. The soft curve of her hip pressed against him. From a few inches away he could count the freckles on her shoulder.

Through the part in the curtains, pale light slanted into the room. For a while Maxwell lay still, watching the slow rise and fall of her breathing. With each exhalation she made a little mewing sound.

He peeked at the clock on the nightstand. Six fifteen. He slipped out of bed, careful not to disturb her, and padded over to the window. The dawn was bathing Jerusalem in an orange glow.

By the dresser lay his cell phone, the screen blank.

Maxwell pressed the power button, then waited while the phone booted up.

There were two voice-mail messages waiting. The first, from last night, was from Hannah Shamir. He skipped it and went to the second. It was half an hour old, from Lev Asher. Maxwell was supposed to call back immediately.

He wrapped himself in one of the large, fluffy hotel bathrobes and took the phone into the sitting room. He closed the door and punched in Asher's number.

"Where the hell are you?" came Asher's voice. "Off the base?"

"Jerusalem."

"You should have told someone where you were going."

"I was on personal business."

"Personal, eh?" He chuckled into the phone. "Anything to do with Hannah Shamir?"

"No."

"Sorry, none of my business. Something has come up. How quickly can you get back to Hazerim?"

"Is it urgent?"

"Too urgent to discuss on the cell phone."

He had to think. The direct route from Jerusalem to Hazerim was only about a hundred kilometers, but that was through the West Bank. Not a good idea. He'd take the long way, west toward Tel Aviv, then south on the highway to Beersheva. Hazerim was six kilometers out of Beersheva.

"Two hours," Maxwell said. "Maybe a little more."

"Better get moving."

He pushed the END button and went back to the bedroom. Claire was sitting up, holding the sheet around her.

"You have to leave, don't you?"

He nodded. "Some things never change."

She took his hand, drew him down beside her, kissed him. "Do we have time for coffee?"

He hesitated, then saw the look on her face. "I'll make time," he said.

CHAPTER 11

BREAKTHROUGH

Southern Israel
0830, Tuesday, 18 October

After he cleared the morning traffic in Jerusalem, it was an easy drive. He kept the rented Fiat at a steady 120 kilometers per hour all the way south to Beersheva. It took another five minutes while the security detail at the gate verified his credentials with the command headquarters.

Asher was waiting in his office.

"This came in last night." He handed Maxwell the printout.

From: ComAirWing Three
To: Cmdr. S. Maxwell, Temporary Duty
    Assignment, Hazerim AB, Israel

Game now in fourth quarter. Players and refs will huddle at U.S. embassy compound Wed 19 Oct., 1400 local. Come ready to play.

Love and kisses,
Battle-ax

Asher waited until Maxwell had finished reading the message. "Hannah Shamir was in here looking for you." A barely noticeable smile flitted over Asher's face. "She seemed upset that you weren't available. Can't imagine why."

Damn, thought Maxwell. Hannah. Should have called her.

"Guess my cell phone somehow got turned off. Sorry."

"You can go with General Zemek," said Asher. "His chopper is leaving for Tel Aviv at thirteen thirty."

Zemek? *Game now in fourth quarter.* Why was Zemek involved? "What's going on?" Maxwell said.

"I think you can guess."

"Something with Pearly?"

"No one's saying. I gather that something has been negotiated."

"I thought Shallutz was refusing to make a deal."

Asher shrugged. "Shallutz is a politician. Maybe someone made him a deal he couldn't refuse."

Maxwell skimmed the message again. *Come ready to play.* What the hell did that mean? Play what? Boyce loved cryptic communications.

Maxwell glanced at his watch. Nearly eleven A.M. "Where do I meet the General?"

"Helo pad outside the command post. Better not be late."

U.S. Embassy Compound, Tel Aviv

"You look like hell, Maxwell."

"Good to see you too, CAG."

Boyce was waiting at the perimeter of the helo pad inside the American embassy compound. He was wearing khakis, no leather flight jacket, no cigar. He exchanged salutes with General Zemek and his two staff officers, then waited until they were escorted inside the compound by the U.S. Marine guards.

"Where'd you spend the night?" said Boyce. "Any-place you want to tell me about?"

"No," said Maxwell.

Boyce turned to watch the Israeli officers vanish inside the compound. "So that's Zemek. I met him once at Point Mugu, years ago. A hell of a fighter pilot, so I hear. Now he's running their whole damn air force."

Maxwell followed Boyce across the pad and into the compound. They passed through another checkpoint, where they showed IDs and passed through a metal detector.

The conference room in the embassy compound was already filled. Maxwell counted at least twenty uniformed officers—Navy, a couple Air Force, one Marine, half a dozen Israeli military. Another twenty or so civilians were present—foreign service, CIA, half a dozen Israelis. A few had telltale cords running from their radio earpieces into their shirts. Secret Service, Maxwell guessed. And Mossad.

At the head of the long table was Rick Solares, smiling and ebullient. Next to him was a short, round-faced man with oversize spectacles and a sour expression.

"Who's that with Solares?" Maxwell asked.

"Sol Kaminsky," said Boyce. "U.S. ambassador to Israel."

"Why does he look like he just swallowed a live cockroach?"

"Because he's been neutered by Solares. He's supposed to be the number one American in Israel, but Solares came to town and stole all the marbles."

Maxwell had met Kaminsky once. He was a New York banker and a heavy contributor to the President's election campaign. Now he was second fiddle to Special Envoy Ricardo Solares.

So far Solares hadn't noticed Maxwell in the crowded room. That was good, Maxwell decided. Sitting to Boyce's right was Rear Adm. Jack Hightree, Commander of the *Reagan* Carrier Group and Boyce's immediate boss. Hightree and Boyce and a half dozen staff officers had flown from the *Reagan* by COD—a C-2 Greyhound—to Ben-Gurion airport, then had been whisked by limo to the embassy compound in Tel Aviv.

Solares rapped on the microphone and a hush fell over the room. A video camera on a dolly rolled into position at the edge of the room.

"Ladies and gentlemen," said Solares, "our hopes for the release of the captured American pilot are about to be realized."

He paused, letting the announcement sink in. The camera dollied closer to him.

"After a very sensitive negotiation, we have reached an agreement between the government of the United States, Israel, and representatives of the Palestinian Liberation Movement. Prime Minister Shallutz has consented to the release of a high-profile Palestinian prisoner, Sheik Rafiq Hamzeh, in exchange for a captured U.S. Navy pilot"— Solares paused to glance at his cue card—"Lt. Christopher Gates."

Spontaneous applause filled the room. Solares nodded and gave the audience an indulgent smile. Even Maxwell found himself clapping. Maybe his take on Solares had been wrong, he thought. Maybe the guy really *was* a diplomat. If he persuaded the Israelis to make a prisoner swap, Solares had just pulled off the diplomatic coup of the year.

Solares went on to explain that the exchange would take place the next morning at the northern checkpoint of the Gaza Strip, a place called Erez. An Israeli Defense Force detail would deliver Sheik Hamzeh to the meeting point. A Palestinian official, Khaled Mohanor, would turn over the American prisoner. Solares himself would be there to take custody of the American and escort him to freedom.

"One American officer who can identify Lieutenant

Gates will be assigned to accompany me," said Solares. "Do you have someone for that mission, Admiral High-tree?"

Maxwell saw Boyce lean over and buzz something in Hightree's ear. The admiral nodded, then said, "Yes, sir. I have assigned Cmdr. Sam Maxwell."

Solares frowned, the name not quite registering. Then his eyes found Maxwell across the room. His face froze. "Perhaps you should assign someone else. Another junior officer who can recognize the prisoner."

Boyce leaned over and buzzed again in Hightree's ear. Hightree gave him a dubious look, then said, "Commander Maxwell is Lieutenant Gates's commanding officer. He is the appropriate choice."

For a long moment Solares held eye contact with Maxwell. Finally he nodded and said, "Okay, if you insist."

Boyce waited until they were outside the embassy, walking along busy Hayarkon Street. He pulled a fresh Cohiba from his pocket.

"Okay, what was that all about?"

Maxwell knew it was coming. "What was what all about?"

"Don't play dumb," said Boyce. "What did you do to piss off Solares? He looked at you as if you carried the Ebola virus."

"Just a little disagreement over the prisoner matter."

Boyce rolled his eyes. "Maxwell, have you ever considered becoming a diplomat?"

"No."

"Smart. Stick to your day job."

Admiral Hightree was still in the compound conferring with Solares and Zemek. The prisoner exchange was scheduled for the next morning at seven o'clock. Boyce had booked quarters for himself and Maxwell at the Dan Hotel, a few minutes' walk from the embassy. Hightree had a VIP room in the embassy compound.

The ground-floor bar of the Dan had a splendid view of the Mediterranean across the busy beachfront street. After ordering two Tuborg drafts, Boyce looked around and declared the area to be a free-fire zone. He pulled out his ancient Zippo and applied flame to his cigar. A wreath of smoke enveloped them.

Maxwell coughed. "CAG, how do you smoke those things?"

"Easy. You light one end and suck on the other. You want one?"

"No, thanks."

"Good. It would be a waste."

Boyce wafted a cloud of gray smoke across the bar. The beers came. They downed them and ordered two more. Boyce gave Maxwell a rundown on his squadron back on the *Reagan*. Bullet Alexander was keeping the troops busy and the jets flying. The Scrotum Scudder affair, instead of going away, was blossoming into an ugly mess. Sticks Stickney wanted the perpetrator identified and court-martialed.

"Why is Sticks getting involved?" said Maxwell. "Hasn't he got more important stuff to do?"

"Covering his ass," said Boyce. "Sticks just got selected for rear admiral. He's not gonna let anything—especially something that smells like a scandal—jeopardize his getting a star."

"Sticks is getting a star?" said Maxwell. "Well, good for him. Guess that means you're next in line, CAG."

Boyce blew a long stream of gray smoke. "Are you kidding? Sticks is the kind of guy the Navy pins the stars on, not me. He's like Hightree. Treads lightly, knows when to shoot and when to hold his fire. I, on the other hand, have left too many bodies around the landscape. All they're gonna give me is my retirement papers."

Maxwell nodded, not bothering to disagree. Boyce was right.

"So where will you go when you retire, CAG?"

"Wherever old fighter pilots go. When I get there, I'll keep a bar stool open for you."

Maxwell grinned and clinked his glass against Boyce's. Red Boyce had been his mentor since he'd returned to the fleet from his stint at NASA. Boyce had stuck his neck out to save Maxwell's career. Maxwell, for his part, had taken more than one outside-the-box assignment from Boyce.

"What do we do with Pearly when we get him back?" asked Maxwell. "Send him back to the *Reagan*?"

"We don't know what shape he's in. They'll keep him here at the compound while the medics check him out and the spooks give him a thorough debriefing. Then he'll get some time off."

For a while they watched the traffic on Hayarkon Street. It looked like the beachfront of any other large Mediterranean city.

Boyce peered back inside the hotel lobby. He glanced at his watch and said, "Yup. Right on time."

Puzzled, Maxwell turned to follow Boyce's gaze. A slow smile spread across his face. He would recognize that sassy, long-legged walk anywhere. She was wearing her work outfit—blue pantsuit, shoulder bag filled with the tools of her trade, silk scarf knotted at her throat. He knew the scarf. It was the one he'd bought for her in Dubai two years ago.

"What a coincidence," said Claire Phillips. "My two favorite fighter pilots, together in the same place."

She's better-looking than I expected.

From her chair in the lobby, Hannah Shamir peered over the magazine she pretended to be reading. The woman walking toward the bar carried herself with the easy, sensual grace of a professional model. Or actress. Or television journalist.

It was easy to see why Maxwell would fall for her. Claire Phillips had it all—looks, brains, glamorous job.

She was probably even a competent journalist. According to the dossier, she had worked her way from junior reporter at a Washington newspaper to broadcast journalist on a local station to her present job as lead correspondent at the world's second-largest television news network. She had to be good.

The file also showed that she had been married to a journalist who happened to be a CIA agent. Hannah, in fact, knew him. He was a charming rogue named Chris Tyrwhitt whom she'd met in Bahrain during an operation to intercept arms shipments from Syria to the Palestinians. Hannah and Tyrwhitt had had a torrid three-day affair.

Tyrwhitt and Claire Phillips were divorced now. Knowing Tyrwhitt, that was no surprise. Phillips had resumed her relationship with Maxwell.

Then, abruptly, they stopped seeing each other.

Why? Other lovers? Career problems? It wasn't in the dossier. And now they seemed to be together again. Why Maxwell? He was good-looking enough, even handsome in a rough-edged way. But a woman like Claire Phillips would have many admirers. Why would she wait for a naval officer to return from the sea? Or worry that he might not come back from the next mission? Or . . .

Hannah knew. She had been there herself. She knew what it was like to love a fighter pilot. Maxwell and Ron Shamir were cast from the same mold.

And that, damn it, was why she was drawn to Maxwell. Despite her good sense.

CHAPTER 12

DELIVERANCE

Gaza, Palestinian Territories
0615, Thursday, 20 October

This is it, Pearly decided.

The bastards were going to kill him. They couldn't cash him in for anything, so they were going to take him out and dispose of him with those beat-up old assault rifles. His eyes were slowly adapting to the darkness. They were prodding him along, jabbing the muzzle of an AK-47 into his ribs, moving him down the rough-cobbled alleyway. On either side were the pocked walls of ancient buildings. Litter covered the ground. From somewhere nearby came the smell of garbage and an open sewer.

Pearly guessed that it was near dawn. He had been asleep for several hours when they kicked him awake, removed his cuffs, allowed him a quick pee, shoved him out into the darkened street. There were six of them, all wearing black fedayeen-style face masks. He was sure that Khaled was not one of them. That was a bad sign. He knew by the look in their eyes that a couple of these young Palestinians had been waiting for the chance to slice his throat.

"Where are we going?" Pearly asked.

No answer. Instead, something hard and metallic

thunked into the back of his head. A Kalashnikov barrel, he guessed.

"Hey, asshole, I'm going to—"

Another thunk, this one almost dropping him to his knees.

"No talk," said a voice behind him. "You go."

For a moment he weighed his options. He could whirl around, surprise this jerk with a world-class right jab, maybe splatter his nose before they turned the lights out on him. It would be worth it. Almost.

Not yet, he told himself. *Wait for the right moment.*

He shuffled through the darkness, stumbling over refuse, stepping on something squishy that made him shiver. His throat was dry. His head throbbed from the blow with the Kalashnikov. Something—a rat?—scurried across the tops of his boots.

They came to the end of the alleyway. Waiting in the darkness was a black Mercedes, motor purring like a sleeping cat. Two men in the front, one in back. As they approached, the rear door opened.

"Get in," said the man in back. Pearly recognized the voice of Khaled Mohanor.

He hesitated, then felt another jab in his back. He glanced back at the man behind him. The eyes glowered through slits in the mask. It wasn't too late. He could still punch the guy's lights out.

He hesitated one more second, then climbed into the backseat next to Khaled.

The Mercedes pulled out of the alleyway into the lighted street. Pearly saw the sky pinkening over the irregular silhouette of the city. Except for the driver, a Palestinian wearing a white kaffiyeh, and another in the right seat, a baldheaded man with a mustache and an assault rifle, they were alone.

"Why the fancy car?" said Pearly. "Are we going to a party?"

Khaled gave him a withering look without bothering to

answer. He lit a cigarette and gazed out at the passing buildings.

The street—Pearly assumed that they were in Gaza City—was coming alive. The place was a slum. Graffiti scarred every wall. Garbage littered the street. Laundry hung from windows. Rusty vehicles stood abandoned, stripped of wheels and every removable part. Hollow-eyed pedestrians stared at the passing Mercedes as if it had just landed from Mars.

Ahead Pearly saw the glow of floodlights and parked vehicles. Military vehicles. Must be some kind of check-point.

The driver continued straight ahead to a low building with a blockade across the road, then stopped ten meters short. On the other side of the blockade, Pearly saw soldiers in battle gear watching them. *Israeli soldiers.*

"Get out of the car on my side," said Khaled. "Stay with me and don't move. Understand?"

"No. What are we doing?"

"If you do not wish to be shot, shut up and do as I say."

Pearly stood next to Khaled. Someone was walking toward them, coming from the other side of the roadblock. He shielded his eyes from the floodlights, trying to see.

Four of them. Who was that? It looked like . . . couldn't be . . . but it sure as hell looked like . . .

Maxwell. The skipper. He was wearing khakis and a piss-cutter uniform cap.

You're hallucinating, Gates.

With him was an Arab wearing an Arafat-style checked kaffiyeh. And some dude in an Israeli Air Force uniform. And another guy who looked familiar . . . *Who the hell?* Somebody from television . . . Rick something. *Solares.* Yeah, that was the guy. *Rambo Rick.*

"Are you okay, Pearly?"

Maxwell's voice. He wasn't hallucinating. The skipper was here.

"Yes, sir. Am I getting out of this place?"

"I'm working on it."

They stopped ten feet away. For several seconds no one spoke. The men stared at each other in the harsh yellow light.

Khaled said something in Arabic. The man in the kaffiyeh—Pearly could see now that he was an older guy, about sixty, with a gray goatee—answered in a hoarse flurry of words.

Solares said, "I have delivered Sheik Rafiq Hamzeh, in accordance with our agreement. Are you prepared to release your prisoner?"

"Do I have your word that the Israeli Army will not interfere with the sheik's movements?" said Khaled.

Pearly saw Solares turn to the Israeli officer. There were two stars on each epaulet. The officer nodded.

"You have our word," said Solares. "Sheik Hamzeh is free to travel as he wishes."

At this, Khaled gave Pearly a nudge. "Go, Yankee. Go home to your soft life."

Pearly felt as if he were sleepwalking. He moved through the puddle of light, vaguely aware of the Arab with the gray goatee walking past him. Someone—Maxwell, he guessed—took his elbow, guiding him. Someone else clapped him on the back. And then Solares—Rambo Rick in the flesh—was pumping his hand, telling him America was proud of him, the President sent his greetings, he was the harbinger of a new era of peace in the Middle East. . . .

Pearly stopped listening. They kept on walking through the floodlit area. They walked past the roadblock and the checkpoint. The Israeli soldiers stared at him as if he were an alien from space.

More floodlights, and at the fringe of the lights another cluster of faceless people. He saw winking cameras, mounted video cams following his movement, silhouettes of people watching him. They were asking incomprehensible questions.

Solares was talking to them. "No, no interviews yet. I will tell you everything you need to know."

Maxwell kept him walking until they reached a large black Lexus guarded by a pair of U.S. Marines in BDUs. One opened the back door. Maxwell stuffed him inside.

Pearly peered out the back window. Solares was in front of the cameras now, delivering his report to the world.

Pearly shook his head in astonishment. *Un-fucking-believable.* Ten minutes ago he had expected to be executed. He had been willing—almost—to trade his last minute of life for one solid punch at the asshole in the ski mask.

Good thing he didn't.

". . . a new relationship between the Israeli people, the United States, and our Palestinian partners."

Palestinian partners? thought Claire Phillips, watching Solares's performance. Amazing. If any other public official, American or Israeli, had uttered those words, his career would be toast by sunset.

It was almost like old times. There was Ricardo Solares, dressed up in his foreign-correspondent costume, mugging for the camera. Stepping all over the poor worshipful journalists who were trying to get their questions answered by the Special Envoy, who sat on the right hand of God. Or the President, or whoever had the highest ratings at the moment.

Meanwhile, the focus of their attention—the *real* reason they were standing out here in the miserable gray dawn—was driving away in the black limo. They'd gotten only a brief glimpse of the released pilot. He was wearing a desert camo flight suit and had a dazed look on his face.

Claire had resisted the urge to call out to Sam Maxwell.

Had Sam seen her? Probably not. It was typical

Maxwell—face expressionless, ignoring the pack of reporters and cameras, eyes straight ahead.

Solares was paying no attention to the waving hands of the reporters. He went on talking.

". . . and for once, the old cycle of death and retribution has been put aside in the interest of peace. Reasonable negotiating partners have succeeded in resolving their differences."

One of the reporters saw an opening. "What reasonable negotiating partners are you referring to?" he shouted.

"One is Khaled Mohanor," Solares said. "He represents the future of the Palestinian people. A rational man in an irrational world."

"Didn't his group shoot down the American pilot in the first place?"

"No. We think Hamas was responsible for the downing of the American jet. Khaled Mohanor is not associated with any terrorist organization. As a highly respected leader in the Palestinian community, he stepped forward to act as an intermediary. He and I"—Solares paused here to let the nearest cameras dwell on his profile—"negotiated the terms of a prisoner exchange."

He nodded toward General Zemek, standing beside him. "With the concurrence of the Israeli government, of course."

Like old times, thought Claire. *She* was the network newsperson, but Solares had taken center stage. For another ten minutes he continued talking about new paradigms and partners for peace and dignity for oppressed people.

And, Claire had to admit, he was doing a damned good job of it. Solares could cast a spell. Even the audience of reporters seemed impressed. Not until he was finished and walked off camera did anyone realize that he had said almost nothing about the release of the American pilot, which was why they had come out to this godforsaken checkpoint on the northern border of the Gaza Strip in the first place.

Solares waited until she had signed off with the network and detached her clip-on mike and earpiece. He walked over to her.

"Good to see you again, Claire." He gave her a smooch and a hug that lasted several seconds too long.

"Congratulations on another winner, Rick."

"It wasn't me," he said. "This was a win for the Middle East peace process."

Yeah, right, she thought. "And what did the President say when you told him the news?"

"The President thinks like I do. He sees this as an opportunity for a new peace initiative."

"Does that mean you'll be heading up the initiative?"

He gave her the old killer smile. "Why didn't you ask me that when we were on camera?"

"You didn't give me the chance."

He laughed. "Guess you're right. I was probably a little overbearing. But, honestly, Claire, I think we're about to make a breakthrough here."

"Sounds like you're teaming up with this Khaled Mohanor. Won't that infuriate the right-wingers in the U.S. and here in Israel?"

"Somebody has to bring both sides to the table. If that somebody turns out to be me, fine. I don't care what they say. Let them be as infuriated as they want."

For a moment Claire let her old feelings about Solares soften. Maybe she'd been wrong about the guy. If he meant what he said, then he deserved all the glory and honor that would come from his accomplishment.

"It would be a wonderful thing if you succeeded, Rick. I wish you well."

His arm was around her again. "Why don't you wish me well in private? How about dinner tonight? In Tel Aviv?"

No, she thought, she *wasn't* wrong about him. Same old Solares. "Sorry, I have an engagement tonight."

He kept his arm around her. "Oh, hell, Claire, you can

get out of it. We need to talk. It's been too long since you and I were together."

Too long since you got kicked in the crotch. Either he'd forgotten, or he thought that she'd forgotten. Or maybe, in his surpassing vanity, Solares thought a knee in the nuts was an invitation to make love.

She remembered that he was selective. In the old days he liked to prey on women who were new in the business and couldn't afford to get into messy he-says-she-says contests. It was the beginning of her career, and her job would have vaporized overnight if she'd accused a superstar like Solares of groping her.

"Sorry," she said. "This is a date I can't break."

He seemed thoughtful for a moment. "I'm trying to recall. Weren't you seeing some military type back in Washington? Some pilot?"

"Test pilot. I'm still seeing him."

"A lucky guy. I'd like to meet him sometime."

"You already have. He was just here. His name is Maxwell. Cmdr. Sam Maxwell."

She felt the arm around her go rigid. The smile remained frozen on Solares's face, but the eyes turned dark and cold.

"Oh, yes, Maxwell," he said. He removed his arm from around her. "Well, too bad about tonight, Claire. Some other time, okay?"

He turned and walked away without waiting for an answer.

Gaza, Palestinian Territories

Khaled Mohanor winced at the sound of gunfire. The collective din of automatic weapons filled the streets of Gaza like the crackle of summer lightning.

Mohanor waved at the adoring crowd. Beside him in the backseat of the Mercedes, Sheik Hamzeh was waving also. The procession—six vehicles in all—was creeping along the main avenue of Gaza City while thousands of ecstatic Palestinians cheered and danced and fired their guns.

It was an insane custom, Khaled thought. Palestinians required almost no excuse to shoot their weapons skyward—funerals, weddings, glorious victories, even inglorious defeats. Not until later would they realize that the bullets hadn't vanished into the atmosphere. Gravity was relentless. Autos, rooftops, awnings, and bare heads would all be hammered by the hailstorm of descending lead.

The gunfire—and the weapons themselves—was outlawed by the Israelis. But the Israeli Army was conspicuously absent today. No armed patrols, no tanks clanking through the streets, no helicopter gunships hovering like birds of prey. The Israelis were being prudent, thought Mohanor. A confrontation today could ignite the mother of all street battles.

Mohanor waved back at the horde in the street. Nothing could diminish the looks of pure ecstasy on their faces. Not only had the Palestinians humiliated the mighty United States by downing one of their vaunted fighter jets; they had forced the U.S. to make Israel release the most important inmate in their prison.

Sheik Hamzeh was more than just a leader. He was a hero of the Palestinian resistance. And now they had a new hero—Khaled Mohanor, who had brought the U.S. and Israel to their knees and delivered Hamzeh from captivity. It was a day for celebration.

The Mercedes moved in small increments through the crowd, starting and stopping, advancing a few meters at a time. The street was filled with joyous Palestinians. Flags waved from doorways and windows. Hastily printed posters bearing the picture of Sheik Hamzeh and of Khaled Mohanor were held aloft. Hands pressed against the windows of the automobile, trying to clasp the hands of the heroes. Tears ran down the cheeks of the overjoyed celebrants.

Mohanor glanced at his watch. Not yet noon. They had another two hours of idling through the heart of old Gaza.

Timing was everything now. Mohanor could feel the currents of history flowing around him. What happened in the next two hours would be followed by an even more momentous event, followed by yet another.

There was no turning back. He, Khaled Mohanor, had launched a succession of events that would change the world.

CHAPTER 13

INCIDENT IN GOLAN

Golan Heights, Northern Israel
0855, Thursday, 20 October

Saleh shivered in the damp cold.

Nearly three thousand meters above sea level, a layer of cumulus clouds covered the upper slope of the Golan Heights. Tentacles of fog crept into the valleys, obscuring the craggy outcroppings.

Crouched in a shallow ditch, Saleh peered down the slope. Through the mist and fog, he could make out the silhouettes of a shattered pillbox. Standing next to it was a burned-out tank—a Russian-made T-55. There was another rusting utility vehicle with a hole blown through its side.

He disliked this place. He disliked it not so much for the penetrating chill and the murky fog, but for what it represented.

Defeat. And humiliation.

Until the 1967 war, the Golan Heights belonged to Syria. It was their high ground from which they could observe the enemy below and, when it suited them, lob artillery shells and missiles onto Israeli settlements. By the end of the Six-Day War, all that had changed. Every Syrian soldier on the Golan Heights had been killed or captured or chased back to Syria. Every item of military value—fortified structures, tanks, artillery—had been converted to scrap.

During the Yom Kippur War in 1973, Syrian armor overran the Golan Heights. For a few glorious days they again possessed the strategic high ground. Then they were repulsed by the Israelis, leaving behind more shattered tanks and vehicles.

Now the Golan Heights was an Israeli amusement park. Weekend hikers climbed the slopes to gaze at the graveyard of Arab weaponry. The Israeli Army sent new recruits up the Heights to observe the artifacts and reinforce their feeling of superiority over their Arab enemies. The subject of returning the Golan Heights to Syria came up at every new peace negotiation, but no one with any sense of reality expected Israel to give up its prize.

All this passed through Saleh's mind as he crouched in the ditch. They had been there for over an hour. The clouds had rolled in and obscured the top half of the Heights.

The fog is our friend, Saleh reminded himself. Israeli gunships couldn't pursue them through the thick bank of fog.

Around him were the ten other members of the unit, each armed with an AK-47. Their commander, Ali Bhouri, only a couple of years older than Saleh, also carried a satchel of grenades.

Saleh shivered again, not so much from the damp cold as from anxiety. This was his first real combat operation. Except for hurling stones at Israeli patrols in the West Bank and dodging their rubber bullets, he had never experienced real armed conflict.

He didn't know the precise reason for the operation. He didn't even know who had given the order, but he could guess. He wasn't supposed to know, for an obvious reason. If he were taken alive, he would have no information of value to the enemy.

What he *really* couldn't figure out was why *now?* Just when everyone in Gaza and the West Bank was celebrating the release of Sheik Hamzeh, dreaming about peace, letting themselves believe that there just might be a—

Ali was signaling something. A hand wave, a finger pointing down the slope.

Saleh peered down through the wisps of fog. He heard someone coming, boots crunching on gravel, the sound of laughter. He sensed his pulse rate accelerating. The Kalashnikov felt cold and alien in his hands. He was beset with doubts. *Why am I doing this? Killing enemy soldiers in combat is one thing. Executing people without reason is—*

He saw them.

In the lead was a young man in olive-drab BDUs. He carried some kind of assault rifle—an M-16 probably. Behind him trudged a column of young people. Unarmed. They wore backpacks, headbands, hiking boots. There were six of them. Three were girls.

One of the girls turned and said something. It must have been funny, because the others all laughed.

Saleh had an impulse to shout *Get out of here! Run back down the hill!*

He kept his silence.

Trailing the group was another young man in BDUs, sleeves rolled up. He, too, was carrying an M-16. On his belt was some kind of radio device.

Get the communicator first, Ali had told him. *Don't let them transmit a warning.*

The trail they were following would bring them within ten meters of the ditch where Saleh crouched. It had to be quick. No communications. If it lasted more than a few seconds, Israeli forces would be summoned. Saleh and all his comrades would be dead within minutes.

Ali was taking his time. The hikers were thirty meters away.

Saleh made himself focus. *Get the last one. The communicator.*

He sighted over the barrel of the Kalashnikov. It wasn't too late. He could still shout a warning.

Twenty meters.

He saw Ali's hand drop. Saleh hesitated one second. He squeezed the trigger. The others were shooting too. The crackle of automatic fire swelled around him, penetrating the fog, seeming to echo from the shattered pill-boxes and tanks.

Saleh's three-round burst struck the young man with the radio in the chest. He stopped, a look of disbelief on his face. For a second that seemed to stretch into eternity, his eyes found Saleh and they locked gazes. His knees buckled and he slumped to the ground.

The gunfire ended as quickly as it had erupted. An eerie stillness settled over the hillside. The acrid smell of spent ammunition wafted over the ditch where Saleh and his comrades were crouched.

Ali ran to examine the bodies. They were all sprawled where they fell. Neither of the young men with the M-16s had gotten off a shot. One of the girls was still alive, feebly trying to crawl away. She had long blond hair, and she had been shot through the abdomen. Ali walked over to her and dispatched her with a single round from his AK-47.

Saleh went to the body of the young man he had killed. His eyes were still open, the look of disbelief frozen on his face.

He felt Ali tugging at his arm. "It is finished," said Ali. "We have to leave."

Saleh couldn't move. Ali slapped him hard. "Move, you sentimental idiot. You'll get us all killed."

Saleh stared at him. He took one more long look at the young man he had killed. He turned and followed Ali up the slope, into the fog.

Gaza, Palestinian Territories

The old fool.
It was just as Khaled expected. Sheik Rafiq Hamzeh

would not speak directly to Khaled. Not to ask how Khaled had negotiated his release. Not to thank him for delivering him from what would have been a lifetime in an Israeli cell.

The sheik rode in silence in the back of the Mercedes, ignoring Khaled's presence in the seat beside him. He waved at the horde of adoring Palestinians in the street. He nodded his head as if he were privy to some secret knowledge.

Khaled knew he should not be surprised. Sheik Hamzeh was a relic from history. He was one of the few figureheads still around who was born in this country when it was still called Palestine. That was before 1948 and before hundreds of thousands of Arabs were driven from their land. Since then Hamzeh had joined in every significant military action against Israel. As a Hezbollah commander he had gained legendary status by conducting multiple successful attacks against Israeli outposts and settlements along the northern border.

Of all the old Palestinian warriors, only Hamzeh was left. All the others, like Arafat, were dead or neutralized by the Israelis and by their own incompetence. And Hamzeh had only one vision for Palestine—jihad. Unending war. He had nothing but contempt for more moderate Palestinians who advocated an accommodation with the Israelis.

Decrepit old goat. The bleary-eyed, addle-brained old fool comported himself as if he were some kind of revered holy man. Waving and nodding to the ignorant peasants who thought he was their savior. The toothless fossil didn't understand that jihad was a failure. A half century of holy war had won them only misery and squalor.

The Mercedes arrived in the main square of Gaza City. The square was filled with hundreds of chanting, poster-carrying, flag-waving Palestinians. Waiting for Hamzeh were three Arabs in military fatigues, wearing bright yellow kaffiyehs. Khaled recognized them. They were senior officers from Fatah. As the crowd cheered, the three

Palestinians gave their leader great deferential bows, then took turns kissing him.

Mohanor kept a respectful distance. Like Hamzeh, the Fatah lieutenants made it clear that they had no use for Khaled Mohanor. Now that he had served the useful function of freeing the sheik, they were finished with him.

Mohanor waited half an hour, and then his cell phone buzzed. He nodded, listening to the excited voice on the other end. He thanked the caller and hung up.

Standing at the fringe of the crowd, he punched another number into the cell phone. While he waited for the phone connection, he watched Hamzeh and his lieutenants moving across the square, toward a black stretch Peugeot with dark-tinted glass. Mounted on the right front was a staff with the flag of the Palestinian Authority, the de facto government headquartered in Ramallah. Hamzeh and his lieutenants would be driving to the West Bank, the other Israeli-occupied territory. There would be more celebrations, kissing, worshipful embraces.

"Yes?" said the voice on Mohanor's cell phone. "Have you concluded your business?"

"I have," said Mohanor. "The shipment is leaving in ten minutes. The client can pick it up at his leisure."

"That is good to know. The client sends his thanks."

The phone went dead.

Mohanor watched Hamzeh and his lieutenants climb into the Peugeot. In a procession with two square-bodied black Renault vans, one in front, one in back, the limousine crept through the throng in the square. It turned onto an open street and disappeared between the rows of crumbling buildings.

Central Israel

It was an abomination, thought Sheik Hamzeh. An insult to Allah.

He was gazing out the window at the green lushness of the Israeli countryside. From the highway he could see cultivated fields, comfortable homes with outbuildings and farm machinery, tidy villages with rows of neat houses and clean streets.

The old anger was heating up inside him. In the four years he'd been locked away, the Jews had continued to prosper. The Palestinians continued to suffer.

Nothing had changed.

On most days it took slightly over two hours to drive to Ramallah, including ten minutes at each of the two Israeli checkpoints. The stretch Peugeot was well-known to the soldiers at the checkpoints because it made the journey between the West Bank and Gaza several times a week.

Depending on the level of hostilities, the official Palestinian Authority government limos were allowed free passage between the two occupied territories. Sometimes the soldiers searched the PA vehicles for hidden weapons. Sometimes they didn't. Today they didn't.

After they'd left the Erez checkpoint on the northern border of the Gaza Strip, the procession veered northeastward and followed the highway to the high plateau of Jerusalem. Hamzeh stared with amazement at the sprawling suburbs on the periphery of the old city. Everywhere there was construction. New buildings, new roads, entire hillsides converted to row houses. The Jews were like ants.

They came to another checkpoint, this one the northern demarcation between Jerusalem and the West Bank. A grim-faced Israeli soldier—he looked to Hamzeh as if he were not old enough to drive—peered through the driver's rolled-down window. Behind him stood half a dozen M-16-carrying soldiers, all in full battle gear. All young and unsmiling.

The soldier took a cursory glance at the travel documents. He stepped back and waved the Peugeot through the checkpoint.

The landscape transformed again. No more construction. The four-lane surface became rough and potholed. On either side buildings were smeared with graffiti. Trash and abandoned vehicles lined each side of the road.

They were in the West Bank.

Hamzeh's anger returned. The Palestinian Authority had accomplished nothing. *Spineless clerks.* In his absence the officials of the so-called government had behaved like castrated dogs, practically begging the Israelis to kick them. They had lived so long in subjugation that they no longer understood what freedom meant.

All that was about to change. Sheik Rafiq Hamzeh was back. A new jihad would begin.

The festering city of Ramallah opened up around them. This section of the West Bank was nearly as poor and squalid as Gaza. Piles of rubble stood where entire buildings had been bulldozed by Israeli wreckers. A cluster of burned-out vehicles marked the site of a street fight. These were the scars of the intifada—the uprising against the Israeli oppressors.

The street widened. Hamzeh recognized the neighborhood. Ahead he saw the walled compound of the Palestinian Authority. Inside the oval-shaped compound were the military, police, and legislative headquarters of the PA.

A crowd had formed outside the compound. Hamzeh saw flags waving and posters bearing his likeness and that of the Prime Minister.

Mahmoud Moghrabi, the senior of the three Fatah officers, was mumbling into his cell phone. He clicked it closed and turned to Hamzeh. "The Prime Minister will meet you outside the compound. He wants to make a speech, I think."

Hamzeh frowned. Another celebration, more kissing, yet another display of undying fraternal love. It was all a sham, of course, but it served a purpose. *Let the peasants in the streets welcome their true leader. It will give them hope.*

The lead car pushed its way through the crowd, while the stretch Peugeot crept to a stop. The crowd surged around the limousine, clamoring for a look at their idol.

Through the tinted glass Hamzeh watched a squad of uniformed policemen opening a path from the front gate of the compound. The smiling, bespectacled visage of the Prime Minister appeared behind the policemen, followed by his entourage of ministers.

Hamzeh took his time. Let the Prime Minister, sycophantic fool that he was, wait on him. He would exit the limousine when he was ready. The throng of Palestinians would—

What's wrong?

The Prime Minister's broad smile was replaced with a look of alarm. He was gazing upward, beyond the parked Peugeot. One of the policeman was pointing at something.

Then they were whirling, trying to run, but there was no place to go. A wave of movement swept over the crowd, pushing it toward the compound.

The gate was closed. The sea of humanity was smashing against the wall of the compound.

Hamzeh lost sight of the Prime Minister. He and most of his ministers were trying to get away from . . . *what?*

The driver had the door open. He was gazing at something behind the car. Mahmoud shoved his back door open, and he too was peering upward.

"What is it?" demanded Hamzeh.

Without answering, Mahmoud shoved the door open on his side and bolted from the car.

Sheik Hamzeh turned to look out the tinted back window of the limousine. The sky was hazy, dotted with puffs of cumulus. Something, a dark blurry object, was out there.

He saw a flash, then another speck detach from the dark object. Hamzeh blinked, confused by what he was seeing.

Then he knew. He lunged for the open door, but he knew he was too late.

Ramallah, West Bank, Palestinian Territories

Capt. Ravi Borok watched the Longbow Hellfire missile streak toward the target. One of the laser-guided supersonic tank-killer missiles would be enough, but he kept his finger on the fire-control selector. He had seven more Hellfire missiles mounted on the two pylons. Just in case.

Watching the fiery tail of the missile, he felt a flash of remorse. There were people down there. Lots of them. A crowd was swarming around the target vehicle.

He dismissed the thought. *To hell with them. To hell with all of them.*

Until minutes before the mission, Borok had been one of a growing contingent in the Israeli Air Force who felt a sense of outrage about what the government called "targeted killings." It was a more respectable term than assassination. What bothered Borok and some of his colleagues was that the killings weren't always targeted. Innocent Palestinians—women, children, old people— were dying along with the Hamas and Islamic Jihad leaders who were being targeted. To Borok, it was murder.

He was over that now. Before takeoff, General Zemek had taken him and his fire-control officer, Lieutenant Zahvi, aside. He showed them photographs of the slaughter in the Golan Heights—eight college students, six of them new recruits in the Israeli Defense Force, all murdered at close range.

Now Ravi Borok was on a mission of retaliation.

Borok and Zahvi, who manned the front seat of the AH-64 Apache gunship, had tracked the PA limousine since it left Gaza. It was ridiculously easy. The GPS transmitter planted beneath the vehicle issued a constant position, which was displayed as a winking yellow triangle in the situation display screen on Borok's instrument panel.

He waited until the limousine was almost at the PA compound. The plan was to catch the target—the newly released terrorist, Sheik Hamzeh—as he was exiting the vehicle.

The timing was intentional, Borok assumed. Whoever drafted the plan knew there would be high-ranking Palestinian officials there to meet the sheik. And, probably, a crowd.

Borok felt another pang of doubt. Killing a killer was one thing. Innocent civilians were something else.

He pushed his qualms aside. Still fresh in his mind was the image of the young Israelis. Boys and girls in the spring of their lives, lying in pools of blood on the Golan mountainside.

An eye for an eye. No, forget that. A *thousand* eyes for an eye.

Someone on the ground had spotted the helicopter. They knew what was about to happen. They had probably even seen the blazing speck of the Longbow Hellfire leave the pylon of the Apache. The crowd was moving like the swell of an ocean wave toward the compound.

Trying to get away from the black Peugeot.

The missile impacted the rear window of the Peugeot, precisely where the laser designator had locked the target. A red-and-black mushroom obliterated Borok's view of the vehicle.

As the smoke lifted and the debris tumbled back to earth, Borok could see the burning shell. An automobile, even if armor-protected and bulletproofed like the PA limousine, was like tinsel to an AGM-114 Hellfire, which was designed to pulverize a thirty-ton tank.

The Peugeot and its occupants were indeed pulverized. So was everyone within twenty meters of the target. Borok could see bodies scattered like cordwood between the shattered Peugeot and the compound wall. Orange licks of flame spewed from the human shapes nearest the shattered limousine.

Even at a range of four thousand meters, Borok imagined he could smell the stench of burning flesh. As he stared at the carnage by the compound, he knew it was an image that would never be erased from his memory.

In his mind he saw again the photo from the Golan Heights.

To hell with them. He banked the Apache into a turn and departed the area.

CHAPTER 14

SUFFICIENT PROVOCATION

U.S. Embassy Compound, Tel Aviv
1820, Friday, 21 October

Ricardo Solares dropped a couple of fresh ice cubes in his Scotch and flopped back in the deep leather chair in his private suite. On the opposite wall, the television screen showed an image of a street in the West Bank. An overturned car was burning. Young Palestinians were taking turns running into the street, hurling stones at a distant enemy, then retreating behind a crumbling wall.

The camera shifted. In the distance an Israeli tank rumbled into view. Behind the tank was a squad of soldiers in battle gear. In the background, a woman's voice described the violence in Ramallah.

It was the same in Hebron and Jenin. Palestinians were in open revolt against the Israeli occupiers. In Gaza it was worse. Pitched gun battles were going on between Israeli troops and Palestinian insurgents. The Palestinians were using RPGs—rocket-propelled grenades—and had already disabled two Israeli tanks.

The camera switched to the announcer. She stood in front of a sandbagged position, and two Israeli soldiers were peering over the barrels of their machine guns.

Solares glowered at the screen. He recognized the woman's face. *Claire Phillips.*

"Prime Minister Shallutz has declared a state of emergency and placed all the occupied territories under martial law," she said to the camera. "A curfew is in effect, but so far it has been ignored by most of the Palestinian population."

Super bitch, thought Solares. He took another hit on the Scotch. Back in the network days, he could have any bimbo journalist he wanted. They used to line up to see who got the honor of screwing Rick Solares. All except Miss Acid-mouth Super Bitch Phillips.

Which was probably just as well, he reflected. He was in the big leagues now. All he needed was some snooty bitch like Phillips reviving some old accusation about him. One whiff of scandal and he could forget sharing the ticket next year with the President.

"The death toll is mounting," Claire Phillips went on. "The massacre of the eight Israeli students yesterday in the Golan Heights provoked an immediate reaction from the Israeli government. The helicopter missile attack in Ramallah killed Sheik Rafiq Hamzeh, Prime Minister Ismail Saad, at least four high-ranking ministers of the Palestinian Authority, and as many as twenty Palestinians who had assembled at the Palestinian Authority compound to greet Sheik Hamzeh."

Solares noticed that she made no mention of yesterday's big news—the exchange of the captured American pilot for the Palestinian resistance leader. Brilliantly executed by Special Envoy Ricardo Solares. *Bitch.*

The camera closed in on Claire Phillips's face. Solares noticed that she was wearing a silk scarf, the same one he seen her wearing in Gaza yesterday morning.

"At least fifty Palestinian protesters have been killed by Israeli troops," she said, "and a dozen Israeli soldiers have been reported killed in separate attacks."

And it's just beginning, thought Solares. A lot more

blood would be shed before either side considered laying down their weapons.

The buzzing telephone interrupted his thoughts.

"Khaled Mohanor for you, Mr. Solares," said Vernon Lewis, manning the duty desk. "You said if he were to call—"

"Put him on."

After a moment, Mohanor's silky voice came over the phone. "I'm sorry to interrupt you. This is a time of great tragedy."

"I agree," he said. "A tragedy for both sides."

"You and I are not only statesmen. We are also pragmatists. We understand that from great tragedy sometimes comes a new beginning."

"What kind of new beginning?"

"Of peace. Perhaps from tragedy will come nationhood for Palestine."

Solares was still watching the screen. The camera was focused on a building in Gaza that was being shelled by an Israeli tank.

"From what I see, Mr. Mohanor, peace is nowhere in sight."

"We should view this conflict as a historic opportunity."

"Opportunity? For what?"

He heard Mohanor take a deep breath. "Consider this. A power vacuum exists on all sides. The Palestinians are without guidance. The Israelis have no one to follow except a stupid and arrogant old general who is taking them over a cliff."

"What has that got to do with me?"

"Only the United States has the power to change the course of events. The right person to exercise that power is you."

"I'm not sure I understand how—"

"We must seize this moment, Mr. Solares."

Solares forced himself to hesitate, not wanting to

sound too anxious. The implications of Mohanor's words had already sunk in. *A historic opportunity.* Yes, he thought, that was what it was. The key to his future. Huge public acclaim. The Nobel Peace Prize. The vice presidency. Maybe more.

"I agree," he heard himself say. "We must meet right away."

U.S. Embassy Compound, Tel Aviv

"Have you noticed," said CAG Boyce, "that junior officers these days can't hold their booze?"

"A deficiency in their training," said Maxwell. "The new breed of fighter pilot. Three beers and they're out."

They were standing at the lounge bar in the U.S. embassy compound. Pearly was wearing a black warm-up suit with convict-style white stripes painted on it, a gag gift from his squadron mates back on the *Reagan.*

Boyce and Maxwell were both in civvies. Boyce was wearing slacks and an ugly flowered sport shirt. Maxwell was in chinos and a knit polo shirt.

"Screw it," said Pearly Gates. "I just wanna get back to the squadron."

It came out slurred, as if he had a speech impediment. *Damn,* thought Pearly. It was true. Three lousy beers and he was shit-faced. He set the empty mug on the bar and stifled a belch.

The embassy physician had warned Pearly this would happen. Something to do with his changed body chemistry. All that adrenaline, the lousy diet, being scared shitless for most of a week.

"Not yet," said CAG Boyce. "You and Brick have to hang in here until the quacks and the intel debriefers are finished with you."

"They're squeezing blood from a stone," said Pearly. "I've told 'em everything I remember."

Boyce had a Cohiba going. He wafted a cloud of gray smoke into the fan over the bar. "Spooks don't care," he said. "They think you have repressed information they can dig out from your subconscious. If they keep asking questions, maybe you'll tell them something they haven't heard before."

Well, he had that right, Pearly thought. He didn't even know the exact job descriptions of some of the debriefers. Some were CIA. You could tell by the haircuts, the supercilious attitudes. There were a couple of uniformed officers, one Navy, one Air Force, and a few goofy-looking guys he guessed were shrinks. He had described for them everything that happened from the time he ejected over the Negev Desert until he climbed into the embassy car and drove away from Gaza.

It wasn't enough. They wanted names and descriptions of each of his captors, what they said, how they behaved. They were particularly curious about Khaled Mohanor and the killing of the two terrorists he knew only as Muhammad and Akram in the Hamas hideaway in Gaza City.

At one debriefing session, two Israelis in civvies were present. One male, one female. She was black-haired and attractive. They didn't introduce themselves, and they asked no questions. They stood in silence, listening attentively while Pearly described the terrorists.

"Hey, Skipper," said Pearly. "Guess who came to visit this morning?"

"I give up," said Maxwell.

"Remember Lebev, the guy I was fighting when I got shot down?"

"The guy we thought *shot* you down."

"Yeah, him. I had him pegged as a snake-eyed little shit who *would* shoot me down if he thought he'd get away with it. Well, I had him wrong."

"Why?"

"He actually said he was sorry, in so many words. He

was almost in tears. Said it was all his fault, busting the hard deck like he did, getting me whacked with the SAM."

"If I recall correctly, *you* busted the hard deck."

"Well, if you want to be technical about it. But Lebev insisted it was his fault. You know why?"

"For Christ's sake, tell the story," said Boyce.

"He said it shouldn't have taken him so long to score a kill on me. Normally, he said, he would have taken me out long before that and we'd never have gotten down to the hard deck."

"And you said . . . ?"

"When we have the rematch, I'm gonna hand him his ass on a platter."

Boyce placed his elbows on the bar and glowered at Pearly. "The hell you are. There's not gonna be any goddamn rematch. We're through playing games with the Israelis."

Pearly was about to argue, when he saw Maxwell giving him the eye. *Leave it alone.*

"Yes, sir," he said.

The Old City, Jerusalem

What the hell am I doing here?

A fresh wave of anxiety swept over Rick Solares. He should have known better than to agree to a meeting here. Jerusalem, of all places. In the distance he could hear the sporadic sound of gunfire, sirens, the whopping of helicopter rotors.

Israel and the Palestinians were at war.

It was Mohanor's idea that they meet in the old city. It would add a historical perspective to their talks, he said. It would be safe because neither of the warring parties—Israelis or Palestinians—had any interest in destroying the ancient buildings.

Solares had brought only one of the Secret Service agents, Chesney, and his aide, Vernon Lewis, who looked like a man on his way to his own beheading. From the Jaffa Gate of the old city they followed the directions Mohanor had given them, to the Muslim quarter, through a narrow passageway to a tobacconist shop with the blinds drawn over a barricaded window.

They were in a long, narrow room, thick with cigarette smoke. Mohanor and Solares sat alone at one end, a wooden table between them. At the far end, Chesney and Lewis watched them, trying their best to ignore the presence of the half dozen nervous-looking Palestinians with them.

"My eyes and ears," said Mohanor. "Don't worry. They are here to protect us."

Solares didn't know how they would protect anyone. One appeared to be a frightened teenager, his expression a mixture of fear and loathing. One was a young woman, whose face was a match of the teenager's. A sister? The other four were lean-faced young men, eyes dark and glowering.

Mohanor and Solares talked about the escalating violence in the streets of the occupied territories. Solares listened to Mohanor's description of the Palestinian frustration over the endless occupation of their territory. Again he found himself impressed with Mohanor's grasp of the deeper cultural issues at stake in the Middle East.

"So why hasn't the Palestinian government called for a cease-fire?" asked Solares.

"Most of the Palestinian government was exterminated yesterday by the Israeli rocket attack. But it wouldn't matter. They never had any real authority to do anything. The people are without leadership."

"What about you?" said Solares. "They respect you as a leader. Why haven't you stepped forward?"

Mohanor shook his head. "A leader must be able to offer hope. At this moment, the Palestinian people have no hope. They have turned to violence because they have nothing to lose."

"What will it take to stop the violence?"

Mohanor kept his voice low. "What is necessary in order to stop the violence," he said, "is for the United States to become involved."

"That's not likely. The United States has always avoided becoming involved in Israeli affairs," said Solares.

"That is because there has not been sufficient provocation."

An alert flashed through Solares's brain. "Provocation?"

"The Americans become militant only when they have been sufficiently provoked. They were not willing to intervene against Al-Qaeda in Afghanistan until after September 2001, when they were directly attacked."

"Are you suggesting that Americans may be attacked again?"

Mohanor gave him a patient smile, like a schoolteacher lecturing a slow student. "Consider this scenario. If the United States thought it was in their national interest, they could depose the corrupt Palestinian government and replace it with one of their own choosing, just as they did in Iraq."

Mohanor's voice was strangely hypnotic. Solares had the distinct feeling that he was being drawn into a web, but he didn't mind. He wanted to hear more.

"How does that involve me. Or you?"

"You, Mr. Solares, would be the natural choice for a benevolent administrator of the provisional government. And, I think you would agree, I would be the logical choice of the people to head up the new independent government of Palestine."

Solares found himself nodding in agreement, even though his good sense was telling him that it couldn't happen. The scenario was too far-fetched. Too over-the-top.

"The Israelis would never allow the United States to intervene here," said Solares.

"They would if they were persuaded that it was the best solution to their terrible burden. The Israelis are as weary of this constant war as the Palestinians. Both sides will be willing to let the United States impose an equitable resolution."

Perhaps it *was* possible, thought Solares. And he, Rick Solares, truly *was* the obvious choice to head up a provisional government. It was the key to his future. He could hardly bring himself to ask the next question. "What sort of provocation would it take?"

Saleh watched from across the room. *What are they talking about?*

The American, the one with the mustache, was someone very famous. Saleh remembered seeing his face on television. A movie star? No, not exactly. His face appeared on news broadcasts.

Why is he talking to Khaled?

Saleh noticed the serious expressions on their faces. They were keeping their voices too low for him to hear what they were saying.

Did the American know about the killings in the Golan Heights? Saleh wondered. Of course he did. That was why he was talking to Khaled. That was what triggered the Israeli rocket attack and the rioting in the streets.

Did he know who carried out the killings?

No. Surely not. With that thought, a fresh wave of nausea swept over him. His mind flew back to the fog-shrouded hillside. He saw again the young man's face gazing at him from across the clearing. Then the pell-mell retreat from the scene. The eleven members of the squad had split into three groups. The first, led by Ali Bhouri, descended the Golan to the west, intending to follow the high ground along the Lebanese border until they found a way to cross into Lebanon. The second group went back down the slope to the Sea of Galilee, planning to slip into the West Bank near Jenin. Saleh and his two companions were to make their way across the border to Syria, then southward through Jordan and cross the river back into Israel somewhere north of the Dead Sea.

While Saleh was ascending the summit of the Golan, still shrouded in thick fog, he heard the crackle of automatic fire from far down the slope. Ali's? No, more likely the second group, led by an excitable teenager named Yusuf. They had run into trouble.

He heard only one distinctive burst from an AK-47; then it was cut short by the chatter of multiple weapons: M-16s, and at least one Tavor assault rifle.

Israeli soldiers. They were already on the slope, hunting the Palestinians. Killing them.

Saleh and his two companions continued up the Heights. Hidden in fog, they buried their weapons, then found a place to slip through the wire at the border. Once inside Syria, they were assisted by resident Palestinian exiles, who arranged their transport into Jordan and back to the West Bank.

The journey had taken two days. The image of the young Israeli with the three bullets in his chest, staring with accusing eyes at Saleh, was seared into his memory. So was the sight of the blond girl, shot in the abdomen, crawling through the fog like a mortally wounded animal. Since then he had not stopped vomiting. Everything he tried to eat came roiling back like lava from his stomach. His head pounded. His knees felt like rubber.

You are warriors, Khaled had assured them before the mission to Golan. *Men, women, civilians or soldiers, there is no distinction. They are the enemy. Kill them all.*

And so they had. Eight of them. Young people, most of them no older than he.

Saleh no longer felt like a warrior. He felt tainted and sick.

He glanced at his sister. He hadn't told her what happened in Golan. Later, maybe, when he'd had more time to think about it.

Hanadi seemed strangely detached. She was watching Khaled and the American. She wore an expression Saleh had never seen before. She was gazing at the Great Leader with a look of pure adoration.

CHAPTER 15

LOSS OF INNOCENCE

Tel Aviv
1015, Sunday, 23 October

"Do you love me, Sam?"

She knew she was pushing him, but damn it, sometimes this guy needed pushing. Life was short. Somebody had to get this romance off dead center.

Claire saw him pretending to think about it. He was rubbing his chin, peering into the hazy sky. It was still morning, and a moist sea breeze was flowing over the beach.

"Well?" she said.

"Well what?"

"Do you?"

"Yes."

She almost laughed. That was Sam Maxwell for you. Articulate as ever.

"Yes, what? C'mon, sailor, you can do better than that."

He stopped and held both her hands in his. He took a moment, then said, "I love you, Claire. Totally, unconditionally, and forever. Always have, always will." Then he gave her a big, crinkly-eyed smile that melted her heart like a summer breeze. The Sam Maxwell smile. It was the real thing.

"Hey, that's good," she said. "Very good. But I still had to ask first."

"I was getting around to it. That's why they call me Brick. I'm slow, remember?"

That made her laugh. "Yeah, I remember."

And then he kissed her, which was what she'd been waiting for. A serious kiss, one that lasted a good thirty seconds, maybe more. Sam Maxwell might be slow, but when he got around to doing something, he did it right.

"Wow," she said. "Does this mean we're going steady?"

"Yeah, sort of."

"Are you going to give me your class ring to wear on a chain?"

"Not exactly. I thought we might do something more permanent this time."

She liked the way this was going. "Do you have anything special in mind?"

"I thought we might go shopping in the souk this afternoon."

"For what?"

"How about a ring?"

She gazed up into his blue eyes, trying to keep her voice from quavering. "We were engaged before, Sam. It didn't work, remember?"

"Yeah, I remember. I was thinking that maybe this time we should just skip the engagement part. You know, cut to the real thing."

Claire stared at him for a long moment, trying to see through his expression. Was he kidding? "Excuse me," she said, "but I would swear I just heard something that sounded a lot like a proposal."

He nodded. "You heard right."

She didn't trust herself to answer right away. Her heart was racing like a runaway train. "Sam, are you sure?"

Another smile spread over his face. "Never been more sure in my life."

She studied his face awhile longer, just to be certain.

"When?" she said.

"You haven't said 'yes.'"

She gave it another moment, then cleared her throat and said it as distinctly as she could. "Yes."

"Are *you* sure?"

She nodded. "Absolutely. Now are you going to tell me when?"

"Whenever you want."

She had to think. This had happened very suddenly. She still wasn't sure she had heard correctly.

"Sam, is it possible . . . do you think we could get married here in Israel?"

"I don't know why not."

Claire felt dizzy. After their roller-coaster ride of a romance, she had thought it wouldn't work for them. Maybe she had been wrong. Maybe they could actually—

Her cell phone was buzzing. She had meant to turn the damned thing off. She reached to mash the power button, then thought again. The network had sent her here to do a job. When they wanted something, they wanted it now.

"Sorry," she said. "This won't take a second." She flipped the phone open.

"Claire?" The voice on the phone was familiar. "It's Rick Solares. Am I interrupting anything?"

"Yes."

"Sorry," he said. She knew better. Rick Solares was never sorry. "Something has come up that you should know about. Can you and your crew cover a happening in the West Bank?"

"Where in the West Bank?"

"Ramallah."

"I thought that was a war zone."

"Only if you're in an Israeli uniform. I'll be there too. We'll be protected by the Palestinian Authority."

"It's not my call. Our bureau chief in Tel Aviv, Ted

Heinemann, has to approve everything we shoot. What kind of happening?"

"A Palestinian leader—you saw me with him that day at Gaza; his name is Khaled Mohanor—is going to talk to the demonstrators outside the Palestinian Authority compound. He's trying to get them to put down the guns and negotiate with the Israelis. Believe me, if anybody can put a lid on this war, it's Mohanor. You're going to see him become the new leader of the Palestinians."

As she listened to Solares, she glanced over at Maxwell. He was gazing out at the ocean with his hands jammed in the pockets of his chinos. His craggy profile was silhouetted against the Mediterranean sky.

They were supposed to have dinner at the Dan Hotel tonight. Just the two of them. She had a noon meeting at the network office in Tel Aviv; then she was free. She wanted to be with Sam.

"I have a schedule conflict," she said.

"Listen, Claire, this is history in the making. The kind of story every broadcast journalist dreams about. If you don't want it, just hang up, and I'll call Derek Sloan at CNN."

She didn't answer. She kept watching Maxwell, that almost-but-not-quite-handsome face that she loved. Today would have been a wonderful day to steer him down to the old Carmel market. To the stalls where they sold jewelry. *How about a ring? You bet, sailor. Nothing fancy, it's the thought that counts.*

She heard Solares's voice. "What do you say, Claire? Do you want this story or not?"

Yes, damn it, she wanted it. She was a reporter. She *had* to cover it.

"I'll call Heinemann," she said. "He'll put the crew together. What time?"

"Two o'clock, in the plaza outside the PA compound. I'll be there to give you an overview of the situation."

She almost laughed. Of course! Rick Solares wouldn't

let this go down without putting his stamp on it. He would help himself to a prime slice of network airtime. Some things never changed.

She told Solares okay, she'd make the call, put a crew together. She clicked the cell phone off.

"Something come up?" said Maxwell.

"A little change in the game plan." She took his arm and tugged him on down the beach. She'd give him the details later.

"C'mon, sailor," she said. "Tell the girl you're going to marry how much you love her. You know, the part about totally and unconditionally."

"Okay."

And so he did. After all these years, Sam Maxwell was catching on.

Arab Quarter, Jerusalem

"I want to see the Great Leader."

"He is not available," said the guard. He didn't move from his position at the door to Khaled Mohanor's private quarters.

Saleh tried to peer around the hulking guard. "It is very important. I have to see him now."

"He's not seeing anyone."

Saleh saw a smirk pass over the guard's face. Saleh knew him. His name was Yasar Tabib. He was a thug from one of the camps in Gaza. He was a Fatah fighter whose specialty was killing suspected informers. Yasar was ruthless and stupid—a bad combination.

Saleh was exasperated. He knew Khaled was in the compound. He had seen the Great Leader here less than an hour ago when he was talking to the American with the mustache.

Yasar was treating him as if he were just another of the rock-throwing juveniles in the Palestinian resistance.

If he only knew. Even this dim-witted thug would be impressed if he knew of Saleh's role in the Golan killings.

Saleh *had* to talk to Khaled. He had to hear *why* it had been necessary to kill the young Israelis in the Golan. How many more massacres would they have to perform?

He knew better than to argue with Yasar. It would just get him a clout on the head. Saleh nodded in submission, then slinked down the hallway and slumped against the wall at the far end. He lowered his chin to his chest and pretended to doze off.

It took less than ten minutes. Yasar was bored, Saleh could tell. By the way he fidgeted, it was obvious that he had to pee.

The guard scratched his crotch and peered in each direction along the hallway. Satisfied that no one was likely to invade the sanctity of the Great Leader's quarters, he darted down the hall and through the door to the outdoor privy.

Saleh was on his feet. He half expected to find the door locked. He tugged on the heavy iron latch. The door swung toward him.

It was dark inside. Saleh entered and softly closed the door behind him.

He'd been in the Great Leader's quarters only once before. That was only three days ago, when he and Ali and the others received their assignment to the Golan. He remembered that the quarters were actually three connecting rooms. The outer room had a large table for meetings. The middle room served as a private office. The far space Saleh had never seen, but he presumed it was the Great Leader's bedroom.

The meeting room was unlighted except for a yellow shaft of sunlight beneath the shuttered window. Saleh stood motionless for several seconds, listening. The quarters appeared to be unoccupied. Perhaps the Great Leader *was* away. He had to find out quickly, then make his exit before Yasar returned.

He tapped on the door to the middle room. If Khaled was in the quarters, he would surely be at his desk.

No reply.

Saleh hesitated. He thought of the beating he would suffer when Yasar found that he had entered the Great Leader's quarters.

But it was vital that he speak with Khaled. A beating was nothing. Not after Golan.

He cracked the door open. The office was windowless, darker even than the conference room. In the gloom Saleh could see the dark shape of a desk, chairs, a row of cabinets.

The Great Leader was not there.

Saleh was about to close the door when he heard a voice. He froze. Forgotten for the moment was the hulking presence of Yasar, who had surely returned to his post.

The voice was coming from Khaled's private room.

Like a sleepwalker, Saleh crossed the room. He stood motionless outside the closed door.

He heard it again. A familiar voice, urgent, muffled, throaty.

He should turn and leave. Confront Yasar and accept his punishment. The meeting with the Great Leader could wait until another time.

He heard the voice again.

Saleh couldn't leave. He tried the door latch. It was unlocked.

Stepping inside the room, he blinked and gazed around. Thick drapes over the high windows diffused the sunlight. A soft yellow light filled the room. At the far end of the room was the bed.

They weren't aware of his presence. The man was kneeling over the woman. Neither was clothed.

Even though the man's back was to him, Saleh knew it was the Great Leader. In the heat of their lovemaking, the two were oblivious to the rest of the world.

Over Khaled's shoulder, Saleh could see the woman's face. Her eyes were closed, black hair splayed on the pillow. She was making the same throaty moaning noise that Saleh had heard from the other room.

Unable to move, Saleh stared at the entwined couple. Rage and disgust roiled like a storm inside him. He felt as though he were suspended in space, viewing the scene from a distant planet.

The woman stopped moaning. Her eyes opened. She sensed that they were no longer alone.

Her gaze found him.

"Saleh!"

For what seemed an eternity Saleh returned his sister's gaze.

"What are you doing here?" Hanadi shouted. "Get out!"

He couldn't move. For several seconds he remained in place. His mind tried to reject what he was seeing. Nothing was making sense.

He whirled and darted back through the door to the office. He ran through the darkened room, stumbling over a chair. He flung the chair out of his path and ran from the office, through the dimly lighted conference room.

As he reached for the latch, the big wooden door flew open. The silhouetted bulk of Yasar Tabib filled the doorway. He was blinking, trying to spot Saleh in the dim yellow light.

"You! You worthless heap of rat dung. I told you—"

Saleh's right foot, sweeping in a wide soccer kick, drove itself into Yasar's groin. The breath left Yasar with a whoosh. He doubled over in pain.

Saleh dashed past him. Yasar was stumbling backward, clutching his crotch with both hands. Saleh ran down the hallway. He ignored the stares and the shouts from the Fatah fighters sitting in a row along the wall of the main entry hall. From the hallway behind him he heard Yasar's incoherent bellowing.

He didn't stop. He darted out the back door of the compound, down the alley to the main road that led to the outdoor market in the Arab Quarter. He kept running, darting between pedestrians and sidewalk stalls. He wanted to put as much distance as he could between himself and his sister and the Great Leader.

Tears of rage flowed down his cheeks. Hanadi had let herself be seduced. So had he. So had all the fighters of the Free Palestine Militia. They had all been seduced by the Great Leader.

Saleh wished he had been killed in the Golan with the others. He didn't want to be a warrior. He wanted to die.

CHAPTER 16

APPOINTMENT IN RAMALLAH

Tel Aviv
1250, Sunday, 23 October

"Are you sure, Sam?"

He looked across the room at her and laughed. It had become a joke between them. Since lunch they had asked each other the same question at least a dozen times. Hell, yes, he was sure. So sure he wondered why he had ever felt unsure about it before. Marrying Claire Phillips would be the most natural and intelligent thing he had ever done.

"No," he said. "The very thought makes me tremble with fear and uncertainty."

"Me too," she said.

"That's why we have to get it over with and become an old married couple as soon as possible."

"Good idea," she said. She laughed and went back to stuffing equipment into her JanSport rucksack for the shoot this afternoon.

Actually, he thought, it *was* a good idea. So good, in fact, that he had already called CAG Boyce, aboard the *Reagan*, who declared it to be perhaps the only brilliant idea Maxwell had ever come up with. Boyce was ready to send a COD to Tel Aviv, transporting himself and half a dozen Roadrunners, accompanied by Lt. Cmdr. Preacher Peebles, the *Reagan*'s chaplain. Peebles would perform the ceremony right there in the compound of the embassy. Boyce had already claimed the honor of giving the bride away. Pearly Gates had been appointed best man.

She finished packing the rucksack. It was almost one o'clock. "Time to go," she said.

"I'll walk you down to the lobby."

She shook her head. "I'd have to kiss you good-bye in front of the crew," she said. "They'll never stop pestering me with questions."

So she kissed him in the room. On the way out the door, she gave him a sly smile. "You could go to the market while I'm away, you know."

He knew. He had caught all the not-so-subtle hints. Never mind the engagement ring, but a girl liked to have *something*. A stroll through the old market . . . you never knew what you might find in those old stalls. Then the smile. Yeah, he knew.

He watched from the window, his breath clouding the glass, until he saw her appear on the hotel entrance ramp six stories below. He saw the chestnut hair bobbing on her head, the no-nonsense blue jumpsuit she favored for this kind of open-air shoot, the JanSport rucksack over one shoulder.

She trotted across the ramp toward the first of the two parked vans. There were no markings on the vans, but Maxwell knew they carried the thirteen technicians and engineers and assistants and all their gear. All going with Claire to Ramallah.

He watched her climb into the open sliding door, almost hearing her saying, "Hi, guys, sorry I'm late." Which she was, by five minutes. That was because lunch arrived late in their room and she insisted—*damn it, they can wait*—that she and Maxwell at least have coffee together.

He stood there until the van had disappeared down the beachfront esplanade, which was filled up with afternoon traffic. He let himself think again about the coming week.

Are you sure, Sam?

Damn right, he was sure. *Never been more sure in my life.*

It was just past one o'clock when he walked out to the sidewalk on Hayarkon Street. The Yemenite Quarter and its marketplace was a ten-minute walk. The narrow passageways between the stalls had not yet filled with the usual bustling crowd. Maxwell pushed his way past the footgear and clothing vendors, past the stalls of fruit and spices, ignoring the singsong patter of the merchants. Most were Palestinian, and they all competed for Maxwell's attention.

Finally he found it. He had no idea what it was really worth—it could be a thousand or twenty thousand shekels, for all he knew. The mustached young Palestinian, who spoke British-accented English, insisted on ten thousand shekels. Maxwell offered four. After more back and forth, they settled on seven.

It was a ring. A gold band with an embedded diamond. Claire had insisted that it not be godawful expensive or ornate. Only that he picked it out himself.

He made it back to the embassy compound just before three o'clock. After the standard ID-card-through-the-slot and five-minute wait while his identity was verified, the electronic latch of the main gate clicked open, and he was in.

Pearly Gates was flopped on a couch in the compound lounge, still wearing the striped convict suit, drinking a diet Coke. He was watching a television screen mounted on the wall.

"Hey, Skipper, you're just in time. Look at that. There's Claire on television."

Ramallah, West Bank, Palestinian Territories

Khaled could feel the woman's scrutiny. The eyes—they were green or gray or some shade in between—were locked onto his. Very disturbing. In the Arab world it was considered an aggressive gesture for a woman to look at a man that way. Women were brought up to avert their eyes from a man's gaze.

"Should I call you the Great Leader?" she asked.

"Only if I can call you the Great Reporter."

"Touché." She extended her hand. "I'm Claire Phillips. I would like to interview you for a special segment of my program."

He looked at her hand for a moment, then took it. Another disturbing mannerism. Arab women didn't initiate handshakes.

"About what?"

"About you. And the future of the Palestinian people."

"Perhaps it can be arranged."

In truth, it was exactly what he expected. She was a reporter. It was normal that she would want to interview him.

But what he had not expected was that she would be so poised. And, yes, attractive. He had seen her image many times on television. He had assumed she was another of those mindless mannequins whom Western networks used to recite their news stories.

This was no mannequin. Here was a full-bodied woman who also seemed to have a brain, one who was brazen enough to consider herself the equal of the men around her. Like most Western women, she wore makeup and a neutral lip rouge, but it seemed natural on her. Her hair was cut in a loose, nonflamboyant style.

She was wearing a tailored jumpsuit that covered her legs and her shoulders, an intelligent choice of attire for an Arab city like Ramallah. But with the wind ruffling the thin fabric over her body, Khaled had no difficulty observing the outline of her breasts or her slim-waisted figure.

"When can we do it?" she said.

Khaled forced himself to look away from her body. "Do it?"

"The interview."

Khaled realized he was still holding her hand.

"Oh, that." He released her hand and glanced at his watch. "After I have addressed these people."

"What if they become angry and begin to riot?"

"They are already angry. But they won't riot. Not after I have spoken."

"Do you really have that much control over them?"

Khaled met her gaze again. "Palestinians don't need control. They need leadership."

"And that is why they call you the 'Great Leader'?"

"A leader is a leader only if he has followers."

"Our viewers would like to hear you say that in our interview."

Khaled glanced at the crowd again. They were getting restless. Time to deliver his message of hope.

"Later," he said. "After I have spoken. Then you can have your interview."

As he turned to leave, he knew her eyes were following him. The woman was intrigued by him. The thought caused him to become aroused.

He glanced back. She hadn't moved. He traced the outline of her body with his eyes. What was she like in bed? Demanding, no doubt. Fiery, perhaps even ferocious. Never submissive. The woman would be an interesting challenge.

Saleh Nazzal heard the lilting, hypnotic voice of Khaled Mohanor. He didn't listen to the words. He had heard the Great Leader's promises for the future. The future no longer had any meaning for Saleh.

While the crowd stood transfixed under Mohanor's

spell, Saleh worked his way through the swarm of bodies. No one paid him any attention. He brushed past one after the other. He kept his arms close to his sides, moving a step at a time.

Careful, he told himself. No abrupt movements. Nothing to attract attention. He nudged his way between spellbound listeners, craning his neck, peering over the sea of heads.

Looking for them.

She would be somewhere close to the speaker's platform. Near the vans that transported the television broadcasting crews and their equipment. It was critical that he maneuver himself close to her before she noticed him.

He was dressed in black trousers and a loose black shirt that covered his arms and draped like a tent over his upper body. He looked as nondescript as anyone in Ramallah.

He felt the pressure of time running out. Mohanor's speech would soon end. The crowd would resume its restless shuffling. The demonstrators would be chanting again, berating Israelis, gesticulating for the television camera.

Where are they? Soon the television crews would be finished with their work. They would climb back in the vans and be gone.

He was almost to the edge of the crowd. Through the line of motionless bodies he saw something that looked like a fence. Except it was some kind of cordon—stanchions with a rope attached. Nothing substantial. And then an open space. Twenty meters at the most.

He edged his way to the rope cordon. He leaned out over the rope and peered around the edge of the crowd. He could see television equipment—lights, cameras mounted on dollies, reflectors. There were people standing with their backs to him, watching something.

He spotted them.

There were security people around the vans. None in

uniform, but still easy to spot. Men with loose-fitting shirts, sunglasses, heads moving in that certain scanning pattern. Looking for trouble.

He could see that the television shoot was nearly finished. The Great Leader was finishing his speech. He saw the American—what was his name? Something Latin. Solares, that was it.

Solares was in front of the television camera.

Saleh had to move quickly. Any minute now the crowd would be in motion. The crew would pack up their equipment. The moment of opportunity would be gone.

He squeezed himself between the roped cordon and pushed his way to the edge of the crowd.

Claire knew now why they called him the Great Leader.

She had no idea what he was saying, but she could tell that it was potent. She could see it in the faces of the audience. They were tilted toward him like sunflowers, hanging on Khaled Mohanor's every word.

Palestinians filled the street from one side to the other. No one was moving. Each was frozen in place, intoxicated by Mohanor's rich baritone voice.

"You're seeing the future leader of Palestine," said the man beside her.

Claire swung her eyes back to Rick Solares. She had almost forgotten that they were on camera.

Solares said, "Khaled Mohanor is the kind of statesman who has been so sadly absent during these years of hatred and bloodshed. He is the Palestinian equivalent of a Nelson Mandela."

Claire hadn't gotten over her nervousness about being in Ramallah. They were shooting in almost the exact spot where the Israeli rocket attack killed Sheik Hamzeh three days ago. Almost as many Palestinians had been killed in the stampede as had died in the missile explosion.

Only a roped barrier and twenty feet of space now separated her and the camera crew from the crowd of Palestinians. Many were holding up posters with pictures of relatives killed in the Israeli rocket attack.

Before they left Tel Aviv, she had argued with Rick Solares about security. They were too vulnerable, she thought. What if the crowd in Ramallah turned hostile? Why couldn't they have the IDF military—tanks and troops—standing by? Just in case things got ugly.

Solares argued that having Israeli soldiers there would *really* provoke the crowd. All they'd get for their trouble was some distant footage of the soldiers fighting with the already pissed-off Palestinians.

The bureau chief, Ted Heinemann, sided with Solares. No soldiers, no tanks. They'd use their own security people. They'd be safe as long as there was no military presence—Israeli or American—to provoke the crowd. Both Khaled Mohanor and Ricardo Solares had guaranteed it.

As it turned out, they were right. No one had threatened them. There hadn't been any gunfire. The sound of Mohanor's voice was lulling the crowd like an opiate.

For the camera, she asked Solares, "What will it take to bring the two sides to a cease-fire?"

"Goodwill from both camps. They have to be persuaded that their goals can best be achieved by coming to the table."

She knew where he was going with this. *Well, get it over with,* she thought. *Give him his opening, then get rid of him.*

"Rick, is it possible that you and Khaled Mohanor might be the ones who can bring the Israelis and the Palestinians to the peace table?"

She was right. It was the question he was waiting for.

He pretended to be contemplating an answer. For a moment he studied the horizon, allowing the camera a view of his profile.

"Khaled Mohanor and I are just ordinary men, Claire. But we share a vision. We believe that ordinary men can accomplish extraordinary feats. A lasting peace can be achieved if we can persuade both sides to regard each other as fellow human beings with needs and aspirations and hopes for the future."

What bullshit, thought Claire. She managed to keep a straight face. Ricardo Solares sounded like exactly what he was—a politician running for office.

She thanked Solares, and was shaking his hand, waiting for him to exit the stage when she noticed someone.

In the crowd. Moving to the roped-off perimeter, toward them.

Someone in black.

CHAPTER 17

LOST CONNECTION

U.S. Embassy Compound, Tel Aviv
1510, Sunday, 23 October

"Hey," said Pearly Gates. He sat upright on the couch. "Look at that."

Maxwell was just settling into one of the deep leather chairs in the lounge. Under his arm was the small package he had brought from the market, a plastic bag with the ring.

His eyes went to the television screen. He saw Claire's face. She was saying something to Rick Solares. Behind them was a crowd of Palestinians. He saw a forest of posters raised high, flags, banners with slogans.

"Look at what?"

"That guy in black. Moving along the edge of the crowd. See him, the one with his face toward the camera? I know that guy."

"You know him? From where?"

"He's one of the bunch that was holding me in Gaza. He's just a kid. What was his name?"

Pearly leaned forward, peering at the screen, scratching his head. "Saleh. Yeah, that's it, Saleh something . . . *Oh, shit!* I remember him, Skipper. That's the kid who wanted to be a martyr."

Maxwell felt a chill run through him. There was an open space between the kid in the black outfit and the set where Claire was talking to the camera. The kid seemed to be watching her, moving on a tangent to the camera. Moving closer.

Where the hell were the soldiers? The security guards? Why wasn't somebody screening the crowd?

The camera closed in on Claire. He could see her cell phone clipped to the belt of her jumpsuit. He snatched up his own phone, stabbed at the speed-dial number for Claire's phone. He kept his eyes riveted on the screen while he waited.

He could hear the phone ringing. Of course she would have the damned thing muted or turned off. Maybe, just possibly—*Please*—maybe she forgot. She would hear it ring. Maybe she or one of her assistants would answer, knowing that it had to be urgent. More than urgent.

An automatic voice in Hebrew came on the phone. It meant, he knew, the party wasn't answering.

He heard the tone prompting him to leave a message. *Damn it!*

He dropped the cell phone and snatched up the house telephone on the coffee table. He punched the zero and waited for the switchboard operator.

"Give me Mooney, the security director," he yelled. "Yes, now. I don't care who he's meeting with. This is Commander Maxwell, and yes, ma'am, it is an emergency. Please hurry."

His eyes stayed fixed on the screen. The camera was still closing in on Claire. The broadcast was almost over. Over her shoulder, barely visible, was the crowd of Palestinians.

He couldn't see the figure in black. He couldn't see Solares either. "Dex Mooney," said a voice on the phone. "I'm in a meeting with the ambassador. This had better be important, Commander. What is it?"

Maxwell told him. Did he have contact with the security detail there at Ramallah? The ones covering the television shoot? Mooney said he thought so. They weren't embassy employees, they were contract people, but yeah, he could communicate. He'd get on it right now. Hang on, he'd need a description of the suspect.

Maxwell hung on. On the screen, Claire was finishing her comments. The camera was zooming out again. The edge of the crowd was visible.

Maxwell still didn't see the kid in black. Maybe he wasn't who Pearly thought. Maybe he had gone away. Maybe . . .

Claire was speaking. Something moved into the background, over her shoulder. Too blurry to identify.

Something in black. He saw on the screen that Claire had noticed it too.

And then Claire looked away.

It was an involuntary habit that broadcast journalists acquired. She took her eyes from the figure in black at the edge of the crowd and glanced at the monitor. She had to, even if it was just for a moment. Where was the camera? Was it following Solares? Was she still on? It was her job to be aware of these things.

During the moment her attention was diverted, she had one of those subliminal perceptions—gut feelings, Sam Maxwell called them—that she had learned to trust. Something was about to happen. Something unthinkable. She also had the sure sense that there was nothing she could do about it.

In the next instant it happened—a flash, brighter than the sun. The wall of concussion moved at the speed of sound, taking less than a second to cross the open space between the crowd and the television crew.

It was a primitive weapon, packed with rusty machine screws, nails, and ball bearings, but it had been constructed with special lethality. The explosive was shaped to direct the blast within a cone of about sixty degrees. Within the cone, nothing could resist the wall of flaming scrap metal. Everything—light stanchions, vehicles, camera dollies, human flesh—was leveled like grain beneath a thresher.

Claire's eyes were still on the monitor when she saw the flash. With instant clarity, she understood what had happened.

Maxwell stared at the screen on the wall. The picture was gone. There was only a blotched, scratchy pattern. No image, no audio, just the sound of static.

After a few seconds, the network announcer in New York appeared. He explained that they were having a technical problem; they'd lost the connection in Ramallah. They'd be back with Claire Phillips's report in a few minutes.

Maxwell was numb, without thought. A commercial was running that featured a talking cereal box. More vitamins in every bowl. He clutched the telephone, holding it with both hands like a weapon.

Vaguely he was aware of a voice crackling in the earpiece.

"Commander Maxwell? Are you there? Answer up, please."

He lifted the phone to his ear. "What happened?"

"We don't know. We're not getting any response from the security detail that traveled with the television crew. The Israeli Defense Forces commander in Ramallah is reporting that a bomb just went off."

"How bad?"

"No information yet. Maybe you should get up here to my office."

Ramallah, West Bank, Palestinian Territories

His ears were ringing.

He lay facedown, nose pressed against the rough stone

surface of the street. His throat and nostrils were clogged with dirt and phlegm and smoke.

Carefully he lifted his head and blinked. Like a curtain lifting on a darkened window, his vision began to clear. He saw a layer of smoke floating a meter above the ground. The acrid taste of nitroglycerin burned his throat like acid.

Through the ringing in his ears he heard sirens. Screams. Pleas for help. From a distance, a rhythmic beating sound. Had to be a helicopter.

He tried sitting up. Nothing was broken; he had no open wounds. His hair was singed, and he could feel burns on the back of his neck. Something wet and sticky was clinging to his sleeve. He plucked at it, rubbed it between his fingers, then yanked his hand away in horror. It was a scrap of flesh. It was warm, oozing blood onto his sleeve.

He felt dizzy and nauseous. His thoughts were coming in disconnected fragments. Why was he alive? He remembered that at the last instant, when he saw what was happening, he whirled and dived for the ground. The explosion caught him from behind, tossing him like a rag doll, scorching his exposed skin and hammering the breath from him with the concussion. Somehow none of the shrapnel had found him.

Flames licked one of the vehicles. It had been a van, one of those used to transport the television equipment. Now it was a twisted steel skeleton. Flames and oily black smoke gushed from the wreckage. Another van lay on its side, all four tires ablaze.

He wobbled to his feet. His instincts were screaming at him to get away. There might be more explosions. More violence. Rage and recrimination would follow as surely as night followed day.

The endless cycle.

He couldn't leave. He shuffled like a zombie through the smoke to where the television equipment had been. He saw silhouettes moving through the smoke, calling to each other, looking for signs of life. Bodies lay like scattered bundles of laundry.

The explosion had cleaved a thirty-meter area of devastation. Nothing remained of the television setup except the destroyed vans and the twisted remains of the camera dollies.

Three men were peering at an object on the ground.

"It always happens that way," he heard one say in Arabic. He was a Palestinian, wearing some kind of uniform. "It blows away their middle. This is all that's left."

Don't look, he told himself. *Turn around, leave this place. Don't stay.*

He had to look. He shuffled toward them. On the ground, between their feet, he saw the object that had captured their attention.

His breath left him in a gasp. A primal scream erupted from his lungs.

The face of his sister gazed up at him. The black hood still covered Hanadi's head. She looked calm, her eyes closed as if she were napping. A crimson pool of blood spread around her severed head.

The man stared at him. "You know her?"

Saleh didn't answer. He stared for a long moment at his sister's face. He remembered the last time he had seen her—her eyes fixed on him, peering at him over the naked shoulder of the Great Leader.

His sister, Hanadi. Hanadi, who until a few minutes ago had a future, who was going to be a doctor. A wife and mother someday. A leader and example for oppressed women when Palestine became a country.

Now she was a martyr. *Why?* Who made her do this terrible thing? The answer came to him.

"I'm sorry," said Mooney.

Maxwell shook his head. He knew it wasn't true. Couldn't possibly be true. No goddamn way in hell was it true.

They were standing in Dexter Mooney's office. Maxwell was clutching the back of the desk chair with both hands. He saw Pearly Gates watching him with wide, worried eyes.

"They made a mistake," Maxwell said. "Tell them to check again."

"They did check," said Mooney. "It was bad. There are at least a dozen dead, probably more."

"Claire wasn't one of them."

Mooney shook his head. "I'm very sorry, Commander, but it looks like—"

"Check again."

"I just told you that they—"

"Just fucking do it!"

Mooney blinked, then turned back to the console that covered one wall of the office. For nearly a minute he exchanged terse dialogue with someone on the other end of the wireless transceiver.

He replaced the unit in its cradle and looked at Maxwell. "It's confirmed. Miss Phillips was killed instantly. So was the bureau chief. So were the technicians in the crew and the security guards and at least twenty Palestinians."

Maxwell stared at him. His hands were gripping the chair so tightly that his fingers punched through the vinyl cover. He closed his eyes, trying to hold back the pain that was cutting like a knife inside him.

Pearly Gates gripped Maxwell's shoulder. "Skipper, is there anything you want me to do? I know what you must be—"

Maxwell shrugged off his hand. He whirled and stormed out the door of Mooney's office, leaving the two men inside staring after him.

Instead of using the elevator, Maxwell took the stairway. He counted each step—twenty-two from the landing on the third floor to the second floor. Six steps on the landing, twenty-two more to the bottom level. In the main passageway, a marine sentry in his service Charlie uniform gave him a curious look.

Twenty-nine more steps to the door of the lounge. He didn't want to stop counting. He wanted to keep walking, ticking off steps, thinking about nothing else. On and on until he was too fatigued to think. No feelings, no dull ache in the pit of his stomach. If he kept walking, he would wake up and find that it was all a dream.

Half a dozen embassy staffers were in the lounge. They were all looking at the television on the wall. The announcer was going through the list of those killed in the suicide bombing in Ramallah. Seventeen Americans—every member of the network news crew, plus the four security agents. No survivors. Six Israelis, including the three drivers and three others, presumably Israeli intelligence officers. At least twenty Palestinians, probably more, members of the crowd.

The bomber, said the announcer, had been identified as a twenty-three-year-old Palestinian woman. She was a medical student named Hanadi Nazzal.

Maxwell stared at the changing images on the screen. He heard the ongoing descriptions of the dead, the outrage being proclaimed in every capital of the world, but none so vehemently as in Washington, where the President was expected to make a statement in the next hour.

A photo of Claire filled the screen. She wore BDUs and a Kevlar helmet. She was riding atop a Bradley fighting vehicle as it entered Baghdad. She had been a brave new personality in television journalism, said the announcer. She would be missed by all who knew her.

Maxwell couldn't hold it back any longer. His chest heaved, and he wept uncontrollably.

CHAPTER 18

NECESSARY LOSSES

Tel Aviv
1415, Tuesday, 25 October

Boyce arrived in Tel Aviv.

They sat in a café called Mike's Place, down the beach from the American embassy. Maxwell had an untouched cup of coffee in front of him. Boyce was nursing a Coke. He gnawed on an unlit cigar.

"No way," said Boyce.

"I have to get back to the ship," said Maxwell.

"You're in no shape to go to work."

"I'm fine."

"The hell you are. Look in a mirror."

It was true, thought Boyce. Maxwell looked like hell. He had dark circles under his eyes and the pallor of a man who had gone without sleep for a day and half.

Boyce knew it would be like this. Brick Maxwell was the best squadron skipper he had. Maybe the best he'd ever seen. He was also, at this point in time, the most dangerous. No way was he going to let Maxwell near any kind of killing machine. Especially an F/A-18 Super Hornet.

Boyce had come in to Tel Aviv as soon as he could get away. He could share some of Maxwell's grief. Claire

Phillips had been like an adopted daughter to him. Smart, funny, sexy—the perfect match for Maxwell, whom he had come to regard as a surrogate son.

Nothing would help Maxwell now. Nothing except time. Time and sleep.

"Take some leave," said Boyce. "A couple weeks, more if you need it. Go back stateside for a while."

"No."

Boyce nodded. They'd been through this once already. The funeral for Claire was in her hometown in New Hampshire. Maxwell had declined to go, and Boyce understood. A funeral would only make his pain worse.

"Go to Europe," said Boyce. "Chill out somewhere."

"I don't want to chill out. I want to get back to my squadron."

"Not yet."

"What about Pearly? Is he going back?"

"He stays too. The intel geeks haven't finished debriefing him, not after this bombing. In the meantime, he's your problem. You guys should do something creative. Try getting drunk."

Maxwell nodded, showing by his expression that he wasn't interested.

The truth was, thought Boyce, he might be wishing he had the services of Brick Maxwell. The Carrier Strike Group had gone to DEFCON 2—the second highest alert status.

Boyce glanced at his watch. "Time I got out of here. The helo is waiting at Ben-Gurion to haul me back to the ship."

Maxwell's face darkened. Boyce knew what he was thinking. Being left behind when the ship—and his squadron—might be going into combat was a fighter pilot's worst dream.

"What is the Strike Group going to be tasked for?" Maxwell asked.

"Probably some bullshit exercise. A show of strength

in case the Syrians or the Hezbollah or somebody gets cocky. Some armed reconnaissance and a lot of combat air patrol. You're not missing anything."

Except that Boyce didn't believe it, and he could tell Maxwell wasn't buying it either. Something was about to happen. A joint task force was assembling in the Mediterranean. When terrorists killed Americans, there was always a payback.

"Get my tab," said Boyce. "Next round's on me." He rose from the table and gave Maxwell's shoulder a squeeze. "I'm very sorry about what happened, Brick. There's nothing anyone can say that will take away your pain right now. Take care of yourself. The Roadrunners are gonna need their skipper back."

On his way out the door, he ran into Pearly Gates. He motioned for Pearly to follow him out to the sidewalk.

"What's up, CAG?"

Boyce nodded inside the restaurant. Maxwell was still at the table, staring out to sea. "Your skipper's gonna need a good wingman for a while," said Boyce. "Stay with him. I'm counting on you."

Pearly nodded his understanding. "Aye, aye, sir. I've got him covered."

USS Ronald Reagan, *Eastern Mediterranean*

Bullet Alexander hated what he had to do. *It's your job,* he reminded himself. *Suck it up; get it over with.*

It was midafternoon. The usual crowd of khaki-uniformed officers was clustered in the officers' wardroom. They sat at the long tables, chatting, drinking coffee, reading mail.

Scrotum Scudder was sitting alone, leafing through a magazine. Since he reported aboard the *Reagan* as the ship's new PAO, Scudder had been a loner. Most of the officers in the ship's company avoided him. They held the opinion that Lt. Cmdr. Norbert P. Scudder was a flaming asshole.

Alexander helped himself to a coffee from the big stainless-steel urn. Balancing his cup and saucer, he walked over to where Scudder was seated.

"Mind if I join you?"

Scudder glanced up. The look on his face left no doubt that he *did* mind. He shrugged and said, "Your choice."

Alexander sat. For a while he sipped his coffee in silence. He noticed that Scudder was still wearing the brace that encircled his neck up to his chin. Scudder read his magazine, studiously ignoring Alexander.

"How's the neck?"

Scudder didn't look up. "No change."

"Sorry to hear about the accident."

"It was no accident, as you very well know."

"Listen, Scro—" Alexander caught himself. "Mr. Scudder. I hope you don't really believe that someone in my squadron intentionally caused you to be injured."

Scudder laid down the magazine and looked up. "It's not a matter of belief. It's a fact. An assault was committed, and the guilty party will be identified and prosecuted."

Alexander nodded. At least Scudder was consistent. Still an asshole.

"Don't you think it's possible that it was just a party prank that went too far? Some of these guys can be pretty immature when they've been drinking. You were drinking with them, weren't you?"

"What are you trying to say? That the assault never happened? I suppose you're one of those cavemen who still thinks that the Tailhook scandal was just a party that went too far?"

Alexander didn't like Scudder's tone. The little prick needed reminding that he was speaking to a senior officer. Alexander took a few seconds, telling himself that what he had to do was absolutely necessary. Even if he hated it.

"Mr. Scudder, on behalf of my squadron officers, I would like to apologize for what happened. I certainly agree that it was unacceptable behavior, and I assure you that—"

"Look, Commander, you should know better than to bring up this matter here in the wardroom. This is an inappropriate conversation."

"What's inappropriate about offering an apology?"

"Each of us is party to an ongoing investigation. And I'll remind you that this is still the U.S. Navy, and as the senior officer present, you were responsible for the conduct of your squadron."

Alexander forced himself to restrain his anger. He picked up his cup and saucer and rose from the table. He should have known better. Scudder was an irredeemable, world-class dickhead. "Thank you for reminding me of my responsibilities." *Scrotum.*

As he walked away, Alexander glanced back at the table. Scudder was buried again in his magazine. He looked like a turtle in the white neck brace.

An image came to Alexander's mind—Scudder flying off the balcony of the Haifa hotel. The vision gave him a moment of secret pleasure.

Tel Aviv

Pearly Gates was shit-faced.

Maxwell knew this for a fact because he had just watched Pearly fall backward off his bar stool. No doubt about it: Pearly's tolerance for alcohol still wasn't up to standard.

Of course, Maxwell wasn't feeling any particular pain either. They had been at a place called the International Bar for nearly three hours, long enough to slam down six or eight drinks apiece. Vodka Collins for Maxwell, Manhattans for Pearly.

That afternoon they had attended a memorial service at the World Wide Network bureau headquarters for the seventeen employees who had been killed at Ramallah. The ordeal had been almost more than Maxwell could bear. When it was over, Pearly declared that it would be a great idea if they changed out of their dress blues and went somewhere for a couple drinks. Maybe more than a couple. Maxwell agreed.

Maxwell watched Pearly climb back on his stool. Pearly wore a goofy grin and a glassy-eyed stare.

"You've just proved that the CAG was right," said Maxwell.

"Whaddabout, Skipper?" It came out in a slur.

"Junior officers. Can't hold their booze. C'mon; I'll walk you home."

Maxwell paid the tab and steered Pearly out the door. He towed him down the sidewalk, back to the embassy compound. After showing their IDs and ignoring the smirk on the Marine sentry's face, Maxwell led Pearly up to his quarters, stuffed him into bed, then went back outside.

Darkness was settling over the beachfront. Maxwell was neither drunk nor sober. The vodkas had only dulled the ache that resided inside him.

He started walking. For an hour he walked northward, then retraced his steps and continued south on the nearly empty beach, past the hotels and glittering storefronts. Twice he was stopped by IDF patrols. The young soldiers checked his ID, then waved him on.

He was still walking, picking his away along the pebbly beach, when he abruptly stopped.

He stared at the hard sand and realized where he was. To his left he could see the bright yellow lights of the city glowing in the night like a new galaxy. The view seaward was black, no horizon, punctuated only by pinpoints of light from distant boats.

It was here, almost on this very spot. He and Claire had

carried their shoes under their arms, holding hands. This was where he had proposed to her.

For a while longer he stood facing the sea, feeling the anger and despair simmer inside him like roiling lava. He walked into the shallow surf, not bothering to remove his shoes or roll up his trousers. He kept walking until the waves sloshed up over his knees.

From his trousers pocket he pulled out the plastic-wrapped package. He removed the ring and held it up, letting the yellow light from the beachfront play on it. The single diamond glinted like a tiny star.

Are you sure, Sam?

Never been more sure in my life.

In a single furious motion he hurled the ring as far as he could into the black void of the ocean. For another minute he stood there, his chest heaving; then he turned away and waded back to the shore.

Ricardo Solares tilted his chin up and to the right. Between the array of cameras he could see his image in the broadcast monitor. He liked what he saw.

He especially liked the bandage over his temple. That had been a last-minute stroke of inspiration. It conveyed exactly the right message. Ricardo Solares, man of action. Bloodied but undaunted. Our man in Palestine, undeterred by terrorist bombs.

He continued speaking to the cameras. "My heart goes out to all the families and colleagues of the Americans lost in the bombing."

He paused, pinching his lips together, making a noble effort to hold back the turmoil of emotion that everyone could see was welling up in him.

"I can only promise them—and every American who is as outraged by this despicable crime as I am—that justice will be done."

Again he paused, letting the full weight of his message

sink in. Then his voice took on a deeper tone, one of righteous indignation.

"We Americans are a generous and peace-loving people. We are slow to anger and temperate in our actions. But when those who hate us wantonly attack our homeland or murder our citizens, we will not shrink from our duty. America will pursue the killers of our people. We will find them in their hiding places and destroy them. And that is a promise. Thank you, and God bless America."

The camera zoomed out. Solares saw himself in the monitor again. Behind him and plainly in view was an American flag. He had turned in his seat so that the sling around his right arm was clearly visible. Another great last-minute idea. Millions of viewers glued to their televisions could see that nothing—not even wounds from a terrorist's bomb—could quench the courage of Rick Solares.

The face of the network anchorman in New York flashed back on the screen.

"That was Special Envoy Rick Solares in Tel Aviv, delivering condolences and what sounded like a suggestion of possible retaliation by the United States. As most viewers know by now, seventeen Americans were killed in yesterday's bomb attack in the Palestinian city of Ramallah, including our own correspondent, Claire Phillips. Rick Solares was among those injured in the blast. As you can see, his fighting spirit is not diminished."

Solares listened to the anchorman's comment as he walked off the set. All in all, an excellent performance. The bandage and the sling, of course, were embellishments, but he'd been in broadcasting long enough to know how the game was played. Little touches like that just cemented the impression that Americans—and the American President—had of their indomitable envoy in the Middle East.

His injuries weren't entirely theatrical. In his hurried

departure from the mobile broadcast set, he had tripped on a loose cobblestone. He tumbled to the ground at almost the exact instant the suicide bomber exploded herself.

Hence the wound on his temple. An inch-wide bruise, actually—but sufficient justification for the bandage. Likewise, a sprained wrist was enough reason for the sling. It was pure bad luck that his only flesh-penetrating wound was a piece of shrapnel—a machine screw as it turned out—in his right buttock.

All in all it had been close. Too damned close. Khaled had not been specific about the "event" that would happen in Ramallah. Only that after Solares delivered his comments to the television cameras, he was supposed to distance himself as quickly as possible from the mobile broadcast set.

He hadn't asked why, but he could guess. His guess had been correct.

Too bad about the Phillips woman, even if she was a viper. He still couldn't visualize her face without feeling all over again the goddamn knee in his nuts. *Vicious bitch.* Maybe it really *wasn't* too bad. *Good riddance.*

He felt badly about Heinemann and the others, but you had to keep things like that in perspective. Sometimes it took the loss of life to rouse Americans off their collective butts. History was filled with such examples. The *Maine.* Pearl Harbor. Gulf of Tonkin, phony that it was. The World Trade Center. By comparison, seventeen bodies was a paltry number.

He was in the A studio of the World Wide Network bureau in downtown Tel Aviv. Black bunting was draped from one corner to the other of the outer office. An American flag was fixed to the wall. The production crew—mostly temps who had flown in from New York last night to take over the duties of those lost in the bombing—normally would be wisecracking and making irreverent jokes. Today they were sober and grim-faced.

Solares's television interview with the evening anchorman had lasted nearly ten minutes. It would show on prime-time news back in the U.S., half an hour before the President of the United States went on nationwide television.

Solares already knew what he would say. He'd been on the phone for fifteen minutes with him this afternoon. The President had been skeptical at first.

"American jets flying combat missions in Israel? The Israelis will never stand for it."

"Not *in* Israel, Mr. President. Over it, on their way to a target in Palestine."

"Palestine?"

"The West Bank and Gaza. It's in everyone's best interest now to call it Palestine. It politically separates the two territories from Israel. That way we can hold the Palestinians responsible for what happens in Palestine."

"The Secretary of State says we'll have the whole Arab community up in arms."

"Yes, sir, we probably will. But we already know that it will just be a show. Getting the Palestinian situation under control is as much in their interest as it is ours."

"What about Shallutz and his cabinet? Can we believe what they say? That they're going to support us?"

"Yes, sir, I'm sure of it. The Prime Minister expects to get a lot of heat from the opposition party about the U.S. conducting military operations in their airspace, but he's a realist. He knows it will take the pressure off Israel for a change. Better for the world to be mad at the United States instead of Israel."

There was silence on the phone, and for a moment Solares thought the President had hung up.

"I'm placing a lot of trust in your judgment, Rick. You'd better be right. Both our futures depend on it."

A thrill ran through Solares like an electric current. *Both our futures.*

"Yes, sir," Solares said. "I appreciate your faith in me."

He heard the line go dead.

That had been only . . . what? Solares glanced at his watch. A little over six hours ago. A joint task force was assembling, a fact that the President would be announcing in his talk to the nation. For exactly what purpose, he would be deliberately vague, but the message was clear: The United States would not let the killing of seventeen of its citizens go unpunished.

He saw Vernon Lewis waiting for him in the outer room. Lewis glanced at the sling on Solares's arm. Solares thought he saw a faint smirk.

"No business like show business," said Lewis.

Solares gave him a sharp look. "What's that supposed to mean?"

Lewis shrugged and averted his eyes from the sling. Solares ignored him and walked past him.

Since the explosion in Ramallah, Lewis had been behaving strangely, almost to the point of insolence. Lewis had been one of the lucky ones. During Solares's interview with Claire Phillips, Lewis had been standing at the edge of the crowd watching the set. He had just turned to walk away when the bomb exploded. The blast singed the hair on the back of his head, scorched his neck and hands, and knocked him headlong into the cobblestones. None of the shrapnel hit him. Despite scraped knees and light burns, he had escaped serious injury.

Now his eyes seemed to bore into Solares. Accusing him. What did Lewis know? Nothing, Solares told himself. Lewis had not been privy to the discussions between Solares and Khaled Mohanor. But by his manner—and those damned accusing eyes—he was behaving as though he suspected something. Lewis was getting on Solares's nerves.

As Solares walked on through the outer room, out to the sidewalk where the blue Lexus from the embassy was waiting, he made a mental note. Lewis was becoming a problem. It was time to get rid of him.

CHAPTER 19

JERUSALEM

Tel Aviv, Israel
1520, Thursday, 27 October

Pearly Gates winced in the harsh sunlight. The glare seemed to penetrate his skull like a laser. *Damn.* Hangovers were a bitch.

It was not yet noon. Even after a massive dose of ibuprofen and orange juice, the frontal lobe of his brain still throbbed in a pulsating rhythm. He'd better learn how to drink again, or give it up altogether.

For the past hour he'd been looking for the skipper. He'd checked the embassy compound, the lounges, and the snack bar. No sign of him.

Finally he spotted him at Mike's Place. Maxwell was sitting at one of the outside tables, a folded newspaper and an untouched coffee in front of him. He was staring out at the Mediterranean.

"Hey, Skipper, I've been trying to call you for the last hour." He saw Maxwell's cell phone on the table. "Doesn't that thing work?"

"Only when it's turned on."

Pearly eased himself into the chair opposite Maxwell. The pounding in his skull eased a bit.

"Here's why I've been looking for you." Pearly laid an

envelope on the table. "This was dropped off with the Marine sentry at the embassy. It's addressed to me."

"Dropped off? By whom?"

"Some Arab dude. He didn't stick around. After the security guys determined it wasn't a letter bomb, they gave it back to me."

Maxwell looked at the envelope for a while. Finally he picked it up and pulled out the note. It had been printed on grainy paper with an ink-jet printer.

Dear Mister Lieutenant Gates,

It is very bad for me since that day you went away from Gaza. We each of us thought life might be good again. You a free man to go home to America. Our Sheik Hamzeh a free man in Palestine. Maybe our people and your people and Israeli people would talk together and make peace and no more killing.

We were wrong. There is no peace, only more killing. You know that Hanadi decided to join the martyrs. You know why? I tell you, but is very difficult. I am not so good writing English.

Hanadi is dead, and so too the American woman. Miss Claire Phillips. I remember she is someone you tell me you know.

I want to talk with you again. Come to my uncle's café in the Jerusalem Old City. In Arab quarter. Al-Quds Café, in al-Hadad Street. Today at four o'clock. Very important that we talk. I will tell you who killed the Americans in Ramallah.

Your friend,
Saleh

A transformation seemed to have come over Maxwell. He was sitting upright. His eyes were fixed on Pearly.

"Who sent this?" he said.

"The kid you saw on the television. The one I thought at first was the bomber."

Maxwell kept staring at him. "This Hanadi, his sister. She was the one who . . ."

"Yeah. She's the one."

Maxwell's face darkened. He read the letter again; then he looked at Pearly. "Who else has seen this?"

"No one that I know of except the security guys who checked it for explosives."

"You didn't tell the debriefers about it?"

"I haven't seen them today. We don't have another session until this afternoon."

Maxwell stared off toward the Mediterranean, seeming to be deep in thought. Abruptly he looked at his watch. "Maybe you should blow off the debriefing today."

"I've already thought of that. That's why I came looking for you."

USS Ronald Reagan, *Eastern Mediterranean*

Wisps of steam gushed from the number one catapult track. Three hundred feet ahead, beyond the blunt bow of the carrier, lay the whitecapped Mediterranean.

Boyce shoved the throttles to the afterburner detent. He felt the two GE engines spinning up, rumbling at military power. The Super Hornet strained against its holdback fitting like a tethered beast.

His eyes made a final scan of the cockpit. No flags, no lights, no messages. The warning/caution panel was clear. Engine parameters all good.

Out the side of the Plexiglas canopy he saw the shooter—catapult officer—gazing back at him through his deck goggles. Boyce snapped Dog Balls Harvey a sharp salute. He shoved his helmet back against the headrest and waited.

A second ticked by. Another. Boyce's pulse rate accelerated as it always did while he waited—

Whoom.

The force of the catapult shot rammed back him in the seat. His eyeballs flattened and his spine dug into the hard back of the ejection seat. He saw the bow of the carrier rushing at him, sweeping beneath his nose.

Abruptly, the violence of the catapult ceased. The nose of the Hornet tilted upward. Boyce took the stick in his right hand, taking control of the jet from its flight-control computer. With his left hand he snatched up the landing gear handle, then the flap switch. He reached up to adjust his half-frame spectacles. They had been yanked askew by the force of the cat shot.

Goddamn glasses. He hated the things. Most of all he hated the fact that he was one of the few pilots in the air wing who had to wear them. One more sign of obsolescence. Thinning hair, thickening gut, spectacles that made him look like a fucking owl. Not only was he already the oldest active pilot on the *Reagan*, Red Boyce was one of the oldest in the Navy still flying fighters off carriers.

Not much longer. Soon they'd muster his air wing on the flight deck. They'd all be in their starched whites. There would be speeches and an exchange of salutes. He'd hand over command of his air wing to his deputy dog, Piles Poindexter. Red Boyce would be history.

"Gipper One-one, switch to Sea Lord," came the voice of the controller on the *Reagan*.

"Gipper One-one switching."

Boyce was leading Gipper flight—four F/A-18E Super Hornets, each loaded with two GBU-32 bombs. The GBU-32 was a thousand-pound JDAM—Joint Direct-Attack Munition—with a GPS guidance system mounted in its tail section.

Back on the *Reagan*, the three other Super Hornets of his flight were already sizzling down the carrier's cata-ult tracks. A pair of EA-6B Prowlers—electronic jammer and detector aircraft—were airborne, though no one expected that they would have much to do. Four more Super Hornets from the VFA-34 Blue Blasters would launch last. Their job was to fly TARCAP—Target Combat Air Patrol.

It was a joke, thought Boyce. This enemy had no fighters.

"Gipper One-one, Sea Lord. Oil Can is on station Bravo, angels twenty."

Boyce acknowledged. Oil Can was the in-flight refueling tanker. Boyce and his Hornets would top off their internal tanks before heading inland to the target.

After one turn at the rendezvous fix, Boyce had his four-ship flight together. The TARCAP was airborne and on the way. The EA-6B Prowlers were already in-country, their electronic warfare equipment monitoring the target.

On each Prowler's wing stations was a pair of HARMs—high-speed anti-radiation missiles. Just in case the enemy surprised them with a SAM acquisition radar. The HARMs would home on the radiation-emitting antennas, locking their exact location into their computerized memory, and pounce on them like avenging angels.

Yet another joke. The Palestinians didn't have target-acquisition radar. Using Prowlers and Super Hornets and GPS-guided bombs against them was like killing ants with a shotgun.

According to the intel briefers, the only opposition might be shoulder-fired SAMs like the SA-16 that whacked Pearly Gates. Which was why Boyce's jets were using the GBU-32 today. Not only was the GPS-guided bomb accurate enough to punch out a gnat's eyeball, it could be dropped from well outside the SA-16's envelope.

The gray shape of the three-engined U.S. Air Force KC-10 tanker filled up Boyce's windshield. He slid into position behind the leftmost hose, dangling from the wing of the tanker. After he'd taken on fuel, he moved to a perch off the tanker's left wing and waited for the res of his flight to top off.

He had a good view of the GBU-32s on the outboard wing pylons of each Super Hornet. Eight GPS-guided bombs in the strike package—enough ordnance to re move the summit of a small mountain. Instead, they were going to eradicate a tiny complex in a village called Tamun, on the far slope of the West Bank.

From his perch behind the tanker, he could see the long, straight shoreline of Israel. The brown patchwork o the interior sloped up to the massif that ran like a spine from Lebanon to the Negev Desert.

"Gipper One-one, your signal is Geronimo. Repeat Geronimo."

"Roger that, Gipper One-one copies Geronimo."

Here we go, thought Boyce. Geronimo was the clear ance to go feet-dry. Cross the shoreline of Israel and pro ceed to the target.

He had seen the intel photos. According to the briefers Tamun was used by terrorists coming down from Syria crossing from Jordan into Israel. The cluster of one-story buildings inside the village was a training and staging area for the same unit of Hamas that carried out the bombing at Ramallah.

And that was reason enough for this little pissan strike. Too bad he couldn't have given it to Brick Maxwell. It would be poetic justice if Maxwell were the one delivering a little payback to the guys who killed Claire Phillips.

Boyce thought again. No, better that he wasn't here Maxwell would be tempted to deliver more than a little payback.

Highway One, Central Israel

"Sure you don't want me to drive?" said Pearly Gates.

"Something wrong with my driving?"

"No, no, just thought I'd offer, that's all."

Actually, Maxwell was scaring the crap out of him. They were going 140 kilometers per hour, which was as good as the Fiat could do on the uphill grade. Maxwell had reverted to fighter-pilot mode, pedal to the metal, darting in and out of lanes. He was passing all the traffic on the sloping highway up to Jerusalem.

Already Pearly was wondering why he had agreed to this. He shouldn't have shown the letter to Maxwell. They were risking a court-martial for taking off on their own. Only in the last couple of days had the intel spooks even allowed him out of the Tel Aviv compound. They had extracted every snippet of information he could recall, but they wanted more. And they definitely didn't want him running loose again in the same theater where he'd been a prisoner.

Tough shit, he decided. He was sick to death of spooks and their questions followed by that cold-eyed gaze only intel officers knew how to use. It had to be something they learned at the CIA school. The gaze followed by a supercilious head nod followed by secretive jotting in a notepad. No jokes, no levity. Never an explanation. *We'll ask the questions, Lieutenant.*

Fuck the spooks. *He* had questions that needed answers. And so did Maxwell.

"Will this kid freak out when he sees me with you?" said Maxwell.

"I think he trusts me. I'll tell him you're the guy who was with me when I got shot down."

Maxwell veered around a slow-moving truck in the center lane. He darted across the lane back to the left. Pearly hunkered down in his seat. *Christ.*

"Really, Skipper, if you want to take a break and let me drive—"

"I'm fine." Maxwell zipped past a Peugeot on the right. The tires squealed as he yanked the Fiat back into the center lane.

The skyline of Jerusalem appeared on the ridge ahead. Yellow and white walls stood out against the brown Judean mountainside. The city looked more like a Disney theme park than the ancient hearth of three major religions.

Pearly had acquired a cursory knowledge of the Old City's history. He knew that Jerusalem's fortifications had been successively constructed and demolished by waves of invaders—Seleucids, Egyptians, Assyrians, Babylonians, Greeks, Romans, Crusaders, Mamluks, Ottomans. Each laid ruin to the culture of their predecessors, then left their own indelible stamp on the city.

Looking at the walls of the city, Pearly felt his doubts returning.

"Has it occurred to you that this might be a setup?"

"You mean, they might want to take us hostage?" said Maxwell.

"Something like that."

"Yeah, it occurred to me."

If Maxwell was worried, he didn't show it. Maybe, thought Pearly, he actually *wanted* to confront the terrorists. Pearly had glimpsed the dark shape of the Colt .45 automatic in Maxwell's canvas satchel when they climbed into the Fiat.

They entered the chaotic traffic of the outer city. Pearly was glad now that Maxwell was driving. Horns blared, trucks belched clouds of black smoke, taxis careened from side streets. Maxwell was handling the Fiat like a fighter, burning rubber at the red lights, going head-to-head with fist-shaking taxi drivers like a native Israeli.

They found a parking garage a block from the Jaffa Gate, the western entrance to the walled Old City. It was five minutes before one when they walked through the big arched gate, down the narrow street toward the Muslim quarter.

Pearly had a street map. At every row of shops they had to fend off the tenacious Arab hawkers selling jewelry and paintings and postcards. It took ten minutes to reach al-Hadad Street, then another five to find the Al-Quds Café.

It was dark inside. The only light came from a stained yellow fixture on the ceiling. Pearly glanced around. Half a dozen tables with checkered plastic covers filled the single room. There were no customers, just a scowling waiter in a white apron, sitting with his legs crossed at the bar. He had a stubble of beard and an untrimmed black mustache.

"Is that him?" Maxwell said.

"No."

The waiter gave them a long, appraising look, then pointed to one of the tables. They each took a seat facing the center of the room. Maxwell placed his shoulder bag on his lap.

After another long scrutiny, the waiter rose from his chair and came to the table. The scowl hadn't left his face. "No English menu. *Shwarma* we have. Also falafel and kebab. You want beer or tea or cola?"

They each ordered a beer. Maxwell ordered *shwarma*, a pita stuffed with thin slices of roasted lamb. Pearly took the falafel—a ball of blended chickpeas and various herbs and spices.

The waiter delivered the beers, a local brew called Taybeh, then disappeared in the back of the café.

"Mr. Personality," said Pearly.

"You sure this is the right place?"

He pulled out the note from Saleh and looked again. "Al-Quds. This is the name of the joint."

Five minutes passed. The waiter still hadn't reappeared.

"The kitchen must be down the street," said Pearly.

"If he doesn't come back—"

A man entered from the back. He was an Arab, younger than the waiter. He was dressed in a loose-fitting chambray shirt and black trousers. He looked vaguely familiar to Pearly.

He stopped at the table. "You are Lieutenant Gates?"

"Yes," said Pearly.

He looked at Maxwell. "Who is this one?"

"My colleague. Another pilot." Maxwell had already warned him: *Don't freak them out with words like* commanding officer.

"He stays," said the young man. "You come with me."

"Come where?" said Pearly.

"You see. Not far."

"Where is Saleh? Will he be there?"

"You come. Now."

Pearly nodded toward Maxwell. "Not unless he comes too."

The young Arab's eyes flicked between Pearly and Maxwell. After a moment he seemed to reach a decision. "Follow me. We must hurry."

They rose from the table. Maxwell slipped the strap of his bag over his shoulder. They followed the young man through the back of the café, out the rear exit. Not until they were outside, standing in the shadows of the dark alleyway, did Pearly realize they weren't alone.

There were six of them. They were grim-faced men with dark eyes and black-stubbled beards. Each held a pistol.

CHAPTER 20

TAMUN

The rough brown landscape of Israel was slipping like a blanket beneath the nose of Boyce's jet. *Amazing,* thought Boyce. It had never happened before. American fighters flying a strike mission over Israel.

But times had changed. Since the events of September 11, 2001, the United States hunted down terrorists who killed Americans. According to the intelligence briefers, the murderers of seventeen Americans were in Palestine.

Boyce guessed that it had taken some high-level pressure on Israel for them to allow the Americans to operate inside their airspace. He guessed, too, that they might be secretly happy that it was someone else bombing the Palestinians today.

This strike ought to be a no-brainer. Undefended target, no known air defense, no target identification problems. The target coordinates—computed within inches—had been loaded in the bombs' GPS guidance units. The pilot's job was to select the weapons station, push the right button, then let the smart bombs do the work. Piece of cake.

He could have assigned one of his other squadron skip-

pers—Gordo Gray, Spike Mannheim, Hairball Shep-
ard—to lead the strike. All good fighter pilots, all savvy
strike leaders.

But not today. Boyce had a feeling about this strike.
Something about it bothered him. This was the kind of mission that could turn into a cluster fuck. If it did, the strike
leader would be hung out to dry. If that happened, it might
as well happen to a washed up old guy like Red Boyce.

The Sea of Galilee came into view beneath his left
wing. To the north rose the high mound of the Golan
Heights, where the killing of the young Israelis had triggered the latest violence. The strike package's ingress
route would circumvent the target to the north, then descend southward along the Jordan valley, attacking the
complex from the east.

The bombs loaded on the four Super Hornets each had
slightly different aim points, allowing a patterned destruction of the target complex. If their intel was correct,
one of the buildings was a Hamas weapons cache. Another was a billeting compound where, if they got lucky,
a hundred or more terrorist trainees would be hunkered
down. Another structure supposedly contained raw chem-
icals—the stuff of bombs like the one that killed Claire
Phillips.

Please, God, thought Boyce. *Just once let the intel
geeks get it right. Let this place be the mother of all
ammo dumps.*

He glanced at his left multifunction display. The symbols of each jet in the strike package were datalinked
from the Hawkeye. Close aboard were the jets of his own
flight—Lt. B.J. Johnson on his left wing, Lt. Cmdr.
Spoon Withers and Lt. Bud Spencer off his right. In a
high station to the south of the target was the four-ship
TARCAP led by Cmdr. Spike Mannheim.

Not datalinked with the strike package, but undoubtedly out there somewhere, were other jets—Israeli F-15s
and F-16s. Watching. Evaluating.

Boyce thought of Lebev, the F-16 pilot who had coaxed Pearly Gates through the hard deck. The cocky little shit was probably hoping the Yanks would screw this one up.

He rolled into a turn to the right, down the Jordan River valley. He saw the green ribbon of the Jordan meandering southward, vanishing into the Dead Sea. It was important not to stray over the river into Jordanian airspace. There would be a loud enough wail from the Arab countries without provoking Jordan.

Off his right wing were the hilly slopes of Shomron. Perched along the high range were the Palestinian cities of Nablus and Jenin—both hotbeds of insurgency. Somewhere between them was—

He saw it. He glanced at his navigational display, just to be sure.

The target. Tamun. The complex was at three o'clock, thirty miles away. It was a barely discernible sprawl of beige-colored structures. A dry stream bed snaked through the village, down the mountainside toward the Jordan River.

Boyce ordered his flight into a combat spread, master armament switches hot, weapons stations selected.

He nudged the Super Hornet's nose down. In formation, the four jets gathered speed in a shallow dive from thirty thousand feet to the delivery altitude of twenty thousand.

The target was easy to see now. A yellow cluster against the sprawling brown hillside. No sign of life. Still no radar emissions. No black bursts of AA fire.

For an instant Boyce let himself think about who was there. Bad guys, yes. Terrorists who killed Americans.

Who else? Women and children? Villagers who didn't have a clue they were about to be bombed? People who consorted with bad guys.

He shoved the thoughts from his mind. This was war. You trusted the planners to select the targets. Your job was to put the ordnance precisely on target. After that, it was up to God.

Twenty miles.

The in-zone cue was illuminated on his weapon stores page. Boyce verified that he had the right aim point selected.

That was another strange and new thing. Dropping from high altitude was an unnatural act, something big ugly bombers did, not pointy-nosed strike fighters.

Instead of rolling in on a target, diving at a steep angle, and using the jet's CCIP—constantly computed impact point—to determine the release of the bomb, you could let this one go in level flight. You could even toss it into the general area over the target. The guidance kit on the bomb's tail steered it precisely to the preset coordinates on the ground. The JDAM didn't care whether it was cloudy or clear.

Boyce depressed the pickle button on his stick. He felt the jolt as the two-thousand-pound load kicked off the starboard wing.

The weapons display page instantly cycled to the next station. Ready for the next bomb.

He hit the pickle button again. Another jolt, this one from the port wing.

He glanced to each side. From each of the other Super Hornets, dark, pointed shapes were separating.

There was no reason to hang around. A pair of F/A-18 recon jets would photograph the bomb hits with their TARPS packages—tactical airborne reconnaissance processing systems. A surveillance satellite would be recording the exact moment of weapon impact.

Still, Boyce had to see. What was the time to impact for a two-thousand-pound Mark-84 shape from twenty thousand feet? It was on his right MFD screen. TTI—time to impact—was twenty-seven seconds.

He saw the first bomb hit. One of the yellow structures down below erupted in a brown and black mushroom.

Then another, a few meters away.

And another.

Boyce couldn't take his eyes off the spectacle. Each bomb sent a fresh eruption from inside the billowing cloud. The village of Tamun disappeared beneath the dirt and debris.

Then he saw what he was hoping for. An orange pillar of fire leaped like a geyser of lava from the debris cloud. Behind it gushed a cascade of black smoke.

Ammo dump. It must have been the last bomb. The spooks finally got something right.

Nablus, West Bank, Palestinian Territories

It took half a minute for the first thunderclap to reach Nablus, twelve kilometers away. Pedestrian traffic in the dusty street came to a halt. Every head swung to the northeast. They gazed at the mountain promontory across the valley.

The village of Tamun. Something terrible was happening there.

More thunderclaps, one after the other, rolled across the valley. Each explosion rattled windows and dislodged plaster. Children and old women wailed. Dogs scuttled for cover. A donkey in the market square reared and overturned a vegetable cart.

Then a final shuddering blast. Every window in every house overlooking the valley was blown inward. The wave of concussion swept through the ancient streets like an invisible tide. Overhead, the red ball of the sun blurred and vanished. The canopy of smoke blotted out the sky.

Khaled Mohanor lowered his Zeiss field glasses and turned his face, but the hot wind still stung his eyes.

How many explosions were there? He had lost count. The last one had to be the nitroglycerin crates smuggled in from Syria. The shock wave overturned chairs and blew the coffee carafe from the table where he sat.

Since early morning Khaled had been waiting on the second-floor terrace of the house in Nablus. It afforded him a view of Tamun, which he could see clearly with the binoculars across the steep valley. He had observed the lethargic comings and goings in the village. Sentries were posted all around the periphery of the compound. The idiots spent their time sleeping or peering uselessly down the mountainside to the Jordan valley.

It never occurred to them to scan the sky.

Every peasant in Nablus knew about Tamun, but none dared speak of it. Everyone knew that some kind of insurgency training went on there. You could hear the shooting and volleys of automatic fire in the night. If you dared get close enough, you might observe the men hauling loads on their backs up the slope from the Jordan valley.

It was not healthy to speculate about such things. You were either a member of the resistance or you claimed to know nothing about it.

There were several places like Tamun. Sooner or later the Israelis always found them out. When that day came, there were shootings and explosions and helicopter attacks. The resistance fighters were ready for them. They would exchange a few rounds of fire, then fade back into the population. Tamun had already seen several such occasions.

But nothing like this. Today was different.

Khaled peered again through the Zeiss glasses. The veil of smoke was lifting. The precision of the bombs had been uncanny. The wall around the compound was mostly intact, but the buildings inside were gone.

He saw no movement in the ruins of the village. Shattered vehicles were burning, including the twisted hulk of the bus that had brought in the families of the Hamas fighters. Fifty of them, mostly wives and children. They had arrived only an hour before the first bomb struck Tamun.

For a while Khaled watched the flames and the smoke gush from across the valley. There was no sign of survivors. Nor did he see ambulances or rescue vehicles racing over from Nablus.

No surprise. No driver would go near such a place until he was certain the bombs had stopped falling.

Bringing the women and children to Tamun had been a brilliant idea, Khaled thought. It was important, of course, that no one discovered it had been *his* idea. Above all else, Palestinians revered martyrdom. It had a mystical attraction for them. It was their route to heaven, their rallying cause for holy war.

Khaled Mohanor had just given them a hundred and fifty new martyrs. With the help of the Americans.

He lowered the glasses and rose from the table. He had seen enough. Let the real war begin.

The Old City, Jerusalem

He still had the satchel.

The gunmen were prodding them down the cobblestone alleyway. Maxwell calculated his chances. He had his hand inside the satchel and on the grip of the Colt. It already had a round chambered, ready to fire. At the right moment he could surprise them, get off two, maybe three rounds.

Not good enough. There were seven of them, three in front, four in back. One would still manage to kill him and Pearly.

Damn. He had known that this could be a setup. Why did he do it? Why didn't he just turn the letter over to the CIA, let them take out these thugs? Or let the Israelis do it? Why did he drag Pearly back into trouble?

Because you wanted the terrorists who killed Claire.

Now what, smart guy?

Stay focused, he told himself. He had the pistol. These guys were amateurs. He could tell by the way they fumbled with their own weapons. They kept looking up and down the alleyway as if they didn't know what might be coming. They were young and scared.

Wait. Wait for an opening.

The walls on either side rose three stories high, blocking out any direct sunlight in the narrow alleyway. The gunmen kept shoving them along. They turned a corner into an even narrower passageway, then ascended a shallow incline. A hundred meters up the alleyway they stopped at a windowless building.

One of the gunmen rapped a sequence of knocks on the wooden door. Several seconds passed. Someone inside replied with another series of raps.

The door swung open. Maxwell was shoved inside. He felt Pearly come stumbling in behind him.

The room had a musty smell, like that of a warehouse. He blinked in the dim light. One side of the room was filled with piles of stuffed burlap bags that smelled of grain or feed. On the other side was a table and half a dozen chairs illuminated by a rusty desk lamp. On the wall was a large framed black-and-white photograph of a man's face.

Maxwell squinted at the photo. The Great Leader. In the portrait, Khaled Mohanor was dressed in a traditional Arab *gellebiah* and checked kaffiyeh. He was smiling his charismatic smile.

Pearly saw it too. He glanced over at Maxwell and nodded.

A man emerged from the shadows of the stacked burlap bags. He looked young, no more than a teenager. He wore a scraggly mustache. With the AK-47 slung over one shoulder, he looked like a kid pretending to be a terrorist.

The young man exchanged a torrent of argument in

Arabic with the others. They gestured wildly with their pistols, pointing them at Pearly and Maxwell.

Maxwell slid his finger inside the trigger guard of the Colt.

"Saleh," said Pearly.

The young man stopped arguing and looked at Pearly. "I am sorry," he said.

"What the hell is this all about?" said Pearly.

The young man broke into a sheepish smile. He motioned for the others to lower the muzzles of their weapons. "They are very angry. They want to kill you."

"Why?"

"You haven't heard? Something happened today. American airplanes bombed a village near Nablus, to the north of here. Many people killed. Women, children, old people. Everyone killed." He glanced again at the glowering Palestinians. "Now they want to kill all Americans."

"We had nothing to do with it," said Pearly.

Saleh turned to the others and rattled off something in Arabic. Their expressions didn't change.

Saleh turned to Maxwell. "Who is this one?"

Maxwell eased the .45 upward inside the satchel. The muzzle was pointed at the belly of the closest Palestinian gunman.

"His name is Maxwell," said Pearly. "My commanding officer. He was with me when I was shot down."

Saleh stared at Maxwell for a moment. "I saw you. You were at Erez when Lieutenant Gates was exchanged for Sheik Hamzeh."

"Yes," said Maxwell.

Saleh spoke again in Arabic. The Palestinians still glowered, but each, one after the other, lowered his pistol.

"I told them that you are here to help us," said Saleh.

"How could we help you?" said Maxwell.

"We have run away from Hamas and the jihad. Now they want to kill us. And the Israelis want to kill us also."

"Why do the Israelis want to kill you?"

Saleh's eyes darted nervously to the gunmen, then back to Maxwell. "They . . . think we were involved in the resistance. In certain . . . killings."

"Were you?"

"Not anymore. We want to leave Palestine."

"Leave? Where would you go?"

Saleh smiled his sheepish smile. "To America. We would like to become rich and famous like you."

Maxwell saw Pearly's eyes roll.

"That may not be easy," said Maxwell. "How would you get a permit to enter the United States?"

"The Americans have to take us."

"Why is that?"

"Because I have information that is very important."

Maxwell nodded. He remembered Saleh's letter to Pearly. *I will tell you who killed the Americans in Ramallah.*

He waited a moment. The young man was smiling. Thinking about being rich and famous, Maxwell assumed.

"Do you know who ordered your sister to blow herself up?"

Saleh's expression froze. He stared straight ahead, avoiding Maxwell's gaze.

Finally he nodded. "Yes."

Several seconds ticked past.

"Tell me."

Saleh didn't answer. He turned and nodded toward the wall.

Maxwell stared at the portrait. "Mohanor? He gave the order to set off the bomb at Ramallah?"

Saleh nodded.

"Did you *hear* him give the order?"

Pearly was watching the exchange with a rapt expression. The Palestinian gunmen looked puzzled.

"I didn't hear him. But I was there when he and the American planned the killing."

Maxwell felt a shock surge through him. *American?*

He tried to keep his voice calm. "Where was this? How do you know they were planning the killing?"

"It was here in Jerusalem. In Khaled's headquarters. It was after . . ." The words seemed to freeze in his throat. He kept his eyes straight ahead. ". . . after the killing in the Golan Heights. I saw them talking. I didn't understand why they were talking. Then, when Hanadi killed herself, I understood. That was what they were talking about. Khaled had already ordered Hanadi to be a martyr."

Saleh fell silent. He seemed to be on the brink of tears.

Maxwell waited. *Don't push. Let the secrets spill out a little at a time.*

Seconds passed. The smiling visage of Khaled Mohanor beamed down from the wall. Maxwell resisted the urge to seize Saleh, to shake him until he got an answer.

Maxwell couldn't wait any longer. "What American?"

Saleh blinked. He didn't seem to understand the question.

"Who was the American?" said Maxwell.

Saleh stared. "American?"

"Who did you see talking to Khaled?"

The harsh tone seemed to shake him from his daze. "You know. The famous one. The television man with the mustache."

Maxwell nodded. It was the answer he expected, but he still didn't believe it. The kid was making a wild presumption. It wasn't possible that Khaled and—

The door smashed inward with a bang, blown from its hinges. Maxwell sensed a blur of motion. He saw the Palestinians whirling, heard a crack of gunfire, the *brrrraaap* of an automatic weapon.

Then a flash of light and another bang. It was the last thing Maxwell remembered.

CHAPTER 21

THE OUTCASTS

The Old City, Jerusalem
1835, Thursday, 27 October

The sound of gunfire had stopped.

Slowly Maxwell regained his senses. He was lying facedown. He could smell the acrid odor of cordite, of gunpowder and spent ammunition. And something else, like phosphorous.

Through the ringing in his ears, he heard barked commands, men answering in a language he didn't follow. Arabic? Hebrew?

His vision was returning in small increments. From a pinpoint of clarity at the center, his field of view was expanding to include the floor around him. He saw boots, the muzzle of an automatic rifle, green camo trousers tucked into boot tops.

Someone was kneeling beside him. "Commander Maxwell?" The voice seemed detached, far away.

His ears were still ringing. He leaned up on one elbow and looked at the man. He wore combat gear—BDUs, a holstered pistol, helmet with chinstrap. The radio on his hip crackled with a voice in the same unintelligible language.

"You'll be okay in a few minutes," said the soldier. He

gestured with his arm around the room. "Which is more than I can say for them."

Maxwell gazed around. A haze of smoke filled the room. He saw bodies, some spread-eagled on their backs, some huddled in fetal positions. Ribbons of blood flowed from the bodies toward a low spot in the floor.

Maxwell wobbled to his feet. "Where's Pearly?" His eyes scanned the room. He saw only bodies. "Oh, shit, what happened to Pearly?"

"I'm here, boss." The voice came from behind. He turned and saw Pearly Gates sitting with his legs crossed. He was shaking his head, a confused look on his face. "What the fuck was that?"

"Stun grenade," said the soldier. His English was accented, and Maxwell saw that he was wearing small black captain's bars on his collar.

"Who are you?" said Maxwell.

"Capt. Ehud Yalon," said the officer. "Special Operations Unit, Israel Defense Force."

Maxwell's vision was clearing, but the ringing in his ears persisted. He looked around the room. He counted a dozen battle-dressed soldiers. Each was carrying a Tavor assault rifle. They were examining the bodies on the floor.

He saw a soldier turning over a bloody, thin-framed shape. Maxwell recognized Saleh's face, still frozen in fear and shock. He had taken a burst of automatic fire in the chest. The front of the cotton shirt was shredded, soaked in fresh blood.

"Oh, man," said Pearly. "Why did you kill him?"

"He was a terrorist," said the Israeli captain. "That's what we do to terrorists. We would have killed them already, but the two of you interfered."

"Interfered?" said Pearly. "Look, pal, we were just—"

"Having a look around," said Maxwell. He gave Pearly a sharp look.

"Looking for terrorists you could exchange information with?" said the captain. The politeness was gone from his voice.

Maxwell shook his head. "That young man there—the one you just killed—had information that would have been helpful to Israel and to the U.S."

"Why didn't you let the intelligence services handle it?"

"Why didn't you? Shooting sources of information is a pretty dumb way to get intelligence."

"You shouldn't have been meeting them. You don't know these people. They would have killed you."

Pearly opened his mouth, about to insert himself back into the argument, but he caught Maxwell's look.

One of the Israeli soldiers had Maxwell's satchel. He pulled out the Colt .45 and showed it to the captain. The captain examined the pistol. He removed the magazine from the grip, then retracted the slide and popped out the chambered round.

He looked at Maxwell. "Yours?"

Maxwell shrugged. "Survival pistol," he said. "I'm a fighter pilot. I'll want that back."

"An unauthorized firearm," said the captain. "A very serious offense in Israel."

He handed Maxwell's pistol back to the soldier. "I'm taking you both to military police headquarters."

"The hell you are," said Pearly. "You don't have any right to—"

"Fine," said Maxwell. "Whatever you say."

His ears were still ringing.

The questions were predictable—and stupid.

Maxwell and Pearly sat on hard metal chairs facing the police commandant's desk. It was obvious that neither the police commandant, an overweight colonel with wet armpits, nor Captain Yalon were trained in intelligence work.

"Why were you and Lieutenant Gates talking to a known terrorist?" asked the colonel.

"We didn't know he was a terrorist," said Maxwell.

This produced a raised eyebrow. "How did you happen to meet this person?"

"Lieutenant Gates met him when he was a prisoner in Gaza."

The colonel couldn't hold back a smirk. He looked at Pearly. "You're telling us that even though you were shot down and taken prisoner by this man, you didn't recognize him as a terrorist?"

"He was a kid. He wasn't one of the assholes who captured me. I never saw him with a gun."

Maxwell saw the Israelis exchange looks, as if Pearly had said something significant. After a moment the colonel said, "What did he wish to talk to you about?"

Before Pearly could answer, Maxwell said, "He wanted to go to the United States."

The Israelis seemed amused. "He wasn't serious?"

"He was," said Maxwell. "As Lieutenant Gates just told you, he was a kid. He didn't know about the real world. He didn't know that he didn't have a future."

Captain Yalon seemed to take offense at this remark. He rose and came around the desk. He stood glowering down at Maxwell. "You Americans are naive. You don't understand what these terrorists do."

"I understand what they did at Ramallah."

Yalon leaned closer to him. "The bombing a few days ago? A minor incident compared to what they have done in Israel. It was more like a publicity stunt for them."

Maxwell decided he didn't like this smart-ass captain. The guy was baiting him, trying to get him to say or do something outrageous. And it was working.

Maxwell said, "You're telling me the murder of seventeen innocent Americans was a publicity stunt?"

"Innocent?" said Yalon. "They were media people. The American media is hardly innocent. Not the way they distort the truth about the Palestinians. The Phillips woman was one of the worst. She was always—"

Maxwell was on his feet, holding Yalon's collar in both hands. Yalon was a short, muscular man, a good three inches shorter than Maxwell. Maxwell yanked him up on his tiptoes.

"Stop!" yelled the colonel, jumping from his seat. "Are you crazy?"

"Hey, Skipper," said Pearly. "Back off. Don't hurt the guy."

Maxwell wasn't listening. All his pent-up rage and grief were boiling up inside him. He held Yalon for a second, then flung him like a rag doll. The Israeli's head ricocheted off the concrete wall, and he slid to the floor, his eyes glassing over.

Maxwell was going after Yalon, about to snatch him to his feet, when Pearly grabbed him from behind. He heard Pearly's urgent voice in his ear. "Cool it, Skipper. You're out of control."

In a distant portion of his brain, Maxwell got the message. It was the first rule of the fighter pilot: *Don't lose control.* The corollary was automatic: *If you lose it, get it back.*

Well, he had definitely lost it. Before he got it back, he wanted to beat the living shit out of someone. Captain Yalon would do nicely.

He sensed another presence close to him. The colonel stood in a crouch, both hands gripping his semiautomatic pistol.

"Stop," said the colonel. "Or I'll put a bullet through your head."

For several seconds no one moved. The sound of heavy breathing filled the room. Yalon blinked, trying to regain his focus. Pearly kept Maxwell's arms pinned from behind.

Then another noise. The office door swung open, banging against the stop. Leather heels clacked like drumbeats on the tile floor.

Hannah Shamir came striding into the police commandant's office, flanked by two M-16-carrying IDF security detail guards.

Maxwell turned his head to stare at her. She was wearing a beige pantsuit, her thick black hair loose down to her collar. She motioned for the security guards to stand back.

"Someone tell me just what the hell is going on here."

"Madame Deputy," said the colonel, "this man assaulted Captain Yalon." He kept his pistol aimed at Maxwell's head.

"Put that gun away."

The colonel's face reddened. "These two are under arrest. We were conducting an interrogation when—"

"I know what you're conducting, and you have greatly exceeded your authority. The Foreign Minister is furious. He has ordered me to take these two into custody."

"That's impossible. We have not completed our investigation."

"Are you a hopeless idiot? Don't you realize you're detaining officers of our most important ally? Why did you not contact the Foreign Ministry immediately? Why was the U.S. embassy not informed?"

The sweat stains in the colonel's khaki shirt seemed to darken. Reluctantly, he holstered the pistol. He exchanged glances with Captain Yalon, whose eyes had regained their focus. He now wore a worried expression.

Hannah pointed to the telephone on the desk. "Call the Minister. Let him explain to you that you had no business arresting these Americans. Ask him if you should hand them over to me."

The colonel stared at the phone as if it were a ticking bomb.

"Call him," Hannah said. "Do it now."

The colonel swallowed hard, then seemed to reach a decision. He turned and stalked into the outer office. Captain Yalon watched him leave, then realized with a start that he was alone with Hannah Shamir and the two Americans. He rose to his feet and wobbled after the colonel.

Pearly released his grip around Maxwell's arms. "You got it back, Skipper?"

Maxwell took a deep breath. He could feel the rage leaving him like escaping steam. "Temporary loss of control. Don't worry; I'm okay."

Hannah studied Maxwell's face for a moment. "Do you have any idea how much trouble you're in?"

"No. How much?"

"More than you can imagine. Why did you assault that officer?"

"He was getting on my nerves."

Hannah shook her head. "You have made some important people in this country very angry."

"Because they're afraid I might learn the truth about Ramallah?"

She sighed, and her face seemed to soften. "Look, Brick, I know what you're going through. You want to find someone you can punish for Claire's death. Believe me, I know. I went through the same thing, lashing out at things, wanting to kill someone, anyone. But you can't bring her back."

Maxwell stared back at her. In his gut he knew she was right. But he didn't care. "What happens now?" he said.

"We get you out of here before the colonel decides to arrest you for assault."

"Where are we going?"

"Not we. You. General Zemek wants both of you out of the country."

"Zemek? What does he have to do with it?"

"Everything. He's just been appointed Defense Minister. That makes him the most powerful man in Israel, next to the Prime Minister."

Maxwell shrugged. "Can't fight city hall."

"What does that mean?"

"An American expression. It's his country."

Hannah nodded. "I'm supposed to take you directly to the American embassy. You and Lieutenant Gates have to pack up and leave. A U.S. Navy airplane is coming to Ben-Gurion airport to pick you up."

Five minutes later, they were standing outside the police headquarters. As they climbed into Hannah's black government limo, she handed him his canvas satchel.

He glanced inside. There was the familiar dark shape of the Colt .45. The clip too.

"And don't get caught with that thing again," she said.

USS Ronald Reagan, *Eastern Mediterranean*

"Those sons of bitches!" roared Boyce.

He glowered at the computer screen as if he were trying to burn a hole through it with his eyes. He was in the flag intel office. He and Cmdr. Harvey Wentz were looking at the online edition of the *Washington News-Journal*. Like yesterday's *International Herald Tribune*, the front page of the *News-Journal* carried a ground-level photograph of the carnage in the village of Tamun.

Boyce was reading the article beneath the photo. "How the hell did they get that information?"

"How do you think?" said Wentz. He made a show of rubbing his fingers together. "The old-fashioned way. Must be a thousand different people who had access to the names of the strike pilots. One of them took a bribe."

Boyce's eyes bulged as he read the story about the Tamun strike. Except that now it was the "Tamun Massacre." The strike leader and perpetrator of the massacre, according to "reliable sources," was the Air Wing Commander aboard USS *Ronald Reagan*, Captain R. S. Boyce.

"I don't fucking believe this," said Boyce. "I thought the media was supposed to keep the names of U.S. military personnel in combat operations anonymous."

"Read the story," said Wentz. "The way they've slanted it, it wasn't a combat operation. It was a calculated destruction of an undefended village. They're calling it a massacre and a slaughter and—look at the last paragraph—an act of homicide. That's freedom of the press for you."

Boyce felt sick to his stomach. He forced himself to look away from the screen, trying to control his anger. *The low-life, scum-sucking . . .* For nearly thirty years he had served his country. He considered the profession of arms to be one of duty and honor. Now this. Vilified in his own country for bombing an enemy target with precision and due regard for collateral damage.

Except, of course, for the innocent civilians.

He saw Wentz giving him his intel officer's owlish gaze. Boyce's anger flared again. He was thinking about the huge gap in their HUMINT—human intelligence—that allowed 120 noncombatants to occupy a target area without his knowing it.

He resisted the urge to lash out at Wentz. He knew it wouldn't do any good. The supercilious little twit would never bring himself to acknowledge that flawed intelligence had caused a calamity of seismic proportions. Wentz wouldn't recognize a calamity if it was gnawing on his leg.

And then Wentz shocked him.

"Have you spoken to your wife?"

Boyce stared at the intel officer for several seconds, not comprehending his meaning.

Then it struck him like a thunderbolt. *Oh, sweet Jesus. While I was sitting here feeling sorry for myself, I forgot about them.*

He was too late. Almost.

"The worst thing is the smoke damage," said Annie.

Boyce could hear the tremor in her voice, and the sinking feeling in his gut worsened. They had been married for twenty-five years. She'd seen some rough times as the wife of a seagoing Navy pilot. But nothing like this.

"The fire was in the guest bedroom," she said. "The firemen put it out before it spread to the rest of the house."

Boyce could barely contain his frustration. The goddamn phone connection via satellite was one of those half-duplex systems that forced him to wait until she was finished before he could talk.

"You're okay," said Boyce. "That's all that matters. You and Julie." Julie was their twenty-two-year-old daughter. She was in her first year as an editorial assistant in a New York publishing house.

"The FBI showed up right after the fire," said Annie. "They're giving us full-time—"

Boyce tried to cut her off, but he couldn't.

"—protection now. Julie too. She still doesn't understand why anybody would do this."

"Never mind," said Boyce. "Don't talk about where you are or how you're being protected. Not on the phone, okay?"

A short silence. "Okay."

"I'm sorry this happened, honey. Just believe it wasn't because of anything we did wrong. It's part of the bigger problem going on over here."

"I know. I'm very proud of you, Roland."

He had to smile, despite his seething anger. His wife was the only human on the planet who was allowed to call him by his real name. She was also his biggest fan and supporter. She had stuck it out through all these years of separation and danger.

Too damn many years. Enough was enough.

"You don't deserve this, Annie. I'm going to retire and take a real job. I'll make it up to you, all the bad times."

Another pause, this one longer. "Bad idea, Roland."

"What do you mean? We don't have to live like this anymore."

"The Navy needs you now. You can't quit."

Boyce nearly choked. "Quit? I'm not quitting. I'm just . . ."

In the short space while he groped for the right words, she supplied them. "Copping out."

Goddamn it. Sometimes he thought Annie was the one who should be running the air wing. Iron Annie.

"It's called retirement," he said. "Everybody does it sooner or later."

"Remember what you always told your junior officers. Don't make important decisions when you're pissed-off or drunk. I think you're pissed-off, Roland."

Well, he had to admit, she had that part right. He was pissed-off. So royally fuming pissed-off he wanted to fly back to the States, find that peckerhead newspaper editor who almost got his family killed, and squeeze his windpipe until his head popped like a balloon.

"Listen, Annie. You and Julie stay out of sight. Do what the Feds tell you to do. I'll be home very soon."

"Don't worry about us."

Boyce sighed. She had just received an anonymous death threat, had her house torched while she was in it, her daughter's life endangered, and she was giving him advice. *Don't worry about us.*

"I love you, Annie."

"I love you too, Roland. Remember that you promised not to smoke cigars on the ship. You know how it sets a bad example."

"I promise," he said, and crossed his fingers.

CHAPTER 22

OVERWHELMING RESPONSE

8,500 Feet, Eastern Mediterranean
0905, Friday, 28 October

The flight in the COD, a Grumman C-2 Greyhound, took less than an hour. In his rearward-facing passenger seat, Maxwell had the old familiar feeling of helplessness. It was the feeling experienced by every fighter pilot when he was hauled aboard a carrier in the nearly windowless cabin of the COD.

Pearly Gates, seated across from him, wore the expression of a condemned man. He kept craning his neck, trying to see the ship through the tiny window in the side of the cabin.

Maxwell heard the whirring hydraulic noises of the COD's gear and flaps extending. He felt the airplane slowing, the moan of the turboprops changing thrust as the pilot flew the glide path. This guy was no smoothie with the throttles.

The whine of the engines abruptly changed. He felt the COD drop from under him. He saw Pearly's body go rigid. His eyes were squeezed shut.

Whump. The wheels slammed into the steel deck. An instant later came the lurching, jostling hard stop as the COD's tailhook snatched an arresting cable.

The COD was rumbling across the deck to its spot forward of the *Reagan*'s island. Pearly's eyes opened. "Home, sweet home," he said.

Maxwell unstrapped from the seat's harness. The clamshell door of the COD's cabin swung open. The whine and din of the flight deck swept into the cabin.

He saw a familiar figure silhouetted in the open doorway. He was wearing the standard Mickey Mouse flight deck helmet and earmuffs. Stenciled in large letters on his float coat was his title—CAG.

"About time you got here," said Red Boyce.

Maxwell followed Boyce down to the CAG's stateroom, which also served as Boyce's office. Pearly was excused to go to the Roadrunners' squadron ready room. Boyce kept a stony silence as he marched down the passageways, leather heels hammering on the steel deck.

Maxwell knew Boyce. He braced himself for one of CAG's eye-bulging, paint-peeling temper tantrums. He'd be lucky if that was all it came to. Getting himself kicked out of their host country by the second senior government minister was enough to get him a severe reprimand. Maybe censured by the Carrier Strike Group Commander. Maybe even relieved of his squadron command.

Boyce peeled off his float coat, then yanked off the headset with the noise suppressors. Still saying nothing, he turned and slammed the headset against the bulkhead.

Here it comes, thought Maxwell. He'd seen Boyce's tirades before, but not like this.

Then Boyce surprised him. "Too bad you didn't hose a couple more of those ragheads before the Israelis threw you out," he said.

And that was it. No more mention of what happened in Jerusalem. Something else was troubling Boyce.

"Take a look at this." Boyce held up the front page of the *International Herald Tribune*. It featured a black-and-white photograph of a bombed-out building. Men wearing face masks were dragging bodies from the rubble. The caption read: *Death Toll Rises in American Bombing of Palestinian Village.*

"A hundred twenty bodies," said Boyce. "And counting."

"I heard about it at the embassy," said Maxwell.

"They're making it sound like the My Lai massacre. Enough dead women and kids to galvanize the whole Arab world against us."

"Why hasn't somebody reported the truth?" he said. "That the place was a terrorist base."

"Nobody gives a rat's ass about the truth. All they know is American murderers bombed a Palestinian village full of innocent people. That puts me right up there with Saddam Hussein and Adolf Eichmann."

"Why didn't the intel specialists know about the civilians in the village?"

"There's no end to the things those idiots don't know. Why didn't they know before we invaded Iraq that there weren't any weapons of mass destruction? Why didn't they know terrorists were planning to attack the World Trade Center? Why didn't the dumb shits know a pharmaceutical plant in Sudan wasn't a nerve gas factory?"

Boyce's voice was rising as his anger mounted. Maxwell knew better than to offer a comment. Boyce needed to blow off steam.

That was one of the downsides of being the Air Wing Commander. Boyce didn't have contemporaries he could talk with. Sticks Stickney, his equal in rank, was not on the same frequency. Boyce's deputy dog, Capt. Piles Poindexter, was an okay guy, but he was a policy wonk. He had degrees in economics and international relations and could drone for hours about zero-sum power balances and bottom-line asset deployments and geopolitical paradigm shifts. True to his call sign, Piles was a pain in the ass.

That left Maxwell. Boyce used him as a sounding board.

"I've killed people before," Boyce went on. He paused to pull a fresh cigar from the humidor on his desk. "But never anyone that didn't richly deserve killing. Until now."

Maxwell just nodded. It occurred to him that he had never seen Boyce like this before. The CAG looked haggard, eyes red-rimmed, like a man who had gone too long without sleep. *Welcome to the club,* Maxwell thought.

Boyce chomped off one end of the Cohiba, spit it in the trash basket, then fired up the Zippo. He caught the expression on Maxwell's face.

"Hey, don't look at me like that. I'm not one of those sensitive types who wears his heart on his sleeve and gets all teary about the inhumanity of war. I've seen plenty of war. I know it's ugly. That's nothing new. People get killed who aren't supposed to get killed."

He paused to aim a stream of gray smoke at the overhead. "The only thing new is this time it was Red Boyce who did the killing."

A silence fell over the room. Boyce studied the end of his cigar. Maxwell looked again at the photo in the newspaper. Boyce was carrying a load of guilt about killing civilians.

But it wasn't just Palestinians who were getting killed, thought Maxwell. Still etched in his memory was Ramallah. Claire and sixteen others. They were innocent civilians too.

"How are the Arabs responding?" said Maxwell. "An eye for an eye?"

"More than an eye," said Boyce. "The Palestinians are blowing stuff up all over the West Bank and Gaza—or Palestine, if you still feel like dignifying that dump with a real name. Syria seems ready to invade the Golan Heights, which they've been itching to do for the last forty years anyway. Egypt just closed the Suez to American shipping.

OPEC has called an emergency meeting to impose an oil embargo. Yeah, things are getting nasty out here."

"The carrier strike group?"

"An op order is coming through as we speak. A contingency plan for coordinated strikes wherever American interests are threatened. Hightree is going to tell us about when—" He glanced at his watch. "Shit," he said, and jumped to his feet. "He's landing in ten minutes."

"Who's landing?"

"Who do you think? A war in the Middle East heating up, who do you think would come out here to share in the glory?"

Maxwell groaned. "Oh, hell. You don't mean—"

"You got it. The one and only."

Maxwell watched from the viewing deck behind the carrier's island superstructure, six stories above the flight deck.

The first of the C-2 Greyhound CODs was already in the groove. The C-2 settled onto the deck, snagging the number two wire. It taxied out of the landing deck area, to the open space forward of the island. The second C-2 swept over the ramp and plunked down, grabbing the number three wire. It taxied forward and joined the first on the forward deck. The first COD's big clamshell doors in the aft fuselage swung open. A swarm of media people—photographers, reporters with bags and recorders slung over their shoulders, crewmen with mobile cameras—spilled out. The flight deck officer herded them into a cluster beneath the forward island structure.

Several minutes passed while the press positioned themselves for the grand event.

On signal, the door of the second COD swung open. From the hatch emerged Ricardo Solares. He was wearing a cranial protector, and a flight suit emblazoned with half a dozen patches and a leather name tag with gold Navy wings.

He flashed a grin. While the cameras whirred, he hopped off the ramp to the flight deck and strode over to grip the outstretched hand of Admiral Hightree. Then he worked his way through the assembled officers, shaking hands with the *Reagan*'s skipper, Sticks Stickney, the Air Wing Commander, Red Boyce, the ship's XO, Capt. Fred Walsh.

Solares plunged into the pack of helmeted deck crewmen, gripping shoulders and high-fiving them. The crewmen responded with surprised grins and happy faces.

Maxwell had to give the guy credit. Solares was a natural. He knew how to work a crowd and how to use the media. His arrival on the *Reagan* would play on every television screen in America tonight.

Maxwell felt a dark shadow pass over him. Through his mind passed an image of smoke and bodies and burning vehicles. Ramallah. Claire.

He heard again the words of the Palestinian teenager. *You know. The famous one. The television man with the mustache.*

Maxwell watched the strutting figure on the flight deck for a moment longer; then he turned and went below.

The lights in the intel compartment dimmed.

Maxwell stared at the illuminated map. It was worse than he expected. The Middle East was going up in flames.

". . . three brigades of Syrian armor assembling here." Cmdr. Harvey Wentz, the flag intel officer, directed his red laser pointer to the territory just north of the Israeli-held Golan Heights. "Another two brigades are moving here, into southern Lebanon."

Maxwell heard a few *Holy shit*s and *Here we go again*s from the squadron COs. "That's the Israelis' problem," muttered a strike leader. "Let them worry about the Golan Heights."

Wentz flashed the mutterer a sharp look. "Listen up," said the intel officer. "You've only heard the beginning."

Maxwell was sitting next to Boyce in the second row.

In the first row of seats were Solares, Admiral Hightree, and their staff officers. Listening to Wentz tick off the latest calamities, Maxwell had the feeling that he was watching a train wreck in slow motion.

Wentz scrolled the illuminated map screen farther to the north, then aimed the pointer at the interior of Lebanon. "A well-armed group—first indications are that it's a unit of Hezbollah—has attacked and destroyed an American missionary hospital in the Bekaa Valley. At least twenty Americans are reported missing or killed.

"Simultaneous bomb attacks have been made on American agencies in Beirut, including a travel office, a contractor's facility at the commercial seaport, and a busload of mostly American tourists. They were stopped and machine-gunned. Apparently no survivors."

More muttering from the assembled officers.

"The insurgents in Iraq have stepped up their activities," said Wentz. "Four roadside bombs went off last night in the vicinity of U.S. convoys, at least a dozen GIs dead. We have reports that several hundred Iranian Shiite jihadists crossed into southern Iraq in the last twelve hours, presumably to join the resistance there."

The laser flicked back to Syria. "Syria is going public with its supply line of arms to the Iraqi insurgents. They're openly supporting all the terrorist and militia groups operating there, including Al-Qaeda, the Islamic Jihad, and Saddam's old Baathist organization."

Wentz continued his briefing. American shipping on either side of the Suez Canal was being denied passage by the Egyptians. U.S. embassies in Beirut, Damascus, and Amman were under siege by mobs and were being evacuated. An American-owned oil tanker had been attacked and set ablaze in the Gulf of Aden by an unmarked gunboat. A U.S. Air Force KC-135 in-flight tanker departing Al Jaber Air Base in Kuwait had been targeted by a surface-to-air missile. The big jet had lost an engine and part of a wing flap, but managed to land safely.

The litany went on until Wentz ran out of material. An uneasy silence fell over the briefing room.

"Jesus," said Boyce. "It's like the goddamn Tet Offensive."

Wentz put away his file folders. Adm. Jack Hightree unfolded his lanky frame from his seat in the first row and walked to the lectern. Behind him, the illuminated map of the Middle East still glowed on the bulkhead.

Hightree gazed around the room, looking at the familiar faces. Most were officers he had commanded during previous conflicts. Iraq, the Taiwan Strait, Iraq again, Iran.

"We will have our tasking order within the next few hours," said Hightree. "The President has made it clear that any attack on American interests in the Middle East will trigger an overwhelming response. The *Reagan*'s air wing will be assigned deep air strike missions at first light tomorrow."

Maxwell watched Hightree. The admiral's voice seemed to be lacking its old familiar placating tone. In the fluorescent light his face looked like that of a man being ordered to do something against his will. Maxwell wondered if Hightree was as troubled by the bombing of Tamun as Boyce had been.

"We will carry out our mission based on the best intelligence available." Hightree paused to glance at the flag intelligence officer. Wentz was busily stuffing files back into his briefcase. "It is imperative that we maintain faith in our leadership and in our intelligence capabilities."

He gazed around the room, waiting for a comment. None came.

"That will be all, gentlemen."

The officers all rose. Hightree made his exit, closely followed by Wentz. The door clanged shut behind them.

Boyce leaned to Maxwell. "Do you think he really believes that shit?"

CHAPTER 23

WALKING WOUNDED

USS Ronald Reagan, *Eastern Mediterranean*
1115, Saturday, 29 October

"Forget it," said Boyce. "You're grounded."

They were on the 0-3 level, on their way from the intel compartment to Boyce's office. Boyce looked like a great shambling bear in his khakis, battered leather G-1 flight jacket with half a dozen faded squadron patches, the fur collar worn to a thin fuzz.

Maxwell stayed right behind him.

"You heard the admiral, CAG. This is a war. If I'm going to lead my squadron, I've got to be on flight status."

"Lead from here on the ship," Boyce said over his shoulder. "You're not ready to fly."

"I'm fine."

"The hell you are. Anyway, you've been around long enough to know the drill. Anyone who suffers a family loss gets a mandatory grounding period while they get their heads straightened out."

"I didn't suffer a family loss." As soon as he said it, Maxwell knew how false it sounded. Losing Claire could not have been more painful if they had been married.

Boyce knew it too. He came to a stop and waited for a couple of sailors to go past in the narrow passageway.

"Look, Brick, I know what you're going through. I'd feel exactly the same way if I was in your shoes. We're warriors, and we don't like being left out of a battle. But it's my job to make the call, and I just made it. Suck it up and follow orders."

"What about Pearly? He didn't suffer a loss."

Boyce rolled his eyeballs. "He stays grounded too. As far as I'm concerned, both you guys are walking wounded."

Maxwell gave it a beat. He knew he was pushing it, but what the hell. "So when *do* we get back on flying status?"

Boyce's face darkened. "When hell freezes over, if you keep running your mouth. You guys are going to give it a few days, get your sea legs back; then I'll think about sticking you in a cockpit again. If this mess plays out the way I think it might, I'm gonna need every pilot I've got. Even basket cases like you and Gates. In the meantime, quit pestering me about it. You got that, Skipper Maxwell?"

Maxwell recognized the look in Boyce's eye. It meant he'd reached the limit of his patience. But at least he had an answer. He'd be flying again soon.

"Yes, sir, I've got it."

"Good morning, ladies and gentlemen," said Cmdr. Harvey Wentz in the video monitor.

It was five minutes before six in the morning. Wentz's visage had just appeared on the screen of every squadron ready room monitor on the ship.

"The *Reagan* is presently steaming northward," said Wentz, "midway between the island of Cyprus and the coast of Lebanon. This morning's strikes will be coordinated to provide simultaneous times on target not only for the *Reagan*'s air wing aircraft, but for USS *Roosevelt*, operating in the southern Med, and USS *Nimitz* in the Persian Gulf. Coordinates of our launch and recovery positions will be delivered by courier to each ready room at the end of this brief."

Here we go again, thought Maxwell. *Another deep air strike. With one minor difference. This time I'm not going.*

He was watching the briefing from his chair in the front row of the Roadrunners' ready room. Next to him sat Bullet Alexander, who was unable to conceal the look of satisfaction on his face. Instead of remaining on the ship as he usually did while Maxwell led a combat mission, Alexander was flying this one.

On the monitor, Wentz continued his briefing. "Since the outbreak of hostilities, Saudi Arabia, Kuwait, Oman, and Turkey have denied us the use of their bases to launch strikes. That means until the Air Force's strike aircraft can be redeployed to friendly bases, the initial burden of this conflict falls on the three aircraft carriers in the region.

"Simultaneous attacks in north Lebanon will be conducted by elements from *Reagan* and *Roosevelt*, while targets in Syria have been assigned to *Nimitz*. U.S. Air Force Strike Eagles and F-16s will be attacking Syrian targets from bases in Iraq. Air Force A-10s based in Iraq will be interdicting Syria's supply routes into the country and chasing down mobile missile launchers."

Maxwell glanced around him in the ready room. The pilots in Alexander's flight were all wearing the alert, sober expressions that airmen always wore when they approached combat. Gone was the flippancy, the smart-ass remarks, the easy laughter of the ready room.

Alexander would lead the BARCAP—barrier combat air patrol. The eight Super Hornets of his flight were tasked to maintain air superiority between the target area and the enemy threat zone. An easy mission—if nothing unexpected happened. In Maxwell's experience, something unexpected always happened. It was the first law of aerial warfare.

"Here are your entry and exit points," said Wentz. His image vanished from the monitor. In its place appeared a map of Lebanon and Syria. A long blue arrow along the northern border of Lebanon showed the ingress route, and another arrow, this one red, depicted the egress route across the southern border, overflying Israel.

Each pilot studied the arrows, scribbling notes and diagrams on his kneeboard pad.

Lebanon, thought Maxwell. He tried to remember the last time Navy jets flew a strike into Lebanon. It was before his time, around 1984 or 1985, a daylight bombing raid against Syrian positions in Lebanon. A-6s and A-7s from *Kennedy* and *Independence* attacked at dawn, into a rising sun—exactly the wrong thing to do. Worse, because of intercepted communications, Syrian gunners were poised and waiting for the incoming strike.

In the debacle that followed, two jets were lost, with minimal damage inflicted on the enemy. It became a textbook lesson on how *not* to run an air strike.

They'd learned a lot since then. One war in the Balkans, two in Iraq, nonstop operations against terrorists from Yemen to Afghanistan. In the process, pilots—and their weapons—had become a hundred times smarter.

But our intelligence is still fucked-up. Maxwell studied the flickering images on the monitor. You conducted a strike based on what you knew. It was what you didn't know that got you killed.

Wentz's face reappeared on the screen. "The *Reagan*'s strike package will be led by CAG Boyce," he said. "It consists of five elements—an element of HARM shooters composed of sections from all three Hornet squadrons, an LGB-dropping element from VFA-36, another LGB element from VFA-34, and an element provided by VFA-35.

"A fifth element will be two reconnaissance jets from VFA-32, who will launch last and make high-speed photo passes five minutes after the last bomb is on target.

"Tanking will be provided by a pair of Air Force KC-10s on stations Chicago and Boston. Those coordinates and altitudes will be included in the package delivered to your ready rooms.

"Syria has continued to update and relocate their surface-to-air capabilities. We know that *all* the target area as well as the ingress and egress routes are within range of multiple overlapping SAM sites. It means our EA-6B Prowlers have to be on station first to jam the enemy radars and air defense communications. It also means that the HARM shooters have to shut down the SAM network before the bombers get close."

Wentz paused and checked the index cards he was using for his briefing. "No enemy air opposition is expected. The Syrian fighter pilots are well aware of what happened to the Iraqi air force. They've also had plenty of bad experiences against the Israelis. If they do decide to join the battle, however, they will encounter Commander Alexander's Barrier CAP elements—one at station Bravo, and the other at Charlie. The BARCAP will be controlled by the E-2C from the *Reagan*. His call sign is Steeljaw."

Maxwell saw Alexander nodding his approval. Given a choice, Navy pilots preferred the control of the carrier-based Hawkeyes over the four-engine Air Force AWACS ships whose controllers answered directly to the three-star who commanded the U.S. Joint Task Force headquartered in Qatar.

Wentz then went over the finer details of the mission—mode one and two transponder squawks, avoidance of collateral damage to nearby buildings and villages, lost-communications procedures, bingo fuel requirements, bull's-eye navigation reference points, code words, weapon load-outs, search-and-rescue contingencies. SAR helos from the amphibious assault carrier *Saipan* would be holding off the Lebanon coast with their Marine AV-8 Harrier escorts.

Maxwell glanced again at Alexander. The XO was scribbling notes on his kneeboard. His brow was furrowed in an expression of intense concentration—and something else. Maxwell recognized the look. It was that heightened sense of awareness a fighter pilot felt before combat, a mixture of anxiety and anticipation, the buzz of pure adrenaline.

Maxwell envied him. He missed the feeling. It would be far better than this deadness that he had felt since Ramallah.

He glanced behind him at the rows of recliner chairs where flight-suited junior officers were watching the video screen just as intently. He met the gaze of Pearly Gates. By Pearly's melancholy expression, Maxwell could tell that he too was unhappy about staying behind.

As if sensing his thoughts, Alexander leaned toward him. "Staying behind really sucks, huh, Skipper?"

Maxwell had to grin. He knew what the XO meant. On previous missions it had been Alexander remaining on the ship while Maxwell led the squadron into action. That was standard air wing doctrine—skippers and XOs didn't fly the same mission. Just in case.

"Don't be so smug," said Maxwell. "I've got a feeling about this. There'll be more missions. Next time you're gonna sit on the bench watching the game instead of me."

Alexander nodded. "There's gonna be lots of glory to go around. More than any of us wants."

On the monitor screen, Wentz's face was replaced again by a map of Syria and Lebanon. The red laser pointer was aimed at a spot in Lebanon, just inside the border from Syria.

"Primary target," said Wentz. "Syrian armor headed for Beirut, or maybe feinting in that direction, then making a sweep to the south into Israel. Doesn't matter. We're going to stop them where they are.

"Battle-ax, led by CAG Boyce, will deliver a mix of GBU weapons, backed up by Slingshot, led by Commander Mannheim. Their secondary target is here"— Wentz's red pointer slid to a spot farther south, toward the northwest corner of Israel—"and here, where more armor and troop convoys have moved into Lebanon overnight from Syria. Intel indicates that they are staging for an attack on the Golan Heights.

"Your targets have been selected to minimize the possibility of collateral damage. With this in mind, do not—repeat, do not—release ordnance without being certain that your target has been positively identified."

Watching Wentz's delivery, Maxwell felt a flash of anger. *How about being certain there are no noncombatants in the positively identified target?* This whole damned war might not have been necessary if the spooks had gotten their facts right in the first place.

Wentz yielded the stage to the meteorologist, a chief petty officer, who showed a synoptic chart of the area. The chief spoke in a high monotone voice. The weather was boringly good everywhere in the Middle East. Puffy clouds over the launch point, a thin bank of low stratus above the coast of Lebanon, high cumulus over the target area. Ingress and egress routes were clear.

The meteorologist finished and left. Seconds later, the face of CAG Boyce filled the screen. He was in flight gear, wearing his battered leather jacket. Maxwell thought Boyce's face looked unusually serious.

"Ladies and gentlemen," said Boyce, "Carrier Air Wing Three is about to carry out the direct orders of the President of the United States. Enemies of our country have killed our citizens and destroyed American property. It is our mission today to respond to those attacks.

"I want you to know that I have the utmost confidence in each of you. We have the best training and the best equipment in the history of warfare. But that is not our great advantage over our enemy today. Our advantage is the certain knowledge that our cause is just and right. We are Americans. We will fight with honor and courage."

Boyce let several seconds pass while he gazed into the camera. "Okay, guys and gals. Let's go kick some ass."

Which provoked a round of applause and whistling in the Roadrunner ready room. Maxwell watched the image fade from the screen. It was an unusual speech for the CAG. Sentimental pep talks weren't Boyce's style. Did Boyce really believe that part about their cause being just and right? Maybe. Maybe not.

CHAPTER 24

BANDITS INBOUND

USS Ronald Reagan, *Eastern Mediterraneun*
0715, Sunday, 30 October

"Good luck, XO," said Hensley, the plane captain. Bullet Alexander watched her climb down from the rail of his cockpit and stow the boarding ladder.

Alexander checked the Koch fittings that fastened his torso harness to the jet's ejection seat. All secure. So were the G-suit attachment, the oxygen hose, the radio jacks, thigh and ankle retention straps. Snug and tight.

His jet was spotted abeam the island next to the other three in his flight. Across the deck, he could see the other plane captains—distinctive by their brown flight deck jerseys—and the yellow shirts—plane directors and handling officers—leaning at an angle against the tilting deck. The *Reagan* was heeling over in a turn, swinging into the wind for the launch.

As the deck slanted further to port, Alexander could look down into the fast-moving green water that was racing past the edge of the deck. Even though his jet was still firmly chained to the deck, his feet instinctively shoved harder on the brake pedals.

The howl of jet engines starting resonated across the deck. The amplified voice of the *Reagan*'s air boss, Commander Bones Needham, boomed down from the flight deck speakers, exhorting the plane directors to get the jets unchained and headed for the catapults.

From the forward deck Alexander heard a *ka-whoom*. He glanced over his shoulder. Dog Balls Harvey was test-firing his number two catapult. A shroud of steam spewed from the catapult track and drifted like wet fog back over the deck.

The *Reagan*'s bow was still swinging into the wind. First to be catapulted would be the bulbous-nosed EA-6B Prowlers, tasked with jamming the enemy's air defense radars and communications. Next went the HARM shooters—a package from all three Hornet squadrons aboard *Reagan*.

Most of the Syrian SAM sites had already been plotted. Some, without doubt, had been moved. New ones would have been erected, still not pinpointed because their radars had never emitted a signal. At the first indication of an acquisition radar, the HARMs would be on their way, the location of the emitting antenna already locked into memory.

At least, that was the way it was supposed to work. But Murphy's law had not been repealed.

Alexander started his engines, left, then right. On Hensley's signal, he actuated the speed brakes, flaps, and cycled all the flight controls, while she darted under and around the jet, checking everything from the outside.

She flashed a thumbs-up. All okay.

Beneath the Hornet's nose appeared the plane director, signaling for Alexander to hold the brakes while the tie-down chains were removed. Seconds later, the signal to taxi.

Alexander nudged the throttles forward, and the heavy fighter trundled across the steel deck toward the number two catapult. The JBD—jet-blast deflector—was raised while the engines of the F/A-18 on the catapult roared at full thrust. Seconds later the jet was hurtling down the track and off the bow.

The JBD lowered back onto the deck. The director was urging Alexander forward, giving him minuscule left and right signals, steering his nose wheel directly over the catapult shuttle. Then a crossed-arms stop signal, while the green-shirted catapult crewmen swarmed beneath the jet, connecting the nose gear to the catapult shuttle.

Out of the corner of his left eye Alexander saw a Hornet go sizzling past from one of the waist catapults. Then another, this one on his right, the number one bow cat.

Beneath the nose, Dog Balls Harvey was giving him the power-up signal. Alexander shoved the throttles forward. He scanned his cockpit, gave the controls a quick check. He snapped Dog Balls a sharp salute.

Two seconds later—*whoom.* The familiar acceleration, spine pressing into the hard seat, gray presence of the carrier blurring past him, off a precipice into the hazy sky.

Airborne. Gear up, flaps up, skimming the sea. Heading for the rendezvous point.

He knew that back on the *Reagan*, peering intently from the glassed Pri-Fly compartment in the island structure, was Maxwell.

Maxwell was a hell of a good skipper. Maybe too good, because when Alexander finally took command of the Roadrunners he would inevitably be compared to his predecessor. Maxwell had a reputation as a cool-handed fighter pilot and top-notch squadron skipper. Alexander was still an unknown quantity. He hadn't yet led a deep air strike, engaged enemy fighters, made the split-second decisions on which his own reputation would forever be staked.

Until today.

Please God, he thought, reciting in his head the fighter pilot's prayer: *Don't let me fuck up.*

29,000 Feet, Coast of Northern Israel

"Burner Two and Burner Six active!"

Steeljaw, the controller in the Hawkeye, was transmitting a warning. Her voice cracked. "East Denver, ten miles."

It was the call Boyce had been dreading. And expecting. Burner Two and Six were Russian-built SA-2 and SA-6 surface-to-air missile sites.

"Burner Six, South Dallas, twenty-five," called Steeljaw. "Burner Two and Six . . ."

Shit. Denver and Dallas were the targets and the reference points from which all hostile activity was identified by direction and range.

The SAM sites were coming online. Why? Where the hell were the HARM shooters?

Four seconds later, he knew.

"Blaster Four-one, Magnum!"

More calls, one after the other, came in rapid succession.

"Runner Three-one, Magnum!"

"Panther One-one, Magnum! Magnum!"

And about damn time, Boyce thought. The HARM shooters were launching the second round of antiradiation missiles at the Syrian SAM radars. The first round was part of the deception package. A wave of decoys had already penetrated Syrian airspace, causing a dozen SAM radars to light up.

Not enough, Boyce knew. But enough to invite a fusillade of missiles on their heads. Now that the real strike package—Boyce's sixteen GBU-carrying bombers—were inbound, the Syrians were motivated to try out the rest of their air defense radars.

And see them snuffed out almost as quickly.

Forty miles to the target. Except for the Burner Two and Six reports, there had been no opposition. No conventional AAA, no fighters. Which was odd. Boyce knew there was no chance the Syrians would be surprised by the U.S. attack. None at all. They had been rolling their own armor and heavy equipment into Lebanon for the past twenty-four hours, practically inviting an ass-kicking from the U.S. or Israel.

"Battle-ax, Steeljaw."

"Steeljaw, Battle-ax. Go."

"Battle-ax and company, signal Ground Hog. Repeat, Ground Hog."

"Battle-ax copies Ground Hog," Boyce acknowledged.

Well, here it is. "Ground Hog" was code. It meant they had clearance from the White House all the way down the chain of command. The strike was a go.

Twenty-five miles. In his situational awareness display, he could see the symbols of the other strike aircraft. They were fanned out, each flight in combat spread. And high above them, on stations to the north and south of the ingressing strike fighters, were Alexander's BARCAP fighters. For a fleeting moment Boyce wished he had assigned the strike lead to Alexander or one of the other squadron skippers and taken the CAP job himself. Let someone else do the killing today.

Knock it off, Boyce. Don't turn into a bleeding-heart wimp now. This might be your last hurrah.

Fifteen miles. He could see the target area. It was in a depression between two ridgelines. There was a complex of single story buildings that, according to intel, contained at least a brigade of Syrian troops and their armor.

According to intel. What if the intel was as wrong as it had been at Tamun? What if the buildings were filled with more noncombatants? If it was hostile, why weren't they defending it with AAA and SAMs? What if—

Then he saw it. Just below his nose, only a few hundred yards. A black, oily smudge. Then another, this one closer.

More puffs, still low, but dangerously close.

Beneath his oxygen mask, Boyce smiled in relief. The

Syrians—*bless the dumb bastards*—were firing antiair-- craft guns. Fifty-seven millimeter, it looked like. Maybe eighty-eight. Real, live, old-fashioned AAA.

Thank you, God. And thank you, Akhmed, Abu, or who- ever you are.

As he pitched up, jinking to avoid the AAA bursts, he flipped his master armament switch to ON. Air/Ground master mode set to Ground. In his FLIR display— forward-looking infrared—he could see the target com- plex. Twenty-two miles to the bomb release point.

Then another warning from the controller in the Hawk- eye.

"Battle-ax, Steeljaw. Pop up contact! Four bogeys, West Denver, forty miles, weeds."

Boyce felt a chill come over him. *Bogeys.* Unidentified fighters, low altitude, forty miles west of the target com- plex. Aimed directly at the strike package.

Bogeys were contacts not yet tagged as bandits, which would have meant they were hostile. But that was a for- mality. Anything coming from inside Syria had to be hos- tile. These guys were bandits, probably MiG-29s.

The Syrians were going to make a fight of it. Boyce shook his head. The craziness never ended.

Okay, we've got bandits inbound. Where are my shoot- ers?

They were on station, twenty miles ahead of Boyce's strike package.

Fulcrums, Alexander decided, even before the excited controller could call out the range and bearing of the in- coming bandits. He could see them in his situational dis- play, and he already had an electronic ID. Russian-built MiG-29 fighters, four of them, still slow but accelerating, probably just airborne. Thirty miles inside Syria.

"Runner One-one," called the controller, "bandits three-five-zero, fifty miles, climbing through ten thou- sand."

Okay, thought Alexander. That matched what he was seeing in his display. "Runner One-one, contact, single group, confirm Fulcrums."

"That's confirmed, Runner. Four Fulcrums, nose hot, climbing through angels fifteen."

The bandits, now identified as MiG-29s, had their noses aimed at Alexander's CAP station. The range was closing rapidly, and there was no question that these guys were hostile. Alexander wondered what they were carrying for armament. AA-10 Alamos and AA-11 Archers, probably. Alamo was the NATO code name for the radar-guided Russian-built missile, roughly similar to an American Sparrow. Archers were heat-seeking missiles, similar to the American Sidewinder—deadly in a close-range fight. The trick was to kill them before they got close enough to fire their missiles.

So far, these gomers weren't emitting a radar signal.

Alexander and his wingman, Lt. B.J. Johnson, were on the eastern leg of the CAP orbit, noses hot—still pointed in the direction of the incoming Fulcrums. His second element, Lt. Cmdr. Killer Keilin and Lt. Hunter Weldon, were on the opposite side, noses cold—pointed away—each two-ship element covering the other's tail.

Forty miles north, on the second CAP station, were Lt. Cmdr. Bat Masters with his two elements. Between the two CAPs, they had the bandits flanked. Unless the Syrians sent up *more* bandits.

For an instant, Alexander let himself think about the Syrian MiGs. According to the air intel estimates, the Syrian fighters were junk, badly maintained, badly vectored by their inept radar intercept controllers on the ground. The Syrian air force had been decimated during the eighties in combat with the Israelis. Their war-fighting capability—and their air force's morale—was destroyed.

So why were these guys coming up to fight? They were like Saracens charging a force of Crusaders, riding into a storm of arrows.

It wasn't too late, thought Alexander. The Syrians could still turn and get the hell out of Dodge.

Alexander glanced again at his display. They weren't turning. The range had shrunk to forty miles. In the display, the MiGs were grouped in a four-ship cluster—geese waiting to be shotgunned.

"Puma leader, contacts bearing one-nine-zero," blurted the Syrian radar intercept controller. "Multiple contacts, going eastbound."

"What kind of contacts?" demanded Capt. Hafiz Faysal, leader of Puma flight—a four-ship division of MiG-29s. "What type aircraft?"

A silence of several seconds. "Fast contacts, Puma leader. Enemy fighters."

"Of course they're enemy fighters, you shit-brained idiot. What distance? What altitude?"

"A hundred kilometers. High altitude." The controller's voice quavered like a guitar string. "More contacts at a hundred fifty kilometers. Low altitude."

Faysal felt the rage bubble up in him like lava. For a moment the heat of his anger overwhelmed his own abject fear. He wanted to reach through the ether and seize the controller's windpipe. By the man's voice, Faysal could tell that he was barely literate. An ignorant peasant, like most members of the Syrian air force.

Why, he wondered for the thousandth time, was Syria plagued by such incompetence? Not only was the air force equipped with obsolete fighters like these Russian hand-me-down MiGs, it was staffed with halfwits like this controller who couldn't distinguish an enemy fighter from a camel turd.

On Faysal's left, more or less in formation, was his wingman, a lieutenant with less than three hundred hours' flying time and whose only qualification for serving in the air force was that his father managed President Assad's stable of horses. The two pilots on his right, a captain and a lieutenant, were almost as hopeless. Each had only a few hundred hours' experience, none in combat. Their fathers were government ministers.

Captain Faysal's own credentials were scarcely more illustrious. During his five years in the Syrian Air Force, he had survived several skirmishes with Israeli fighters, mainly by using the mighty acceleration of the MiG-29's Tumansky engines to remove himself at supersonic speed from the combat zone. The tactic had served him well.

Now Faysal was possessed with a single burning ambition. He wanted to live long enough to attain senior rank so that he could remain on the ground during future battles. It was a matter of practicality. An officer of his immense talent was simply too valuable to be lost in aerial combat.

Now the unthinkable had occurred. A war. Not another dung-slinging feud with the Israelis, but a real war with the most dangerous enemy on earth. No one, not even the fanatics of the Islamic Jihad Party, could have any doubt about the outcome of such a war. The United States had demonstrated in Iraq—twice—what it could do to an Arab adversary.

Of the entire fighter wing based at Shayrat, only Captain Faysal's fighters had made it into the air. This phenomenon was due to the urging of Faysal's squadron commander, an ill-humored colonel, who, for emphasis, had shoved the muzzle of his Makarov semiautomatic pistol against Faysal's forehead.

"Faysal, you worthless specimen of fly shit, you will engage the enemy today or I will blow your brains out. Do you understand?"

Faysal nodded. "Yes, yes, Colonel, I do."

Possessed with this new understanding, Captain Faysal climbed into the cockpit of his MiG-29. Minutes later he and his three gloomy wingmen were roaring off to engage the enemy. Wherever they were.

"Battle-ax One in hot," called Boyce.

"Two."

"Three."

Down the line, the Super Hornets in Boyce's flight were rolling in on the target. The U-shaped complex of buildings had a long camouflage net drawn between them. Beneath the net, according to the intel briefing, were at least a hundred armored vehicles.

Boyce felt the satisfying *thunk* of the two bombs leaving the pylons beneath each wing.

He pulled the nose of the Super Hornet up and to the left. Several thousand feet below he saw puffs of antiaircraft fire, neither high nor close enough to pose a threat to the bombers. Just another zealous Syrian gunner making a statement.

Boyce peered back over his shoulder, trying to spot the impact of the first bombs. For a moment he felt himself filled with a sense of dread. These were the same weapons—GPS-guided iron bombs—that he had dropped on Tamun. Autonomous, mindless killers.

He saw the first two bombs hit. One end of the U-shaped complex erupted in a mushroom of smoke and flame. More bombs exploded, working methodically around the complex. The building vanished beneath the cloud of smoke.

Next came the cluster bombs, delivered by Spike Mannheim's Slingshot flight. The canisters would open and the whirling bomblets would shred everything—armor or flesh—inside the compound.

It was over in less than a minute. His bombers were all pulling off the target, egressing on their assigned tracks. A column of smoke was billowing into the sky over the target area.

Boyce called the controller in the Hawkeye. "Steeljaw, Battle-ax. Say the picture." *Where are the bandits?*

"BARCAP has the bandits engaged, Battle-ax. Battle-ax is green west."

Good, thought Boyce. Alexander's shooters were dealing with the MiGs. All egress routes to the west were clear.

"Battle-ax copies."

CHAPTER 25

MAD DOG IN A MEAT LOCKER

24,000 Feet, Western Syria
0810, Sunday, 30 October

"Puma lead, contacts range fifty-five kilometers," called out the radar intercept controller. Then he added, unnecessarily, "Multiple contacts."

Captain Faysal didn't bother to acknowledge. His disgust with the inept controller was now eclipsed by the fear that gripped him like a vise. He could sense the nearness of death. It was close, very close. Fifty-five kilometers, to be precise.

A thought flashed through Faysal's head. Before he died, he hoped that an enemy antiradiation missile would descend on the head of the bumbling air intercept controller. At least the incompetent dung gatherer would be greeting Allah in the company of the pilots whom he had just caused to die.

What Faysal needed now was hard information—altitude, bearing, aspect, type aircraft. He had only one tool for such a purpose—and it was the most dangerous. The MiG-29's own onboard radar.

He reached for the toggle that would activate the N-019 radar; then he pulled his hand back. A fresh wave of fear overcame him. The instant his radar emitted a signal, the Americans would know precisely who, what, where he was. They would pounce on him like terriers on a rat.

But didn't they already know? With the vastly superior equipment they possessed, they surely had been tracking him since he left the runway at Shayrat. He was blind, but they were not.

A plan was forming in Faysal's mind. It wasn't a good plan, but by now his brain was shriveled with fear. He would employ the most basic of fighter tactics, the kind that even his idiot wingmen might remember from their training. Perhaps Allah would grant them success. Just this one time.

His left hand trembled as he reached again for the toggle.

There. The green monochrome screen flickered to life. He waited for several sweeps of the antenna. Then he saw them—little yellow triangles in the display.

Two pairs, in some kind of orbit. What were they? The ancient Russian radar didn't have electronic identifying capability. He forced himself to think. The enemy fighters had come from somewhere offshore. An aircraft carrier.

F/A-18 Hornets.

The thought triggered another round of trembling. The fear oozed into his stomach, causing a sudden wave of nausea.

It took all the discipline he could summon to roll the MiG into a hard turn to the right. At the same time, his voice a raspy croak, he transmitted the order to his wingmen. "Puma three and four, radars on. Enemy contacts at twelve o'clock high. Hard turn forty-five degrees left. We will flank the enemy on either side."

He heard his wingmen acknowledge in quavering, barely discernible transmissions. Faysal recognized the peculiar inflection in their voices. It was the sound of men waiting to die.

*   *   *

"Runner One-one spiked at two o'clock," Alexander called.

His RWR—radar warning receiver—had just come to life. It meant that the MiG leader, or one of his wingmen, was targeting Alexander's flight. Alexander's display was showing the distinctive signature of an elderly Russian Phazotron N-019 air-to-air radar.

"Sea Lord copies, Runner One-one. You are weapons-free. Acknowledge weapons-free."

"Runner copies weapons-free." The weapons-free call was a formality, mostly for the tape recorders. By the rules of engagement, any contact who was foolish enough to paint you with his targeting radar became a legitimate target.

The Syrian MiGs had just made themselves fair game.

Range forty. What the hell were they thinking? Alexander wondered. The Syrians had to know by now what they were getting themselves into. They must be hoping to get close enough to engage the Super Hornets in a classic turning fight. Close enough to shoot an Alamo or an Archer. Maybe close enough for guns.

It wouldn't happen. Even though the Syrians had little chance against the Hornets in a four-versus-four dogfight, Alexander had no intention of letting them get that close. The days of high-G swirling and turning air combat were mostly over. This would be a BVR fight—beyond visual range.

Using his right thumb to mash the weapons selector switch on the stick grip, Alexander selected AIM-120. This was the AMRAAM and it was the great equalizer, a radar-guided missile that could be launched from over thirty-five miles away.

"Thirty miles."

"Roger, Runners committing. Runner One-three," Alexander called to Keilin, "turn hot and join me." He wanted Keilin and his wingman to come hard left and join his right flank. They would present a wall of fire-power to the oncoming MiGs.

Maybe the Syrians would get the picture and bug out.

In his display he saw the two symbols of Keilin's element moving toward him to join on the far right. And there were the symbols for the MiGs, still in a cluster. They weren't bugging out. They were still coming like—

Whoa, what's this? Not anymore.

"Runner One-one," called the controller, "Steeljaw shows the bandits maneuvering. Steeljaw shows a bracket."

"Runner One-one concurs." Alexander could see it in his own display—the MiG flight splitting, taking divergent headings. *Bracketing.* Trying to get on either flank of the Super Hornets, then close the pincers. Not very imaginative, but better than presenting a single fat target. Maybe the gomers were smartening up.

"Runner One-three flight, take the south group," Alexander called. "One-one has the north."

"Runner One-three, roger, south group," Pearly answered.

He hauled the nose of the Hornet hard to the left, held the heading for five seconds, then pulled back to the right. He had a good radar image of the two Syrian MiGs, still climbing, still accelerating. Alexander was using the Hornet's scan mode in order to avoid locking up the bandits and setting off their radar warning receivers. The MiGs were unaware that they were about to be toast.

Range twenty-five. Close enough. Alexander's display indicated that each of the bandits was correctly sorted and targeted by members of his flight.

Squinting into the hazy desert sky, Alexander still didn't have a visual on the bandits. He saw specks and shimmers and puffs of cloud. No Fulcrums.

"Runner One-three, Fox Three!" he heard Killer Keilin call.

"Runner One-four, Fox Three," called his wingman,

Hunter Weldon. Keilin and Weldon had just fired two AMRAAMs.

Alexander knew that the two had privately agreed how they would handle the shots. Standard doctrine called for the element leader to fire *both* missiles at a resolved enemy group. But MiG kills in modern warfare were almost the stuff of history. Keilin was sharing the bandits with his wingman.

Because of the geometry of the merging fighters, Keilin's element was now closer to their targets than Alexander was to his.

In his HUD, Alexander superimposed the target-acquisition box over the radar symbol of the closest Fulcrum. In range, within the missile's envelope. All parameters satisfied.

Alexander's finger wrapped around the trigger.

He hesitated another second. Fighter pilots called the AIM-120 a "mad dog in a meat locker." Once locked on, the missile's autonomous guidance system took it to the target like an unleashed animal. It needed no further inputs from the pilot.

"Runner One-one has the leader," Alexander called. He'd already decided to share his own kills with B.J. He'd worry about the criticism later. "One-two, take the trailer."

"One-two has the trailer," answered B.J. Johnson. Alexander could hear the excitement in her voice.

Alexander squeezed the trigger. "Runner One-one, Fox Three!"

As he released the transmit button, he saw a blur of movement off to his left. A missile left its rail on B.J. Johnson's Super Hornet. An instant later, he heard her voice. "Runner One-two, Fox Three!"

Two more AMRAAMs in the air. Four missiles moving at triple the speed of sound toward the Syrian MiGs.

"Runner One-three, Pit Bull." The first AMRAAMs had just gone active. The rest would follow in seconds.

*   *   *

Chirp. Chirp. Chirp.

Captain Faysal winced at each aural alert from the Sirena radar warning receiver. The steady chirping was making his skin crawl. He could almost feel the enemy radars probing and examining his airplane, selecting the exact spot at which they would aim their air-to-air missiles.

But he still had time. The slow chirping of the Sirena indicated that they were in search mode, not active targeting. The distance was closing rapidly, almost within range of the AA-10 missiles on his wings.

For a moment, Faysal's abject fear was supplanted by a vision of glory. What if he succeeded in shooting down one of the enemy fighters? Ah, the great honor that would come to him! His squadron commander, insensitive pig that he was, would finally understand that Capt. Hafiz Faysal was a true warrior. Faysal would be decorated in Damascus by the President himself.

The image swelled in Faysal's imagination to panoramic proportions. He could hear the blare of trumpets as he stood tall and erect in the presidential palace, waiting to receive the grateful nation's highest accolade. He would be instantly elevated to the rank of colonel, perhaps higher. A squadron command would be his. His future would be—

Chirrrrrrrrp. Chirrrrrrrrrrp. Chirrrrrrrrrrrrp.

The image vanished. Faysal's heart nearly leaped from his chest.

The *Sirena* was chirping like a deranged parrot. The American radar was no longer searching. It had gone to an active *targeting* mode.

Targeting whom?

All of us. All four of his MiG-29s were being locked up by the enemy fighters.

Faysal hunched down in his cockpit, frozen with fear. What to do? Break hard and run? Fire his own missiles?

They were not yet in range. Just a few more kilometers. Perhaps he should launch an Archer missile anyway. He could pray that the enemy pilots would be forced to evade the radar-guided missiles. It might startle them enough to—

The thought froze in Faysal's brain. A ripple of panic reverberated through his entire body. He stared disbelieving at the specter out the left side of his canopy.

A fireball.

Three seconds later, another fireball.

His second element was gone. Two MiG-29s and their pilots converted to molten metal and scraps of flesh.

Alexander saw the first fireball. Then the next. Two roiling orange blobs of flame and black smoke. They looked like Roman candles, arcing downward toward the desert.

"Runner One-three, splash one!" The exultant voice of Killer Keilin.

"Runner One-four, splash one!" called Hunter Weldon.

Two MiGs down. That left the north element.

Alexander had a visual on the two northern MiGs now. Through the HUD he saw twin fins jutting from the tail of each MiG. Tiny brown silhouettes slanting upward like sharks swimming to the surface.

The silhouette on the right exploded. An ugly black and orange mushroom against a tan desertscape. Then a secondary explosion.

"Runner One-one, one-two," he heard B.J. Johnson call. "I think we shot the same MiG."

Shit. Alexander saw it too. Both their missiles had targeted the wingman. B.J. Johnson's missile had arrived a second after his.

The leader was still alive.

"Roger that. Runner One-one has the leader. I'm padlocked." Meaning he was not going to take his eyes off the contact, and he expected his wingman to clear the sky around them.

In his HUD, Alexander slewed the target-acquisition

box over the remaining Syrian fighter. He wrapped his finger around the trigger and squeezed.

"Runner One-one, Fox Three." The AMRAAM streaked away from Alexander's jet.

Faysal was still staring at the black smudges where the two MiG-29s of his second element had been. Something, a reflection on the canopy glass, a subliminal cue, caused him to swing his head to the right. With a dreadful certainty, he knew what he would see.

Another fireball.

His wingman. Pieces of the flaming MiG-29 were whirling through space. The carnage was so close Faysal could see the flaming shape of Husni still in his cockpit. He imagined he could feel the heat of the explosion.

Faysal's brain shriveled to the size of a pebble. In a tiny flea speck of his brain, he heard a voice talking to him. *It's useless, Faysal. You can't outrun the missile. You are a dead man.*

Faysal tried to shut out the voice. He couldn't. *Another missile, Faysal. It is only a second away. You have only one chance to live.*

To hell with the war, thought Faysal. To hell with his homocidal squadron commander. To hell with this decrepit Russian fighter.

With both hands he grabbed the ejection handles between his legs.

Alexander couldn't believe what he was seeing.

He had a visual lock on the lead Fulcrum. Something—it *had* to be what he thought it was—had just separated from the top of the fighter.

In the next instant the AMRAAM struck the Syrian jet in its forward left quarter. The bat-shaped silhouette of the MiG-29 dissolved into a shimmering orange blob. Pieces of the shattered fighter whirled through the sky like flaming confetti.

"Runner One-one, splash one!" called Alexander.

The nose of his jet was still pointed toward where the Syrian MiGs had been. Now there was only a descending debris field. It was spreading downward like a dirty cloud.

And something else.

Alexander squinted against the harsh glare. Yes, definitely, he *had* seen something. It was several thousand feet below, fluttering like a streamer, blossoming into something round and beige-colored.

Captain Faysal hung in his harness, too numb to feel the chill of the thin air.

He was dead. Of that there could be no doubt. There was not the slightest chance that he had escaped the hellish fury of the American missiles.

Then he felt the straps of the harness biting into his crotch. His testicles ached. So did his nose, and he discovered that it was because his helmet was shoved forward over his face.

Gingerly, Faysal pushed the helmet back over his forehead, released the chinstrap, and hurled the helmet into space. Then he wriggled in the harness, adjusting the straps that were binding between his legs. The aching in his testicles subsided.

His hands were undamaged. So, apparently, were his eyes, now that he had gotten rid of the clumsy Russian helmet. But the Russians had gotten one thing right. The Zvezda K-36 ejection seat had functioned perfectly.

Beneath him he could see the brown, undulating landscape of Syria. Or was it Lebanon? What did it matter? He was alive and—

His heart nearly stopped.

Above him, not more than a few thousand meters— *fighters.* Two of them, and he could tell by the long-snouted profile that they were Hornets. Undoubtedly the same ones who had just killed his wingmen—and would have killed him. Now they were going to shoot him while he hung in his parachute.

For nearly a minute Faysal didn't breathe. He watched the Hornets pass over him, turn and fly westward. They paid him no attention.

As the brown patchwork of earth spread beneath his boots, Faysal's thoughts turned to the future. It occurred to him that it might be good—*very* good—if this were not Syria rising up to meet him. Anyplace would be better than Syria. When his ill-humored squadron commander learned that Capt. Hafiz Faysal, leader of Puma flight, had just lost all four of his MiG-29s, he would be transformed into a sputtering, incoherent maniac. Worse, when he learned that Faysal alone had survived the engagement, he would waste not a second before reuniting Faysal with his wingmen in heaven.

Faysal gazed around him. He thought he recognized the high ridge that separated eastern Lebanon from Syria. If so, it meant he was coming down inside Lebanon. He allowed a smile to spread over his face. Today was a glorious day.

Good decision, bubba.

Alexander peered over his shoulder, taking one last glance at the MiG pilot's parachute. The guy was either incredibly lucky or he possessed perfect timing. Alexander was glad that at least one of the Syrians had survived. Shooting down enemy fighters was one thing. Killing the pilots was another.

He checked his display again. The RWR was no longer showing the telltale signal of an enemy's acquisition radar.

"Runner flight," he called, "anyone spiked?"

"Runner One-two naked," called B.J. Johnson.

"One-three naked."

"One-four naked."

No one spiked. No one targeted with an enemy air-to-air radar. Four MiGs engaged, four splashed. It was turning into a very good day.

After another twenty minutes on station, the CAP flights were ordered back to the ship. Egressing over southern Lebanon was uneventful, but no cause for relaxing. Another visit to the tanker to take on fuel, then the long descent back to the visual landing pattern over the *Reagan.* Alexander stayed busy with the tanking, the frequency changes, authentication procedures, then the ritual of landing back aboard the carrier.

A long white wake trailed behind the *Reagan,* moving at twenty-two knots through the eastern Mediterranean. Alexander rolled his wings level in the groove, picking up the yellow blob of the ball at the left deck edge.

"Three-oh-seven, Rhino ball, four point six."

"Roger ball," answered the LSO.

Alexander recognized the voice of Pearly Gates. Pearly, he could tell, was not at all happy that he was waving jets aboard instead of flying one himself.

Alexander flew a steady pass, requiring no sugar talk from the LSO, down to a three wire. An okay pass, no comment. As good as it gets, and a fitting finale to a flawless combat mission.

Well, *almost* flawless, he thought, as he followed the director's signals to his parking spot forward of the island. Someone was sure to ask why he hadn't initially fired two missiles at the bandit group. And what would he say?

What the hell, he decided. *Tell 'em the truth.*

CHAPTER 26

THE NEXT PHASE

USS Ronald Reagan, *Eastern Mediterranean*
1050, Sunday, 30 October

Boyce unwrapped a fresh Cohiba. He took his time snipping the end, rolling it around in his mouth, applying an even flame with the Zippo. He blew a stream of smoke at the far bulkhead, then directed his attention back to Bullet Alexander.

"Tell me again why you didn't take both shots at the bandit group."

Alexander held Boyce's gaze. "Because I was the flight leader. I wanted my wingman to take the follow-up shot."

"Even though our shot doctrine specifically says the leader will take *both* shots at a resolved bandit group?"

While Boyce waited for Alexander to answer, he caught Maxwell watching them both from the far end of the small conference table. Maxwell seemed as interested in Alexander's answer as Boyce was.

Alexander took his time. His flight suit was still damp from sweat. The indentation from his oxygen mask was still on his face. "Let's say, I, ah, called an audible."

"And, quite coincidentally, so did Killer Keilin," said Boyce. "You guys both let your wingmen take shots right behind you. I must be missing something. Is that what they're teaching now at fighter weapons school?"

"Not exactly. But they do teach that fighter tactics is a dynamic environment. We're supposed to be flexible, right?"

Boyce knew that Alexander was bullshitting him, but the truth was, he didn't care. He didn't give a damn who took the shots. Alexander's flight engaged four MiGs and killed four MiGs. It didn't get any better.

It was Alexander he was wondering about.

Boyce said, "So now you get to paint two MiG symbols on your jet."

"Just one. B.J. Johnson gets the other one."

"I saw the HUD tapes. It was your missile that got there first."

"Begging your pardon, CAG, but B.J. hit the target that she was assigned. She gets the credit."

"Doesn't matter what she was assigned. The kill goes to the guy who scored first."

Alexander's face hardened, and he leaned forward. A fire seemed to ignite in his dark brown eyes. "With all due respect, sir, I was the flight leader. It's my call. B.J. killed the MiG. I won't have it any other way."

He said it forcefully enough to cause Boyce's eyes to narrow. They both knew that Alexander was pushing the limit. For half a minute, no one spoke. The tension in the room crackled like electricity.

Boyce abruptly turned away and busied himself with his cigar. He pretended to be ruminating over something, gazing moodily at the bulkhead.

He looked at Maxwell. "What the hell's going on with your squadron, Brick? Everyone wanting to share kills, like a pack of hyenas splitting up a carcass."

"Hyenas? Mmm, how about wolves? Has a nicer ring to it."

Boyce shot him a look, then turned again to Alexander. "All right, all right, goddamn it. Give the MiG to Johnson. Now I suppose you all expect to get DFCs out of this." The Distinguished Flying Cross ranked just below the Legion of Merit.

Alexander shrugged. "Not my call."

"Not mine either," said Boyce. "I'll let your skipper handle that."

Boyce yawned and made a show of looking at his watch. "In the meantime, I think we've all got work to do."

Alexander caught the cue and rose to his feet. He was on his way out the door when Boyce said, "Oh, one more thing, Bullet."

"Sir?"

"It's not every day a flight bags four MiGs. Well done. Tell your troops it was damn good shooting."

Alexander nodded. "Yes, sir. I'll pass it on."

The steel door closed behind Alexander.

Boyce looked at Maxwell. "Well?"

"You were pretty hard on him."

"For good reason."

"Because he let his wingman shoot the MiG?"

"No. Because I wanted to see what Bullet was made of. Until today, I wasn't sure. Then he sat here and looked me in the eye and told me his wingman was getting the kill. Said he wouldn't have it any other way. That's when I knew."

"Knew what?"

"That Bullet has balls. He's gonna make a good squadron skipper."

"I believe I told you that six months ago."

"So what? I'm the CAG. I gotta have proof."

Maxwell just shook his head. Boyce ignored him and puffed his cigar in silence, thinking again about the day's operation. The strike had been a huge success. Four MiGs downed, no American losses. The target—a Syrian armor depot and command headquarters—obliterated. All in all, a banner day for the USS *Ronald Reagan* and its Air Wing Commander.

But something still wasn't right. He ought to be experiencing a feeling of euphoria, but it was missing. Maybe he was losing his warrior's spirit. Or maybe he had just seen too much war in the Middle East.

Time to retire?

Maybe, but not yet. He couldn't quit in the middle of a war, and he had the feeling that this one had just begun. There would be more targets, more MiGs, more lives to lose.

"By the way," he said, "don't make any plans for tomorrow."

Maxwell's eyebrows went up. "Because . . . ?"

"Because you and I are flying over to the *Saipan*. The President's Special Envoy, the honorable Mr. Solares, has called a joint planning meeting. The senior military officers—Navy, Air Force, Marine, the Israelis, and some suits from Washington—will be flying out. Looks like Solares is taking control of this phase of the war."

Maxwell nodded. The USS *Saipan* was a *Tarawa*-class (LHA) assault ship. It had an 820-foot flight deck with nine helicopter landing spots and two aircraft elevators to the hangar deck. It also had a large conference compartment that strike group commanders favored for high level meetings.

"I can't go. I'm persona non grata with the Israelis, remember?"

"That's been fixed. Now that we're in a shooting war, the Israelis are willing to forgive minor transgressions like yours. I need a deputy at this meeting, and Piles Poindexter has to stay here to run the air wing. Since you're grounded anyway, you can come along and help me answer all the suits' dumb questions."

He watched Maxwell's face for a reaction. Maxwell just returned his gaze, showing no change of expression.

500 Feet, Eastern Mediterranean

Sitting upright, Maxwell dozed in his seat. It was a short flight, only fifteen minutes, from the deck of the *Reagan* to the *Saipan.* In the HH-60 Seahawk helicopter with him were Boyce, Wentz, and Capt. Guido Vitale, the flag operations officer. Ricardo Solares and his staff, with Admiral Hightree, had departed earlier aboard another Seahawk.

Maxwell snapped awake when the wheels of the helicopter thumped down on *Saipan*'s deck.

Maxwell followed Boyce and Vitale through the open hatch, ducking instinctively beneath the still-whirling rotor blades. They fell into step behind their Marine guide, who led them across the deck and into the island structure.

Maxwell and Boyce both wore khakis beneath their G-1 leather flight jackets. Vitale, always more formal, was wearing service dress white uniform. Maxwell was removing his cranial helmet and float coat when he spotted a familiar face. It belonged to a muscular young man with tiny, dark eyes. He was wearing the uniform of an Israeli air force captain.

"Lebev? Is that you?"

"Yes, sir," said Capt. Yuri Lebev. "General Asher thought I should be the one who came to greet you. To show there are no hard feelings."

"*General* Asher? Since when?"

"A week ago, when he took command of the fighter wing," said Lebev. "How is Lieutenant Gates?"

"Pearly's okay. He'll be flying again soon."

"That's good," said Lebev. A sly smile crept over his face. "You can tell him that I'm looking forward to our rematch."

Boyce's head swiveled when he heard this. He thrust his face within a foot of Lebev's. "Rematch, hell. Listen to me. Next time one of you peckerheads breaks the hard deck and loses one of my jets, I'm gonna kick your ass from here to Baghdad."

Lebev's face froze. He looked at Maxwell, who just grinned.

"Captain Lebev," said Maxwell, "meet Captain Boyce, our Air Wing Commander. He's heard all about you."

Lebev shook Boyce's hand, looking as if he'd just grabbed a snake. "I, uh, am pleased to meet you, sir."

"Look who's here," said Vern Lewis.

Hannah Shamir looked up and peered over Lewis's shoulder. The *Saipan*'s conference room was crowded. It took her a moment to sort through the swarm of new arrivals coming in the big double door.

Then she spotted him—taller than his companions, wearing one of those Navy leather jackets—coming into the main lobby. With him was an older man, heavier, also in a flight jacket. His boss, she presumed. And the young IAF fighter pilot—what was his name? Oh, yes, Lebev. The one involved in the shoot-down of the American jet.

Hannah detached herself from Lewis. She threaded her way through the cluster of officials. As she crossed the room she could sense the not-so-discreet glances. Even though she wasn't wearing the short leather skirt, her tailored blue skirt with the white, low-cut blouse still displayed her bosom and flowing hips. *Why not? Use all your assets.*

He saw her coming. A smile creased his face, making little crinkles around his eyes.

"I was hoping you'd be here," she said, offering her cheek to be kissed.

"Why?"

"Silly question. I wanted to see you again."

He seemed to be embarrassed. "Uh, Hannah Shamir, meet my Air Wing Commander, Capt. Red Boyce."

She took Boyce's hand. "I've heard about you, Captain. All good, of course."

Boyce gave her an appreciative look-over. "Now I know what it is that Brick likes about Israel. May I ask how the two of you happened to meet?"

"Hannah's with the Foreign Ministry," Maxwell said. "She worked on the deal to get Pearly back."

"I'm also a major in the air force reserve," she said. "I was trained as a helicopter pilot."

"I'm impressed," said Boyce. "You're much better-looking than any of our helicopter pilots."

She laughed, instinctively liking the older man. She had already checked his dossier. Boyce had a reputation as a hard-nosed, curmudgeonly commander. His subordinates seemed to hold him in high esteem.

She led them to a table where there was coffee and tea and pastries.

"This has got to be a first," said Boyce. "Israelis coming to a joint military planning session with the United States."

"And there are the two men responsible," said Hannah. She nodded toward the front of the compartment, where there was a raised dais and a row of chairs. On the dais were Ricardo Solares and Gen. Nathan Zemek, huddled in conversation.

She watched Maxwell's face. He was gazing at Solares and Zemek. His face seemed to harden, and his eyes narrowed. She could sense his mind whirring.

She wondered how much he knew. What would he do if he knew the truth?

"As you already know," Ricardo Solares said from the speaker's lectern on the dais, "attacks are occurring throughout the area against American and Israeli interests. We consider these to be terrorist-inspired actions. Both countries have resolved to act in concert against them."

Polite applause rippled from the audience.

Solares smiled and continued. "The war against terrorism has reached a new level of intensity. There will be no sanctuary for terrorists who murder Americans, Israelis, or any other freedom-loving people."

Another round of applause, this time less subdued.

Seated on the dais were a dozen high-ranking U.S. and Israeli officers, including Lieutenant General Penwell, the U.S. Air Force three-star who headed the joint task force in the Middle East, Rear Admiral Hightree, who commanded the Carrier Group that included USS *Reagan*, Vice Admiral Dinelli, who commanded the Fifth Fleet headquartered in Bahrain, and General Zemek, now officially installed as the Israeli Defense Minister.

Maxwell sat with Boyce and several other staff officers from the *Reagan* near the back of the room. He thought he heard a low groan coming from Boyce as Solares went on.

"—more strikes conducted by American and Israeli units against terrorist bases in Syria, Lebanon, and the Palestinian territories. Where necessary, mobile ground forces will be utilized to neutralize and occupy enemy bases. In the case of the Palestinian territories, our ultimate goal is to replace the current Palestinian Authority with an interim military government, which will then preside over an independent and democratized state of Palestine."

Solares paused, and this time there was no applause. A stunned silence fell over the crowd.

Boyce whispered, "Did he say what I thought he said?"

Maxwell nodded. "I think he said we're going to occupy the West Bank and Gaza."

"Who's 'we'?"

"I don't know."

And then Solares told them. "A historic agreement has been reached between the Israeli government and the United States. After Hamas and Fatah and all other insurgent groups have been neutralized in the Palestinian Territories, a U.S. peacekeeping force will enter with the purpose of implementing a new Palestinian government."

"Oh, no," Boyce groaned, this time not so quietly.

Solares finished his address, then yielded the lectern to General Zemek. Zemek gave his own version of the same scenario, speaking alternately in English and Hebrew. The senior U.S. officer in the Middle East, Lieutenant General Penwell, took the stage and explained in deliberately vague detail how coalition forces would operate jointly against the known terrorist threats.

The meeting concluded. There was no further applause. The audience seemed to be in shock. Most of the military officers were looking at each other with dubious expressions.

Boyce pulled a half-gnawed cigar from the pocket of his flight jacket. "It's gonna be Iraq all over again. Only worse."

Hannah Shamir was waiting at the big watertight door that led to the hangar deck. She tugged at Maxwell's arm, pulling him aside. "When are you coming back to Israel?"

"I don't know. Sounds like we're going to be busy."

"Brick, I know it's too soon to be saying this. You haven't come to terms with losing Claire. That will take time. I just want you to know, I'll be there when you're ready."

He nodded, giving her a smile.

She said, "You still want to know why it happened, don't you?"

"Not why. Who."

She nodded, then looked up at the dais. He followed her gaze. Solares and Zemek stood on the dais, still in deep conversation.

"Those two?" Maxwell stared at them. "Do you think either of them had something to do with it?"

She didn't answer. Her expression remained blank.

He looked at the dais again. No, he thought. Certainly not Zemek. What about Solares? Would a man in his position indulge in a conspiracy?

The words of the Palestinian teenager played like a mantra in his head. *You know him. The famous one. The television man with the mustache.*

He turned to Hannah. "How could I prove it?"

"I don't know. I'm only a bureaucrat in the Foreign Ministry."

She stood on her toes and gave him a quick kiss, causing several passing officers to stop and stare. Maxwell felt her press something—a folded envelope—into his hand.

"Don't open it until you're alone," she whispered.

She turned and strode away, blue silk skirt swaying hypnotically about her hips.

The blades of the HH-60 Seahawk helicopter bit into the damp air, sending a spiral of vapor from the tip of each blade. Through the cabin window, Maxwell watched the deck of the *Saipan* drop away beneath them.

Over Boyce's objections, Maxwell had exchanged rides with Lt. Sally Bowen, Admiral Hightree's aide. Now Maxwell sat across the cabin from Ricardo Solares. Hightree was on the opposite bench engrossed in a newspaper.

Solares was staring moodily out the cabin window. Maxwell could tell by his tense expression that he didn't like flying. Maxwell waited until the helo had leveled in cruise and the air smoothed. He unbuckled his straps and made his way across the cabin. He slipped into the empty bench seat next to Solares.

Solares glanced up, not recognizing him at first. He noticed the leather flight jacket. He squinted at the leather name tag.

"It's you again."

"Yes, sir. I'm the skipper of the pilot who was shot down and held in Gaza."

"The one who thought I wasn't doing enough to get your pilot back."

"I owe you an apology. You negotiated the deal that got him released."

"A lot has happened since then."

"The bombing in Ramallah, for one thing."

Solares nodded gravely. "A terrible tragedy."

"You were there."

Solares gave him a sharp look. "Yes, I was. What about it?"

"Who do you think was behind it?"

"I know who was behind it. Islamic terrorists. Who else?"

"That's what I'd like to know. Who else?"

Solares's eyes narrowed. "What are you driving at?"

"You were there when the bomb went off. How close were you to Claire Phillips when she was killed?"

"Close enough to have been nearly killed. Why do you want to know? Were you acquainted with the Phillips woman?"

"In a manner of speaking. We were engaged to be married."

Solares nodded. "You have my condolences. Now, if you'll excuse me, I have work to do." He made a show of fumbling with his leather attaché case, pulling a sheaf of papers from it, positioning his reading glasses over his nose.

Maxwell waited a moment.

"Was it Khaled Mohanor?"

"Who?"

"Your negotiating partner. Did he order the bombing that killed Claire and the others?"

"Look, Commander, you're way out of line here. I advise you to back off and keep your mouth shut while you still have a career."

Maxwell could tell by Solares's constricted face that he had stuck a nerve. *He knows.*

The discussion had come to an end. Solares was glowering as if he'd like to put a bullet through Maxwell's head.

Maxwell gave him a smile. He rose from the bench seat. "Thanks for your time, Mr. Solares."

Solares didn't reply.

CHAPTER 27

ADAGIO

Maxwell had never seen Hightree so furious.

"—an absolutely preposterous display of arrogant behavior," said the admiral. "To berate a senior government official—one who happens to be our guest at this moment aboard the *Reagan*—is the most unbecoming conduct I can possibly imagine from one of my subordinate officers."

The admiral's tirade went on for five minutes. Flecks of spittle dotted his lower lip as he paced the deck of the flag bridge. He paused long enough to wipe his lip with his handkerchief.

Boyce was observing the scene with a curious look on his face. He took advantage of the break.

"Ah, may I ask what Commander Maxwell said that so annoyed Mr. Solares?"

"It's not *what* he said so much as how he said it. A commander in the U.S. Navy does not have the privilege of asking impertinent questions of presidential envoys."

Boyce turned to Maxwell. "What impertinent question did you ask?"

"I asked him if he knew who was behind the bombing at Ramallah."

"And Mr. Solares said . . . ?"

"Terrorists. I asked whether Khaled Mohanor was involved. That's when he went ballistic."

Boyce shrugged. "Doesn't sound impertinent to me."

Hightree glowered at them both. "Mr. Solares is the highest-ranking American in the Middle East. He talks to the President every day. He doesn't expect to be cross-examined by a middle-ranking naval officer whose only job out here is to run a squadron."

"Okay," said Boyce. "I'll take care of it. Brick will get a letter in his file. No more impertinent questions or we send him to sea."

Hightree's face darkened. "Don't presume to make light of this, Captain Boyce. Mr. Solares was quite emphatic. He wants Maxwell transferred. Off the *Reagan*, out of theater, to another assignment."

"I apologize, Admiral. I didn't mean to make light of it, but let's wait a moment here. How does this guy—presidential envoy or whatever he is—get to dictate officers' assignments in the Navy?"

"He represents the Commander-in-Chief. He can dictate whatever he likes."

"With all due respect, sir, aren't *you* in command of this carrier group?"

"Yes, I am."

"Why don't you tell Solares to go fuck himself?"

Hightree stared at Boyce. They both knew the answer. The suggestion was so contrary to Hightree's nature that he was without a reply.

Finally he said, "I'm going to forget that you said that, Red. I know you don't mean it. We've been in the Navy long enough to know how the system works. We are all responsible to higher authority."

Boyce nodded and glanced at Maxwell. They both knew where Hightree was going with this. He had every intention of keeping his two stars. While he was at it, he wanted to add a third.

"Would you really relieve Maxwell over a thing like this?" said Boyce.

"I may."

"Then maybe you should relieve me too."

A look of surprise came over Hightree's face. He shook his head. "This is not a subject for negotiation. It's my decision, not yours. After I've thought it over, I'll let you know what I intend to do. In the meantime, I suggest you get on with your duties."

Boyce looked him the eye. "Aye, aye, sir. Will that be all?"

Hightree sighed. "I certainly hope so."

Boyce stopped in the passageway outside the flag bridge. He glanced around, making sure they were alone.

"Has it ever occurred to you, Maxwell, that sometimes it would be better if you kept your mouth shut?"

"Once or twice."

"Of all people to pick a fight with, why Solares?"

"A hunch. I think he knows what really happened at Ramallah."

"You've got yourself in a mess that I may not be able to get you out of."

"Do you think Hightree will really have me relieved of command?"

"If he thinks it's in his own best interest, yeah. In a heartbeat."

"Did you mean what you said, that he should relieve you too?"

"I don't know." Boyce removed his cap and rubbed his scalp. "All I know is that this isn't fun anymore. Maybe it's time we both looked for another job."

"Before we're both fired, how about putting me back on flight status?"

"We've already been over that. You're still—"

Maxwell pulled a folded sheaf of paper from his jacket pocket and handed it to Boyce.

"What's this?"

"My up chit. And Pearly's too. The flight surgeon gave us both a complete physical. He says we're good to go. Physically and mentally."

Boyce didn't bother looking at the papers. "When did Knuckles become a practicing psychiatrist?"

"Approximately the same time you did."

Boyce's right eyebrow arched. "You're pushing your luck, Skipper Maxwell."

"Yes, sir, sorry. I'm just suggesting that if I'm going to be relieved, this may be the last chance I have to fly with my guys."

Boyce nodded. Maxwell was right. Hell, it might be the last time either of them got to fly. Still, he had to go through the motions of thinking about it. He rubbed his head, scowled, turned to gaze in each direction down the passageway.

He gave it another beat, then said, "All right, goddamn it. If that's what it takes to shut you up, then go for it. Put yourself back on the schedule. Just don't decide you're going to take revenge on the whole Arab world."

"What about Pearly?"

"What about him?"

"Is he back on flight status too?"

"Maxwell, are you deliberately trying to piss me off?"

"No, sir. But I *am* the squadron skipper and—"

Boyce waved his hand. "Okay, okay, don't bother me with that crap. It's your call. I've got more important stuff to deal with."

He turned and marched on down the passageway toward his office.

The idea had been growing in Solares's mind like a germ since he arrived aboard the *Reagan*. He could see it in all its glory. It was brilliant.

"It's a grandstanding play, if you ask me," said Vernon Lewis.

Solares whirled on him. "I don't recall asking you."

They were in Solares's office, which was an extension of the stateroom he occupied one deck beneath the admiral's quarters. Lewis sat in his work cubicle in a corner of the compartment.

"I'm supposed to be your adviser," said Lewis. "My advice is forget it. You'll be the laughingstock of the late-night shows."

Solares's face reddened as he struggled to control his anger. Since the bombing in Ramallah, Lewis was becoming more and more quarrelsome.

"It doesn't matter what you think. This is a critical time in the war. We have to have public support for the strikes against the Arab insurgency and for the occupation. It will be a huge morale booster for Americans to see the President's envoy flying an actual combat mission from the *Reagan*. I've discussed it with Admiral Hightree, and he concurs."

Of course, that wasn't exactly what the admiral had said, but it was close enough. Hightree had given him some military gobbledygook about unnecessary exposure and the inherent danger of carrier operations and the unpredictability of air combat. Solares had countered by offering to put him on a direct line to the President.

Hightree had caved in, just as Solares knew he would. He had already pegged Hightree as an officer with a keen interest in preserving his own career. While Solares stood beside him on the flag bridge, Hightree ordered the Air Wing Commander to provide Solares a ride in one of the two-seat F/A-18F strike jets on a mission over Syria.

But Lewis was probably right about one thing. His enemies in Washington *would* rant and beat their chests about his using a $100 million fighter for a photo op. Let them. Didn't Bush get away with landing aboard a carrier after the invasion of Iraq? Despite all the criticism, he came off looking like a hero, climbing out of the jet in his flight gear, swaggering across the deck like Tom Cruise in *Top Gun.* Of course, Bush *had* been a fighter pilot once upon a time.

Well, Rick Solares could do the same thing, only better. This would be a *real* combat mission. Not that he would actually get shot at, God forbid. But real enough to show the world that the future leader of the United States was one hardball-playing tough—

"Rambo Rick rides again," he heard Lewis say in a low voice.

Solares looked over at his cubicle. "What did you say?"

"Nothing." Lewis rose and walked toward the exit. "Thinking out loud."

Solares let the comment pass. He had already decided that something would have to be done about Lewis. If a recent report from the Tel Aviv CIA section chief was to be believed, Lewis might even be a security risk. The CIA chief suspected that Lewis had leaked material—possibly damaging information about Solares—to the media. Maybe even to a foreign agent.

"Someone from this staff has to attend the meeting tomorrow with the Israeli Foreign Minister," said Solares.

Lewis had the door open, about to leave. "Foreign Minister? That's something you ought to attend in person."

"I have to stay here on the *Reagan* because of the strike operation tomorrow. I want you at the meeting."

For once Lewis didn't offer an argument. He shrugged. "Sure. I'll be happy to be off this boat."

Not as happy as I'll be, thought Solares.

He waited until Lewis was gone; then he went to the secure phone. He punched in the code sequence that would connect him with Khaled Mohanor.

Maxwell passed up dinner in the wardroom and instead picked up a slider—a Navy-issue hamburger—from the dirty shirt wardroom, the eatery reserved for pilots in flight suits and deck officers still in working jerseys.

He let himself into his stateroom and flicked on the overhead light. The steel bulkheads seemed closer, more confining than ever. How long had such a compartment been his home? He had to think. Of his nearly twenty years on active duty, eight had been spent on sea duty. If he stayed, he could expect to spend at least half of his remaining career aboard a ship.

That had been one of the divisive issues between him and Claire—the long times at sea, the separations, the nomadic life of the Navy man. She had balked at marrying him because of it. When she finally relented, it was too late.

Ramallah.

As it did every night, the scene replayed itself in his head like a recurring nightmare—roiling smoke, screams of the maimed and dying, the wail of sirens, the clatter of helicopter blades. In a single millisecond, their future snuffed out like a candle.

Maxwell flopped down in the desk chair. He kicked off his shoes. Without looking he picked a CD off the stack and inserted it in the player. He listened for a moment, then nodded as the somber strains of Albinoni's "Adagio" washed over him. The darkly beautiful baroque music suited his mood.

Listening to the music, he reflected on the day's events. Maybe Hightree was right. He *was* out of his league, badgering Solares like a crazed terrier barking at a bear. For no valid reason. Solares might be devious, ambitious, probably corrupt. He wouldn't be a conspirator in terrorism.

Then he remembered. The envelope. It was still in his shirt pocket, where he'd stuffed it after Hannah had pressed it into his hand. *Don't open it until you're alone.*

Well, he thought as he opened the envelope, this was about as alone as he had ever felt in his life.

The envelope contained a three-by-five photograph, creased in the middle. The image was blurred, and he had to hold it up to the light. It took him several seconds to recognize what he was seeing.

The breath left him in a rush. He felt a throbbing in his temples and the familiar ache of loss. The image in the photo blurred as his eyes misted over.

Claire.

He blinked away the tears and stared at the photo. She was wearing that serious, furrowed-brow expression she put on whenever she was on camera. The little tortoise-shell fake spectacles were in place.

She was standing on the set. He could see that it was Ramallah. The video equipment was arrayed around her. Visible in the background was the crowd of demonstrators in the plaza. A sea of black hair, gray and brown clothing, upraised fists, banners and flags.

And something else.

Maxwell pulled a magnifying glass from his desk drawer. He leaned over the photo and examined the image closer. He could see the backs of heads. They were directed toward the far end of the plaza where a speaker—it had to be Khaled Mohanor—held the crowd in thrall.

But not all the heads were turned toward the speaker.

At the edge of the crowd was a figure in black. Maxwell recognized her. It was Hanadi Nazzal, the about-to-be martyr. She had her eyes fixed on Claire Phillips.

Another face, thirty yards distant from both Claire and Hanadi. Maxwell recognized him. He was a familiar figure, a tall, dark-featured man with a mustache, wearing a bush jacket.

Rick Solares.

Solares was scanning the crowd. He appeared tense, as if he were about to bolt and run.

Maxwell felt his pulse quicken.

He knew he was seeing one of the last images of Claire Phillips before she died. In the next few seconds, the man watching the woman in black would whirl and distance himself from the horror that was about to be released.

Maxwell's eyes were clear now. The ache from deep inside was replaced by something else—the rising heat of anger. The murder of Claire and the other Americans wasn't just the act of a single terrorist. They were all conspirators—Palestinians, Israelis, even an American.

Maxwell tilted back in the desk chair and gazed at the empty bulkhead. The solemn strains of Albinoni swelled and filled the stateroom. The pieces of the puzzle were coming together.

It wasn't proof, of course, but his gut feeling was sending him an unmistakable message. What Saleh had told him in Jerusalem was the truth. What began as a vague suspicion was becoming a belief.

He needed proof. And what would he do then?

He didn't know yet. He only knew that somehow he would find a way to kill Ricardo Solares.

CHAPTER 28

COOL HAND LUKE

USS Ronald Reagan, *Eastern Mediterranean*
2130, Monday, 31 October

Boyce stared at his computer screen. The e-mail was still there, saved in his in-box where it had been for nearly two weeks.

From: Hwendell@Wendelltech.org
To: Rboyce.CAW3@USSRonaldReagan.Navy.mil
    Dear Red—(Why am I still calling you Red when most of your hair has fallen out and the rest is turning gray?)
    It was good to see you during my trip to the Middle East last month. As you know, the emirate air forces are among my prime customers and I have to give the sheiks some one-on-one time.
    A lot has changed since you and I were at the Naval Academy. I've never been sorry I got out after my first squadron tour. Smartest thing I ever did was decide not to work for anyone, including the Navy, and start my own company. Wendell Technologies is the third-largest supplier of American-built air-to-air and air-to-surface missile components. Our contracts with the Defense

Department extend into the next decade and total something over $6 billion.

Which brings me to the topic I raised with you back in Dubai. I still want you to come to work for me. Never mind that you think you're just a fighter pilot, not an engineer or a salesman. It doesn't matter. Of all the guys I've known in or out of the Navy, you are the world's champion arm-twisting, finger-poking, manipulating salesman. You are also a first-class bullshitter, which counts for a lot in the Pentagon.

But that's not why I need you. I know I could trust you implicitly to represent me and my company. You understand what our equipment does—you've fired enough of these missiles to know—and you have credibility with the Pentagon brass. You are probably the best leader of men I've ever known, and that's why I want you to head up our government affairs department (we don't call it lobbying anymore).

Oh, yeah, the compensation part. Well, with salary, bonuses, and stock options, you should make about four times what you presently earn as a Navy captain. Never mind what a rear admiral makes, because I've done some checking and you're not going to be one. Surprise, surprise. Too many fragile toes out there that you've stepped on. The Navy's loss, Wendell Technologies' gain.

This is the logical time to retire from one splendid career and start a new one. Annie will love it. She'll be the hottest new hostess in Washington.

I need an answer soon. Can't keep this job open forever. Let me hear.

Best regards,
Harv Wendell

Boyce sat back in his steel chair and massaged his balding head. A few weeks ago, leaving the Navy would have been an unthinkable act. He knew about jobs like the one Wendell was offering. In his own Pentagon tours he had seen those guys—retired captains and admirals and their counterparts from the other services. It was an old-boys' club. They wore button-down shirts and striped ties and talked about their goddamn golf game.

How the hell would a beat-up old fighter pilot like Red Boyce fit in there?

He didn't know, but he was going to find out. He returned to the keyboard, hit the REPLY button, and began typing.

From: Rboyce.CAW3@USSRonaldReagan.Navy.mil
To: Hwendell@Wendelltech.org
Harv—
After considerable thought, I have decided to accept your offer of employment. I will tender my request for retirement tomorrow. Don't know how long the process will take (I've never retired before), but expect that it should not be longer than about a month. My Deputy Commander, Carrier Air Wing Three, Captain Poindexter, is already on board and is ready to relieve me on short notice.
I appreciate your confidence in me. Annie and I look forward to joining you and Faye.
Your classmate and bud,
Red

Boyce read the note again. Then he opened his safe and withdrew his stash of liquor. He poured himself a vodka, splashed some tonic into it, then ignited the already gnawed cigar in his ashtray.

He studied the screen for several more minutes. "What the hell," he said, and pushed the SEND button.

* * *

Khaled Mohanor smiled and clicked the cover of his cell phone closed. He turned to the man seated across from him.

"It's done," he said. "The Palestinian Authority is finished."

The man nodded his approval. "How was it accomplished?" he asked.

"A bomb, delivered by a fighter plane."

"Israeli or American?"

Mohanor shrugged. "Does it matter?" At this, both men laughed.

Actually, thought Mohanor, it *did* matter, but not to Suleiman Kharazi, who was the current secret leader of Hamas. The leadership of Hamas, like that of Hezbollah and Islamic Jihad, was a revolving title, because Israeli assassins managed to kill each new leader within days of his appointment.

"So that leaves Hamas to lead Palestine," said Kharazi.

"And Hezbollah, and Fatah, and Islamic Jihad, and the Al-Aksa Brigade. All loyal fighters in the war for independence."

Kharazi shook his head. "Palestinians will have to decide who is most fit to lead them. They should understand that Hamas has done the most to resist the oppression of the Jews."

Mohanor didn't bother disputing this view. Let him believe that his ignorant gaggle of killers could actually run a government. As long as each of the fanatical organizations believed that they were Allah's appointees to lead Palestine, then none of them was likely to succeed. They would replace the war against Israel with a Palestinian civil war that would leave the country in ruins.

Mohanor had no intention of letting that happen. When the day of independence approached, he would unify all the warring parties into a single political faction. Those who refused to be unified would be eliminated.

It was very simple, actually.

USS Ronald Reagan, *Eastern Mediterranean*

Maxwell saw Boyce come in the back of the ready room.

"Well?" said Maxwell. "Am I fired?"

"Not yet," said Boyce. "Hightree has been too distracted with the war and the presence of Mr. Solares to get around to it. But don't get your hopes up. He has a memory like a bull elephant."

Boyce stood looking at the roster board with the names of the squadron pilots grease-penciled in. Maxwell's name was at the top of the list.

Boyce said, "Who's assigned to lead the strike package on the Golan border target tomorrow morning?"

"Me."

"Why am I not surprised? Okay, who's leading the second flight?"

Maxwell pulled the folded schedule from his flight suit breast pocket. "Flash Gordon."

"Perfect," said Boyce. "Gordon's a solid aviator with a couple hundred combat missions under his belt. Tell him he's gonna be flying the two-seater on the strike tomorrow."

Maxwell looked at him for a moment. "The two-seater? Why?"

"He's gonna have a VIP in the backseat."

Maxwell thought for a second. Only one of the squadron's Super Hornets was an F/A-18F model—a two-seater. *A VIP?* Then it came to him.

"Solares?" he said. "Rambo Rick wants another notch in his belt?"

Boyce nodded. "A mega–media event. Tell Flash that it's no big deal, just that the fate of the free world depends on his getting Solares back in one piece."

"Flash will be thrilled."

"The breaks of naval air." Boyce contemplated the end of a fresh cigar for a moment. "By the way, don't get any

cute ideas. My advice to you is to stay the hell out of Solares's sight. Maybe he'll forget about shipping you off to
Kodiak or wherever."

Maxwell did his best to maintain a neutral expression.
"Yes, sir."

The cameras purred.

Rick Solares strode across the steel deck, taking long,
deliberate steps, pausing to grin for the nearest video
camera. That would be a hell of a shot, he thought—the
long-snouted jet fighter behind him, the massive structure
of the *Reagan*'s island towering in the background, the
blue expanse of the Mediterranean in the distance. Cool
Hand Luke in his fighter jock outfit, flying into the teeth
of the enemy.

The trouble was, his heart was beating like a jackham-
mer. An ice-cold puddle of fear was swirling in his gut.
But, thank God, he still knew how to fake it. It was a trick
he had learned back in his rookie days of broadcast journalism. This was show business, and illusion counted for
more than reality. He learned how to take those long bold
strides without revealing the tremor in his knees. He developed the knack of mugging for the photographers.
Give them that cool, cocksure grin, never revealing the
terror that was gnawing like a beast at his guts.

The gnawing worsened as he approached the huge gray
killing machine—the F/A-18F Super Hornet. He was already regretting this stupid idea. It wasn't too late to tell
the pilot—what the hell was his name?—that he had
taken ill, that they should just discreetly find something
wrong with the airplane and cancel this whole—

"Hey, Rick," called out a reporter whose name Solares
couldn't remember, "aren't you worried about enemy
missiles over the target?"

"Not a bit," said Solares, his voice brimming with
feigned bravado. He pointed at the racks of ordnance
mounted beneath the wing of the jet. "Look at those.

We're going to teach the terrorists what happens when they kill Americans."

"Give 'em hell, Rick," yelled a sailor from the edge of the deck.

"That's exactly what I'm gonna do." It was a Harry Truman line that Solares didn't mind appropriating. He flashed a grin and a thumbs-up for all the media.

As he arrived at the parked jet, the brown-jerseyed plane captain—a *female*, he observed as he saw her face behind the eye protectors—snapped to attention and gave him a smart salute.

He returned the salute, holding it long enough for the press to capture the moment. *Perfect,* he thought. There was a cover shot for *People* or *Newsweek.* So perfect that for a moment he almost forgot the terror that was swelling inside him.

The plane captain helped him slide his boot onto the bottom rung of the cockpit boarding ladder. Solares swallowed hard, then hauled himself up the ladder, moving quickly before his trembling legs betrayed him. He settled into the backseat of the Hornet, observing that the pilot was already in front, wearing helmet and oxygen mask.

The plane captain attached the seat strap fittings to his torso harness, plugged in his radio and oxygen and G-suit connections, helped him attach his oxygen mask. She pulled something with a red flag attached from the top of the seat.

"Ejection seat pin," she said, showing it to him. "You're good to go, sir. Have a great flight."

Solares gave her a feeble grin. He watched her descend the ladder and disappear beneath the jet. *Shit.* This thing was progressing faster than he wanted. He could hear jet engines starting. Deck crewmen were swarming around the fighter. The swarm of media people was being ushered back to the shelter of the carrier's island.

He could hear raspy breathing over the intercom. He remembered from his briefing that the microphones in both seats, front and back, might be audible all the time. He was hearing his own breathing as well as the pilot up front. What the hell was his name? One of those stupid comic-strip call signs they gave each other in the Navy.

It came to him. Gordon. Flash Gordon.

Solares was still thinking about telling Gordon that he'd fallen ill when he felt the jet begin to trundle over the deck.

"Ah, I'm not sure I want to do this," Solares said on the intercom. "Maybe we ought to—"

"You'll be fine, Mr. Solares," came the pilot's voice. "Trust me; you'll be okay."

Solares frowned inside his oxygen mask. He didn't like what he was hearing. He wasn't at all sure he would be fine. In fact, he wasn't sure he even trusted this clown with the comic-book name. There was something wrong with this whole goddamned setup.

He felt the nose wheel pass over a hump, some kind of object on the deck; then the jet lurched to a stop. Out the side of the canopy he could see a man in a yellow jersey, his hand held up as if he were directing a symphony. Stenciled on his jersey was a label: DOG BALLS. Another idiotic name.

Solares felt the rumble of the Super Hornet's engines increase to a thunderous roar. The man on the deck—Solares knew now that he was the catapult officer—was waving his hand in the air.

"I've changed my mind," said Solares. "Stop this damned thing."

"Too late. You wanted a ride in a jet; you're gonna get one."

Solares felt a shock of recognition. *That voice.* He knew it.

"You're not Gordon," said Solares.

"No, sir, I'm not."

Solares's loud wail was cut short by the firing of the catapult.

CHAPTER 29

ATTITUDE ADJUSTMENT

27,000 Feet, Eastern Mediterranean
1330, Wednesday, 02 November

"You're going to lose your job over this," growled Solares in his oxygen-mask microphone.

"Really?" replied Maxwell. "Why?"

"You're not supposed to be the pilot on this jet."

"Lieutenant Commander Gordon came down with stomach cramps just before the launch. As his squadron commanding officer, I had to assign someone at the last minute. I was the best choice."

Which was not too far from the truth. At Maxwell's suggestion, Flash Gordon had discovered that he might possibly feel too ill to fly the mission. It would be prudent to have someone else take such an important assignment. Since Maxwell had attended the briefing and already had the data, he was the logical choice to take Gordon's slot. Lt. Cmdr. Bat Masters, who was the standby flight lead, was assigned to Maxwell's slot.

They were at twenty-seven thousand feet, just coming off the tanker, an Air Force KC-10 on station fifty miles off the coast of Lebanon. One after the other the Super Hornets in Maxwell's flight were leaving the tanker, joining him in a high left perch.

Solares had fallen silent in the backseat. By the rapid, raspy breathing in the intercom, Maxwell could tell that he was still agitated. Or furious. Or scared to death, which was even better.

Maxwell reached into the breast pocket of his flight suit and retrieved the envelope. He slipped out the photograph and laid it on the left cockpit console. The face of Claire Phillips smiled up at him.

He swallowed hard and blinked his eyes. He didn't need the magnifying glass to recognize the man in the blurry background behind Claire, observing the last few seconds of her life. The rapt, expectant look on Rick Solares's face was imprinted in Maxwell's consciousness like an indelible stamp.

The target was a Syrian artillery battery. It had moved in during the night along the border of the Golan Heights. The tactical planners were worried that the big guns would support an infantry thrust across the border. They would also threaten the Israeli settlements and military outposts along the slope of the Golan.

According to the intel briefers, no serious air defense batteries were active in the target area. Over the past three days U.S. and Israeli strike fighters had converted most of Syria's SAM and AA batteries to smoking ruins. The only threats along the border were small and hard-to-detect SA-7 and SA-16 man-portable missile systems. These were low-altitude weapons with little chance of hitting fighters armed with standoff weapons like Maxwell's flight was carrying today.

"Runner Zero-one," called the airborne controller from the E-2C Hawkeye, "Storm King clears you feet-dry."

"Runner Zero-one, cleared feet-dry," Maxwell acknowledged. Cleared in country. He and his strike package would cross the Lebanese coastline a few miles north of the Israeli border, then descend over the Golan to attack the targets just inside Syria.

"Runners, check switches, knockers up," Maxwell called.

Each pilot in the flight acknowledged. Weapon stations selected, master armament switches on.

"What's happening?" said Solares in the backseat.

"We're crossing the beach," answered Maxwell. "Heading into Indian country."

He heard the raspy breathing in the intercom quicken.

"Do the Syrians know we're here?" said Solares. "Are they shooting at us?"

Maxwell peered into the hazy eastern sky. A few puffs of cumulus, a high layer of stratus, nothing more. "Yeah. They're blazing away with everything they've got."

The breathing in the intercom escalated to a furious tempo.

"Don't hyperventilate," said Maxwell. "You'll pass out and miss the whole show."

Already on station was the BARCAP, a flight of Super Hornets from USS *Roosevelt*. Also in the area were two EA-6B Prowlers and the airborne FAC—forward air controller—in another F/A-18F two-seater. The FAC's job was to identify and update the position of the Syrian artillery emplacements for Maxwell's bombers.

Maxwell swung his flight to the north. Peering down at the high promontory of the Golan Heights, he saw the first feeble puffs of antiaircraft fire. Small-caliber, he observed. Probably a twenty-three millimeter towed-gun system. The gunners wouldn't use a radar-fire control system. They had learned the hard way that the first emission caused HARM missiles from on high to come down on them like lightning from a thundercloud.

Maxwell rolled into a shallow dive. The dark outlines of the Syrian emplacements were visible in his HUD.

"What are you doing?" demanded Solares from the backseat.

"Diving on the target," said Maxwell. "Pay attention. This is what you wanted to see."

Seconds later, a *thunk* rattled the jet's airframe. Both one-thousand-pound bombs were en route to their target.

Maxwell hauled the Super Hornet's nose up in a four-G pull. He rolled into a hard right bank so he could observe the bomb impact.

"*Ooohh, shit*," grunted Solares under the load of four Gs.

One after the other, the flight called clear of the target. Already Maxwell could see the eruptions on the ground. His two bombs had obliterated the westernmost gun emplacement, nestled in the slope of the hill. The eruptions continued eastward. Mushrooms of dirt marked each gun emplacement. Black smoke roiled into the sky.

As the last pair of GBU-32s tore into the emplacements, Spoon Withers's division of four Super Hornets appeared over the target, laying down their CBU-59 APAMs. At preselected altitudes, each of the bombs dispensed a swath of 117 BLU-77 bomblets—vicious weapons that sliced through trees, vehicles, armor, and human flesh like tiny cleavers.

Over his shoulder Maxwell could see the target area. For a stretch of a mile and half, the earth looked as if it had been hit by a meteor shower. Flames licked through the sparse scrub brush. A rain of dirt and vegetation and destroyed machinery was descending back to earth. A cloud of black smoke was drifting east toward Syria.

The airborne FAC reported that the target had been destroyed. No more ordnance was required. Even the small-caliber AA guns had fallen silent.

"Holy shit," muttered Solares. "How can anyone live through that?"

They can't, thought Maxwell. He knew he should feel satisfied. The strike package had missed none of its assigned targets. They'd taken no hits, lost no jets to enemy fire. It was a successful strike. The rest of the flight would be routine. They had only to join the tanker, top off with fuel, then recover aboard *Reagan*.

With that thought, he remembered the rest of the mission.

"Runners, loosen up and stay clear," Maxwell called to his flight. "I'll be maneuvering."

Maxwell watched the other Super Hornets spread out in a loose, wide formation.

"What are we doing?" asked Solares. His voice had nearly returned to normal. Even his breathing rate had slowed down.

Maxwell didn't answer. He yanked the nose of the Super Hornet up in an abrupt six-G pull.

"*Whuuuhhhhhh,*" came the strangled voice in the back. "What the—"

He didn't finish. The jet was inverted, the nose dropping back toward the earth.

"*Stop! Stop! Are you crazy?*"

Maxwell ignored him. Passing through the horizon, he snapped the wings back to level flight. Same altitude, same heading as before the violent maneuver.

Solares's breathing sounded like the gasps of a dying cow.

"Tell me about Ramallah, Mr. Solares."

"What are you talking about? Land this airplane immediately. That's an order."

"You know what I'm talking about. The bomb, remember? The one that killed Claire Phillips."

"I don't know what you mean. You have no right to—"

The six-G pull cut him off. It was even more abrupt than the first. The breath left Solares's lungs in a single long wheeze.

He kept the Gs on this time, pulling the Hornet's nose up to a nearly vertical attitude. The horizon disappeared below the jet's long snout. The hazy blue Middle East sky filled the windscreen.

"*Sto-op!* Goddamn it, stop!"

Maxwell didn't stop. He rolled inverted and pulled the nose of the Hornet back toward the horizon—then stopped.

With the Hornet still inverted, he shoved the nose back up. The sudden negative Gs threw him hard against the shoulder straps, causing blood to rush to his head.

He heard a *thunk* from the back cockpit. It was the sound of Solares's helmet slamming into the canopy.

Imagine that, thought Maxwell. Solares's straps must not have been tight enough.

He snapped the Hornet back to level flight. Back to one G.

He heard a new sound over the intercom. *"Rooooooo-aaaaarrrrk."* It was the sound of Solares's breakfast being ejected into his oxygen mask.

"Oooooorrrrrooaarck."

The sound changed in volume. Maxwell saw in the mirror that Solares had unfastened his mask. He was barfing over the front of his torso harness.

"Are you okay, Mr. Solares?"

"Nuh-nuh-nooooooo."

"Would you like to talk about Ramallah?"

"No! I want to— No, please, no more of—"

Too late. The Hornet was inverted again. Maxwell shoved the nose back toward the open sky.

Another *thunk* from the back. Solares's head again met the hard Plexiglas of the canopy.

"Okay! Okay! Stop. *Please* stop."

Maxwell rolled the Hornet level again.

"You knew about it, didn't you?"

"About Ramallah?" Solares's voice was weak, a gurgling whisper. "Yeah, I knew."

Maxwell felt the anger sweep over him like scalding water. He wanted to kill Solares. He wanted to eject him from the jet. Blow him out over the Mediterranean. But the Hornet's ejection seat system didn't work that way. One crewman couldn't eject the other without also punching himself out. *Pity.*

Claire's face smiled at him from the photo on the console. Oblivious to the horror that was about to take her life. In the background was the face of Solares. Watching. Waiting for an explosion.

"Who else?" said Maxwell.

Several seconds passed. No answer.

"Khaled Mohanor?" said Maxwell. "Did he know?"

More heavy breathing. No answer. Maxwell moved the Hornet's wings, rolling toward the inverted position.

"Yes, yes, goddamn it! Khaled knew."

"Why? Why did you do it?"

Solares had trouble answering. He was gagging and retching. His voice was a ratcheting croak. "Why do you think? It was the only way to get the United States engaged in Palestine."

Maxwell stared through the windshield at the sky ahead. In his gut he had known the truth. Until now he didn't want to believe it. They killed Claire because they needed an excuse to start a war.

Solares's breathing had slowed down. For the moment he had stopped puking. "Okay, hotshot, you heard what you wanted to hear. But it's your word against mine. You can do anything you want with this airplane, but you'll have to kill me before I go on record."

Beneath his mask, a smile spread over Maxwell's face. Killing Solares would be sweet. A pleasure, actually. But it wasn't necessary.

That didn't mean the fun had to end. He yanked the nose of the Hornet up and rolled inverted.

"Noooooooo!"

Maxwell ignored Solares's scream. He gave the stick a vicious shove forward. From the backseat came another satisfying *thunk*. Good, solid Plexiglas. Amazingly hard stuff.

"Runner Zero-one, this is Zero-two. We see you doing some pretty hard maneuvering. Are you having a problem?"

"No problem," answered Maxwell. "No problem at all."

*   *   *

"Runner Zero-one, Rhino ball, four-point-three."

"Roger ball," answered Pearly Gates from the LSO platform.

No more calls from the LSO. Except for a tiny lineup correction, Maxwell flew a steady pass. Not bad, he thought. Not bad for not having landed aboard a carrier for over two weeks.

The jet slammed onto the deck. Maxwell felt the reassuring bite of the straps on his shoulders as the tailhook snatched an arresting cable. The jet lurched to a stop.

From the backseat came a long, rasping moan.

It was the first sound he had heard from Solares since the violent maneuvering had stopped. His breathing had slowed to a dull wheeze. He sounded like a man with a terminal lung disease.

The cable dropped free of the tailhook. Maxwell followed the deck crewman's hand signals out of the landing area. He crossed the foul line and taxied toward the parking spot forward of the island.

He saw them clustered beneath the towering island structure. The flight deck officer was holding them back. There were half a dozen cameras on wheeled dollies, rolling booms and reflectors, and a horde of reporters. There were at least fifty of them. Each was wearing the obligatory cranial protector and float coat.

After Maxwell cut the engines and raised the canopy, the plane captain appeared on the boarding ladder. She was smiling as she peered inside at Solares. The smile froze on her face.

"Are . . . are you okay, sir?"

"No," said Solares.

The plane captain made a gagging sound. Holding her hand to her mouth, she helped Solares unstrap and climb down the ladder.

The flight deck officer released the pack of media reporters. They surged toward the parked fighter, shoving camera dollies, dragging coils of black cable.

Solares was already on the deck when he saw them coming. "Oh, shit. Tell them to go away."

"No way," said Maxwell. "These guys came all the way out here to interview you."

The first reporter arrived as Solares's feet reached the deck. He shoved a microphone at Solares.

"Congratulations, Rick. You've certainly given us—"

He saw the mess on Solares's torso harness and flight suit. Solares's oxygen mask was still dangling from his helmet. It appeared to be filled with regurgitated Spanish omelet.

The cameras rolled up. Solares tried to wave them away. They wouldn't leave. They were wheeling into position around him. Reporters crowded around him, shoving each other to be close to their subject.

"Please," said Solares. "Let's do this some other . . ."

He was overcome with another wave of nausea. He leaned against the fuselage of the Super Hornet and tried to throw up. The spasms racked his body.

The reporters loved it. One stuck his boom mike close enough to capture every fresh heaving noise. A photographer got a close-up with his Nikon of Solares's contorted face.

"Tell us about your combat mission, Mr. Solares," said a reporter.

Solares didn't tell him. He turned from the camera and made a long retching sound.

CHAPTER 30

FOR THE RECORD

USS Ronald Reagan, *Eastern Mediterranean*
1610, Wednesday, 02 October

"In front of the entire world," said Hightree, his voice
rising to a crescendo, "you humiliated the President's
Special Envoy."

Hightree's eyes were burning with a fury that Boyce
had never seen in twenty-some years of knowing the
man. They were alone on the flag bridge, just Hightree,
Boyce, and Maxwell. Hightree had sent his staff out of
the compartment.

Maxwell stood with his hands at his side, not bothering to offer a rebuttal. He was still in his flight suit. The
lines of his oxygen mask were still imprinted on his
face.

Hightree ranted on. "With the liberal, antiwar press
corps out here breathing down our necks, looking for any
excuse to undermine our mission, you—a senior air wing
officer—pull a stunt like this!"

Boyce knew better than to interrupt. He understood
Hightree. The way to handle him was to let him blow off
steam, get all the bullshit and thunder out before he gave
him the facts.

Hightree went on. "After your first display of bad

manners with Solares, I told you it could cost you your command. If I had had any idea that you would do a thing like this, I would have fired you on the spot. Now you've given me no choice. You will consider yourself relieved as skipper of your squadron."

Boyce cleared his throat, not so much to interrupt Hightree but to let him know that he was getting into a matter of protocol. Relieving a squadron commanding officer was the responsibility of the Air Wing Commander, not the admiral who commanded the carrier strike group.

Hightree ignored Boyce. He paced the deck of the compartment, stopping every few steps to glower again at Maxwell. Maxwell didn't seem intimidated. He wore a pleasant expression, keeping his eyes straight ahead.

On the deck below, flight operations had ceased. Tugs were hauling jets around the deck, spotting them for the next cycle.

Hightree stopped pacing. He glowered again at Maxwell. "Mr. Solares wants you court-martialed for deliberately endangering his life."

"Good," said Maxwell.

Hightree stared. "Did you say *'good?'* You *want* a court-martial?"

"Yes, sir. More than Mr. Solares does, I'm sure. I don't think he'll want our discussion in the cockpit revealed in public."

"Discussion?" said Hightree. "Did you badger him again about the Ramallah thing?"

"Yes, sir. This time he was more forthcoming about what he knew."

"Forthcoming? Why?"

"Because I whacked his head on the canopy."

Hightree looked like he was choking. "Commander Maxwell, I'm beginning to suspect that you are mentally ill. Do you think your word will hold up against that of the President's envoy?"

"Yes, sir. If there's a record of what he said."

Maxwell nodded to Boyce. Boyce pulled a cassette from the pocket of his leather flight jacket.

"This is the HUD tape from Brick's jet," said Boyce. "Brick yanked it when he climbed out of the jet. I've already heard it, and I think you should too, sir."

Hightree stared. "What the hell are you talking about?"

Boyce walked over to the tape machine on the bench with the flag staff's media equipment. He slid the cassette into the machine and pushed the PLAY button.

Hightree stood transfixed while the tape played.

The two voices—Maxwell's and Solares's—were clearly recognizable. When the sound of Solares's vomiting came over the speaker, Boyce had to turn to the window so Hightree wouldn't see him chuckling.

The tape played on. They heard Solares groan as Maxwell yanked the Super Hornet around.

"Okay," said Boyce. "Here comes the good part."

"You knew about it," said Maxwell on the audio. *"Didn't you?"*

"About Ramallah?" Solares's voice was a raspy croak. *"Yeah, I knew."*

"Who else?" Maxwell asked.

A silence of several seconds passed. Solares didn't answer.

Maxwell's voice again. *"Khaled Mohanor? Did he know?"*

Another pause. Boyce watched Hightree's face. The fury was gone, replaced by a look of disbelief.

"Yes, yes, goddamn it! Khaled knew."

"Why? Why did you do it?"

More retching noises on the tape, then, *"Why do you think? It was the only way to get the United States engaged in Palestine."*

For a while there was only the sound of Solares's labored breathing. Then his voice seemed to regain some of its old haughtiness.

"Okay, hotshot, you heard what you wanted to hear. But it's your word against mine. You can do anything you want with this airplane, but you'll have to kill me before I go on record."

Boyce pushed the STOP button.

"There it is. What he didn't know was that he *was* on record. The tape is time- and date-stamped, by the way."

Hightree didn't seem to be listening. He was staring at the tape machine.

Boyce extracted the tape and held it up. "I guess this proves that Brick was right."

Hightree shook his head. "It doesn't prove anything. Only that a very frightened man was coerced into saying something under duress."

"Maybe it won't hold up in court," said Boyce, "but it ought to change a few minds about Rick Solares. Maybe even the President's. Don't you agree that it should be forwarded up the chain of command, Admiral?"

Hightree blinked, looking startled. "Forwarded? Well, I suppose it could."

He walked over to the window and peered down at the activity on the flight deck. "But I warn you not to expect anything to come of it. It won't change anything."

Boyce and Maxwell exchanged glances. It was predictable. Hightree was being Hightree. The buck didn't stop with him, and he rarely missed an opportunity to pass it along.

"What about Commander Maxwell?" Boyce said.

"What about him?"

"Is he still relieved of command?"

Hightree avoided Boyce's eyes, keeping his gaze on the flight deck below. "Yes," said Hightree. "Nothing has happened to change my mind."

Tel Aviv

"Just like the old days," said Vernon Lewis.

Hannah Shamir smiled and raised her wineglass in a way that gave Lewis encouragement.

Okay, he thought, *maybe not just like the old days. Not yet anyway.* They had a long way to go. At least they were moving in the right direction.

They had an outside table at the Carlton bar with a splendid view of the sunset. On the water were silhouettes of the ubiquitous Israeli patrol boats. Everywhere were signs of heightened security—roving military patrols, body searches at the entrance to every public facility, helicopters thrumming overhead.

Since the escalation of the war, Tel Aviv had been untouched by terrorists. A suicide bomber had attacked the market in the Old City of Jerusalem, killing a dozen shoppers, half of whom were Arabs. Another bomber was intercepted in Haifa, killing himself and a security guard.

To no one's surprise, the Arab world was reserving most of its rage for the United States. The U.S. embassy on Hayarkon Street was cordoned off to thwart car bombers. Americans in the Middle East had been advised to conceal signs of their nationality. They should refrain from flashing greenbacks, Yankee baseball caps, Harley Davidson T-shirts.

"How long are you in Tel Aviv?" Hannah asked.

"For a while. Until I decide to leave." *Or until Solares fires me, which could be anytime.*

He hoped she would take it to mean that he was available. In the old days, which in the Middle East could mean as recently as last year, Lewis and Hannah Shamir had been an item. Not a holding-hands-in-public item, and not the kind that got them invited as a couple to embassy functions. It was the kind of discreet liaison that foreign service officers conducted for the purpose of exchanging information and, sometimes, for no other reason except getting laid.

It didn't last. He was realistic enough to know that she hadn't been infatuated with him, at least not physically. Sure, she liked his brain, maybe even his looks. But he knew what she really wanted from him: information.

For his part, he was crazy about her. Too much so, because when she'd gotten what she wanted and then broke it off, he was despondent for a month.

As far as he could tell, Hannah admitted one man at a time into her life. Before him, there had been Asher, the Israeli air force colonel who was now a general. There was a succession of diplomats, including a Russian ambassador. Most of her lovers were married, which Lewis guessed was her way of never becoming committed.

Now it was the American, Maxwell. Lewis doubted that they were sleeping together. The word was that Maxwell had been involved with Claire Phillips, the woman killed in the Ramallah bombing. He'd supposedly been carrying a torch for her for a long time. Of course, that had always been Hannah's taste in men—the ones who were off-limits.

In the meantime, there was Vernon Lewis.

Just as he expected, the conference at the Foreign Ministry was a waste of time. It had been all Lewis could do to stay awake while old Joffe, the Israeli Foreign Minister, rattled on about occupational responsibility and joint custodianship of occupied territory. And then the American ambassador, Kaminsky, who was probably relieved that Lewis had shown up in Solares's place, did his own share of pontificating about the magnificent Israeli–American bond of friendship.

Which was all bullshit, Lewis reflected. Both men knew they were only figureheads. The real players— General Zemek, the new Defense Minister, and the U.S. Special Envoy, Ricardo Solares, whose title might as well be "Deputy President"—had skipped the meeting.

The only good result from the conference was running into Hannah Shamir.

"I almost forgot," said Hannah. "Thank you for the photo."

Lewis nodded. The photo from Ramallah of Claire Phillips—and the face in the background. It was a chance shot, snapped by one of the secret service agents, who gave it to Lewis without realizing what it contained. On a hunch, Lewis decided not to include it in the files of evidence accumulated from the Ramallah bombing. Something told him it would vanish.

So he passed it to Hannah Shamir, hoping that it might somehow be used against the perpetrator of the Ramallah tragedy.

Solares.

As the image of that grinning face flitted through Lewis's mind, he felt the anger return. *That preening, posturing, treasonous sonofabitch.* Solares and his Arab cohort, Mohanor. Lewis had no doubt that they were the ones who set this bloodbath in motion.

With the connivance of Zemek.

Even that by itself wouldn't have aroused Lewis's antipathy. Vernon Lewis was a pragmatist. As a career bureaucrat, all he had to do was put in his time. The bureaucracy would outlast the politicians and appointees like Rick Solares. There was no need for him to get caught up in every passion of the hour. All he had to do was wait.

But that was before Ramallah. Something snapped inside Lewis when the bomb killed Claire Phillips—and nearly killed *him.* It was the end of pragmatism.

Solares had to be stopped.

Lewis wanted to ask Hannah what she had done with the photo. Handed it over to Mossad? Channeled it back to the CIA? Maybe she gave a copy to her current boyfriend, the Navy commander.

He knew better than to ask. She wouldn't tell him, and

anyway, that wasn't how the game was played. When you passed information, you didn't ask how it would be used.

The bottle of wine—one of those bland sauvignon blancs from the Mt. Carmel vineyards—was nearly empty. Lewis was about to suggest that they open the next one in his suite on the Carlton's sixth floor when he saw her eyes. She was staring at the television over the lounge bar.

"Is that who I think it is?"

His eyes went to the blurry image on the television. He saw a figure in some kind of costume, wearing a helmet. Standing beside a jet fighter.

Lewis mounted his spectacles on his nose. The image swam into focus.

"Hey, that's my man Solares. Returning from his heroic combat mission."

"What's he doing?" said Hannah.

Lewis squinted at the screen for another moment. Then he cracked up.

"I believe it's called hurling."

The journalists were having fun at Solares's expense. Relentlessly the camera zoomed in on Solares. He kept trying to wave it away. Over the audio was the whine of engines, the rustle of wind over the microphone, and the distinct sound of a man barfing his guts out.

"The poor man," said Hannah. "He's not well."

Lewis glanced to see if she was serious. She wasn't. Hannah was doing her best to suppress a giggle.

Lewis wondered who on the *Reagan* was responsible for making Special Envoy Solares toss his cookies. Good job, whoever it was. Too bad that the guy was probably on his way to a new assignment in Antarctica.

The news program flashed to a new location. The announcer was speaking in Hebrew. He was describing a scene on the Jordan River where Israeli troops were engaged with a force of Arab insurgents.

Lewis turned back to the table. He had seen enough of

this stupid, unnecessary war. The sun had descended beneath the horizon, leaving a shimmering gold crescent on the sea.

He looked at Hannah. The rays of the faded sun were giving her hair a soft, diaphanous halo. Lewis felt his heartbeat pick up.

"How about a walk? One circuit of the beach; then we can have dinner ordered up to my suite."

It was a long shot, but what the hell. Get the preliminaries over with, lay your cards on the table.

She shook her head and smiled. "Thanks for the invitation. Not tonight, Vern."

"Guess that means you have a better offer." He said it with a grin, letting her know he was okay with it. She might still change her mind.

"Just a long day and a lot of work left." She patted the leather attaché case beside her chair. "Another time."

He nodded. *Another time.* He could always hope.

He stood and watched her gather up the attaché case. "I'll walk you to your car."

"No need. My driver is waiting."

Before he could argue, she leaned over and gave him a kiss, holding it just long enough to send his hopes soaring again. Abruptly she turned and left. He watched her cross the lounge, swishing the short skirt in that distinctive stroll of hers.

Lewis sighed and turned to gaze again at the sea. The shimmering crescent was gone. There was only a purple band of horizon. The scent of Hannah Shamir hovered over the table.

He was close, he told himself. Life was getting better. All he had to do was wait.

It was too early to go home. With that thought, he signaled the waiter. He needed a drink, a real drink, not another lightweight Israeli wine. He'd have a Stoli martini. If that went down well, he might even have another. It would clear his head of the unpleasant images—Ramallah, the smoke-filled square littered with the dead and dying, the upturned, knowing visage of Ricardo Solares.

Ricardo Solares looked terrible.

The man's pallor was a ghastly shade of yellow. The dark Latin eyes were red-rimmed and glassy.

They were alone in Hightree's stateroom. Solares had gone to clean himself up and get out of the puke-splotched flight gear. He returned wearing a velour warm-up suit and running shoes. His knees still wobbled, and a sheen of perspiration glistened from his forehead.

"I apologize again for the rough flight you had," said Hightree in his most conciliatory voice. "It was not part of the—"

"Never mind the apologies. I expect that pilot—"

"Maxwell. Commander Maxwell."

"Yes, him. I expect that by now he has orders to the most desolate duty station in the U.S. military establishment."

Hightree kept his expression blank, concealing his annoyance. He was as furious at Maxwell as Solares was, but, damn it, this was still *his* carrier group. Political appointees didn't tell admirals how to deal with officers in their command.

"It's being taken care of," said Hightree.

"Good. As you know, a rotten apple like Maxwell can cause us all to look bad."

Especially if he causes you to puke in front of eighty million television viewers, thought Hightree. He struggled to maintain his blank expression.

Hightree's eyes were drawn to his desk. In the second drawer of the starboard shelf lay the cassette tape from Maxwell's HUD recorder. For the past hour Hightree had agonized about what to do with it. No one knew that the tape existed except him, Maxwell, and Boyce.

Did Solares know? Did he suspect that his admission of complicity in the Ramallah bombing had been recorded on tape? Hightree wondered if he shouldn't simply hand the tape over to Solares. Let him do with it as he wished.

No. The best course of action was to simply make the tape disappear. It was in the best interest of everyone. Such a damning recording would only derail the carefully crafted operation now under way in the Middle East. Revealing the tape would be a disservice to the Commander in Chief and, by extension, to all in the chain of command beneath him.

Something still wasn't right. Solares *had* conspired to kill Americans in order to start a war. At least, he implied as much in the confession that Maxwell had gotten out of him.

Hightree wished the tape had never come into his possession. *Damn you, Maxwell.*

Solares still looked shaky. He lowered himself into a chair and dabbed at his brow with a handkerchief. He gazed for a moment at the bulkhead, on which was spread a map of the eastern Mediterranean and the Middle East.

"I was wondering, Admiral. Did Maxwell, ah, offer any explanation about why he behaved as he did?"

"No, only that some of the maneuvering he did during the mission had made you ill."

"Did he, umm, mention anything that we may have discussed in the cockpit?"

Here it comes. Hightree could feel Solares's dark eyes on him. *He wants to know how much I know.*

"No, sir. Why do you ask?"

The dark eyes remained on him. Solares seemed to be assessing Hightree's veracity. *That goddamn tape,* thought Hightree. How did he let himself get caught in such a trap? The very fact that a Presidential appointee's incriminating statement had been captured on an F/A-18 HUD tape—without his knowledge—was enough to put Hightree's own career in jeopardy. And if he forwarded the tape up the chain of command, it would cause a whole new set of even more serious problems.

All because of Maxwell.

Jack Hightree's ascent in the Navy's pyramidal rank structure had been the result of careful, noncontroversial decision making. As a junior officer he had learned the fine distinction between fawning obsequiousness and respectful obeisance. You didn't contradict your boss; you didn't disagree with policy. Senior officers learned that they could rely on him to handle every thankless task. *Give it to Hightree,* was the watchword where he was assigned. *He'll take care of it.*

And so he did. Hightree's diligence had taken him all the way to the rank of rear admiral, upper half. By the same proven method he intended to add the third star of a vice admiral.

"It occurs to me," said Solares, "that this fellow Maxwell might continue to be a problem."

"A problem? What sort of problem?"

"Oh, you know. We've all seen it before. A disgruntled officer or employee will make an outrageous claim after he's been dismissed. He might come out with some accusatory statement about the Navy or his superiors. Or, who knows, even about me."

Hightree again felt the dark eyes on him. Still probing. Trying to learn whether Maxwell had revealed anything.

Hightree kept his face impassive. "I don't think Commander Maxwell would do that."

Solares slowly rose to his feet. "You'd better be correct, Admiral. We both have too much at stake to let it be jeopardized by some cowboy fighter pilot."

For a long moment, Hightree and Solares held eye contact. Hightree understood Solares's meaning. If Maxwell took Solares down, Hightree was going down with him.

Hightree's eyes again went to the second drawer of his desk. The tape was a ticking bomb. It had the potential to destroy them all.

"I'll take care of it," said Hightree.

CHAPTER 31

A SENSE OF HONOR

USS Ronald Reagan, *Eastern Mediterranean*
2140, Wednesday, 02 October

"Are you out there, Deb?"

No reply came from the blackened sky. The stars twinkled back at him.

Maxwell held the rail of the catwalk, leaning into the twenty-knot wind that burbled over the bow and spilled down the catwalk. Flight operations had ceased. From sixty feet below came the hiss of the carrier's hull slicing through the sea.

This was his favorite place on the ship. The forward port catwalk was a recessed walkway just beneath the edge of the flight deck. It was where he came to be alone with the sea and the sky and the stars. It was a good place to think.

"What should I do, Deb?"

His words were caught in the wind and flung into space. He peered into the moonless sky. A shooting star arced across the void, tracing a white pencil line of light. He could imagine that Debbie was out there listening to him.

How long had it been? Six years? No, going on seven since the morning at the cape when his astronaut wife waved to him from the gantry of the space shuttle *Atlantis*. It was supposed to be a dress rehearsal. A mock countdown for the real launch in four days.

When they carried her out forty-five minutes later, she was dead. Debbie and another astronaut had perished in the fire that flashed through the crew's oxygen system.

For Maxwell, the glamour of space flight was finished. He'd already flown one mission and was in training for his second. He resigned from NASA and returned to active Navy duty.

It was a tough transition. During his years as a test pilot and astronaut, he had skipped the normal progress a naval aviator makes through the billets of a seagoing squadron. He checked into VFA-36 as the new operations officer, the number three job in the unit. Within a few months both the CO and XO were dead. Brick Maxwell received the prize every naval aviator coveted—command of his own squadron.

Now they were taking it away from him.

It seemed to be the pattern of his life. If he loved something too much, he lost it. He loved Debbie, and when he lost her, he lost his desire to be an astronaut. He loved Claire Phillips. She was taken from him in an instant of horror at Ramallah.

And yes, he had to admit, he loved his squadron. He had led the Roadrunners in peace and in combat, grieved over their losses, taken pride in their victories. For a fighter pilot, it didn't get any better.

Sometime after eighteen months, every squadron skipper was rotated. Maxwell had been scheduled to be relieved by his XO, Bullet Alexander, in a few weeks. He could have expected a Pentagon job, or war college, or perhaps an assignment to the Naval Air Warfare and Strike Center. Within a year or so, he would be screened for the ultimate flying job—command of a carrier air wing, the job held by CAG Boyce.

Well, he could kiss that job good-bye. Getting peremptorily relieved of your squadron was the kiss of death. His career was finished. They'd give him a nonflying job in some backwater air station where he might be allowed to finish his twenty years and retire.

Or he could just quit. Go be a civilian.

And do what? Be a new-hire airline copilot? Not an attractive prospect. Go to work for some defense contractor with his obsolescent degree in aeroengineering? Even less attractive.

The truth was, he had few marketable assets. There was little demand for guys whose only skill was killing people with precision weapons from a strike fighter.

Maxwell gazed for a while longer at the sky. The stars looked like pinpoints on a black canopy.

Okay, he thought, *you forced Ricardo Solares to admit his role in the Ramallah bombing. And it cost you your job. Was it worth it?*

After a moment the answer came to him. No, probably not. He knew how the system worked. Solares would get away with it. Maxwell's career had been trashed for nothing.

And then he corrected himself. Actually, something good had come of it. He had scared the living hell out of Ricardo Solares. He'd made him puke in front of eighty million people.

With that thought, he laughed. As if in response, a shooting star arced across the sky.

"Is this important, Red?" Admiral Hightree glanced at his watch. "I've got a conference call in five minutes with Fifth Fleet and the Joint Task Force Commander."

"I just need a minute." Boyce glanced around the flag bridge compartment, noting the presence of Senior Chief Pearson, the flag yeoman. "In private, please."

Hightree hesitated, then nodded to the senior chief, who picked up a stack of file folders and exited the compartment.

When the steel door clanged shut, Boyce pulled out the stub of a cigar and stuck it in his teeth. He gazed around the red-lighted compartment. Through the thick glass panes he could gaze down on the deck, where tugs were respotting strike fighters for the early morning launch.

"What is it, Red? I hope it's not about—"

"Yes, sir. Do you really intend to have Maxwell relieved?"

"It's already in process. His orders will be coming in a day or two, and another set of orders will be cut for the new squadron commanding officer."

"You understand, Admiral, that you're undercutting the Air Wing Commander's authority in this matter."

"We've already been over that. You had your chance to fire Maxwell. Now I'm doing it."

Boyce clamped his teeth down on the cigar and turned back to the window for a moment. He was on the verge of telling a two-star admiral that he was a pompous, pinheaded dipshit. It would be an honest statement, he reflected, but the timing was bad.

He turned back to Hightree. "What about the tape, Jack?" He'd known Hightree for a long time, since they were both junior officers in the same air wing aboard the *Enterprise*. He addressed Hightree by his first name when they were alone.

"What about it?"

"Did you forward it?"

Hightree was giving him that icy look that Boyce had come to recognize. He guessed that it was something they taught senior officers when they gave them their first star.

"The matter of the tape is no longer open to discussion."

"Since it's not open to discussion, can I assume it's been passed up the chain of command?"

Hightree's eyes blazed. "All you have a right to assume is that it's being handled in the best way."

"Okay, just tell me this. Is Special Envoy Solares going

to get his nuts kicked up between his eyeballs for his complicity in the Ramallah murders?"

"I can't answer that. Whatever happens, I'm sure that neither you or I will ever hear about it."

Hightree took a deep breath, and his voice mellowed. "Look, Red, we've both served in the military long enough to know how these things play out. Whatever happens with this matter, it's best if you and I are totally removed from it."

Boyce nodded. He had the picture. Hightree was covering his ass, which was exactly what he had done for the past twenty-five years. But Boyce had also seen another side of Hightree. If you pushed him into a corner, he could dig inside himself and call upon his inner steel. There was a time when Jack Hightree could make a tough call.

Hightree had changed.

"What I'm hearing, Jack, is that you caved in to Solares. You've always been a politician, but you were never a toady. Not until now."

Hightree looked like he had been slapped. "Captain Boyce, I'm going to give you one chance to save your career. You can retract what you just said and then leave this compartment immediately. Otherwise I'll have you relieved for insubordination."

Boyce nodded. He had expected that it might come to this. There was a line between disagreement and disrespect. He had just crossed it. He had crossed it on purpose.

"Never mind, Admiral, I'll save you the trouble."

He pulled an envelope from the pocket of his leather flight jacket. He tossed in onto Hightree's desk.

"What's that?"

"My letter requesting immediate retirement. You can ship me out on the same COD with Maxwell."

Hightree looked at the envelope as if it were about to

explode. "You can't quit. We're in the middle of a combat operation."

"Then you'll have to fire me."

Hightree picked up the envelope and held it out to Boyce. His voice sounded conciliatory. "We've both been under a lot of stress, Red. Take some time to think it over. Let's not do anything we'll be sorry about tomorrow."

Boyce ignored Hightree's outstretched hand.

"I don't need any time. The only thing I'm sorry about is that my old friend Jack Hightree has lost his sense of honor."

Hightree's face hardened. He held Boyce's gaze for several seconds; then he turned back to his desk. "That will be all, Captain Boyce. You're dismissed."

Boyce gave it another beat, then turned on his heel. "Yes, sir."

Another explosion. This one was close enough to rattle the shuttered windows of Khaled's bedroom. He saw pieces of plaster fall from the cracked ceiling.

It occurred to Khaled that having sex with a terrified woman wasn't particularly pleasurable. This one's name was Leila, and she came from Jenin. She had been an assistant pharmacist in Ramallah before quitting to join the Free Palestine Militia.

The girl sat upright in the bed, trembling. "What was that?"

"The same as before. Another bomb."

His relaxed tone didn't seem to calm her. "They're bombing the compound," she said.

"No. They're hitting the warehouses in Hebron. Probably trying to blow up the weapons stockpiles."

The girl wasn't convinced. She trembled again as another explosion, this one farther away, caused more plaster to fall. She sat with the sheet gathered about her waist, brown-skinned arms clasped about her breasts.

Women were as essential to Khaled's well-being as

food and sleep. But not the same woman, nor even women from the same background. The young Palestinian women he bedded came mostly from the educated class, daughters of merchants or physicians or ambitious politicians. They regarded cohabitation with the Great Leader as a logical route to respectability and influence in the new Palestine.

The trouble was, they bored him. Palestinian women— even the bright ones with degrees and professional credentials—were too deferential and submissive. Intimate conversation with them amounted to prattle about family or fashions or mindless television programs.

For pure, unfettered sexual diversion, he preferred European women. German, Scandinavian, French, it didn't matter. They knew how to distinguish sex from politics and social problems. Best of all, they had no illusions about becoming the future Palestinian first lady.

Someday, he reflected, he would take a wife. When he became the Great Leader of a free Palestine, it would be necessary. A new country needed a first lady, but not just another woman from one of the refugee camps. She would have to be special.

Of course, he once *did* have a wife, a stocky woman named Fatimah, whom he had married because her father was a powerful Beirut gold trader. Ultimately, Fatimah became a burden to him, and it was necessary to remove her. This became possible during a border clash between the Hezbollah and Israeli forces. An errant artillery shell flattened the house where Khaled had sent Fatimah to find shelter. Even though secret evidence revealed that the shell had come from a Hezbollah gun, it suited Khaled's purpose to blame the Israelis. He could declare his beloved lost spouse, Fatimah, a martyr.

Since then he had been in no hurry to replace her. His role as Great Leader—and grieving widower—provided him with a ceaseless supply of willing bedmates. Some were more difficult than others to get rid of. The medical student, Hanadi Nazzal, was one whose attachment to him became particularly burdensome until he found the perfect solution. He had persuaded her to accept a martyr's death to prove her eternal devotion to the Great Leader.

And so she had, taking with her the American TV reporter, Phillips. Which, Khaled reflected, was a great pity. Given different circumstances, he would have enjoyed adding the Phillips woman to his list of conquests. He still fantasized about the reddish-brown hair, the gray-green eyes that seemed to penetrate his thoughts.

From outside came the staccato rattle of antiaircraft fire, then a string of explosions. Five-hundred-pound bombs, he guessed. Precision-guided, undoubtedly. American, but maybe Israeli.

"Shouldn't we be in a shelter?" said the girl.

"We're safe here."

"Why?"

"Because I said so."

The girl looked at him, not comprehending. She was frightened, but her somber brown eyes showed that she was willing to trust the Great Leader.

He couldn't explain, of course, that the compound here in Hebron was off-limits to the bombers. As recently as last night, Solares had assured him that the American F/A-18s and the Israeli F-16s would respect the sanctity of his headquarters.

It was a complex game they were playing. From this very headquarters, Khaled was directing his militia against enemy forces in East Jerusalem and the Golan. It was necessary that the Palestinians see him as their courageous commander against the invading enemy. At the same time he had to cooperate with the Americans and Israelis in order to remain in their favor. When peace came and Palestine was free, Khaled Mohanor would still be the Great Leader.

The end would justify the means.

He knew that at any time the enemy could obliterate him and his headquarters. It would be easy with precision weapons delivered from the air. The fact that his headquarters had not been touched was sufficient evidence that the pact between him and Solares was holding.

No, he was not worried about an aerial attack. More likely was an assault from the ground, and that was why he had ringed the compound with a two-hundred-meter-wide band of razor wire and embedded mines. A network of machine-gun nests guarded the compound, and a garrison of loyal militia stood ready to defend the headquarters.

Against whom? Not the Americans or Israelis. He was concerned about a betrayal from inside Palestine. Any of the warring factions—Fatah, Islamic Jihad, Hezbollah—could turn on him like feral animals. He expected it, and he was ready for them.

The explosions had stopped. Khaled rose and went to a window. He cracked open a shutter and saw a column of black smoke rising from the eastern perimeter of Hebron. The warplanes had found a target, destroyed it, and left.

"Is it over?" said the girl.

Khaled turned to look at her. Now that the bombing was finished, she no longer seemed terrified. She was kneeling, facing him. The shaft of light from the cracked shutter fell across her bared shoulders and breasts.

"Yes, it's over," he said, and returned to the bed.

With four martinis buzzing inside him, Vernon Lewis shambled down the steps of the Carlton. He tried to remember where the hell he'd left his car.

After half a minute of befuddlement, it came to him. He hadn't driven his goddamn car. His automobile was still in the underground garage of the American embassy compound, where he'd left it last week before flying out to the *Reagan* with Solares.

Yeah, he needed a walk all right. Clear his head and give him an appetite for dinner, which, unfortunately, he'd be having alone in one of the beachfront restaurants. Maybe the Regatta, which had good seafood and a view of the sea.

He angled inland, distancing himself from the lights and commotion of the beachfront. Despite the battles along the borders and the danger of an expanded war, young Israelis were determined to have fun. Lewis had a grudging admiration for them. This was a country that had learned to live with the threat of extermination. Israelis refused to be intimidated by two intifadas, a legion of suicide bombers, incoming Scud missiles, coordinated attack by the armies of every adjoining Arab nation. Tough people.

Still walking northeastward, he left the hotel and storefront district. He was in a neighborhood of small shops and low-rise apartment buildings. The evening had cooled. Lewis felt the breeze from the sea as it flowed inland between the rows of buildings.

Yes, the martinis were a brilliant idea. He was floating. His feet propelled him along the brick sidewalk as though they were directed by some remote guidance unit. They always did that when he was shit-faced. The buzzing in his head had settled down to a fine hum.

He turned the corner and headed south, back toward the central district. He was on a narrow street with few lights. Each intersection was marked with a stop sign. He was feeling good enough that he might even consider another martini before dinner at the Regatta. It would get him over the disappointment of not sleeping with Hannah Shamir. It might flush Ricardo Solares's smirking face from his memory.

Bless you, Mr. Stolichnaya, from whom all happiness flows.

His feet were still marching along of their own accord. He stopped for a second at an intersection. His mood had

brightened to a state of near-happiness. Fixed in his imagination were the sultry features of Hannah Shamir, black
hair splayed on a pillow, tanned bare skin moist from the
heat of lovemaking.

What the hell. It didn't hurt to fantasize.

He was halfway across the empty intersection when he
realized that it was not empty. There was an automobile.
It was coming from behind him.

He whirled and saw it. The car was coming very
damned fast. Something about it was peculiar. What the
hell was it?

Oh, shit. The fucker's lights were out.

Lewis's feet performed a skittering, hopping maneuver, receiving no clear command from his brain. His eyes
remained fixed on the approaching vehicle. It was black
and swelling large in his blurred vision.

He didn't feel the impact. In a flash of awareness, he
sensed the car ramming his body. He heard the snapping
of bones, felt the crushing of organs, knew that the mass
of the automobile was rolling over him. Then came
blackness.

CHAPTER 32

PERP ROLL

USS Ronald Reagan, *Eastern Mediterranean*
0935, Friday, 04 November

Something had changed.

Rick Solares couldn't put his finger on it, but he could sense it from the dispatches that were coming to him. There was nothing about an occupation of Palestine. Or an interim government.

"When is the Marine Expeditionary Unit landing in the West Bank?" he asked Admiral Hightree.

"The landing has been put on hold," said Hightree. "We're waiting for the new op plan from Central Command."

The admiral seemed distant this morning. Not his usual compliant self.

"New op plan?" said Solares. "Why wasn't I informed about a new op plan?"

Hightree gave him a wary look. "We presume that you have your own information pipeline."

Hightree was referring, of course, to the President, with whom Solares had at least one SatComm conference every day, and lately more than one. Until today. He hadn't been able to get through to the White House, not even to Chad Barkley, the President's weasel-faced little chief of staff, who hated Solares's guts.

Something had changed, goddamn it, and he still didn't know what.

"What about the airstrikes on Damascus and Halab?"

"They're on hold also," said Hightree. "The only tactical assets airborne at the moment are surveillance and CAP aircraft."

"Why? We've got the enemy routed, practically groveling at our feet, and we're *not* following through with the invasion of the West Bank? What the hell's going on?"

Hightree ignored him and turned back to the situational display screen on the bulkhead. On it was an array of little green triangles showing the disposition of the ships in the carrier group.

Solares felt the anger swell in him. He was about to remind this impudent, snot-nosed flag officer that if he wanted to continue occupying his little aerie in the loft of a seagoing bird farm, he had better—

"Yellow phone, Mr. Solares," said Baxter, the State Department specialist who had come out to take Lewis's place. He was young, thirty-something, but he already had a belly and a bald spot.

Solares nodded and followed Baxter into the private compartment where he could take the President's call. And about damn time. The President needed to know that these military square-heads were on the brink of royally fucking up the Palestinian takeover.

Solares nodded for Baxter to leave the compartment. He waited until the steel door clunked shut before he picked up the cordless yellow telephone. For another long moment he stared at the phone, not sure what to expect.

Solares and the President had always enjoyed an easy familiarity. They joked and kidded like old chums. In Solares the President seemed to see qualities that he admired—the aura of self-confidence, coolness under fire, boldness of action. The tricks of the clever broadcast journalist.

But all that was before the regrettable incident on the flight deck of the *Reagan*, when the cameras caught him vomiting beside the Super Hornet. As the recollection came back to him, Solares again felt a hot wave of nausea in the pit of his stomach.

That goddamn Maxwell.

Potentially more damaging was the gagging, half-delirious statement he had made to Maxwell while being thrashed around in the air like a rag doll. He doubted that anything would come of it. It would be Maxwell's word against his. Even that cowboy fighter jock had enough sense not to challenge the word of the President's Special Envoy.

Or did he?

Solares continued to stare at the yellow phone, his self-confidence eroding like sand in a tide. Had the President seen the images of his Special Envoy standing on the deck of the *Reagan*, retching like a drunk sailor?

Yes, decided Solares, he probably had. Someone on his staff—that meddlesome little shit Barkley, for one—would make sure he saw it.

He picked up the phone. "Yes, Mr. President."

"Just a minute," said a man's voice. It sounded like Chad Barkley, which added to Solares's uneasiness. "He'll be with you when he has a free moment."

Solares waited in the closed compartment, phone pressed to his ear, his anxiety mounting like a summer storm. This was not like the President, whose telephone style with Solares was friendly and informal. Until lately. A day and a half had passed since Solares's last dialogue with the President.

"Ricardo?"

Not Rick, or Rico, which was the President's nickname for him. A bad sign.

"Yes, Mr. President."

"Things have gotten shaky out there."

"Shaky? Actually, we're right on target. We have the Palestinians and their allies on the run. In a few more days I'll be—"

"You don't have a few more days. I'm going before the United Nations general assembly on Thursday to ask for a peacekeeping force in Palestine. In the meantime, I'm sending Frank Talmadge out there to get a handle on the situation."

Solares nearly choked. Frank Talmadge was the Deputy Secretary of State and a veteran troubleshooter who had built his reputation by extracting the United States from untenable conflicts in the third world. Talmadge had twice been nominated for the Nobel Peace Prize.

"Talmadge?" Solares felt his world crumbling beneath his feet. "Mr. President, that will send the wrong message to our adversaries. They will interpret it as a change in our policy."

"It *is* a change in our policy. Instead of a military solution to this mess we've gotten ourselves into, we're going for a diplomatic solution."

"Sir, I should have been consulted before any sweeping changes were made out here. After all, I'm the Special Envoy and the—"

"That's all changed," said the President. "In light of . . . uh, recent disclosures, I'm removing you from the Palestinian initiative."

"Disclosures?" Solares tried to keep the panic out of his voice. "May I ask what disclosures you're referring to?"

Several seconds passed. Solares thought that they had been disconnected. Then he heard the President's voice. "I'm sure you know what I'm talking about, Mr. Solares. If not, you'll find out soon enough. I want you in Tel Aviv to brief Talmadge when he arrives tomorrow. He'll enlighten you about anything you don't already know."

Solares's mind was racing to catch up with this sudden development. *I'm sure you know what I'm talking about, Mr. Solares. What the hell happened? Mr. Solares?* That wasn't the way a President addressed his potential running mate.

He could feel it slipping away. The Nobel Prize. The brilliant political future. It was a shattered dream. He had to save it before it was too late.

"Mr. President, I believe you have been misinformed. I need to speak with you in person as soon as possible."

In reply he heard only the crackle of static. The line was dead.

"You guys have to get a handle on this," said Boyce. "Or it's going to take your whole squadron down."

Maxwell and Alexander exchanged glances. They were in Boyce's stateroom. Boyce was telling them what they already knew. The Scudder affair was becoming a bottomless quagmire.

Bullet Alexander sat on the opposite end of the narrow table from Maxwell. He seemed preoccupied, staring moodily at the far bulkhead.

Maxwell coughed and waved away the smoke cloud from Boyce's cigar. "What are you saying, CAG? Offer them a head to chop?"

"That, or everyone else's head gets chopped."

"Got any suggestions whose head it ought to be?"

By now it had become a squadron joke. In the Roadrunner ready room someone put up a poster labeled PERP ROLL OF HONOR. The list of names had swollen to twenty-two, including two ship's company officers and three pilots from VFA-34. They all wanted the honor of having catapulted Scrotum Scudder.

"Look, I'm just the CAG. You guys run the squadron.

Bullet here is taking over as skipper. If you don't figure out—"

"I've got it figured out," said Alexander.

Maxwell and Boyce swiveled their heads to Alexander.

"You've figured out who's going to take the hit?" said Boyce.

"Yeah," said Alexander. "Me."

"Hang on a minute," said Maxwell. "You weren't even there when—"

"I was the guy in charge. If I had done my job, it wouldn't have happened."

"You can't take the hit," said Boyce. "You've got orders to take command of the squadron."

Alexander reached inside his flight jacket pocket and pulled out a folded sheet of paper. "This letter says it all. I take full responsibility for what happened to Scudder. The whole affair was a matter of failed leadership. No one is to blame except me."

Maxwell scanned the letter, then tossed it on the table. "This is bullshit. I'm the commanding officer. If anyone takes the blame, it's going to be me."

"Won't sell," said Alexander. "You might be the skipper, but even those half-assed JAG lawyers aren't that fucked-up. They know that you weren't in town and couldn't have done anything about it. I was the guy in the hot seat, and that makes me responsible."

"That letter has to be endorsed by me," said Maxwell. "I'm not going to sign off on anything that incriminates you alone."

"Doesn't matter whether you endorse it or not." Alexander picked up the letter and stuffed it back in his jacket pocket. He rose and walked to the door. "I've already cut a deal with the JAG guys. If I take the hit, they won't press charges against the junior officers. Case closed."

Alexander had his hand on the doorknob. Boyce said, "Bullet, when that letter goes up the chain of command, those orders giving you command of the Roadrunners go straight down the crapper. Your career is toast."

Alexander shrugged. "Better that than all our young tigers losing their own shot at a command. Don't worry about me, CAG. I've had a great ride, and I don't regret a damn minute of it." He gave them a nod. "See you, gentlemen."

Boyce and Maxwell stared in silence at the closed steel door.

"This is bullshit," said Boyce.

"Yes it is," said Maxwell.

"What's happening to this outfit? You've been canned. I'm leaving right behind you. Now Bullet. For no good reason at all."

"I believe it's called attrition from the top."

"This Scudder mess is out of control. You'd better come up with a miracle, Maxwell."

"Yes, sir. I'm working on—"

The jangling of the phone interrupted him.

Boyce snatched up the receiver. "Boyce," he said. He listened for several seconds, nodding his head. "Yes, sir. I'll be right up."

He rose and put on his uniform cap. "Something's up," he said. "We'll finish this later."

Maxwell knew where he was going. There was only one officer aboard the *Reagan* whom Boyce had to call "sir."

As Boyce arrived on the flag bridge, he noticed wisps of vapor swirling from the rotor blades of the CH-53 below. The helo lifted from the flight deck, rising nearly to the level of the flag bridge before turning its nose to port.

For a moment Boyce could see faces in the windows of the cabin. One looked familiar. Boyce waved, and the face abruptly turned away. The helicopter dipped its nose and accelerated toward the open sea.

Boyce turned around and saw Admiral Hightree watching him from across the compartment.

"Was that who I thought it was?"

"Yes," said Hightree. "And good riddance."

It was the first conversation between the two men since their dispute over Ricardo Solares and the HUD tape. That was two days ago. Since then Boyce had conducted all his communications with the flag staff through the ops officer, Capt. Guido Vitale.

Now Solares was gone.

Boyce looked out the window again. The Sea Stallion was skimming the water, gathering speed.

"We're two hundred miles at sea." said Boyce. "Why doesn't a big shot like him fly off in a COD?"

"Mr. Solares's last words to me were—and I quote him verbatim—'I'll never set foot on another fucking Navy airplane as long as I live.'"

"Good news. Let's hope he keeps his word."

"He may not have a choice. Looks like Solares is out of the warlord business."

Boyce wanted to ask what was going on, but he knew better. The admiral had summoned him without giving a reason. When Hightree had something on his mind, you had to give him time to get it out.

Boyce said, "My pilots needed this break. So did the maintenance crews and the ordnance hangars. They've been working twelve-hour shifts around the clock."

"It's not exactly a break," said Hightree. "More like a change in game plan. We've suspended air strikes. The President is gambling that the Arabs will sit down and talk. But we're prepared to respond to any further attacks."

"Meaning we're still going to insert troops?"

"That's on hold," said Hightree. "Our Marine expeditionary units are still out there, waiting for the order to land in the West Bank. The President is going to ask the

U.N. to mandate a peacekeeping force to take over the Palestinian territories."

Boyce glanced out to sea. He could see the *Reagan*'s accompanying warships cruising in a distant formation. The dull gray shapes of the two amphibious assault ships, *Saipan* and *Tarawa*, were visible. Over three thousand marines were embarked on the two warships.

"And get the Prez off the hook. What if there's no peace there for them to keep?"

"Then we're back where we started."

"Bombing the shit out of them, turning every Muslim on the planet into a wannabe martyr?"

Hightree shrugged. "You said it, not me."

For a while both men gazed out the thick glass over the flight deck. On the far side of the compartment, the flagstaff yeomen and two lieutenants were in conversation, ignoring the two senior officers at the window.

Hightree fell silent. Boyce waited. Sooner or later Hightree would say what was really on his mind.

It took half a minute.

"What is Commander Maxwell's status?" said Hightree.

Boyce looked at him in surprise. "You fired him, Admiral. Remember?"

Hightree seemed to be studying a spot on the horizon. "Well, figuratively perhaps. I believe I said he *would* be relieved of command."

"There's a difference?"

"Umm, in a manner of speaking. What I meant was that Commander Maxwell should be rotated in due time, which is to say, he should continue to command the squadron until his successor has received specific orders, at which time he would be relieved in an appropriate fashion."

Hightree looked at Boyce. "Why are you frowning, Red? Didn't I make myself clear?"

Boyce shook his head. *As clear as stewed owl shit.* He

remembered that Jack Hightree was a legend in the Pentagon for his ability to convolute a simple sentence into an incomprehensible maze. This time he had outdone himself.

"Yes, sir, perfectly clear. Should I tell Maxwell he's not fired?"

"You're the Air Wing Commander. Tell him whatever you please."

Well, thought Boyce, at least they had that little technicality cleared up. Imagine that, letting the Air Wing Commander actually run his air wing. Miracles did happen.

Hightree seemed pleased to have the subject closed. He clasped Boyce's shoulder and steered him toward the far corner of the compartment. "Let's get a coffee. I want to tell you about the change in the op plan."

Boyce was one pace behind Hightree, following him to the coffeepot, when it came to him. He stopped and stared at Hightree's back.

"You did it, didn't you?"

Hightree reached for a mug. "Did what?"

"Forwarded the HUD tape."

Hightree didn't seem to hear. He was holding the cup under the spigot of the stainless-steel urn. "Senior Chief Lester just brewed this ten minutes ago. Fresh as it gets."

"The tape went up the chain of command."

Hightree filled the cup, inspected the contents, then handed it to Boyce. "Black, right?"

"It went all the way to the White House. That's why they pulled the plug on Solares."

"Tape? I don't know what you're talking about." Hightree filled his own cup, then took a trial sip. "How's the coffee, Red? Strong enough for you?"

CHAPTER 33

HISTORIC OPPORTUNITY

U.S. Embassy, Tel Aviv
2005, Friday, 04 November

Ricardo Solares slammed the telephone back down in its cradle. Another "Please hold. It will be a while longer," followed by the same maddening silence. Ten minutes of maddening silence, after which Solares had reached his flash point. The idiot operators who directed calls at the White House didn't even use soothing background music for the poor patient bastards who were waiting to speak with the leader of the free world.

The message was clear. The President wasn't taking calls from Rick Solares.

Even the ambassador to Israel, that toad-faced hack Kaminsky, was shunning him. The ambassador was in a meeting, on his way to a meeting, in a conference call, or otherwise engaged. Taking his daily dump, maybe. He was too busy to meet with Solares.

That was the most noticeable change. Being the President's Special Envoy no longer carried any clout. When he asked for an intelligence briefing from the station CIA section chief, he was told that he wasn't on the cleared list. Even Solares's aide, the mincing little bureaucrat Baxter, was treating him as some kind of social inferior.

In less than three hours Talmadge would be landing at Ben-Gurion. Frank Talmadge, in Solares's opinion, was a thickheaded bully. He would come sweeping into the Tel Aviv embassy like a conquering general, trailed by an entourage of lackies and gofers, barking orders and making pronouncements. Talmadge didn't know his ass from his elbow about the Palestinian situation.

Fuck Talmadge. Fuck all the bureaucrats in the State Department.

Solares was pacing the tiled floor of the office, which adjoined his two-room suite in the embassy compound. Through the shatterproof window, he could look down on the busy street below. Traffic was flowing like it always did in Tel Aviv—in frenetic bursts between lights, horns blaring, fists shaking. Israelis acting out their anxieties with road rage.

The sight of a car darting across the intersection made him think of Vernon Lewis. A good thing that Lewis was no longer here. He'd be taking sadistic pleasure in Solares's humiliation.

Lewis had been a troublemaker. It was entirely possible, Solares reflected, that Lewis had even had something to do with discrediting him in Washington. He should have had Lewis removed sooner.

Someone at the embassy had shown him the photo of the body, and it was all Solares could do not to vomit. Whoever did the job—Solares guessed that it was someone from Hamas—didn't bother with neatness. The wheels of the heavy vehicle had rolled over Lewis's torso, converting it to a gory pulp. A nasty solution to the Lewis problem, but it left open the possibility that Lewis was the victim of a hit-and-run driver instead of an assassin.

Too bad. Lewis was a smart guy. If he'd simply shut up and played the game, he would have been an asset to the team.

What team? he thought, and his mood darkened.

Solares forced himself to stop staring out the window. He had to think. His career had run into roadblocks before. He always found a way around them. What he needed was another opportunity to demonstrate his statesmanship in—

A rap on the door. Baxter stuck his head inside the office. "A visitor, Mr. Solares."

Solares was caught off balance. "Who is it?"

He thought he saw a smirk flit across Baxter's face. "An official visitor."

Before Solares could demand the visitor's identity, the door was flung open. Into the office marched a black-haired woman in a short leather skirt.

"I thought the war was on hold," said Maxwell.

"The insertion of troops in Palestine is on hold," said Boyce. "We have one more tactical air operation to handle."

He and Boyce were in the flag intel compartment. They were peering at an illuminated map of Israel on the bulkhead.

Maxwell had to shake his head in amazement. Events were moving too fast for him to keep pace. This morning he'd been cleaning out the desk in his stateroom, preparing to hand over command of the VFA-36 Roadrunners to Bullet Alexander. Then the call from Boyce.

Forget the command change. Unpack your bags, get back into flight gear. He was still the squadron skipper. He would remain so until his scheduled end of tour.

Okay, thought Maxwell, but he knew there was more. There had to be. Rambo Rick Solares had abruptly departed the *Reagan*. Almost simultaneously the war had come to a halt. Too much coincidence there.

Boyce was aiming a laser pointer at the map. The beam was playing on a spot south of Jerusalem, along the high ridge that traversed the length of Israel like a serpent's spine.

"The complex is near Hebron," Boyce said. "The planners have designated it a high-value target."

"High value?"

"That's as much as you need to know," said Boyce. "You can ask the intel geeks in the briefing, but they won't tell you any more than that, even if they know."

High value? That was a generic term that meant anything from a weapons stash to a head of state. Maxwell's mind was running over the possibilities. There were few targets anywhere in Palestine that could be tagged "high value." It wasn't likely that the Palestinians had acquired weapons of mass destruction.

That left one real possibility. The target was human.

"What's the load-out?" said Maxwell.

"One JSOW."

Maxwell nodded. This was getting even weirder. The AGM-154 JSOW—Joint Stand Off Weapon—was a recently developed, precision-guided glide bomb. It could be released at a distance of more than forty miles and fly itself through a three-foot-wide window. It was a special-purpose weapon, employed against special targets.

What special target?

Maxwell looked at Boyce, who was gnawing on a cigar stub, studiously ignoring him. He'd seen Boyce in this mode before. Boyce had another surprise up his sleeve. He always did.

"Ah, may I ask who's been assigned to the mission, CAG?"

"Who do you think?" said Boyce.

It all came back to him. He had almost slept with her. They had gotten as far as the outer room of his suite in the King David. As it turned out, what she wanted was information, not sex. Details about the deployment of a Marine unit along the border of Iraq. He'd blabbed a few innocuous facts about the operation. That was enough. The devious bitch picked up her bag and left.

That was over a year ago. The memory of the incident still caused him to seethe with anger.

"How have you been, Rick?" said Hannah Shamir.

"I've been better."

She smiled, and he felt the anger coming back. He remembered that she had some kind of title with the Foreign Ministry, deputy something or other, but he had been tipped—too late—by the CIA. She worked for the Mossad. If she slept with you, it wasn't for love or even lust. It was business.

For Solares it had been a maddening experience. Women gravitated to him. He preferred to think it was for his looks and aura, not his celebrity status. There were aspiring journalists and studio interns and even some established anchorwomen who tumbled into the sack with him.

Of course, he'd been careful since taking the Special Envoy job. He knew all about the kind of scrutiny a public figure received. As an investigative reporter, Solares had exposed more than a few politicians who were careless about where they slept.

Hannah Shamir looked good. Long legs, tan and exposed beneath the thigh-length skirt. Black hair worn loose to her collar. The kind of olive-skinned face that barely required makeup.

Without asking, she sat in the leather chair beside his desk and pulled out a pack of cigarettes. She lit one, waved the smoke away. "The Prime Minister is worried, Rick. So is the Foreign Minister. They think that you and I"—she flashed a smile—"might be friends, so they suggested I have a word with you."

"Worried about what?" He knew perfectly well what they were worried about, but he'd play the game.

"The attitude in Washington. There's been a climate change. The White House is not being forthcoming about what direction they intend to take."

Solares nodded. She hadn't changed. Still fishing for

information. Apparently the Israelis hadn't been informed that Special Envoy Ricardo Solares was in the diplomatic shithouse.

For a moment he let his gaze dwell on the tan legs. They were crossed, one trim ankle over the other. It occurred to him that he might be in a position to negotiate a session in bed with Hannah.

Not now, he told himself. With the world falling around his ears, screwing an Israeli spy was far down on his wish list.

"The strategy has changed," said Solares. "Instead of U.S. troops occupying Palestine, the President wants the U.N. to insert a peacekeeping force."

"So the agreement that you and my government and Khaled Mohanor put together has been canceled?"

Solares shrugged. "So it seems."

She drew on her cigarette, appearing to be deep in thought. Most women who smoked turned him off, but not this one. He had to admit, Hannah Shamir was sexy.

"It may not be too late," she said.

He tilted his head, looking at her. "For what?"

"The Palestinians are not responding to the U.S.'s call for a cease-fire. That's because no strong authority figure is telling them *how* to respond."

"They're terrorists. Who can tell Hamas or Hezbollah what to do?"

"You."

Solares blinked, not sure he heard right. "Excuse me?"

"You and Khaled Mohanor. You are the only ones who have the power to make something positive happen in Palestine. The two of you can negotiate an armistice that the Palestinians and Israelis will observe."

"I haven't spoken with Khaled in several days. I don't even know if he's alive."

"He's alive. He is very aware of this historic opportunity. He wants to meet with you immediately."

"You're in communication with Khaled?"

"Of course. We share information."

Solares stared at her. Khaled and the Israelis? How much more was there that he didn't know?

"Why doesn't he contact me himself?"

"He's in a heavily guarded shelter in Hebron. At least two of the Palestinian resistance factions want him dead because they suspect him of cooperating with the Americans and the Israelis."

Solares's mind was filling with new scenarios. *This historic opportunity.* Maybe it wasn't too late. He could present the President with a fait accompli—a negotiated acceptance by the Palestinians of an interim government that would lead to their statehood. He could still emerge from this quagmire as the greatest peacemaker of his time.

For several seconds, he let the images parade across his consciousness. Governor of a peaceful Palestine. Head bowed, clasping in his hands the newly awarded Nobel Peace Prize. Balloons and banners and streamers over the convention floor as delegates acclaimed his nomination as Vice President.

It was still possible.

"How do I find Khaled?" he said.

CHAPTER 34

JSOW

20,000 Feet, Coast of Israel
0945, Saturday, 5 November

From his perch off the port wing of the KC-10 tanker, Maxwell watched Pearly finish taking on fuel. The refueling probe of Pearly's jet disengaged from the drogue that was dangling behind the big three-engine tanker. Pearly glanced over to his left, then slid his F/A-18 outboard and beneath Maxwell's jet, taking a position off his port wing.

They were a two-ship element, Maxwell and Gates. No second element, not even a TARCAP flying air cover for them. They were observing strict EMCON—emissions control. No radar, no electronic signaling, no radio chatter between pilots.

They had only a one-way communication with Steeljaw, the controller in the E-2C Hawkeye, in his orbit off the coast. Everything else was transmitted by silent datalink. Steeljaw would issue a coded signal, which would clear Maxwell to launch his JSOW glide bomb. Pearly Gates carried an identical weapon beneath his jet as a backup.

The secrecy surrounding the mission was the strictest Maxwell had seen since the Black Star operation in the

Taiwan Strait. No one outside the intel briefing was privy to the nature of the mission. Not the pilots attacking air defense positions along the Syrian border, nor the VFA-34 crews tasked with the armed reconnaissance mission up the Jordan Valley.

Those were diversions. The real target—the one Maxwell and Pearly Gates were attacking—was to the south. Its coordinates were already programmed into the guidance units of their JSOWs.

Finished with the tanking, Maxwell and Pearly climbed away from the KC-10 and turned back toward the coastline of Israel. No clearance would be issued for them to enter Israeli airspace. In radio silence he and Pearly would enter an orbit over the Negev Desert, roughly between the Hazerim air base and the ancient fortress of Masada on the Dead Sea.

Throughout the intel brief and the final flight brief back on the *Reagan*, Boyce had remained tight-lipped about the identity of the target. It didn't matter. Maxwell knew Boyce. He knew there was one compelling reason why Boyce had handed him this mission.

It was the same reason Maxwell had tagged Pearly to be his wingman. It was an obvious choice. Pearly Gates had almost as much reason to kill Khaled Mohanor as he did.

Hebron, West Bank, Palestinian Territories

"Excellent," said Khaled Mohanor. "I look forward to the meeting."

He smiled and clicked the cover of his cell phone closed. He turned to Suleiman Kharazi, seated opposite him at the small octagonal table.

"He's coming?" said Kharazi. He wore a checked kaffiyeh and an olive-drab military tunic.

Mohanor nodded. "He'll be here within the hour."

"It is dangerous for him. Palestinians are enraged at the Americans."

"He is being escorted by loyal militia. The flag of Palestine will be on the vehicle."

For the first time in two days, Mohanor was feeling optimistic. The war had not gone as he had expected. U.S. troops were not storming into Palestine, occupying the country, setting up a provisional government. Instead, the U.S. had pulled back.

Worse, his American negotiating partner, Solares, had dropped out of sight. There were rumors that Solares had fallen out of favor. There were even rumors that Zemek, his ally in the Israeli government, had abandoned his support of Mohanor.

It was clear now that the rumors were false. An agent of the Israeli Mossad—a woman—had just assured him that Zemek was still promoting a Mohanor-led Palestinian government.

Strange bedfellows, reflected Mohanor.

Looking across the table at the unshaven, scowling face of Suleiman Kharazi, he wondered what Kharazi would think if he knew the truth—that Mohanor was negotiating not only with the Americans but with the Israelis. When Mohanor took the reins of power in Palestine, all the Hamas and Hezbollah and Islamic Jihad organizations would be disbanded. Thugs like Kharazi would be arrested and shot.

The Mossad had even connected him with Solares again. Now Solares was on his way to Mohanor's headquarters in Hebron, thirty-five kilometers south of Jerusalem. It meant that the Americans still intended to establish new leadership for Palestine. He and Solares would work out the details, ensuring a smooth transition of power from the interim governor, Solares, to the new President, Khaled Mohanor.

It would be glorious. After the years of humiliation and oppression, he would emerge as the leader of a new nation. He would be celebrated around the world as a champion of peace and dignity.

The path had not been easy. Terrible risks had been taken and many lives snuffed out, but the end would justify the means. The killing of the Americans at Ramallah had been the spark that ignited the blaze. The rest was merely a matter of fanning the flames.

One of his aides, Jamil al-Busti, entered the room. He bowed his head in respect. "The caravan with the American is passing though Hebron. They will be here in a few minutes."

Khaled nodded to the young man. He could feel his excitement growing. He had not met with Solares since the United States entered the war. Their telephone communications had been necessarily formal and strained. Both Israeli and American intelligence eavesdroppers could be monitoring every word.

"Get the photographers," Khaled ordered. He waved at the disorderly group of Palestinians slouching at the far end of the room. "All of you, come see this. We want this moment to be remembered."

Khaled rose and put on his leather jacket. He straightened the kaffiyeh on his head. His image would be seen by millions. It was important that he convey the correct impression.

A feeling of ebullience surged through him as he strode toward the door. Palestinian schoolchildren would read about this day for the next century.

A young, AK-47-armed Palestinian rushed to open the steel-plated door for him. Khaled strode out into the yellow, waning light of the courtyard. It was late afternoon, still warm, but the air would cool quickly in the approaching dusk. Hebron had the same climate as Jerusalem. Both cities straddled the high massif that stretched from the north of Israel to the edge of the Negev Desert.

"They're coming," shouted a young man.

And so they were. Khaled could see the caravan, three black Citroëns, laboring up the winding road. The lead automobile had a flag mounted at the driver's side. Even at this distance, Khaled recognized the black-white-and-green bars and red triangle of the Palestinian flag.

A two-hundred-meter-wide belt of razor wire, tank traps, and land mines lay between the main road and the headquarters building. The belt of defenses required visitors to leave their vehicles and approach the headquarters by foot along a prepared walkway. This was a precaution Khaled had ordered on the day the Americans began bombing.

The caravan came to a stop at the entrance to the walkway. Doors opened; passengers disembarked. From the front and back Citroëns emerged a squad of Palestinians. All wore yellow kaffiyehs. Each carried an assault rifle or a submachine gun.

A man climbed out of the middle automobile. He was taller than the others, hatless, wearing a khaki bush jacket. He stretched, gazed around him.

Khaled waved. The man recognized him and waved back.

Solares. Khaled could feel the nearness of victory. Solares was here. Together they would write the final chapter in Palestine's struggle for independence. Soon they could dispense with the assault rifles and land mines and tank traps. They would attend to matters of state.

He watched Solares and his escort start up the path through the defenses, toward the headquarters complex.

Why the hell was he doing this?

Solares stood beside the Citroën and stared at the maze of trenches and razor wire that lay between him and Khaled's headquarters.

It had seemed like a brilliant opportunity back in Tel Aviv. Now he knew it was a long shot. A *dangerous* fucking long shot. He was already persona non grata at the White House, and from what he gathered, Khaled Mohanor was not enjoying any great popularity of his own.

He wondered how much Khaled knew about recent developments in Washington. Did he know that Solares no longer represented the President?

Perhaps not.

Okay, so he had no official bargaining chips. But he still had his reputation, which was considerable, and he could still get a spot on network television whenever he wanted. If he and Khaled could put together a deal before a peacekeeping force got their boots on the ground, then go public with it, there was still a chance. The President would have to sign off on it. If the United States had learned anything from its wars in the Middle East, it was not to try to replace a government that worked.

He and Khaled would install a government that worked.

"Do they expect me to walk through *that?*" Solares pointed at the path through the wire.

"It is no problem," said Zahir, the taciturn Palestinian who had driven the lead Citroën. "You follow me."

Solares didn't move. Follow a Palestinian terrorist who considered land mines as an express route to heaven? *Fat fucking chance.*

"It is nothing," Zahir insisted. "We all take this path. It is the only way to reach the Great Leader."

15,000 Feet, West Bank, Palestinian Territories

Ten seconds.

Maxwell watched the digital elapsed timer.

Five seconds.

Three . . . two . . . one . . .

Thunk.

He felt the jolt of the ton-and-a-half weapon leaving its

station beneath his wing. The JSOW was on its own now, guided by a GPS coupled with an inertial guidance unit. It was a launch-and-forget weapon, designed to keep the delivery pilot removed from the battle zone.

Or keep him anonymous.

Maxwell reefed the Super Hornet's nose up in a climbing turn to the left. He couldn't see the bomb yet, which was beneath and behind his jet. Nor could he see the target, forty miles away and obscured in the mottled brown patchwork of the Judean range. The JSOW's thin wings would carry it like a bird of prey through the pale sky, its tailfins making tiny course corrections on its long glide path to the target.

Still no radio communication. Steeljaw, of course, knew that the weapon was away. Maxwell guessed that she was already beaming the news, via a scrambled satellite link, to all interested parties on the far side of the Atlantic.

This was the part of modern warfare that Maxwell disliked the most. The invisible, impersonal killing—no enemy in his gunsight, no face to impose over a bull's-eye.

But he had no trouble conjuring up the face. It was a handsome Arab face, black mustache, dark eyes that glowed like embers, with a mesmerizing voice that inspired a brigade of young killers to strap explosives onto themselves.

He saw Pearly maneuvering to stay with him. From his vantage point, Pearly could observe the flight of the JSOW. If something was wrong—a guidance unit gone dumb, or a failed control fin—Pearly would know. He'd launch his own bomb.

The JSOW was good. Maxwell checked his display panel to confirm it. No blinking symbols, no failure alerts.

He reversed the turn, keeping the Hornet's nose above the horizon. He squinted in the glare of the afternoon sun.

He tried to pick up the slender profile of the JSOW. He couldn't see it. It blended into the brown landscape of the—

There. Slanting downward, flying straight and true as an arrow.

Maxwell knew they should exit the area. Get the hell out, maintain their anonymity. But not yet. He wanted to see what happened.

Hebron, West Bank

Solares glanced around. The drivers were all standing beside their cars. So were the half dozen Palestinian fighters who had ridden with them. The group was bristling with automatic weapons.

But now there were more Palestinians. Villagers were appearing beside the road. They were coming from the slums at the foot of the hill. Solares could feel their curious stares. He was glad the Palestinian flag was mounted on the lead Citroën.

"Hey, this really sucks," said Baxter, standing beside him. He had just seen the villagers, whose numbers seemed to be increasing. "I don't think they like Americans here."

"Why would you think that?" Solares was doing his best to sound nonchalant. "Just because we've been bombing their homes? They probably want our autographs."

Baxter wasn't amused. Solares had brought him along because he spoke Arabic, which would be useful if things got dicey. But there was another reason. Baxter was still a bona fide employee of the U.S. State Department. His presence added a tiny bit of officialdom to Solares's meeting with Khaled.

At the last minute, he'd had to bully Baxter. The fat little twit protested that he had to check with the ambassador. Luckily, the ambassador was in yet another meeting. Baxter hedged his bets and came with Solares.

"I don't like the looks of this," said Baxter.

"Looks don't mean anything. Get over it."

One thing about having Baxter along was that the younger man's fear actually made Solares feel not as shit-scared as he might have been.

He gazed up the hill. Khaled was still there, surrounded by his entourage. Khaled was beckoning to him. *Come on.*

Solares summoned all the resolve he had left and motioned to Zahir. Zahir nodded in turn to the armed men behind him. They all began walking toward the path that led to Khaled's headquarters.

Solares walked with his head down, intent on watching each spot on the ground where his feet would step. He was careful to stay at least fifteen or twenty feet behind the Palestinian directly in front of him. Khaled's men could have planted mines anywhere. If this bunch was in a hurry to meet Allah, let them. He'd take his time.

They came to within a hundred feet of the headquarters. Solares looked up. There was Khaled, watching, arms folded over his chest Il Duce–style. For a few seconds Solares and Khaled held eye contact.

It was the last glimpse Ricardo Solares had of the Great Leader.

Solares saw a flash, then an orange curtain of flame. The wall of concussion rolled down the hill like a flaming tidal wave, sweeping away everything in its path.

CHAPTER 35

THE MOST PRIMITIVE WEAPON

Hebron, West Bank, Palestinian Territories
0942, Saturday, 5 November

His vision was returning.

He saw smoke. Tendrils of flame were leaping from the great cavity where the front of the headquarters building had been. Where Khaled Mohanor and his staff had been standing.

The easterly wind was sweeping the smoke from the shattered building, away from where Rick Solares lay huddled.

What the fuck happened? Solares's brain was barely functioning. Nothing made sense. There had been some kind of explosion. Why?

Someone tried to kill Khaled Mohanor. And succeeded.

And tried to kill me with him.

The thought stirred his brain to alertness. He was still in danger. He was somewhere in Palestine. He couldn't remember the place, but he knew he had to get out.

He tried to move. Something was restraining him. His bush jacket. It was singed and torn, the back of it tangled in strands of barbed wire.

Solares reached around behind him, trying to free the

jacket. He couldn't. The effort was too much. He unbuttoned the front of the jacket and slipped out of it.

Carefully he tried moving his legs. Nothing broken, no serious injuries. His face felt burned. His ears were pounding from the concussion, but his vision had returned. He peered around.

A body was spread-eagled on a coil of wire, motionless. Farther up the hill was another body—one of the Palestinians—facedown on the path.

Amazing. No one had survived the blast except—

A voice came from behind him. Solares turned to see Baxter wobbling to his feet.

"Baxter, are you injured?"

"Unnnnnhhhhh." It was an animal sound, coming from somewhere in the gut. The young man's eyes were wild and uncomprehending.

"Wait a second." Solares rolled over onto his knees, then struggled to his feet. He lurched toward Baxter. "We've got to get help so we—"

Baxter saw him coming and panicked. He turned and fled, half trotting, half limping down the hill.

"Stay where you are," yelled Solares. "Stop! Listen to me, Baxter."

Baxter wasn't listening. He was running pell-mell down the barren hillside. He stumbled over the trenches, picked himself up, ran again. The rolls of barbed wire had been swept away by the blast. They were tumbled into piles, exposing an open area in the raw, sandy earth.

"Baxter!" Solares called. "Stop, damn it! You're running through—"

The explosion drowned out his words. The earth beneath Baxter's running feet erupted. Dirt and debris and body parts rose thirty feet above the ground. Muffled by the layer of earth, the explosion made a deep, resonant sound.

Solares stood paralyzed, too stunned to move. He watched the rain of carnage. Baxter's shattered body—

the largest part of it—landed in a smoking heap ten feet from Solares. The odor of cordite reached his nostrils, then the stench of scorched flesh.

Silence fell over the hillside. Already the wind was wafting the smoke and dust eastward, in the direction of the Dead Sea.

In the distance Solares heard a metallic whine. It changed in pitch, then faded. The sound of jet engines.

His brain was processing information at a slow pace, but it was coming to him. He knew what happened to Khaled Mohanor. And he knew *who* made it happen.

At the foot of the hill were the three Citroëns. They didn't appear to have been damaged. Without moving, Solares studied the landscape between him and the cars. The razor wire was strewn over the hillside, but he could still see the pathway. It was a different color, hard and packed by pedestrian traffic.

He took his time, being careful to stay on the path. It took nearly five minutes to retrace his steps. He was still thirty meters from the first car, the one with the Palestinian flag, when he saw them.

Heads. Some were wearing kaffiyehs; some were bareheaded. They were appearing over the edges of the ditches on either side of the road. Dark Arab eyes blazing at him. The Palestinians were coming from the village at the base of the hill.

This is not good, Solares thought. In fact, this had the potential to be very bad. It would be an excellent time to be someplace else.

He gazed around, looking for the drivers of the Citroëns. They were nowhere in sight. Also not in sight were any of the armed bodyguards, which meant that those not killed in the bomb blast had either deserted or already been dispatched by villagers.

And then Solares heard a new sound. It was a buzzing noise, like a distant swarm of insects. Then it grew louder, and he knew.

Voices. Angry voices, chanting in Arabic. From the ditch Solares saw the villagers pointing at him, yelling in their incomprehensible language. He didn't understand what they were saying, but he had no doubt about the meaning.

Despite the sense of growing danger, he knew he could still handle the situation. When they saw who he was—Ricardo Solares, the television journalist—they would welcome him. They knew that he was a man of peace.

He heard a word he recognized.

"American!"

His blood ran cold.

More yelling, and now they were climbing out of the ditch. Coming toward him.

"Hey, hey." He held out his hands, palms up. He tried smiling. "I came here to help—"

A stone hit him on the cheek.

The shock and the pain ended all rational thinking. He whirled and ran. He had no idea where he was running, only that he had to get the hell away. *Run. Run from these fucking wild-eyed animals.*

Stones were hitting the ground around him, kicking up plumes of dirt. Behind him he heard voices, the sound of feet on the hard earth. Propelled by adrenaline and terror, he charged down the road. His chin was tilted high, his knees pumping like pistons.

A stone caught him in the back of the head. His vision blurred, and his momentum carried him several more paces before his knees buckled under him.

Another rock thudded into his left ear. His face hit the earth. His nostrils filled with dirt and blood. In a distant corner of his remaining consciousness he heard yelling and the pounding of feet near him and, somewhere not far away, a familiar rhythmic whopping sound, like the beat of helicopter blades.

He lifted his head. The stones had stopped coming. In

the blurry distance he saw the dark shapes of helicopters. Three of them, closing fast.

Thank God.

"There he is," said the pilot in the right seat of the Blackhawk. He was a baby-faced young IAF captain named Shemerev. "We're not too late."

The pilot in the left seat didn't answer. From the cockpit, they had a clear view of the scene on the ground. They could count at least two hundred of them, maybe more. A mob, not an organized military unit. What did they have for weapons? A few AK-47s maybe, and a handful of old pistols.

And stones. The most primitive of weapons.

The Blackhawk pilots saw the stone throwers gazing up at the approaching helicopters. The cheeky bastards were standing still, apparently not intimidated by the choppers. They could have either of the two Cobra gunships on their flanks open up with their Gatling guns. Or they could use the Blackhawk's own 7.62 guns to disperse them. A few bursts and the insurgents would disappear like rats back into their crevices.

The armed reconnaissance flight—the Blackhawk escorted by the two Cobras—had been waiting behind the ridge. Waiting for the telltale gush of smoke and debris from Mohanor's headquarters. The precision-guided weapon had arrived on schedule.

"Shall we open fire?" asked Shemerev.

No answer. The pilot in the left seat was still studying the scene on the ground. Wondering who had been assigned the mission. Did the American pilot, whoever he was, suspect who the real target was?

It would be best, of course, if he—or she—never learned. Americans were squeamish about such things. They had no stomach for targeted killings.

Though the precision guidance of the American weapon had been perfect, the timing was off. The Palestinian caravan had arrived late. Apparently the occupants of the three Citroëns had dawdled, not quite reaching Khaled Mohanor's headquarters before it ceased to exist.

One of them had escaped the blast. They could see him looking up, waving at them. His face was bleeding, but he displayed a huge smile as the helicopters came nearer.

The Palestinians were coming out of their hiding places. They were close to the man on the ground. It was still possible to disperse them with a few bursts from the gunships.

"Shall we open fire?" Shemerev asked the pilot in the left seat.

"No," said Hannah Shamir. "Hold your fire."

It will be a hell of a story, Solares thought. The kind of adventure tale that would elevate him to legendary status not just in the United States but throughout the world.

The banner headline flashed across his mind. *Heroic Envoy Escapes Death in Palestine.*

Even the President would have to give him his due. What greater asset could a politician have than a running mate who was admired—no, *idolized*—by voters who loved nothing so much as a movie star-handsome, real-life hero?

Of course, less than a minute ago he had expected that it would be his bloodied corpse, not his handsome features, that they would see in the tabloids. It had been a close thing, the goddamn ragheads slinging rocks at him, chasing him across Palestine, and then—

What the hell are they doing?

The helicopters. They weren't coming any closer. They weren't firing their guns. Damn it, they were leaving!

The Palestinians saw it too. The heads were rotating back toward the man who was just wobbling to his feet.

Dark eyes blazing at him.

"Hey, guys, enough is enough, right?" He tried smiling

again. "Let's not do anything silly or those choppers will—"

A stone struck him in the cheek. Then another. The next one hit him in the forehead, knocking him senseless, which was fortunate for Solares. He didn't feel the next one, or any of the hail of stones that followed, pounding his body to a gelatinous pulp.

CHAPTER 36

REQUIEM

Maxwell could see Scrotum Scudder's jaw muscles working. Scudder was sitting at rigid attention in the chair on the far side of Maxwell's gray steel office table. His face was pale and clammy. His head protruded from the neck brace as if it were being squeezed.

From the far bulkhead, Bullet Alexander sat watching the two men. On the table lay the nineteen-inch video monitor. Scudder was watching the fuzzy images on the screen with rapt attention.

The voices coming from the video were scratchy, almost indecipherable. The speakers sounded inebriated.

"Stickney?" said a slurred voice. *"You mean the old man?"*

"Yeah, him, the captain," said another man's voice. *"What kind of a guy is he?"*

"A world-class prick, that's what. Lemme tell you somethin'. You guys love call signs so much. Know what his call sign oughta be?"

"No. What?"

"Prickney. Prickney Stickney." The man broke out in a

frenzied chortle, pleased with his cleverness. *"Whaddya think of that?"*

"Hey, that's good. That's really good, Scrotum."

Maxwell stopped the recording. The video screen turned to a gray snowstorm.

Scrotum Scudder's jaw muscles were working at a furious rate. He said, "Whose voice was that on the tape?"

"Who do you think?" said Maxwell. "How many guys are named Scrotum?"

"That's not my name."

"Call signs are as good as names. I don't think we have an identity problem here."

"That's illegal. You can't tape someone's conversation without their permission."

"It was a party. Someone probably wanted to remember how much fun they had."

"Who made the video?"

Maxwell shook his head. Scudder didn't need to know the origin of the VHS cassette. It bore neither a date or time stamp, and it came in a standard reusable Navy routing envelope.

"No one in particular," said Maxwell. "The camcorder belongs to the squadron admin. Apparently someone at the party just left it running and forgot about it."

At the far bulkhead, Bullet Alexander sat in his own steel chair, keeping his silence. The overhead fluorescent light glistened off his slick, brown skull. He followed the discussion with a sober, curious expression on his face.

"The video is lousy quality," said Scudder. "So is the sound track. It could be anyone's voice on the tape."

"Yeah," said Maxwell. "Anyone named Scrotum who looks and sounds like you. Why don't we just let Captain Stickney decide who it sounds like? He'll particularly like the new call sign you've given him. Prickney? Has a nice ring to it."

Scudder's jaw muscles were pulsing like tiny motors. After several seconds, he said, "I believe this is called blackmail."

"I prefer to call it a sharing of information."

"I know what this is about. You want me to drop the assault charges."

"Do whatever you want. I certainly wouldn't want you to think you're being pressured one way or the other."

Another period of silence passed. Scudder stared at the snowy screen. He took a deep breath and said, "What if I tell Captain Stickney and the JAG team that my complaint is withdrawn?"

Maxwell kept a blank expression. "That's your call."

Scudder breathed an audible sigh. "Okay, I'll do it." He looked again at the screen. He had the look of a man reprieved from a death sentence. "But I want that tape."

"You'll get it in due time. For now, it stays in my safe."

Scudder stared at him, then shifted his gaze to Alexander. Alexander flashed him a toothy smile.

Scudder's face hardened, and he rose from the steel chair. "I hope you two are pleased. You've gotten what you wanted. Will that be all?"

"No," said Maxwell. "There's one more thing."

A wary look flashed over Scudder's face. "What?"

"That neck brace. Get rid of it. It makes you look like a turtle."

Scudder's face reddened. He stood motionless, glowering at Maxwell. Abruptly he reached up with both hands and unclasped the brace. He yanked it off his neck.

"There. Does that make you happy?"

"Ecstatic."

"Now I have a request."

"What is it?"

"That disgusting call sign your squadron hung on me. Make them stop using it."

"Sorry. I can't do that."

"Why not? You're the commanding officer."

"You know what they say about call signs. They're like diamonds."

Scudder's eyes narrowed. "Diamonds? What does that mean?"

"They're forever, Mr. Scudder."

A wave of pure enmity spread over Scudder's face. He started to say something; then his eyes darted back to the flickering screen. He wheeled and stormed from the room.

Alexander waited until the sound of Scudder's footsteps had stopped reverberating down the steel passageway.

"You know, Skipper, ol' Scrotum had a point there. That video was pretty fuzzy."

"Yeah, it was."

"Could have been anyone's voice on that tape."

"Could have been."

"Are you sure it was Scudder saying those things?"

Maxwell tilted back in his chair. He played for a moment with the ballpoint on the table.

"Look at it this way. If Scrotum didn't exactly say it, then he obviously thought it. Otherwise, he wouldn't believe he said it, right?"

"Right."

"So, in any case, it comes down to the same thing."

Alexander reflected for a moment. "Hmm. I think I see your point."

"I figured you would."

"Guess this means I owe you one, huh, Skipper?"

Maxwell glanced at his watch. He rose and picked up his uniform hat. Boyce was waiting for him on the flight deck. Their COD was leaving in ten minutes for Tel Aviv.

"Yeah," said Maxwell. "That's what it means."

U.S. Embassy Compound, Tel Aviv

". . . whose indomitable courage will serve as an inspiration to future generations of Americans. Ricardo Solares was an American hero who gave his life so that . . ."

Boyce stifled a yawn. It was warm inside the U.S. embassy rotunda, crammed now with over three hundred mourners. The Secretary of State was ten minutes into his eulogy and still hadn't run out of ways to describe the undaunted heroism of Special Envoy Ricardo Solares.

"Do you think he believes that shit?" Boyce said.

He was standing next to Maxwell in the back row of military officers. Admiral Hightree, on Boyce's right, gave him a scowl. All three naval officers were wearing their dress white uniforms with high collars and rows of decorations.

"Sure," whispered Maxwell. "Same as the President believes it."

The President of the United States had already gone on television the previous evening to deliver his own eulogy to his tragically departed friend and colleague. Rick Solares was a man who had a brilliant future ahead of him, the President informed the nation, leaving the clear hint that Solares *would* have been his choice of running mate if, of course, he hadn't been pounded into a gory mess in Hebron.

"Smart guy, the President," said Boyce, ignoring another sour look from Hightree. "He gets it both ways. He gets the ghost of the departed Rick Solares on his ticket without having to put up with the sonofabitch."

The Secretary of State droned on. ". . . distinguished journalist and statesman whose name had already been mentioned for the Nobel Peace Prize . . ."

Boyce tuned the rest of the Secretary's speech out. His eyes scanned the audience that ringed the podium where the Secretary stood. The U.S. military contingent formed one side of the throng around the dais. Opposite them

were the Israeli dignitaries. Boyce spotted the Prime
Minister in the front rank, flanked on either side by the
Foreign Minister and the President of Israel.

He looked for other faces he recognized. Missing was
General Zemek, the recently appointed Defense Minister.

His eyes stopped on a familiar face. She stood at the
edge of the group of Israeli officials. No short skirt today.
She was wearing a demure black suit, with conservative
elbow-length sleeves and black gloves. Maxwell's Israeli
friend. She looked good.

Hannah Shamir saw him looking at her. She nodded
and flashed a smile.

Directly in front of the podium were the cameras, more
than a dozen, all capturing the mourning of Rick Solares
for tonight's broadcasts. It was ironic, Boyce thought.
Only a few days ago they were running footage of Rambo
Rick barfing his guts up on the deck of the *Reagan*.

Now all that was forgotten. In a few days Solares had
made the transition from distinguished Special Envoy to
laughingstock to deceased hero. Amazing.

The exact circumstances of Solares's death were un-
clear. Khaled Mohanor, as both Boyce and Maxwell suspected, had been the target of the JSOW mission, though
no such report would ever be released to the public.
After-action intel confirmed that the Great Leader had indeed been dispatched to Allah, to the immense satisfaction of all parties, including the Palestinian resistance.

But no one seemed to know what Ricardo Solares was
doing there in Hebron, or how he became the victim of a
mob of rock-throwing Palestinians. Even Hightree insisted that he knew nothing about it. Boyce believed him.

The Secretary was building up steam for his finale.
". . . a lasting peace for Israel and the Palestinian people.
With the example of Ricardo Solares to guide us, let us
rededicate ourselves to . . ."

His voice swelled to a crescendo, urging all peace-
loving people to remember the sacrifice of the departed

Special Envoy. The United States would erect a monument in his honor right here in Israel.

The eulogy came to an end. A grateful silence fell over the crowd.

As the throng of mourners made their way toward the long tables where refreshments were being served, Boyce saw Hannah Shamir coming toward them.

He turned to Maxwell. "Looks like you're gonna be tied up. I've got to attend a meeting with Hightree and the Secretary of State. And don't ask what it's about because I don't know. I'll catch you later at the bar."

He saw the eyes following her across the room. Israeli, American, civilian, and military. All watching Hannah Shamir.

She stopped in front of him. "You look very handsome in your white uniform, Brick."

"Thank you."

She glanced around. "Are you allowed to talk to me?"

"Depends. Are you on duty or off?"

"On," she said. "But for you I'll make an exception."

"In that case, let's have a drink."

"I don't need a drink."

"I don't either. How about a walk?"

She nodded, and he observed that she looked good in black. Very good, actually. Even without displaying those superb legs, the neatly tailored suit revealed her narrow-waisted figure. He'd never seen her in high heels before. He liked the way she walked with that hip-swaying sashay.

More sets of eyes followed them across the rotunda. Maxwell glanced back at the podium. The Secretary of State was still shaking hands with the assembled dignitaries. Ambassador Kaminski was beside him, looking cooler and more sure of himself than the last time Maxwell saw him. Now that the overbearing presence of

Solares was gone, Maxwell guessed, Kaminski could go back to being a real ambassador.

In the center of the rotunda, surrounded by six Marine guards standing at parade rest, lay the coffin of Ricardo Solares. It was draped in an American flag. Banks of flowers were heaped on each side. Solares's remains would be flown back to Washington aboard a C-5 that night, to be interred after yet another ceremony in Arlington.

An open-casket funeral, of course, was out of the question. From what Maxwell had heard, there hadn't been enough left of Ricardo Solares to fill a shopping bag, let alone a coffin. Certainly not the kind of farewell event Solares would have scripted for himself. *Too bad about that, Rick.*

He led Hannah out of the rotunda and across the courtyard to the Hayarkon Street gate. Maxwell returned the Marine sentry's salute. They walked out into the coolness of the evening.

A gentle breeze was wafting in from the sea. The sun had descended beneath the rim of the Mediterranean, leaving a purplish glow in the western sky.

Hannah stopped at the edge of the beach and pulled off her shoes. With a shock, Maxwell stood frozen, watching her. He had the feeling of being transported in time.

When was he last here?

It came to him. Almost this exact spot. Claire had removed her shoes, leaning against his shoulder just as Hannah was doing now. Same kind of evening. Same purplish glow over the Mediterranean. Different girl.

A lifetime ago.

Hannah was giving him a worried look. "Are you all right?"

"Yeah. Yeah, I'm fine."

He took off his uniform shoes, then rolled up the bottoms of his trousers. They walked across the hard, grainy sand. The feeling of déjà vu stayed with him.

They walked in silence for a while. A few couples still
sprawled on beach towels in the gathering dusk. Maxwell
could see the shapes of the boats patrolling the coastline.
Terrorists had once tried to sneak ashore on this beach.

"Why were you at the memorial service?" Maxwell
asked. "Were you a friend of Solares's?"

She didn't reply for a few seconds. "That wasn't why I
came."

"Why, then?"

"I knew you'd be there."

Maxwell tried to come up with a reply, but he couldn't.
He kept his gaze on the darkened sand ahead. He felt
Hannah slide her hand inside his. They continued walk-
ing in silence, hands clasped between them.

It occurred to Maxwell that he was comfortable with
her. More than comfortable, actually. He liked walking
with her. He liked the feel of her hand in his.

"I didn't see General Zemek," he said.

"He wasn't there. According to rumor, Zemek is gone.
Dismissed."

"That's a surprise." Maxwell tried not to sound
pleased. "How did he fall out of favor so soon?"

"I'm off duty, Commander. Remember?"

"Just wondering if you had an opinion."

"Mm, maybe. If I did, my opinion would be that General Zemek might have made some . . . let's say, inappropriate alliances during the recent war."

Maxwell nodded. A scene was replaying itself in his
mind. Zemek and Solares huddled on the dais at the Ben-
Gurion military complex. And in the background, out of
sight, the visage of Khaled Mohanor. *Inappropriate alliances.* More like an unholy trinity, and the result of their
alliance was a war and over five thousand casualties,
most of them Palestinian, most of them unnecessary.

And nothing had changed. Palestinians and Israelis
still hated each other.

"So Zemek will go back to running the Air Force?"

"It doesn't work that way. He's finished. The other rumor is that your friend Lev Asher will take command of the IAF."

"Things move quickly in Israel."

"It's not over yet," she said. "The Prime Minister may not survive a confidence vote of his party. Firing Zemek was an attempt to salvage his own credibility, but it probably won't save him."

Maxwell shook his head. What a strange country. Full of beauty and history and contradictions.

Darkness descended over the western horizon. Lights of fishing boats twinkled on the black water. They passed the marina, opposite the brightly lit Carlton Hotel. They walked in silence, their footsteps synchronized. Her hand was still clutched in his.

"And you, Sam? You are leaving the *Reagan*?"

"In three weeks. My executive officer has been itching to take command of the squadron. It's time."

"And then what?"

Good question, he thought. He still had no orders. "A new assignment. Probably in the States."

"Will they give you a leave before you report?"

"Maybe." He looked at her. "Why?"

"You could come to Israel. Take a real vacation. I can show you the beautiful parts. No strings attached, honest."

He didn't answer. He didn't trust his feelings yet. It was too soon. The memory of Claire Phillips was too close, too painful.

But the notion of spending time with Hannah Shamir felt right. It was feeling better by the minute. Okay, so she was a spy. So what? Everybody needed a job.

"The Navy Distinguished Service Medal?" said Boyce. "You've gotta be kidding, Jack."

They were alone, so he could drop the formality of addressing Hightree by his rank. He was retiring anyway.

"You heard me," said Hightree. "The Secretary of State wants to pin them on us himself."

Boyce stared at the admiral. Something was wrong here. Hightree was looking too pleased with himself.

"Medals for what?" said Boyce. "All you and I did was—"

"He knows what we did, and there will never be an exact record of it. But he wants us to receive some kind of recognition."

"Why us? What about Maxwell and my other guys?"

"If you want Maxwell or anyone else to get a medal, that's your business. You and I were the senior commanders, and for some reason the President thinks that we had something to do with ending the shooting war in the Palestinian territories."

Well, thought Boyce, *maybe we did, maybe we didn't.* All he knew was that his wife was in protective custody somewhere because her husband was responsible for the deaths of 120 innocent Palestinians. Now they were giving him a medal. The world was going batshit.

As ordered, Boyce had accompanied Hightree to the ambassador's reception room. The spacious room contained a row of padded leather chairs, a long table with a lectern at the end, and several unrecognizable paintings, which looked to Boyce like the leftovers from a kindergarten art class. Ambassador Kaminski, it was said, was an avid collector of modern art.

"When is this supposed to happen?"

"In a little while. But first, I have something for you."

Hightree fumbled in his attaché case, then came up with an official Navy-issue brown envelope. "Seems that your orders have come in."

"Orders?"

"To your next assignment."

Boyce's eyes narrowed. "What's going on, Jack? I'm retiring, remember?"

"Oh, that." Hightree fumbled again in the attaché case.

He came up with another envelope. He handed it to Boyce. "Gee, I'm sorry, Red. I meant to forward this, but I must have forgotten."

Boyce tore the envelope open. His request for retirement. It hadn't been endorsed or forwarded.

Boyce's anger burst to the surface. "Goddamn it, you didn't have any right to do that. I promised Annie I was getting out. I've put her through enough—"

He caught himself. Someone had entered the room and walked up beside Hightree. Boyce stared, unable to believe what he was seeing.

"There you go again, Roland, using me as your excuse to do what you want."

He continued to stare. Nobody—absolutely *nobody*—was allowed to call him Roland. No one except . . .

"Ah, how . . . I mean . . . Annie, what the hell are you doing here?"

She looked at Hightree. "Isn't he a romantic soul? Hasn't seen his wife in six months and he opens with a line like that." She turned back to Boyce. "Damn it, Roland, stop behaving like a clod and give me a kiss."

Boyce was too stunned to protest. He opened his arms and swept her to him. For most of the next minute he held her tightly, unable to speak, a torrent of emotions flooding through him.

It didn't make sense. *Annie. Here in Tel Aviv.* He felt as if he were dreaming. It was wonderful.

Hightree was clearing his throat. "Umm, the Secretary will be along any minute now to pin those silly medals on us. I think you'd better read your orders before he gets here."

Boyce looked at the paper in his hand. Orders? He had already forgotten them.

He squinted at the paper, tried to fake it, then gave up and pulled the half-frames from his uniform shirt pocket.

He read the orders. They still didn't make sense. Nothing was making sense today.

From: OpNav, Flag Assignments Desk
To: Captain Roland S. Boyce, USN
Subj: Permanent Change of Station

Upon receipt of these orders, and following
relief as Commander, Carrier Air Wing Three, and
subject to presidential confirmation of promotion
to rank of rear admiral (lower half), you will
proceed to NAS Fallon, NV, to assume command
of U.S. Naval Special Tactical Operations Unit.

He looked up. Hightree was grinning like a baboon. Annie was smiling too, and her eyes were wet.

"Okay, you two. What's the game here?"

"No, game," said Hightree. "To the absolute astonishment of everyone in the Navy who has ever served with you, including me, you have been selected for promotion to flag rank."

Boyce read the orders once again. They looked real, but they couldn't be. No way. Guys like him didn't get promoted to admiral. Not in the U.S. Navy.

There was something else he didn't understand. "What the hell is the Naval Special Tactical Operations Unit?"

"A new concept," said Hightree. "STOU is a black program, an unconventional warfare unit, using conventional assets. Guess that's why they tapped a guy like you to run it. You're about as unconventional as they get."

Boyce removed the half-frames and looked at his wife. She looked back at him. Little by little, it was coming together, like tiny pieces of a jigsaw puzzle.

"You knew, didn't you?"

She nodded. "Jack asked me to be here when he sprang it on you. He was worried that you might do something stupid, like say no."

"I'm going to retire, Annie. You and Julie were nearly killed by terrorists. I won't have anything like that happen to you again."

"Oh, balderdash. The FBI has already caught the thugs who burned our house."

"There are lots more where they came from."

"They were part of a terrorist cell in the U.S. that the FBI had been tracking for months. I'm not worried about them anymore, and neither is Julie."

"I've seen the FBI in action. We ought to be worried."

"You have to take this job, Roland. Besides, I've been training for years to be an admiral's wife."

Boyce could see where this was going. When Annie made up her mind, he might as well be arguing with Mount Rushmore.

But his brain was already sifting through the possibilities. He could feel a familiar old excitement tugging at him. Something very interesting was happening out there in the wide-open spaces of Nevada. *A new command. An unconventional way of fighting wars.*

Well, America had plenty of unconventional enemies. Maybe the way to beat them was with unconventional warfare.

Perhaps Annie had a point. He could stick around a little longer. Just to see what happened.

Of course, he would need some good guys working for him. Special guys who could think outside the box. The kind who didn't mind kicking in doors without asking permission.

With that thought, he smiled to himself. Yeah, Maxwell would have a fit when he heard where he was going. Too damn bad. He'd get used to it.